Northwest Vista College
Learning Resource Center
3535 North Ellison Drive
San Antonio, Texas 78251

D1527581

An American Girl, and Her Four Years in a Boys' College

Olive San Louie Anderson,
Class of 1875.

An American Girl, and Her Four Years in a Boys' College

By *Olive San Louie Anderson*

EDITED BY

Elisabeth Israels Perry and
Jennifer Ann Price

THE UNIVERSITY OF MICHIGAN PRESS   *Ann Arbor*

Copyright © by the University of Michigan 2006
All rights reserved
Published in the United States of America by
The University of Michigan Press
Manufactured in the United States of America
♾ Printed on acid-free paper
2009   2008   2007   2006   4   3   2   1

A CIP catalog record for this book is available from the British Library.

Library of Congress Cataloging-in-Publication Data

Anderson, Olive San Louie, 1842–1886.
   An American girl, and her four years in a boys' college / by Olive
San Louie Anderson ; edited by Elisabeth Israels Perry and Jennifer
Ann Price.
      p.   cm.
   Originally published: New York : D. Appleton and Company, 1878.
(under the pseudonym of Sola)
   "An annotated edition of An American girl, and her four years in a
boys' college"—T.p. verso.
   Includes bibliographical references.
   ISBN-13: 978-0-472-09916-0 (alk. paper)
   ISBN-10: 0-472-09916-7 (alk. paper)
   ISBN-13: 978-0.472-06916-3 (pbk. : alk. paper)
   ISBN-10: 0-472-06916-0 (pbk. : alk. paper)   1. Women college
students—Fiction.   2. College students—Fiction.   3. Coeducation—
Fiction.   I. Perry, Elisabeth Israels.   II. Price, Jennifer Ann.
III. Title.
PS1039.A368A83   2006
813'.4—dc22   2005017906

An annotated edition of An American Girl, and Her Four Years in a Boys' College
by SOLA (pseudonym of Olive San Louie Anderson)
Originally published in 1878 by D. Appleton and Company, New York

Frontispiece art: F99–536: Class of 1875, Classes by Year, Individual, University of
Michigan Photographs Vertical File, Bentley Historical Library, University of Michigan.

Contents

List of Illustrations

Introduction

In 1870, the University of Michigan reached a major turning point. In January of that year, the university—one of the oldest, largest, and most prestigious public universities in the United States—admitted its first woman student. The Board of Regents, which governed the university's affairs, had been debating this step for fifteen years but had refused to take it on the grounds that the admission of women would jeopardize Michigan's reputation as offering top-notch professional training to men. Pressured by the state's teachers, taxpaying parents of daughters, and activists in the woman's rights movement, the regents at last voted to accept women. Madelon Stockwell immediately presented herself for admission to the university's literature department. Stockwell earned her degree in less than two years and was chosen a commencement speaker, a singular honor for any senior, male or female. In fall 1870, the university admitted thirty-four women. By the following year, sixty-four women were studying at Michigan: three in law, thirty-three in medicine, and twenty-eight in the Department of Science, Literature, and the Arts. Thus began what some observers called Michigan's "dangerous experiment" with coeducation.[1]

What was it like to be a member of this tiny group of brave "coeds," who made up just 3 percent of the university's twelve hundred students? Two historians, Dorothy Gies McGuigan and Ruth Bordin, have published detailed studies of the experience. For documentation, they used a variety of primary sources, including records of the regents' debates, the testimony of eyewitness participants, and accounts and comments in contemporary newspapers.[2] They also used *An American Girl, and Her Four Years in a Boys' College*, the novel presented here for the first time since its original publication in 1878.

The novel's author, Olive San Louie Anderson, was a member of the small class of women students who entered the university in 1871. She graduated in 1875, wrote the book two years later, and published it under the pen name SOLA, an anagram of her initials. Her novel is, on the surface at least, a roman à clef, a literary genre in which the author disguises actual people and events by giving the main characters fictional names and altering the course of events for dramatic purposes. But it was never meant to be a realistic portrayal of women's experiences at Michigan. Instead its goal was to tell the story of the emergence into maturity of a highly independent, modern "American girl."

Anderson's American girl is an early rendering in fiction of the "new woman" of the late nineteenth century. Such a woman challenged many of the moral, religious, and cultural values of her day. In Anderson's time, people would have called this woman unconventional or perhaps strong-minded. Today we would call her a feminist, that is, an individual who refuses to be subordinated to men, who desires as many opportunities for education and achievement as men enjoy, and who seeks a life of meaning and purpose beyond domesticity. Anderson's American girl is a feminist who throughout her experiences of coeducation retains a strong feminine core. As such, she is a character whom modern readers will find both engaging and provocative.

The Narrative Structure of *An American Girl*

Anderson built her novel around the character of Wilhelmine Elliot, the rebellious daughter of a freethinking surgeon who had died during the Civil War. Her family and friends call her Will. As this is a name that could also belong to a boy, it captures not only the heroine's "tomboyish" behavior but also her obstinate and sometimes impulsive temperament. As the novel opens, Will is telling her mother that she cannot accept a Christian catechism that emphasizes damnation. She has already declined to attend a "fashionable boarding school" that merely "finishes off" girls instead of taking their academic training seriously. Envious of her male classmates' talk of college, she is thrilled when she hears that "one of the finest universities in the country has opened its doors to women." Her mother, secretly proud of her unconventional daughter, allows her to go.

Will sets off for the "University of Ortonville," a stand-in for Michigan. The school's president welcomes her warmly but the town less so. Like all students in that day, Will must arrange for her own lodgings. Several landladies refuse to board women. Eventually a kind steward helps her find accommodations, and the next morning she presents herself for her entrance examinations.[3] These are in mathematics, history, geography, Latin, and Greek, all subjects in a "classical" curriculum usually taken only by those destined for professional careers—in other words, men. Will does well in all the subjects but needs tutoring in Greek.

Daily "persecutions" follow. She is almost injured by sophomore men hazing the freshmen. Her Greek tutor presses attentions on her that are both unwanted and worrisome. Won't people think the girls have come to the university only "to flirt"? She worries about going alone to hear a famous former abolitionist speak. Professors praise her academic work and that of the other women but predict that the strain will soon break down their health. Will's beloved younger sister, long an invalid, dies.

Matters improve in Will's second year. The town's landladies now welcome female boarders because they are neater and quieter than the boys. Will, gaining in self-confidence, organizes a successful debate on woman suffrage. To stay healthy she takes up rigorous physical exercise, including chopping wood, and soon wins a reputation for being an "Amazon." She decides to take her degree in literature and then study medicine. A romance develops with Guilford Randolf, who at first disdains the "tomboyish" Will but is soon "smashed." By the end of Will's third year, the two are steady companions, but his negative reaction to her plan to become a physician is not a good sign.

During her senior year, when she accidentally overhears Randolf disparaging her to another girl, she breaks off the affair. In the end, she finds her career goals thwarted. An uncle, who had invested her legacy, has lost it. Will must find a teaching post to earn her living. One school rejects her for not being a member of a church, but another in Wisconsin promises her a post teaching Greek and Latin. At commencement, Will is the only woman student chosen to speak. Her oration, "Women in the Professions," calls for an "open career for talent." As Will leaves for her teaching post, her remorseful former beau begs her to write him. She says she will, as in her heart she still loves him. And thus she keeps open the possibility, but not the promise, of personal fulfillment.

An American Girl as Autobiography

Many of the details of Will Elliot's life resemble those of the novel's author, Olive San Louie Anderson.[4] Born in Lexington, Ohio, in 1852,

Anderson was (like Will) the daughter of a doctor, Dr. Hugh P. Anderson, who died when she was seventeen. One year of her schooling was spent with her mother (Alice Cook) and sister in the house of her maternal grandfather. The sister was ill (in Olive's case she was older; in Will's, younger). As this illness preoccupied the family, young Olive was left to romp and play sports with her brothers. The family spent some time on the Iowa frontier but later returned to Ohio, where Olive graduated from the Mansfield, Ohio, high school in 1869. After teaching in public schools for a while, she began to prepare for college. Her fictional character, Will, entered the "classical course" at Ortonville in 1870, but Olive did not enter Michigan until 1871.

Like Will, Anderson had a masculine nickname. According to Sarah Dix Hamlin, who was one class ahead of Anderson at Michigan and would later write a lengthy obituary of her friend, Anderson's friends called her Joe. "A certain air of frankness," Hamlin wrote, "a way of saying original and unexpected things, a certain style in Miss Anderson at this time, reminded her friends so much of the 'Jo' in Miss Alcott's 'Little Women,' that almost unconsciously the name of 'Jo' was given to her, and she became known every-where in Ann Arbor as 'Joe Anderson.'"[5]

Also like Will, Anderson was the only woman honored with an "appointment," as it was then called, to speak at commencement. The title of her talk was "The Next Century." According to one report, the theme of her speech was the nation's young age. She predicted that in the next century Americans would see improved machinery and faster locomotion. She emphasized, however, that "neither the twentieth century nor the fortieth would see the world redeemed unless women were granted the rights and privileges which belong to them."[6]

According to Hamlin, Anderson was known throughout the university for "her bright, original manners, her clear reasoning powers, her witty and concise way of expressing herself." These qualities "rendered her a favorite both within and without the class room." Anderson "constituted herself a champion of woman," using "her bright wit and . . . sarcasm" (as opposed to "ranting") to make her "onslaught upon old customs and opinions." "Her orations and essays," Hamlin added, "were seldom without some allusions to the 'woman question,' expressed with a great deal of original force, and many were the students who flocked to the lecture-room when it was known that she was to speak."[7]

Sarah Dix Hamlin, Class of 1874. Hamlin was a year ahead of Anderson at the University of Michigan. Like Anderson, she settled in San Francisco, where she founded the Hamlin School for Girls. In 1886, she wrote Anderson's obituary, the basis for most of what is known about her friend's short life. (F99–535: Class of 1874, Classes by Year, Individual, University of Michigan Photographs Vertical File, Bentley Historical Library, University of Michigan.)

Anderson, again like Will, planned a career in medicine. She had every intention of returning to the University of Michigan to fulfill this ambition but instead, like her protagonist, became a teacher. She did not move to Wisconsin, however, but to California. After staying in San Francisco for a while she took up a post teaching Greek and Latin at a college in Santa Barbara. While there, she wrote short sketches, which were published in some eastern newspapers, about the "quaint" Spanish life of the place. She also wrote *An American Girl*. When the college at which she was teaching closed, she taught in various private schools until she became a partner in a private school in San Rafael in May 1882. She later served as this school's principal.

Hamlin describes Anderson as an inspiring teacher, writing that she believed that "life was holy, that it was possible to make it divine through dedication and devotion to high aims, though the labor might be humble." "What matters [is] the work and who can measure the results," Hamlin reports Anderson as saying. "They are all the same, if one's own conscience is clear. Is it not better than all else to have one's own approval than the applause of the world if you stand convicted before your true self?" An advocate of physical training, Anderson carried herself with a step that "had the spring of the deer." "Certainly few have seen that splendid form," Hamlin wrote, "that graceful carriage, that high bearing, without feeling that here was a 'perfect woman, nobly planned.'" Anderson (again like Will) was "an accomplished and fearless horse-woman, able to bring a horse into perfect obedience to her will; expert with the rifle, able to bring down a bird on the wing; a good swimmer and skilled in all athletic and out-of-door games." She loved nature and the West Coast, once writing, "How I love this coast, the part made by nature. The ocean and the islands form a picture which can never cease to be a source of pleasure."

In her religious views, Anderson "despised all artificiality and superficiality, believing that the voice of conscience speaking to the heart and soul and mind was the voice of God." She "despised all cant and avoided all expressions savoring of sentimentality." Hamlin reported that she once exclaimed passionately, "I would be that which it is right for one to be, but I must think for myself, I cannot be bound by religion's shackles." She never found a theological creed that satisfied her more than an "intense practical religion" that entailed "devotion to duty and consecration to high aims."

In June 1886, Anderson spent a month with an "Artistic League" on San Francisco Bay, partly on a boat and partly on shore. She was collecting materials for a "California" book and preparing for foreign travel and study. While planning a series of panel sketches for which she was to have written the literary material, her party went up the Sacramento River on a yacht called the *Ariel*. On June 5, the excursion's last morning, Anderson left the yacht with five members of the party to take a swim in the river. Seized with cramps, she sank before anyone could help her.[8]

Anderson's body was sent to Mansfield, Ohio, where it was buried by her father's side. A friend, Elizabeth C. Curtis, collected some of her last writings, which Anderson probably never would have published, and printed five hundred copies in remembrance of her in a book entitled *Stories and Sketches*. *An American Girl* was thus "Joe" Anderson's first and last novel.

The Historical Context

Educational Opportunities for Women in the Nineteenth Century

For young American women like Olive Anderson, the opportunity to attend a major state university was a welcome development. Few of their mothers and even fewer of their grandmothers had enjoyed such a privilege. In the early nineteenth century, hardly any colleges accepted women students at all. Most educators then saw little point in sending women to college, since the professions requiring a college education, such as law, medicine, and the ministry, were open only to men; grade school teaching, the one profession women could enter, required only a high school education. Moreover, most parents assumed their daughters would marry, bear children, or otherwise devote themselves to domestic pursuits. Contemporary prejudices against intellectual women led many parents to believe that no man would want to marry a woman more interested in study than in taking care of a household.

Not all Americans agreed with such attitudes. Advocates of higher education for women argued that it would make women better wives and mothers. Educated mothers could properly train their sons for citizenship and their daughters to fulfill the same role in relation to their own children. They also argued that wives knowledgeable about the world would run more efficient, harmonious households, thereby relieving their husbands of domestic cares and freeing them to pursue the family's living in the competitive marketplace.[9] Thus, the whole society would benefit from educated mothers.

But what of single women or those who married "badly," perhaps finding themselves wed to a gambler, an alcoholic, or an abuser? And what of women who lost their husbands to illness, accident, death, or desertion? Independently wealthy women might fare well enough, but for those who needed to make a living an advanced education would certainly increase their chances of avoiding destitution.

To these practical reasons for women's education, others added more feminist arguments. Many nineteenth-century American women yearned for more fulfilling intellectual lives. They claimed a "right" to an education equal to that of men. Most of these egalitarians did not believe that educated women would or could compete on equal terms with men in the public sphere. Pointing to the physical and moral differences between women and men, they predicted that the two sexes would always play different social roles. Some egalitarians, however, were active in the rising woman's movement, which had begun officially with the convening of the first "Woman's Rights Convention" at Seneca Falls, New York, in 1848. These women were eager to enter the professions that continued to exclude them. By midcentury, they were mounting energetic campaigns to win admission for women to college and university training.[10]

Women who wanted to teach also put pressure on educational establishments to admit them to college. In the early nineteenth century, the American population grew dramatically, increasing the need for schoolteachers. As the nation's growing communities could rarely pay enough to hire male teachers, they turned with increasing frequency to women, whom (they rightly assumed) they could pay one-half to one-third of what they paid men. As the teaching profession became feminized, women's opportunities for higher education expanded through the founding of private seminaries (so-called in order to distinguish them from the "academies" meant for boys) and state-funded "normal," or teacher-training, schools. Although these were open to both sexes, women's enrollment exceeded men's.[11]

The most prestigious of the early women's seminaries included Emma Willard's, which was established in Middlebury, Vermont, in 1814 and moved to Troy, New York, in 1821, where it is still a boarding school for girls; Catharine Beecher's, founded in 1824 in Hartford, Connecticut; and Mary Lyon's Mount Holyoke, founded in 1837 in South Hadley, Massachusetts, and now a college for women. Schools such as these generally offered a three-year course roughly equivalent to today's secondary education. After 1850, growing numbers of these schools upgraded their curricula to emulate those of men's four-year colleges. Finally, after the Civil War, several elite colleges for women opened in the

East. These included Vassar (1865), which claimed to offer a curriculum equal to that of elite male colleges in the arts and sciences (it actually provided laboratories); Wellesley (1875); Smith (1875); and Bryn Mawr (1885).[12]

Early Coeducational Opportunities

Oberlin, a private institution in Ohio, was the nation's first coeducational college. Initially founded to train ministers, after 1833 it also accepted women students. Convinced that women were more spiritual than men, Oberlin's founders hoped that women's presence would raise the campus's moral tone, help the future ministers learn to work with female congregants, and be a source of the ministers' future wives.[13] Thus, at Oberlin coeducation at first aimed less to meet the needs and ambitions of women than those of men.

Instead of taking the courses in Hebrew, Latin, or Greek expected of the college's future ministers, Oberlin's early women students were enrolled in a "ladies' course," which was heavy on religion, French, poetry, and modern literature. To its credit, Oberlin did not offer the "ornamental" courses, such as embroidery or wax working, popular in the eastern finishing schools that Anderson's protagonist rejects. In 1841, the college ended women's obligation to take the ladies' course, but for some time it still denied women the right to deliver orations or conduct debates before mixed-sex audiences.[14]

Antioch College, founded in 1853 in Yellow Springs, Ohio, as a nonsectarian college, was coeducational from the start. The famed educator Horace Mann, then the first secretary of the Massachusetts Board of Education, was attracted to Antioch's presidency not only by the school's nonsectarianism but also by the idea of giving women the "equal advantages of education." Mann held a narrow view of the purpose of higher education for women, however. Concerned with overall community improvement, he saw higher education as preparing women primarily to become teachers, not professionals who might compete with men in their spheres. He once told a rebellious woman student that he would not remain president of a coeducational college if as a result of higher education women might seek to enter the professions.

Worried about the potential for moral transgression at Antioch, Mann drew up an elaborate set of rules governing the relations between the sexes. He allowed them to take classes together but separated them everywhere else, even on college walks. Women could not live off campus but only in Ladies' Hall, a residence supervised strictly by a matron. When advising the University of Michigan on whether to admit women, Mann warned that they would need to prevent all clandestine correspondence and meetings between the sexes. In his view, if Michigan's administrators could not do this they should abandon coeducation altogether.[15]

In the 1850s, small midwestern church denominations, such as the Methodists, Baptists, Disciples of Christ, Friends (Quakers), and Universalists, also established coeducational colleges. The chief reason was financial: their rural congregations were generally too poor to afford separate institutions for their sons and daughters. Even if church members could have paid the tuition of an elite eastern institution, they rarely were willing to send their daughters so far from home. Moreover, they wanted to provide their offspring with a practical, scientific education. Neither the classical training offered in the East nor the finishing school atmosphere of many female seminaries was adequate. And, finally, coeducation appealed to small denominations because it held out the hope that offspring would marry within their faiths.[16]

The colleges established for African Americans after the Civil War were also coeducational. Like the small denominational colleges, these institutions could not afford to maintain separate schools for men and women. As the African American educator Anna Julia Cooper wrote in 1893, "These schools were almost without exception co-educational. Funds were too limited to be divided on sex lines, even had it been ideally desirable; but our girls as well as our boys flocked in and battled for an education."[17]

Some denominational colleges believed in coeducation on principle. In 1873, Edward Hicks Magill, president of the Quaker college Swarthmore, extolled coeducation as liberating to women. In an "Address upon the Co-education of the Sexes," he quoted a father of one of his students, who said he was pleased that her associations with young men in "a competitive way" had strengthened her "rather yielding character," which had lacked self-esteem, and now she was "better able to understand, weigh and value them at their *real worth*, and not be dazed by her first contact with the other sex." Magill asserted that women do just as well if not better than men in scholarship and without detriment to their health.[18]

Coeducation Comes to the University of Michigan

In general, coeducation was more the rule in the Midwest and Far West, where it was fostered by the populist and evangelical denominations most active in the development of the multipurpose college. The land-grant institutions founded by the Morrill Act of 1862, which granted public lands to states in order to fund agricultural and mechanical education for all classes, accepted women from the start.[19] By 1867, twenty-two American colleges and universities were admitting women as well as men. By 1870, eight state universities, including those of Iowa, Wisconsin, Kansas, Indiana, Minnesota, and Missouri, were coeducational. Cornell University, which opened in Ithaca, New York, in 1865, admitted its first woman in 1870 as well.[20]

All of Michigan's elementary and high schools, as well as the university's preparatory branches, which readied students for university study, were coeducational. The state's land-grant institution in East Lansing and its Normal School in Ypsilanti were also coeducational. But the university in Ann Arbor held out. The institution's 1837 charter declared that it "shall be open to all *persons* who possess the requisite literary and moral qualifications."[21] The regents granted that women were persons but argued that, since the purpose of university training was to prepare men for the professions, women should not be admitted. When in May 1855 the State Teachers' Association passed a resolution in favor of admitting women, the university's president responded only by proposing that the state establish a "Female Seminary" across the street.

In the spring of 1858, twelve Michigan "ladies" informed the university's Board of Regents that they planned to apply for admission the following fall. The regents appointed a committee to prepare a response. Over the summer, the committee wrote to leading educators (all of whom were male) to ask their views. All wrote back saying that they opposed coeducation.

President Woolsey of Yale commented, "Of what use degrees are to be to girls I don't see, unless they addict themselves to professional life, and I should expect the introduction of such a plan would be met with ridicule." President Walker of Harvard pointed to the "immense preponderance of enlightened public opinion against this experiment," one that should never be undertaken unless society proposed educating females for "public life." In making his argument against women's admission, Dr. Nott of

Union College also called attention to the "difference of sex and of destination." Women, he said, were delicate of sentiment, dependent, and shrink from the public view, while men were decisive, self-reliant, independent, and willing "to meet opposition and encounter difficulties." In short, the sexes were so different that he could not envision their studying together "without endangering alike their virtue and their happiness." The Yale-educated evangelical minister Lyman Beecher was positively alarmist, expostulating, "This Amalgamation of sexes won't do. If you live in a Powder House you blow up once in a while."

These views, taken along with those of Antioch's Horace Mann and Oberlin's Charles Finney, both of whom warned that coeducation would require constant supervision, persuaded the regents once again to refuse the admission of women. Yes, women were persons, their report conceded, but they had a right to withhold admission from those "whose presence would detract from the character of the Institution, or prevent it from attaining to the proper rank of a University." They were careful to disassociate the twelve "young ladies" from "the political or social movements known as 'Women's Rights,' 'Free Love,' etc. etc.," but the mere suggestion that the women *might* be linked to those movements was enough to quash the idea of admitting them.[22]

Still the issue would not go away. In 1859, almost fifteen hundred Michigan citizens petitioned the regents to admit women. In response, the regents distributed two thousand copies of their report of the previous year. Suspended during the Civil War, the debate recommenced afterward. Advocates of women's admission, many of them Michigan suffragists, pressed the regents to change their minds. They won over one, George Willard, an Episcopal rector and Latin professor at Kalamazoo College, and several of the university's faculty. In 1866, one faculty member's daughter, Alice Boise, audited Greek classes at the university, including her father's. Her presence on campus, where (as she later wrote) "no woman's foot was known," may have helped accustom the university community to the idea of coeducation. Favorable comments, such as that women's presence might make the students "less boorish in their manners and less profane in their conversation," began to appear in the student press. In the spring of 1867, the state legislature passed a resolution in favor of admitting women to all of the university's "rights and privileges." Still university leaders said no. Calling the idea of coeducation "a radical revolution," President Erastus O. Haven insisted that the wiser course for the state would be to build a separate women's college.[23]

In the end, economics made that proposal unrealistic. The state's legislators knew that Michigan taxpayers would never approve such a plan. Even so, the regents continued to oppose coeducation until, following another legislative resolution in favor of it and the appointment of two new members to the board, in January 1870 they finally agreed to admit Madelon Stockwell.

As Olive Anderson describes so vividly in her novel, the townspeople were unhappy with the first appearance of women students in the town of Ann Arbor. One student, Caroline Hubbard Kleinstueck, felt that the "antagonism of the townspeople" was harder to bear than that of the male students. Others reported that, despite women's presence in classrooms, some faculty members persisted in addressing their students as "Gentlemen." The *Michigan Argus,* a local weekly, made sneering remarks about the "academic" subjects women students might pursue, such as "a little piano and guitar . . . pencil-sketching . . . light gymnastics and calisthenics, with all the accomplishments of a modern belle."

Members of the medical faculty were especially resistant to women applicants. Expressing views widely held in their day, they argued that, as "woman is during a large fraction of each month a quasi-invalid" and "childbearing must incapacitate her during a large part of the period of *utero* gestation," medical coeducation was "an experiment of doubtful utility, and one not calculated to increase the dignity of man, nor the modesty of woman." The medical faculty acquiesced only after receiving approval to instruct male and female students separately and be given an extra five hundred dollars in salary for this purpose. By 1871, the medical faculty dean reported that the "experiment" of coeducation had proceeded well and that Amanda Sanford, the faculty's first woman student, was graduating with honors. Still, male students hooted when she crossed the stage to receive her diploma.[24]

Michigan's women students had a powerful defender in James Burrill Angell, who became university president in 1871 and remained in that office for thirty-two years. Often asked his opinion of coeducation, Angell took many opportunities to point to the "brilliant successes" of Michigan's women students. To his mind, they had both the intellectual gifts and the physical stamina to do well in a university course of study. Moreover, he denied that the women had experienced any "danger" to their virtue by coming to a "boys' college." "The relations of the sexes to each other here are those of well-bred men and women, and are not, in fact, in the least degree embarrassing to us," he wrote in 1881.[25]

Michigan did not hire women faculty for many years. After 1877, Louisa Reed Stowell held a minor appointment teaching microscopical botany, and after 1881 Dr. Lena C. Leland was an assistant demonstrator in anatomy in the Medical Department, but no woman held a full faculty appointment until Dr. Eliza Mosher (Michigan, Class of 1875) became dean of women in 1896. Mosher at first refused the deanship because the Medical Department had denied her a full professorship in gynecology. She later accepted the post of dean when President Angell appointed her a lecturer in hygiene in the Literary Department, a post that carried with it the rank and salary of a full professor. By the turn of the twentieth century, twelve women were teaching at Michigan, primarily in the sciences and all at low rank and salary. Alumnae and other women's advocates raised money for endowed chairs to be held by women, but the regents never approved such a use for these funds. The university did not make its first "chaired" appointments of women until the 1950s.[26]

After getting past the original discomfort of her minority status in "Ortonville" (Ann Arbor), Anderson's protagonist, Will Elliot, enjoys life at her coeducational university. The townspeople grow accustomed to the sight of women "co-eds" and welcome them in their homes. Will's increasing comfort in Ortonville seems to reflect the reality for women students who joined the university community in later years. At one point in the novel, Will contrasts the "free and easy life" she felt she could lead in a coeducational environment to the "strict boarding-school atmosphere" of single-sex schools such as Vassar. She develops strong and lasting platonic friendships with men such as Charlie Burton, who becomes engaged to her friend Nellie Holmes, and Tom Phelps, whose life she saves in a skating accident. In her letter to a friend at Vassar, she brags that "we have the most unbounded liberty" and she was "a pattern of decorum."[27]

Indeed, for this first generation of college women, campus life at Michigan was "free and easy." As the historian Dorothy McGuigan notes, Michigan "had devised no special rules for women nor created any special authority to supervise their actions."[28] This changed, however. By the 1890s, the university's deans of women had established strict rules of behavior, some of which lasted to the 1960s. The introduction of a system in loco parentis (in the place of parents) may have been due to the declining age of women students. The first generations of college women tended to be three to five years older than the men students, and thus they were perceived as being less in need of such supervision.[29]

Opponents of Coeducation

Despite the high standing of supporters of coeducation such as President Angell, opponents continued to raise objections long into the decades surrounding the turn of the century. In the mid-1870s, these opponents took arguments from a highly popular book by Dr. Edward H. Clarke, a prominent Boston physician and former member of the Harvard Medical School faculty. Clarke's *Sex in Education; or, A Fair Chance for Girls* (1873), was an expanded version of a speech he had delivered before the New England Woman's Club the previous year. In it, he charged that women did irreparable physiological harm to themselves when they undertook a higher educational curriculum designed for men. Hungry for reasons not to proceed any farther with coeducation, many readers seized on Clarke's book as a definitive answer to advocates of women's professional advancement. Its first printing sold out in a week.[30]

Clarke asserted that women's "periodical movements" (i.e., menstruation), "which characterize and influence woman's structure for more than half her terrestrial life," consume a large part of her "vital forces," or energies, especially between the ages of fourteen and eighteen. Young women who try to ignore this periodicity, instead focusing their energies on intellectual work, flout the immutable "laws of nature," drain sustenance from their reproductive systems, and inevitably fall ill, even to the point of sterility and lifelong invalidism. Clarke concluded, "Appropriate education of the two sexes, carried as far as possible, is a consummation most devoutly to be desired; identical education of the two sexes is a crime before God and humanity, that physiology protests against, and that experience weeps over." His solution? "Educate a man for manhood, a woman for womanhood, both for humanity. In this lies the hope of the race."[31]

Two sets of contemporary scientific ideas supported Clarke's polemic. The first concerned the differences between the sexes. Charles Darwin's recently published *Descent of Man* (1871) had presented a theory of sexual divergence as an integral part of the evolutionary process. Darwin theorized that because motherhood forced females into periodic dependence on males, during the evolutionary process their brain development fell behind. Male brains became not only larger and heavier but more "evolved" than the female's. Darwin granted that females developed strong intuitive powers, rapid perception, and quick reflexes but insisted that they rarely could compete with the more "advanced" ability of men to reason and do imaginative work.

The second set of ideas informing Clarke's theories derived from thermodynamics. According to its law of the conservation of energy, energy spent in one part of a system had to draw energy from another. The British sociologist Herbert Spencer had argued that all physical systems, including the human body, were subject to this law. Clarke concluded from Spencer's work that excessive brain work for women during the years of puberty drew energy away from their reproductive systems at a crucial time in their physiological development.[32]

In making this argument, Clarke was not denying women a "right" to education. He was asking only that their education suit their biology. Nor was he saying that women's pursuit of education was the sole cause of the physical weaknesses he observed in some of his young women patients. Some patients, he said, fell victim to "irrational cooking and indigestible diet." "We live in the zone of perpetual pie and doughnut," he complained. To make matters worse, women strap "artificial deformities" (corsets) to their spines. But Clarke's chief argument was that educating girls in the same way as boys "arrested" the development of their reproductive systems, thereby destroying their maternal instincts and turning them into sexless "Amazons."[33]

Clarke's "biological reductionism," the belief that human beings are defined by their biology, infuriated women's advocates. They immediately set out to refute him, first by contrasting his mere seven examples of highly educated women who had become invalids with dozens of counter-examples of physically fit and fertile college women. In 1885, the Association of Collegiate Alumnae published a scientific survey of its membership to show that female college graduates were not the invalids Clarke had predicted they would become. Others responded by taking his predictions of women's invalidism seriously but then offsetting them by establishing mandatory physical education programs for women at both women's and coeducational colleges.[34]

Olive Anderson's *An American Girl* was also a response to Clarke. She opens the novel with Will's mother protesting her daughter's plan to attend a "boys' college" on the grounds that it will ruin her health. Will dismisses her mother's fears, taking up the topic again (chap. IV) when she hears that Clarke's book sold more than two hundred copies on its first day on the market in Ortonville. Will then engages in a lively discussion about Clarke with her women friends.

Will begins by asking what Clarke would "do with us after he has cajoled us into believing that we are born and predestined to be invalids. . . .? Send us home to embroider chair-covers and toilet-sets, I suppose." She continues with a paean to female strength.

> Women have washed and baked, scrubbed, cried and prayed themselves into their graves for thousands of years, and no person has written a book advising them not to work too hard; but just as soon as women are beginning to have a show in education, up starts your erudite doctor with his learned nonsense, embellished with scarecrow stories, trying to prove that woman's complicated physical mechanism can't stand any mental strain.

Of course, Clarke was not accusing women of weakness but of misdirecting their vital energies. Will's response is similar to that of many of her contemporaries, which was to insist that women are *not* weak and then go out and prove it.

For herself, Will takes to heart Clarke's tirades against the harmful effects of wearing corsets, throws hers into the fire, and launches into a regime of rigorous physical exercise that includes chopping wood. She remains a paragon of physical health through the rest of her college days, earning admiration when she uses her strength to rescue Tom Phelps from drowning during a skating accident.[35]

The Debate over Coeducation at the Turn of the Twentieth Century

By 1890, the National Council of Education decided almost unanimously that "both theory and practice confirmed the wisdom of coeducation." According to the council, coeducation "led to better discipline, more balanced instruction, and a healthier psychological and sexual development of both boys and girls. Women had proved themselves equal to men in intellectual capacity, and the apocalyptic fears that study would undermine their health had been shown to be 'groundless.'" It concluded that the notion that studying the same subjects together would make women mannish and coarse and men less strong and courageous "will soon be numbered among the infinite host of dead theories that lie strewn all along the path of human progress."[36]

Debates over the wisdom of coeducation continued, however. Elite private colleges in the East persisted in their refusal to admit women. In response to continuing pressure, they instead opened up "annexes" or "coordinate" women's colleges such as Harvard's Radcliffe, Brown's Pembroke, and Columbia's Barnard. No additional "boys' colleges" opened up to women until the 1950s. Equally significant, in the early 1900s a number of coeducational colleges returned to the idea of separate curricula for women or applied a quota on the number of women who might enroll in certain programs. The motivation behind this step was a fear that certain fields were becoming "feminized," especially those in the humanities such as English, history, modern languages, and classical studies.

By 1900 at Michigan, the proportion of women students had risen to 22 percent of the student body. They comprised about 47 percent in literary studies, while men remained the majority in scientific, technical, and professional fields such as law and medicine. Opponents of coeducation used this disparity as proof that the sexes required different curricula and that unless women were directed toward fields more "suitable" to them, such as domestic science or "home economics," men would be "driven out" of the humanistic fields altogether.[37] In the early twentieth century, of course, women's opportunities for professional attainment in scientific, technical, or professional fields were extremely limited. Women gravitated toward the humanities primarily because they could find employment in these fields. Nonetheless, coeducation's opponents continued to raise alarms about women "taking over" fields in the humanities.

Other fears played into renewed debates over coeducation. In the early 1900s, social commentators noted the decline of birth rates among college-educated women. In contrast, census data were suggesting that less well-educated peoples, including immigrants and people of color, were reproducing at much faster rates. Concerned that "the old native American stock" would soon lose its ascendancy, President Theodore Roosevelt warned of "race suicide." Although he did not blame higher

18

education for women's failure to reproduce, other social commentators did. In his monumental study of adolescence, an influential Clark University psychologist, G. Stanley Hall, devoted an entire chapter to "Adolescent Girls and Their Education." Following Edward Clarke, Hall accepted the idea of sexual divergence and saw motherhood as a girl's greatest fulfillment. "To be a true woman means to be yet more mother than wife," he wrote. He despaired of an educational system that persisted in training women for "independence and self-support," leaving matrimony and motherhood to "take care of itself." As periodicity, or the menstrual cycle, was "perhaps the deepest law of the cosmos," he argued that women of high-school age ought to be educated in separate schools "primarily and chiefly for motherhood."[38]

As a result of such concerns, a number of colleges and universities began either to set up separate curricula for women and men students or to initiate quotas on women's admission. The University of Michigan was one of few major universities that refused to adopt policies of segregation, but after President Angell, the school's most ardent defender of coeducation, passed from the scene, Michigan set up a quota on women's admission to some programs.[39]

Religion and Feminism in *An American Girl*

In addition to addressing the specific issues raised in Clarke's book, *An American Girl* develops two interrelated themes, those of liberal religion and feminism. Over the course of the nineteenth century, American Christianity had become increasingly liberalized. Like some other women of her time, Will Elliot rejects the strict view of salvation that marked the Presbyterian faith in which she had been raised. A key feature of Presbyterianism was the Westminster Catechism, a "confession of faith" rooted in seventeenth-century Calvinism that saw human beings as "naturally depraved" and predicted the salvation of only a select few of the "righteous." Will finds this theology repellant. Moreover, unlike pious churchgoers of her era, she refuses to seek a "conversion" experience through which she would commit her soul to Jesus. This "failure" gives her mother great anxiety. In the novel's first chapter, after Will's mother opposes Will's plan to attend college because it will ruin her daughter's health, she makes a second objection, "one outweighing all the others":

going to college will ruin her daughter's soul. Indeed, she predicts that, because Will has "never had a change of heart" and "never taken Jesus as [her] Saviour," her being "away from the restraints of home," where she will be "exposed to the temptations of college-life," will lead to her destruction.

Will never had the conversion experience her mother wished for her in part because of the influence of her mother's father. As we learn in the novel's first chapter, Will had spent some time in her grandfather's house after her mother was widowed. Her grandfather had "startled" his community by leaving the church at the age of thirty-five. Although he lived a charitable and moral life, his neighbors (and Will's mother) still think of him as an "infidel."[40] Will adored her grandfather. After his death, she finds his copy of Ernest Renan's *Life of Jesus*, a biography published in 1863 that treats Jesus as a human being, not God. Drawing her even closer to her grandfather's humanistic views, this discovery alienates her further from her mother's Presbyterianism. Even as her mother presses a Bible, a hymn book, and a copy of the "Confession of Faith" on her and her local minister warns her to avoid the skeptical books she is bound to encounter at college, Will sets off for Ortonville hoping to leave religion behind.

Religion, however, follows her to college. In Ortonville, she is rarely free of social pressure to accept some denominational affiliation. Before Will's personal effects arrive at her new residence, her roommate, Clara, offers her the use of her own Bible (chap. II). When Will declines, Clara expostulates: "Aren't you a Christian, and don't you love Jesus?" Will manages to get along with her "churchy" roommate, who is the daughter of a Methodist minister and intends to become a missionary. But she pulls away (chap. III) when Clara insists that she attend a Sunday school class and almost breaks off the friendship when Clara tries to convince her that the imminent death of Will's sister "is intended . . . to draw you nearer to the Saviour." Will cries out in despair:

> If that is the way your God treats those he loves, I don't want to know him. Pretty way to fill up heaven, by making earth so lonely and cold and wretched that we don't want to stay! Oh, it is too hideous to think of!

After attending a campus religious revival, again at Clara's urging, Will resists pressure (chap. VII) from a local minister to declare her religious faith.[41] Their heated discussion serves only to reinforce in Will her deci-sion to interpret the Bible on her own and to refuse to accept a religion that condemns unbelievers to hellfire.[42]

Some scholars have seen American women's rejection of a strict Calvinistic outlook as having feminized American religious culture. But Olive Anderson's protagonist is as tough-minded in her moral and spiritual outlook as any fire and brimstone cleric. Her sense of self is so strong that she is sure that neither a formal creed nor a conversion experience is a necessary condition for leading a good and pious life. Her free will and deeply held personal convictions are, to her, sufficient.[43]

Will's religious nonconformity is of a piece with her social non-conformity. Although Anderson never shows her protagonist making an explicit link between these two aspects of her highly individualistic personality, she gives equal treatment to Will's religious independence and her strong commitment to "woman's rights." This was the term used in Anderson's time to designate an entire spectrum of social, educational, economic, and political privileges that "strong-minded" women were hoping to win.[44]

Anderson's novel shows the extent to which the social ferment of the woman's movement had permeated university life by the early 1870s. It also demonstrates the strength of the resistance to the movement. The University of Michigan had admitted women medical students, but according to Anderson they had to fight their way through not only "bigoted opposition from men" but from women, too. "People were slow to believe that a woman could be truly womanly and work in the dissecting-room, attend clinics, and hear lectures on all sorts of dreadful subjects," she writes. Guilford Randolf, Will's beau, shares this view, as does a rural woman who takes Will in while she recovers from being struck by lightning (chap. IX). Being a doctor is "man's work," the woman avows, "and a woman that'll do it is not modest." Will's friend Nell approves of her plans to go to medical school, not because such a career would be fulfilling but because, if Will is ever widowed, she will be able to support herself. And, finally, a local doctor "welcomes" Will into the ranks of medicine when he sees how well she has cared for Randolf when he is injured, but when he perceives Randolf's love for her he says to himself, "I guess her practice of medicine will be limited to one household." In short, no one in Will's circle can accept the idea of a woman combining a medical career, or any career for that matter, with marriage.

Will's attitudes toward marriage are pertinent here. She claims (chap. V) that the "starch" goes out of girls when they become engaged to be married. "She loses ambition right away, and don't amount to anything forever after," Will says. She feels that girls should get married but despairs that "they settle right down and lose their individuality, and are as good as dead and buried." As for herself, she wants to "do something, have an object, be somebody." Mrs. Lewis, Will's landlady, gets the last word. As Will departs after graduation Mr. Lewis predicts that in the end their lodger will marry "that pair of handsome eyes," a reference to Randolf. Mrs. Lewis chides her husband for his conceit. "You think a woman never has an aim in life that she won't leave to go at your beck and call. I have more faith in our Will than that, and we'll see if I'm not right."

The novel explores other gender conventions of the day, including courtship customs and "tomboyism." In late-nineteenth-century America, girls were not supposed to talk to boys to whom they had not been formally introduced. Although Will Elliot and Guilford Randolf see each other in classes for almost two years, they do not have an extensive conversation until Nell and her boyfriend bring them together for a croquet game (chap. VIII).

Will's tomboyism reflects her independent spirit, but, as boyishness is not always attractive to men, it troubles her mind. When we first meet Randolf, he is disparaging her to his friends for "aping boys," criticizing her from her nickname down to her "boyish" hats. Her roommate Clara worries about Will's use of boys' slang and observes her hopelessness with a needle. To her, Will needs "taming," a conclusion reinforced when Will takes part in traditionally male-identified activities such as breaking a horse, hunting birds, and chopping wood.[45]

Throughout the narrative, Will either takes issue with or breaches traditional feminine boundaries. She burns her corset. She cuts her hair short and shortens her skirts to keep them out of the mud. Randolf accepts these breaches until a society girl makes him feel ridiculous for liking Will as she is. When as a consequence he asks Will to wear longer dresses and a "switch" in her hair (to make it look longer) when they "go out," it is a clear sign of trouble. And when the society girl teases Randolf by suggesting that Will would make a husband care for the babies while she presides at a woman suffrage convention, the end of the relationship is at hand.

The Literary Dimensions of An American Girl

An American Girl is a roman à clef, an imaginative treatment of real people and events. Although such novels are often associated with satire, Anderson's was not designed to ridicule. Nor was it intended to present an entirely realistic portrayal of college life for Michigan co-eds in the early 1870s.

Some readers have taken the novel as realistic or at the very least an attempt at realism. In her history of women at Michigan, for example, Dorothy McGuigan accepts Will Elliot's tale of freshman year "persecutions" as historically accurate. Ruth Bordin, in her later study of the same subject, dismisses the tale as unrepresentative. Citing the testimony of Alice Freeman (later Palmer), who graduated from Michigan a year after Anderson, Bordin admits that Freeman felt she had been treated as a "curiosity" by townspeople. She then counters this admission with Freeman's insistence that Michigan professors "nurtured" her and her male student colleagues treated her with friendship.[46]

Two decades after graduating from Michigan in 1876, Vassar College historian Lucy Maynard Salmon received a copy of The Inlander, a Michigan student paper, which carried a story written by Mary Louise Walker Hall about the early days of coeducation at Michigan. Hall mentioned Salmon's difficulty in finding housing when she arrived on campus in 1872, an experience purporting to echo that of Will Elliot in the novel. Hall wrote, rather dramatically, "Of that brave little band of girls, one, who subsequently became the wife of a professor in our University, tells how she and Miss Salmon (for many years since a professor at Vassar), wandered up and down the streets of Ann Arbor for three whole days trying to find a boarding place." In a private letter written to President Angell, Salmon denied the implication of the story. "I have no recollection of ever 'walking the streets three days to secure a boarding place,'" she wrote. "If I did so, it was because I could find no place to suit me not because no one would take me in. Of the six years I lived in Ann Arbor, four were in the same house so that my trouble could not have been excessive."[47]

Two factors may account for the difference between the experiences of Anderson's character Will Elliot and those of the other Michigan women students. First, both Freeman and Salmon arrived at Michigan in 1872, not only a year after Anderson but two years after Will's fictive arrival. By 1872, the town and student body had become more accustomed to women students. Second, Freeman had a "sunny" disposition that endeared her to townspeople, faculty, and students alike. Thus she might have had an easier time than Anderson in adjusting to life in Ann Arbor.[48] Although Anderson describes Will as also having many admirers, Will's personality—her strong convictions, unconventional behavior, and occasional bursts of hot temper and moodiness—set her apart from some of the other women in her class. Will's critical view of her first-year experiences was, for novelist Anderson, perfectly consistent with the temperament her creator had given her.

Salmon's denial of a hard time finding a welcome in Ann Arbor may have reflected a concern about the effect of Mary Louise Walker Hall's article. "I am growing fairly nervous over it," Salmon wrote President Angell, "for at every knock at my door I expect to see someone who asks, 'Did you walk the streets of Ann Arbor three days looking for a boarding place?'" Salmon worried that such accounts of the early days not only exaggerated women's early struggles, but were most of all "humiliating" and, for those readers not familiar with the real situation, "one more proof of the general disagreeableness and undesirability of coeducation." Given the turn-of-the-century backlash against coeducation, Salmon's insistence in 1896 that she had experienced nothing unpleasant in her first days in Ann Arbor is understandable.

Even though Anderson was not writing a history of coeducation at Michigan, students had fun deciphering the names of faculty, students, and events alluded to in her story, and therefore in our annotations to this edition we identify as many of these as possible. A copy of the novel in the University of Michigan's rare book collection contains the marginal notations of one of Anderson's friends, Cora Agnes Benneson, who made many of these identifications.[49] In addition to noting what she felt was "true," however, Benneson also noted what she saw as "exaggerated," or "no longer true" in her friend's portrayal of college life. Surely Benneson understood that Anderson had written an imaginative work, one based in a lived reality but tempered by a highly individualistic perspective.

Some students lauded the novel as a just account of the university's women pioneers. The editor of The Chronicle, Michigan's student newspaper, gave an enthusiastic assessment.

All of us have felt that some book (and of course a novel would be the *best* book) ought to be written, which should preserve some record of how Michigan University took the great step which gave to women educational advantages equal to those of men, and which should recount the story of the brave young pioneers who were the first to push their way into new and untried realms of action, and make straight the paths of learning, that all their weaker sisters might follow without fear. The story of these heroines of civilization has in this book been well told. . . . It is written in a clear, sparkling style, and has such a piquancy and dash about it that one could well believe that the heroine, "Will," or her prototype, was the author, who has penned a story so unique, so brimming with wit, and so far removed from the conventional novel of the day.[50]

Any first-time author would have been well pleased with such a review.

Other reactions to the novel were less enthusiastic. "H.," who wrote to *The Chronicle*'s editor anonymously, found the novel offensive and lashed out "at the frequent displays of poor taste in the treatment of real personages and happenings."

The description of the faculty is in point. It is unnecessary to particularize; even a stranger, if possessed of any delicate sense of propriety, would discover the things to which I allude, and would only be spared intense feelings of disgust because he did not know that real individuals were the subjects of this free handling. More than this, worn out gossip is introduced, which no one has any business to rehearse, least of all to publish.

H. then quotes from a review that appeared in the *Cornell Era*, Cornell University's student newspaper, which chided the novelist for the "weakness of the plot" and "the wearying recurrence of religious discussion."[51] Despite Anderson's many references to student reading, H. also chided SOLA (Anderson's pen name) for failing to give any

hint of the intellectual life of study and reading which absorbs the average woman in college, but implies that match-making is the principal business. Without doubt the objection is well founded, although it did not occur prominently to myself. There are some of both sexes, perhaps, who take up the development of the tender passion as a sort of special elective, and with some ambitious souls it may form even a fifth study, counting possibly for ten hours a week. But such cases are phenomenal—purely phenomenal.[52]

Finally, H. quotes from a letter written by a Michigan alumna that had appeared in a local newspaper: "On the whole," the alumna wrote, "the book, which might have said so much that is interesting to recall and of advantage to know, is a little volume that the University girls who have read it look upon as a dishonor to the University, and one through which they have been deeply wronged. In every respect it is quite unworthy of the author."[53]

We can only speculate whether Anderson, who by then was residing in California, received news of these comments. If she had, this might explain why Sarah Dix Hamlin, the writer of Anderson's obituary, claimed that Anderson had come to regret "deeply and bitterly" having published the novel. She certainly was not the kind of person who took joy from the pain of others.[54]

In addition to being a roman à clef, An American Girl is also a sentimental novel. This kind of novel uses the feelings of a main character and his or her emotional relations with others to move the plot along. By the mid–nineteenth century, both men and women had written sentimental novels, but they were especially popular with middle-class women readers. This popularity prompted some male writers and critics to associate such novels with women, domesticity, and all things trivial and overdone.[55]

Some writers, however, used the sentimental genre to tremendous effect. As one scholar has shown, writers with social agendas and little publishing clout could use the genre as a vehicle for "legitimating conventions" and "engendering solidarities."[56] In the 1850s, Harriet Beecher Stowe achieved widespread sympathy for the abolition of slavery with Uncle Tom's Cabin, the epitome of the agenda-based sentimental novel. In her concluding remarks to the novel, Stowe directly addresses her readers, instructing them to "feel right": "There is one thing that every individual can do,—they can see to it that they feel right. An atmosphere of sympathetic influence encircles every human being; and the man or woman who feels strongly, healthily and justly, on the great interests of humanity, is a constant benefactor to the human race. See, then, to your sympathies in this matter!"[57]

In *An American Girl,* Wilhelmine Elliot is the only character whose thoughts and feelings readers are privileged to know. As they go through the novel, readers "feel" along with Will, empathizing with her in her struggles and triumphs.[58] Perhaps Anderson intended her novel to engender solidarity among women or at least to make an emotional argument against the opponents of coeducation and in favor of freeing women from oppressive social conventions. In any case, Anderson wields the accepted formulas of the sentimental novel in a way that creates empathy in her readers for those who violate accepted social norms.

Will is a rebel. She rejects many social strictures, from her church catechism to her own corset, too binding for her to bear. By placing her strong-minded character within the conventions of the sentimental novel, Anderson wins sympathy for her. One contemporary charge against the woman's movement was that it "unsexed" women, that is, made them into putative men. Will might cut her hair and burn her corset, chop wood, go hunting, and tame ornery horses, but she can still be beautiful to look at and can fall in love with a man. The advocates of coeducation argued similarly: women could study with men and take the same academic courses without losing their femininity or harming their reproductive capacity. Ironically, the literary limits of the sentimental novel reflect the larger cultural limitations of the post–Civil War woman's movement, which insisted that women constantly had to prove that they could take on larger public roles without becoming Amazons.

The conventions of the sentimental novel are all present in *An American Girl.* The invalid yet angelic younger sister, Hally, who is very much like the precocious Little Eva in *Uncle Tom's Cabin,* provides the necessary religious and sympathetic foil to Will. As Will's confessor, conscience, and advocate, she softens Will's untraditional character. With her body broken in a carriage accident, Hally presents the antithesis of the healthy and strong-minded Will. Hally is all heart (emotion) and soul (she has been "saved"). In short, Hally "feels right" on Will's behalf. As *The Chronicle* reviewer wrote, "The story of Hally's death [is] as pathetic and touching as though [it] had come from the magic pen of Bret Harte."[59]

Homosocial intimacy is another feature of the sentimental novel that is prominent in Anderson's novel. Will shares domestic space with many other female characters, her sister Hally at home and her roommates Nell and Clara at Ortonville. Her relationships with them express the importance of female bonding (with both verbal and physical expressions of love) and reflect the gender-specific world of the sentimental novel. Furthermore, they temper Will Elliot's rebellious nature, with each presenting various aspects and degrees of respectable femininity (from her best friend Nell, who is highly marriage-conscious yet religiously liberal, to her roommate Clara, a missionary type who is deeply devoted to saving others). These women, along with the distant influence of her invalid sister, repeatedly come to Will's rescue whenever she goes "too far." And when she does transgress boundaries she either suffers the consequences and engenders sympathy in the reader through the sympathy of her friends or she triumphs and fills her family and friends—and thus the reader— with empathetic pride. As part of the story, then, these female characters keep the headstrong Will safely within the confines of sentimental literary conventions.

While the issue of racial prejudice is an important theme in some sentimental novels of the era, most notably, of course, in *Uncle Tom's Cabin*, it is barely present in *An American Girl*. Only two persons of color appear in the novel, a lisping servant boy who turns Will away from a boardinghouse and a "trickster" barber to whom she repairs when she decides to cut her hair. The novel is about a middle-class white woman from a small town in Ohio, and the small cultural universe in which Will Elliott and Olive San Louie Anderson moved seems to have lacked meaningful interactions with African Americans. Perhaps, like other feminists of her era, Anderson was more concerned with issues of gender than with those of race. Thus, she provides her readers with only stereotypical black characters, a lisping servant and a "trickster" barber.

Of these two encounters, the one with the barber is the more interesting. Will goes to the "dusky son of Ham,"[60] as Anderson describes him, on impulse (chap. VIII). The barber registers her instructions about length with a grin, saying "Yes, miss; all right." She is so busy memorizing an ode for class that she pays no attention to the results, merely throwing a scarf over her head at the end and heading for home. Back at her boardinghouse, the horrified faces of her friends register "the crime." He had sheared her hair so short that "one could not catch it with thumb and finger." "Will Elliott! what have you done?—you're ruined!" her friends shriek. Will is mortified: "O girls! he has ruined my head for life—ruined!"

The word *ruined* carries sexual connotations. A ruined woman is one who has lost her virginity and is thus unfit for marriage. Will has been tricked, but she has also been violated, as "the rape of her locks" implies. The declaration of her landlord, Mr. Lewis, that he will horsewhip the barber makes the act all the more redolent of a common white male response to a presumed black violation of white womanhood. The barber has not raped Will, of course, but he has nonetheless violated her by depriving her of her femininity. The next day Will must display this fact to her male classmates. The boys in her class guffaw at the sight of her shorn head and tease her with the name Captain Elliott. In the end, Will takes the blame for her impulsiveness, Mr. Lewis is talked out of his urge to commit racial violence, and her friends' sympathy for her plight tames the teasing boys. The Michigan women bond with Will in female empathy, later admitting that she looks better with short hair. The aesthetics of sentiment (feeling Will's pain and redemption) thus diffuse the potential explosiveness of race and even vindicate her nonconformity.

As in all sentimental novels, domesticity itself plays a key role. Despite the university setting, the important character interactions take place largely within private, domestic spaces: Will's home and her boarding-house rooms. Will has adventures outside of these spaces (in the classroom, on horseback, on ice skates, at the debate podium), but she always returns to the private spaces where womanly feelings dominate. There she finds refuge in the sympathy and support of female bonding. Moreover, domestic concerns hover in the near future. Her stormy relationship with Guilford Randolf—whose promises of love come with the certainty of more social conventions to bind Will—ends bitterly, and Will is freed for the rest of the story from this future of domestic limitation by Randolf's own (as she sees it) inability to empathize with her nonconformity. Yet as the novel ends a future partnership between Will and Randolf is still a possibility. Limited by the social constraints of late-nineteenth-century gender expectations, Anderson allows at least some of the conventions of the sentimental novel to prevail.

As we know, the conventions of sentimentality did not prevail in the life of Olive San Louie Anderson. After her graduation from Michigan, she moved to California to become a teacher and school administrator. At the time of her death, she was planning a trip abroad and reaching for new heights as a creative writer. She enjoyed many warm friendships and the companionship of a group of like-minded, creative young adults of both sexes. She had not married. Was this because in entering a marital relationship she would have had to subordinate her own interests and ambitions to those of her husband? Possibly. Many intellectual women of her era felt that heterosexual marriage was too constraining. Some chose instead to enter into the lifelong romantic partnerships with women that were often called "Boston marriages."[61]

We do not know whether Anderson enjoyed such a relationship. It is possible that Elizabeth Curtis, who edited her final writings, or Sarah Dix Hamlin, who wrote her obituary, were special friends. But the pen name Anderson chose for An American Girl, SOLA, seems to hint otherwise. In addition to being an anagram of her initials, the word suggests a strong commitment to independence. Thus, Anderson may have planned a life course as a teacher and writer completely "on her own."

Olive San Louie Anderson was certainly of an independent mind; the mere act of writing and publishing a novel takes both independence and courage. We are grateful to her for having left us An American Girl, a novel to enjoy and appreciate on several levels. As a testament to middle-class women's desires for higher education, it makes a singular contribution to the intellectual history of late-nineteenth-century American women. As a feminist novel, it brings to life a period, not so far in the past, when Americans took for granted women's exclusion from the halls of academe as well as from the professions. Finally, as an imaginative depiction of the coming "American girl" it portrays a heroine with whom we can identify. Will Elliot may be a character rooted in the Victorian era, but she harbored within her soul aspirations for personal and intellectual fulfillment that many modern readers will recognize in themselves.

NOTES

1. See Dorothy Gies McGuigan, A Dangerous Experiment: 100 Years of Women at the University of Michigan (Ann Arbor: University of Michigan Press, 1970), chaps. 3–4; and Ruth Bordin, Women at Michigan: The "Dangerous Experiment," 1870s to the Present (Ann Arbor: University of Michigan Press, 1999), 1. The phrase "dangerous experiment" comes from the regents' own description of coeducation: "By many it is regarded as a doubtful experiment, by some as a very dangerous experiment . . . certain to be ruinous to the young ladies who should avail themselves of it . . . and disastrous to the institution which should carry it out" (quoted in Bordin, Women at Michigan, xvi).

2. Both historians wrote their studies under the auspices of the University of Michigan's Center for the Education of Women. Bordin wrote hers in order to bring McGuigan's up to date and to apply insights drawn from works in women's history

published since McGuigan completed her study. See also Bordin's biography of Alice Palmer, a Michigan graduate who went on to become president of Wellesley College, *Alice Freeman Palmer: The Evolution of a New Woman* (Ann Arbor: University of Michigan Press, 1993, and online at http://www.press.umich.edu/bookhome/bordin/).

3. In this era, students who had not graduated from Michigan high schools accredited by the university presented themselves to its professors to be examined orally. Students with deficiencies could make them up by working with senior tutors. See Bordin, *Women at Michigan*, 14.

4. Most of the following information comes from Sarah Dix Hamlin's "Olive San Louie Anderson, Class of '75, Obituary" (June 5, 1886), 20 pp., Sarah Dix Hamlin Paper, Bentley Historical Library, University of Michigan, Ann Arbor, Michigan (hereafter BHL). In soliciting subscriptions for a memorial booklet of stories and sketches Anderson's friends intended to publish, Hamlin gave her address as 1606 Van Ness Avenue, San Francisco. This suggests that the friendship she began with Anderson at Michigan continued in California.

5. The reference here is, of course, to Jo March, the protagonist of Louisa May Alcott's famous novel, *Little Women* (1868–69). Apparently some members of Olive's family called her "Louie," another masculine name. See note 8.

6. This description of Anderson's talk comes from "The University, Concluding Proceedings of the Board of Regents, the Exercises of Commencement Day," *Tribune* (July 1, 1875), p. 31, Scrapbook Vol. III, Box 22, Alexander Winchell Papers, BHL.

7. As Hamlin points out, Anderson was not alone in her views. She writes, "Scarcely a girl at the University was not strong-minded, in that she disdained weak-mindedness, and had a contempt for affectation, silliness, and inactivity. . . ."

8. In a diary entry dated June 25, 1886, Anderson's sixteen-year-old cousin Nina Cook wrote, "We got word last Sunday of cousin Louie Anderson's death. It did not seem possible that she could die, for she was so strong and daring and brave. She was bathing in the Sacramento river and was drowned. We have had no word since. Her body was not found until quite a while afterwards. I believe she got in sort of a whirlpool. This is the ending to her book, *An American Girl and her Four Years in a Boy's College*, which itself had no end." See www.stumpranchonline.com/skagitjournal/S-W/Pioneer/Cook/Cook02-NinaDiary.html (accessed May 9, 2005).

9. For an extensive discussion of these attitudes, see the classic work of Linda Kerber, *Women of the Republic: Intellect and Ideology in Revolutionary America* (Chapel Hill: University of North Carolina Press, 1980).

10. Today we would use the term *women's movement*, but in the nineteenth century activists used the term *woman*, calling their movement the *woman's movement* and their meetings *woman's rights conventions*. For an introduction to the nineteenth-century woman's movement, see Eleanor Flexner and Ellen Fitzpatrick, *Century of Struggle: The Woman's Rights Movement in the United States* (Cambridge: Harvard University Press, 1996). For the text of the "Declaration of Sentiments and Resolutions," on which those attending the Seneca Falls convention (held in Seneca Falls, New York, July 19–20, 1848) voted, see Mari Jo Buhle and Paul Buhle, eds., *The Concise History of Woman Suffrage: Selections from the Classic Work of Stanton, Anthony, Gage, and Harper* (Urbana: University of Illinois Press, 1978), 91–97. The declaration can also be found in almost every anthology of feminist historical documents. For information on women intellectuals of the early nineteenth century, see Susan Conrad, *Perish the Thought: Intellectual Women in Romantic America, 1830–1860* (New

York: Oxford University Press, 1976); and Charles Capper, *Margaret Fuller: An American Romantic Life* (New York: Oxford University Press, 1992).

11. See Jurgen Herbst, *And Sadly Teach: Teacher Education and Professionalization in American Culture* (Madison: University of Wisconsin Press, 1989). In the United States, normal schools trained primary-school teachers. The first was founded in Massachusetts in 1839; others followed in the 1840s. Many of today's major universities began as normal schools, but the term is no longer used today. Most teacher training now takes place in college or university education departments or graduate schools.

12. For more on the history of women's education, see Ellen F. Fitzpatrick, *Endless Crusade: Women Social Scientists and Progressive Reform* (New York: Oxford University Press, 1990); Roger Geiger, ed., *The American College in the Nineteenth Century* (Nashville: Vanderbilt University Press, 2000); Lynn D. Gordon, *Gender and Higher Education in the Progressive Era* (New Haven: Yale University Press, 1990); Helen Lefkowitz Horowitz, *Alma Mater: Design and Experience in the Women's Colleges from Their Nineteenth-Century Beginnings to the 1930s* (Boston: Beacon Press, 1984); Carol Lasser, ed., *Educating Men and Women Together: Coeducation in a Changing World* (Urbana: University of Illinois Press in conjunction with Oberlin College, 1987); Janice Lee, "Administrative Treatment of Women Students at Missouri State University, 1868–1899," *Missouri Historical Review* 87, no. 4 (July 1993): 372–86; Mabel Newcomer, *A Century of Higher Education for Women* (New York: Harper and Bros., 1959); Pat Palmieri, *In Adamless Eden: The Community of Women at Wellesley* (New Haven: Yale University Press, 1995); Rosalind Rosenberg, *Beyond Separate Spheres: Intellectual Roots of Modern Feminism* (New Haven: Yale University Press, 1982); Barbara Miller Solomon, *In the Company of Educated Women: A History of Women and Higher Education in America* (New Haven: Yale University Press, 1985); David B. Tyack and Elisabeth Hansot, *Learning Together: A History of Coeducation in American Schools* (New Haven: Yale University Press, 1990); and Thomas Woody, *A History of Women's Education in the United States* (New York: Science Press, 1929). Chapter 3 of Kathryn Kish Sklar, *Florence Kelley and the Nation's Work: The Rise of Women's Political Culture, 1830–1900* (New Haven: Yale University Press, 1995), offers a good description of coeducational life at Cornell University in the early 1870s.

13. Lori D. Ginzberg, "'The Joint Education of the Sexes': Oberlin's Original Vision," in *Educating Men and Women Together*, edited by Carol Lasser, 67—80 (Urbana: University of Illinois Press in conjunction with Oberlin College, 1987); and Ronald W. Hogeland, "Coeducation of the Sexes at Oberlin College: A Study of Social Ideas in Mid-Nineteenth-Century America," *Journal of Social History* 6, no. 2 (1972–73): 160–76.

14. In the nineteenth century, mixed-sex audiences were called "promiscuous," a meaning for the word no longer in current usage.

15. For more on Antioch's early days of coeducation, see John Rury and Glenn Harper, "The Trouble with Coeducation: Mann and Women at Antioch, 1853–1860," *History of Education Quarterly* 26, no. 4 (winter 1986): 481–502; and McGuigan, *A Dangerous Experiment*, 21.

16. See Doris Malkmus, "Origins of Coeducation in Antebellum Iowa," *Annals of Iowa* 58 (spring 1999): 162–96. According to Malkmus, conservative midwestern denominations raised money from eastern philanthropists to found all-male colleges in

the West, but these were never successful. Neither were all-female seminaries. In 1853, noted educator Catharine Beecher went West to offer money to communities interested in establishing a female seminary. Only Dubuque, Iowa, followed through, but the seminary that opened there in 1857 attracted only eighty students to a building designed for two hundred and soon failed, as did other "genteel" female seminaries founded in Iowa (170, 174). See also pages 178–79, where Malkmus writes: "Since many students found spouses while at college, educating sons or daughters at the college of another denomination meant risking that their children would marry outside the faith."

17. See "Discussion of the Same Subject (The Intellectual Progress of the Colored Women of the United States since the Emancipation Proclamation) by Mrs. A. J. Cooper of Washington, D.C.," in *The World's Congress of Representative Women*, edited by May Wright Sewall, 711–15 (Chicago: Rand McNally, 1894). The schools Cooper mentioned in her 1893 speech included Hampton, Fisk, Atlanta, Raleigh, Wilberforce, Livingstone, Allen, and Paul Quinn.

18. Edward Hicks Magill, *An Address upon the Co-education of the Sexes* (Philadelphia: Charles A. Dixon, 1873), 5–6. Helen Magill, his brilliant daughter, was the first woman in the nation to earn a Ph.D. See her biography in *Notable American Women, 1607–1950: A Biographical Dictionary*, edited by Edward T. James, Janet Wilson James, and Paul S. Boyer, 3:588–89 (Cambridge: Harvard University Press, 1971), under Helen Magill White. In her forties, Helen Magill became the second wife of Cornell University's president, Andrew Dickson White; White and her father had been college colleagues.

19. Signed into law by President Abraham Lincoln on July 2, 1862, the Morrill Act (named after Congressman Justin Smith Morrill of Vermont) was designed to fund practical education for the nation's farmers and workers. The act granted public lands to states in the amount of thirty thousand acres for each member of a state's congressional delegation. The states were to sell the land and use the proceeds to endow colleges that would teach agriculture and "the mechanic arts" (such as engineering) in addition to regular academic subjects. As a result of the act, more than seventy land-grant colleges were established in the Middle and Far West. A second Morrill Act, passed in 1890, extended its provisions to sixteen southern states, with the grants divided equally between white and black schools.

20. Roger L. Geiger, "The Era of Multipurpose Colleges in American Higher Education, 1850–1890," in *The American College in the Nineteenth Century*, edited by Roger L. Geiger, 141–42 (Nashville: Vanderbilt University Press, 2000); Bordin, *Women at Michigan*, 3–4.

21. The university was founded in 1817, but its state charter dates from 1837.

22. Except for the quotation from Lyman Beecher, this reconstruction of the regents' discussion is based on McGuigan, *A Dangerous Experiment*, chap. 3; and Bordin, *Women at Michigan*, chap. 1. The Beecher quotation comes from Robert Samuel Fletcher, *History of Oberlin College from Its Foundation through the Civil War* (Oberlin, Ohio: Oberlin College, 1943), 377.

23. Among the faculty members favoring coeducation were Alexander Winchell, Professor of Geology, and James Robinson Boise, Professor of Greek. In 1866, Winchell pondered the question of women and wrote an essay entitled "Woman: Her Actual Place and Her Rightful Place," which he read at a "Senate Social" on January 26. Boise,

the father of the brilliant Alice, had been the only faculty member to favor women's admission in 1858, saying that "No reason urged against the admission of ladies is sufficient for its denial." See McGuigan, *A Dangerous Experiment*, 26–29.

24. These anecdotes all come from McGuigan, *A Dangerous Experiment*, chaps. 4 and 5. The quotation from the *Michigan Argus* is on page 33. For similar views on the debilitating effect of women's menstrual cycles, see the subsequent discussion of Dr. Edward Clarke's famous book, *Sex in Education*.

25. Quoted in McGuigan, *A Dangerous Experiment*, chap. 6.

26. Ibid., chap. 9 and p. 87; Bordin, *Women at Michigan*, 31–34. Mosher remained at Michigan for only six years. For a biography of her, see *Notable American Women, 1607–1950: A Biographical Dictionary*, edited by Edward T. James, Janet Wilson James, and Paul S. Boyer, 2:587–88 (Cambridge: Harvard University Press, 1971). The chaired appointments that the University of Michigan made in the 1950s were in the Psychology and History Departments.

27. See McGuigan, *A Dangerous Experiment*, 50. In *An American Girl* (chap. VI), Will debates the virtues of coeducation in an exchange of letters with a friend, "Mame," who is a student at Vassar. In her response, Mame claims that she is "as free here as it is possible to be in an institution of the kind. I'd like to see you put four hundred girls together, and leave no particular rules and no one in particular to see that they behave!"

28. McGuigan, *A Dangerous Experiment*, 61. She quotes the university's president, James Burrill Angell, who in 1883 wrote: "We have no rules prescribing their conduct in the hours of recreation, save the general rule that their conduct shall everywhere be such as is becoming."

29. The first generations of college women tended to be older because they enjoyed less financial support from parents and usually had to spend several years teaching to earn enough to meet their college expenses. In the novel, Will's roommate, Clara Hopkins, is two years older than Will and had taught in a primary school before being able to afford college tuition. The introduction of a regulatory system in the 1890s may also have been a response to pressure from the young women themselves, who enjoyed the experience of homosocial bonding in separate women's facilities. The first dean to establish "approved" rooming houses for women was Eliza Mosher's successor, Myra Beach Jordan; the first dormitories appeared after 1915. See ibid., 111; and Bordin, *Women at Michigan*, 35–37.

30. The book saw seventeen printings in all. The last was in 1886, by which time the controversy had died down but not ended. Clarke published a sequel, *The Building of a Brain*, in 1874, which provided supporting evidence from educators for his conclusions. The copy we refer to here is the fifth printing, published in Boston by James R. Osgood and Company in 1874.

31. Clarke, *Sex in Education*, 27, 127, 19.

32. For informative discussions of Clarke and his ideas, see Sue Zschoche, "Dr. Clarke Revisited: Science, True Womanhood, and Female Collegiate Education," *History of Education Quarterly* 29, no. 4 (1989): 545–69; Patricia A. Palmieri, "From Republican Motherhood to Race Suicide: Arguments on the Higher Education of Women in the United States, 1820–1920," in *Educating Men and Women Together*, edited by Carol Lasser, 49–64 (Urbana: University of Illinois Press in conjunction with Oberlin College, 1987); McGuigan, *A Dangerous Experiment*, chap. 8; and Rosalind Rosenberg, *Beyond Separate Spheres: The Intellectual Roots of Modern Feminism* (New

Haven: Yale University Press, 1982), 5–27. Rosenberg notes that Clarke himself had to drop out of Harvard due to a "hemorrhage from the lungs" (10, n. 22). For more on evolutionary biology, see Cynthia Eagle Russett, *Sexual Science: The Victorian Construction of Womanhood* (Cambridge: Harvard University Press, 1989).

33. Clarke, *Sex in Education*, 23, 92–94.

34. Writer and poet Julia Ward Howe was one of the first feminist respondents to Clarke. See the book she edited in 1874, *Sex and Education: A Reply to Dr. E. H. Clarke's 'Sex in Education'* (New York: Arno Press, 1972). The scientific survey appeared in Annie Howes, "Health Statistics of Women College Graduates: Report of a Special Committee of the Association of Collegiate Alumnae" (Boston, 1885). This association was the forerunner of today's American Association of University Women. Sue Zschoche notes that the publication of their statistics ended Clarke's popularity, though an obituary for his views was premature. For Clarke, "periodicity" was the law of women's biology. Feminists might argue that women's "will" could overcome the force of this law, but according to Zschoche the idea that it dominated women's physiological makeup "remained central to medical and psychological views of women and their education well into the twentieth century" ("Dr. Clarke Revisited," 563). Concerned about declining birth rates among educated women (which surely were more the result of choice than sterility brought on by excessive brain work), by the turn of the century educational reformers were arguing that "most" women wanted to fulfill their "femininity" through an education that was "different" from that given to men. By the second decade of the twentieth century, educators had rejected the "ungendered" education craved by the first generations of college women.

35. Although townspeople interpret the physical failures of two women students in Will's sophomore year as proof of Clarke's premises, Anderson is quick to point out that male students fell ill as well (chap. VIII).

36. Tyack and Hansot, *Learning Together*, 104.

37. In 1908, Julius Sachs, a professor of education at Teachers' College, Columbia University, reaffirmed sex differences when he argued that women should not "duplicate the effort and pursuits of young men when other subjects for which they are particularly fitted are still ignored." Unless they are redirected toward fields (which he never names) for which they are "fitted," men will continue to voluntarily segregate themselves from literary courses because they think of them as feminized. See Julius Sachs, "In the Educational World," *Literary Digest* 37, no. 4 (July 25, 1908): 125–26.

38. G. Stanley Hall, *Adolescence: Its Psychology and Its Relations to Physiology, Anthropology, Sociology, Sex, Crime, Religion, and Education* (New York: D. Appleton, 1904), 2:627, 632, 635, 639. Clarke announced his concerns about the future of "the race" in his *Sex in Education:* "If the culture of the race moves on into the future in the same rut and by the same methods that limit and direct it now; if the education of the sexes remains identical, instead of being appropriate and special; and especially if the intense and passionate stimulus of the identical co-education of the sexes is added to their identical education,—then the sterilizing influence of such a training, acting with tenfold more force upon the female than upon the male, will go on, and the race will be propagated from its inferior classes" (139).

39. McGuigan, *A Dangerous Experiment*, 104–6.

40. For a discussion of a famous nineteenth-century woman who also rejected Calvinism, see Kathryn Kish Sklar, *Catharine Beecher: A Study in American Domesticity* (New Haven: Yale University Press, 1973), 246ff.

41. On religious revivals at Michigan, see Philip Harrold, "'A Transitional Period in Belief': Deconversion and the Decline of Campus Revivals in the 1870s," in *Embodying the Spirit: New Perspectives on North American Revivalism*, edited by Michael J. McClymond, 109–24 (Baltimore: Johns Hopkins University Press, 2004). Reinforcing Harrold's observation of "decline," the campus reviewer of *An American Girl* wrote: "The religious ideas in the book are not subjects for a criticism in this place, although we must say that it is refreshing to read a novel which introduces religious discussions in the story without converting all the characters to orthodoxy in the last chapter." See "An American Girl and Her Four Years in a Boys' College," *The Chronicle* 9, no. 8 (February 2, 1878): 117–18 (hereafter *Chronicle* review).

42. "I beg to be spared further persuasion, Mr. Allison," an indignant Will exclaims (chap. VII), avowing that "I shall never be brought to become a Christian on the terms you present; they only repel my affections and degrade my reason." Through her friendship with Nellie Holmes, who attends a Unitarian church, she thinks she might find solace in a religion that emphasizes a loving God. But she remains skeptical, especially when she is feeling miserable over the end of her relationship with Randolf. "If I believe in any almighty Power," she says in despair, "it is in one who delights in our wretchedness—one who loves to make us trust in people, and then show us how foolish we are to do so" (chap. XI).

43. Ann Douglas's *The Feminization of American Culture* (New York: Knopf, 1977) takes a dim view of the nineteenth-century rejection of Calvinism, which she blames on "effeminate" ministers and sentimental women writers. Olive Anderson's protagonist defies this stereotyping. Unlike the "weak" and "sentimental" women Douglas studied, Anderson was a feminist who both rejected Calvinism and remained strong-minded; in addition, she sometimes behaves in stereotypically "masculine" ways. For more on the controversy aroused by Douglas's book and sexual stereotypes in literature, see David S. Reynolds, "The Feminization Controversy: Sexual Stereotypes and the Paradoxes of Piety in Nineteenth-Century America," *New England Quarterly* 53, no. 1 (March 1980): 96–106.

44. By the time Anderson was writing, many woman's rights activists had, in varying ways, set themselves up against institutionalized religion. Frances ("Fanny") Wright (1795–1852), one of the early-nineteenth-century's most notorious "freethinkers," linked women's subordination to the influence of priests. Later in the century Elizabeth Cady Stanton (1815–1902) published *The Woman's Bible* (1895), a critique of scripture and the church for having limited women's sphere of action. Anderson's protagonist took a more moderate position, never directly attacking either priests, church, or Bible but simply declaring her independence from all "confessions of faith." On Wright, see Celia Morris Eckhardt, *Fanny Wright: Rebel in America* (Cambridge: Harvard University Press, 1984); and Lori Ginzberg, "'The Hearts of Your Readers Will Shudder': Fanny Wright, Infidelity, and American Freethought," *American Quarterly* 46, no. 2 (June 1994): 195–226. On Stanton and the Bible, see Kathi Kern, *Mrs. Stanton's Bible* (Ithaca: Cornell University Press, 2001).

45. On tomboyism in the nineteenth century, see Sharon O'Brien;, "Tomboyism and Adolescent Conflict: Three Nineteenth-Century Case Studies," in *Woman's Being, Woman's Place: Female Identity and Vocation in American History*, edited by Mary Kelley, 351–72 (Boston: G. K. Hall, 1979), a study of the conflicts endured by Frances Willard, Willa Cather, and Louisa May Alcott between their free and independent childhoods and the lessons in submissive domesticity they had to learn after puberty.

46. Bordin, *Alice Freeman Palmer*, 44; *Women at Michigan*, 10–13. See also Helen Lefkowitz Horowitz, *Campus Life: Undergraduate Cultures from the End of the Eighteenth Century to the Present* (Chicago: University of Chicago Press, 1987).

47. Lucy Salmon to President Angell, April 29, 1896, Folder 155, Box 4, James B. Angell Papers, BHL.

48. Bordin thinks that Anderson was describing Freeman when she wrote the following of one of Will's friends, Nellie Holmes: "At first glance you would say she had not a single element of beauty. Her hair was red, and her nose had a decided inclination to turn up; she had freckles and light eyebrows, and yet no person became acquainted with Nellie Holmes who did not think her beautiful, and before her college life was over, more than half a dozen boys had fallen hopelessly in love with her, and raved about her beauty, while she was a paragon of loveliness to all the girls in the class." One problem with ascribing this description to Freeman is that "Nellie Holmes" was a Unitarian while Freeman was a Presbyterian. As Bordin writes (*Alice Freeman Palmer*, 51): "Until she married, Alice Freeman's formal religious affiliation was always with the Presbyterian church. She joined the Windsor congregation at fourteen, and in January of 1873 transferred her membership by letter to the First Presbyterian Church of Ann Arbor. Again in 1875 when she interrupted her Ann Arbor years to teach in Illinois, she attended the Presbyterian church in Ottawa as a matter of course." In any event, Nellie Holmes may have been a composite character.

49. The copy of the novel that we originally obtained through Interlibrary Loan from the University of Missouri Library also had penciled notations in the margin but by an unknown hand.

50. *Chronicle* review, 117.

51. The *Cornell Era*'s review concluded, derisively, "Although we are neither 'a prim old lady, who spent our maiden days in needle work, or proper waiting, until some man should come along and marry us,' nor are we 'a young lady pursuing the same career,' nevertheless for ourselves we can merely say, Providence and the maiden permitting *we* will never marry that kind of girl."

52. "Correspondence," *The Chronicle* 9, no. 11 (March 16, 1878): 166–67.

53. The *Post and Tribune*, January 31, 1878.

54. Hamlin, "Olive San Louie Anderson," 9.

55. For more on sentimental literature, see June Howard, "What Is Sentimentality?" *American Literary History* 11, no. 1 (1999): 70–71, 75. Other works that tackle the subject of sentiment as a social construct and literary device include Nina Baym, *Woman's Fiction: A Guide to Novels about Women in America, 1820–1870*, 2d ed. (Urbana: University of Illinois Press, 1993); Douglas, *The Feminization of American Culture*; Shirley Samuels, ed., *The Culture of Sentiment: Race, Gender, and Sentimentality in Nineteenth-Century America* (New York: Oxford University Press, 1992); Glenn Hendler, *Public Sentiments: Structures of Feeling in Nineteenth-Century American Literature* (Chapel Hill: University of North Carolina Press, 2001); Lori Merish, *Sentimental Materialism: Gender, Commodity Culture, and Nineteenth-Century American Literature* (Durham: Duke University Press, 2000); and Jane Tompkins, *Sensational Designs: The Cultural Work of American Fiction, 1790–1860* (New York: Oxford University Press, 1985). The writer Henry James derided sentimentality as affectation in opposition to "real" human feeling. Twentieth-century literary scholars describe sentimentality as "emotional response in excess of the occasion; emotional response which has not been prepared for in the story in question." Critics continue to

cast sentimentality in literature and other narrative forms, such as theater and film, as unreal, exaggerated, and manipulative. This is true even of those scholars who seek to redeem its value as a valid area of inquiry.

56. See Howard, "What Is Sentimentality?" 74.

57. Harriet Beecher Stowe, *Uncle Tom's Cabin* (New York: Bantam, [1852] 1981), 442.

58. The reviewer wrote that "all through the book are little gems of description and deft transcriptions of human feeling which show no ordinary power in the author" (*Chronicle* review, 118).

59. Ibid. According to June Howard, Bret Harte was one of the few male writers critically condemned for employing the language of sentimentality. Cleanth Brooks and Robert Penn Warren, in *Understanding Fiction* (New York: F. S. Crofts, 1943), deride Harte for his sentimentality when, as Howard sees it, they are actually most offended by Harte's "failure to defend family values" by allowing wife stealing to be forgiven and an elopement to stand unchallenged. See Howard, "What Is Sentimentality?" 75.

60. This is a biblical reference to the presumably "dark" sons of Ham, descendants of Ham, the son of Noah, and the progenitors of Africans. See Gen. 9:25.

61. The term may have come from Henry James's novel *The Bostonians* (1886), which satirized strong female friendships in the Boston woman's movement. Scholars agree that some, though not all, of the female "marriages" of this era involved not only romance but also sexual intimacy. For more perspectives on these relationships, see John D'Emilio and Estelle B. Freedman, *Intimate Matters: A History of Sexuality in America* (New York: Harper and Row, 1988), and Lillian Faderman, *Surpassing the Love of Men: Romantic Friendship and Love between Women, from the Renaissance to the Present* (New York: Morrow, 1981).

AN

AMERICAN GIRL,

AND HER

FOUR YEARS IN A BOYS' COLLEGE.

BY

S O L A.

NEW YORK:
D. APPLETON AND COMPANY,
549 & 551 BROADWAY.
1878.

A note on our method of annotation:

We have provided two kinds of annotations to Anderson's novel: glosses that define or explain obscure references, and endnotes that provide further background information on issues and individuals discussed in the novel. Glosses appear at the bottom of the pages of the novel; the endnotes can be found at the end of the novel, organized by chapter.

—The Editors

CHAPTER I

The Bending of the Twig

A child of thy grandmother, Eve—a female;
Or for thy more sweet understanding, a woman.

— SHAKESPEARE

"O mother, just listen to this that I found in to-day's paper! Here's my chance to go to college: 'Recognizing the equal right of both sexes to the higher educational advantages, the Board of Regents have made provision for the education of women, and they are now admitted to all the departments of the University of Ortonville on the same conditions that are required of men.'*[1] There! if that doesn't come as near being a special Providence as anything that ever happened to me! Won't it be glorious, mother? I'll study hard, and win honors, and you'll be as proud of me as if I were a boy." And Wilhelmine Elliott stood with expectant face, while her mother said, quietly:

"You know, Willie, that we have never quite agreed upon this subject of the higher education of women, and I could never give my consent to have a daughter of mine make herself so conspicuous as to enter an institution founded and designed only for young men. Then, if there were no other objection, it could be condemned because of the ill-effects that would result to their health; for girls cannot tread the same path that boys do without detriment to their health, as the highest medical authority may be brought forward to prove."†

"O mother dear, how can you say that?—for not all the high medical authority in Christendom can make me believe that I was born and

*University of Ortonville: Anderson's fictional name for the University of Michigan.
†the highest medical authority: Mrs. Elliott is referring to Dr. Edward H. Clarke (1820–77), a prominent Boston physician and the author of *Sex in Education; or, A Fair Chance for Girls* (1873).

41

Along the Diagonal Walk, the University of Michigan, 1870s. The campus of the University of Ortonville, the fictitious setting of the novel, was "not accustomed to resound with the tread of girlish feet, and the steps had hitherto been worn only by male devotees in their pilgrimages to the temple of learning." (Bentley Historical Library, University of Michigan, BL001936.)

destined to be an invalid, all my life, because I happen to be a girl. Have I ruined my health by keeping up with Frank's class in the high-school? Look at me," and she drew herself up proudly, but a moment after she burst into a merry laugh as she caught sight of her face and form in the mirror opposite; for they were, certainly, a glowing refutation of the theory that girls cannot do the same work that boys do, as far, at least, as the end of a high-school course.

"I know that you are an exception in the way of health, Willie," replied the mother, "for which you should be very thankful; indeed, you have always been more like a boy than a girl, but now it is time that you were settling down, and paying attention to things that essentially pertain to woman's sphere."

"You look at things so differently from most mothers," said the girl, "for it was only yesterday that Mrs. Denton said to me that she would be perfectly happy if Ella were as much interested in getting an education as I seemed to be, instead of spending her time in flirtations, balls, and parties; and, on the other hand, you wish that I was like somebody else's daughter, and yet if I were like Ella you would not be satisfied with me."

"Mothers are queer things," she continued, laughingly; "they take opposite ground from the crow who always thinks her own are the whitest, for mothers think other people's children better than their own, mine does at least; but, now in regard to this college business, you know that, since father's death,*² we have all been brought up with the idea that we must make our own way in the world, and what could be a better preparation for this than a good classical education; and when it is offered for the taking, it seems to me the blankest stupidity to refuse it. If you needed me at home to help you, mother, it would be different, but you do not; and why can't I take my part of father's estate and put it into an education, which will be my stock in trade?"

"You oblige me, my daughter, to give another reason, and one outweighing all the others, that makes me unwilling to have you go away from the restraints of home, and be exposed to the temptations of college-life; and that is the fact that you have never had a change of heart, have never taken Jesus as your Saviour, and, without this, education can be nothing but a curse. I have watched your growing tendency to unbelief with the anguish that only a mother can feel, who sees her loved ones going to destruction, and I say now and here that you can never have my consent to any step that will only make you a greater power for evil, because not begun in the fear of the Lord, which is the only true beginning of wisdom."

"I may as well tell you now, mother," said Will, "something that I have been going to tell you for a long time. I don't think that I ever can believe as you want me to in those things. I try to, but it grows more impossible every day. You have almost forced me to accept certain forms of religious belief; but, mother, I must be free." And the proud lip quivered. "I do love Jesus, although I have not been able to accept all the doctrines that you

---

*father's death: Olive San Louie Anderson's own father died when she was seventeen, just before she graduated from Mansfield High School in 1869.

have taught me. What do we judge people by, if not by their every-day lives; and what have I done that is so bad, mother? Have I ever done a dishonest or dishonorable thing? And yet you deny me your consent and blessing when I want to do something entirely proper, and that some would even call praise-worthy, simply because I am not a professing Christian; and, therefore, you cannot trust me away from home for fear that I will bring disgrace upon you. I cannot disobey you, mother, but I feel that I am right, and once more I ask your consent to my going to college." And she stood with flushed cheeks before her mother.

As she looked at the bowed head, where threads of gray were fast taking the place of the darker locks, and as memory brought back the years in which she had been watched over and cared for tenderly by this mother, her conscience smote her, and slowly the gray eyes filled with tears at the thought that she had been the cause of adding a new pang of sorrow to that mother's heart.

"Wilhelmine," began Mrs. Elliott in a sad voice, "I never thought to hear such things from the lips of a child of mine, least of all from a daughter. You have in effect denied the Bible and Saviour; and, my child, such a thing cannot but bring its own curse. These long years have I looked forward to the time when I could lean upon your arm, but I cannot lean upon an arm that does not draw its support from the God of Abraham."

Will threw herself on her knees before her mother and took her hands as she said, pleadingly: "Mamma darling, why can't we live happily, and each believe what seems best? You know that I want to be good and true, and believe what is right; but I can't be forced."

It was a common situation, but one of deep interest. The mother, with deep lines of care upon her face, the inward struggle of the true mother's love and tenderness, as it tried to break through the hard shell of doctrinal religion with which it had surrounded itself; the one prompting her to clasp the child in her arms and assure her of confidence and belief in her, while the other prompted her to feel that her daughter was under God's wrath and curse, and must have no encouragement in plans for the future until, by conversion, she had been passed up into the light of God's smile.

The kneeling figure was in some respects a contrast. There were no lines of care upon the youthful face, and fresh, joyous life leaped in every vein; but there was the same firm mouth, the dark eyebrows, the finely-cut, sensitive nostril, and, more than all, the same strong will, so that Mrs.

Elliott was arrayed against herself when opposed to her daughter. She answered the pleading tones:

"Yes, Willie, you talk about each one believing as he thinks best; but there is only one right way, and if you do not take it you are lost. I should be willing to consent to anything in the way of education, if you were only a Christian, for then I would know that you could not go wrong. You talk about being true and noble, and so you are, my darling child; but you lack the one thing needful, which will keep you from falling into sin when you are tempted. What have you to keep you true and noble when you come to the trials of life?"

"Why, mother, I have the honor that I have inherited as my birthright, and the moral teachings that you have given me by precept and example, and I feel sure that they will keep me."

"But you must have God's blessing, or you will fail. I hope you will go to your room and ask him to forgive and help you, for your sin is against him in rejecting his offers of mercy."

Mrs. Elliott was a Presbyterian of Scotch descent, and she kept the law to the letter, believed to the uttermost the five points of Calvinism,*[3] and, with the true Calvinist's spirit, would have forced her children to Christ at the point of the sword, thinking it was for their eternal happiness; while all the time she was doing it her mother's heart would have bled for their sufferings, so strangely do hearts and creeds sometimes clash. She had been for ten years a widow; for, when the rebellion broke out, William Elliott went as surgeon, and received a mortal wound in one of the early engagements, so that he only reached home in time to give his little family a parting blessing, and express the hope that he would meet them in heaven.

He left four children—Henry and Frank, the two elder; Wilhelmine; and the youngest, little Harriet, who, from an injury to the spine, was condemned to the life of an invalid, however long or short it might be.[4] Mrs. Elliott, who was an only child, went home to live with her parents, and the home of her own childhood became that of her children. Here she had passed the days of her widowhood, taking care of her aged parents as long as they lived, and devoting herself to her family. Above all things she prayed that they might be kept from the growing skepticism and irreligion

*five points of Calvinism: These points form the core of the ideas of the religious reformer John Calvin (1509–64).

of the day,[5] and brought to see the truth as it is in Christ. At the time the story opens the elder son was engaged in business in a distant State. Frank and Wilhelmine had just graduated from the high-school of the place; and while her brother immediately took a situation as book-keeper in one of the banks of the city, Will was waiting for further developments to determine her career. She declined going to a fashionable boarding-school to "finish off,"*[6] and heard with longing heart the boys of her class talk of going to college, for she was a good scholar, and had stood shoulder to shoulder with the best boys of the school.

When one of the finest universities in the country opened its doors to women, it seemed to her, as she said, a special Providence in her behalf, and she had not expected opposition of such a character as she found in her mother. One great source of anxiety concerning skeptical influences thrown around her children had come from the bosom of her own family; for Mrs. Elliott's father, during his lifetime, had been called an unbeliever.

Adam Conway had startled the community in which he lived when, at the ripe age of thirty-five, he had his name taken from the church-books, having been a member from his youth. A life of the widest philanthropy and purest morality was necessary to enable him to outlive the prejudice caused by such an extraordinary step, and such a life was his. No tale of distress was ever told to him in vain, and in every benevolent enterprise his name stood first on the list of subscribers.

Good people would often say, "'Squire Conway lacks only one thing of being perfect, and even as he is I guess he will not come far short of the kingdom." He was an aged man when Mrs. Elliott, their only daughter, came to live at the old home after the death of her husband.

Mrs. Elliott knew, of course, of her father's peculiar way of thinking, and much grief it gave her to feel that her dear father was still out of the ark of safety and city of refuge. She feared the influence, too, upon her children, but hoped to shield them by prayer and correct teaching. Not long after they were settled in the old house, Will, who was a mere child, came in from play one day and, with big-eyed wonder, asked what an infidel was, for Jennie Irwin had said that her grandpa Conway was one; and her mother would not allow her to play with Will for that reason. Mrs. Elliott took the little one upon her knee, and tried to explain the meaning

*fashionable boarding-school to "finish off": Boarding schools, or female academies, allowed well-to-do young women to spend a few years learning the "feminine" arts before coming home to find a husband.

of the word in language suited to the understanding of the child. "Oh, he is like the man in my catechism that is going to be burned 'cause he won't believe as they want him to, and they can't make him. Will they burn my grandpa?" and the little face grew troubled, and tears gathered in her eyes at the thought.

Mrs. Elliott explained to her that they did not burn people now, and that the men who had been burned were not all bad men; and, while she took care that the child's trust in her grandfather should not be shaken, she yet made the best of the occasion, as she never failed to do, to show her her obligation to love and serve God.

"But what has grandpa done that is bad?" persisted the child; and she was greatly relieved when the mother assured her that her grandpa was a man of the noblest character. Her mother kissed the eager face, and told her that she would understand these things when she grew older.

When she got down from her mother's knee, the puzzled expression was only half gone, and, taking her little catechism, she was soon lying full length in the grass, looking at the picture of John Rogers,* who is about to be burned at the stake, while his family gaze at the painful spectacle. "Poor man!" she murmured; "how bad those people are to burn him so! and there are lots of his little children seeing their father die in the fire, and pretty soon he'll be all gone, and then they will not have a father. I wonder why he did not believe as they wanted him to, and they would not have him burned him so? What makes people believe things? When I grow big I will not believe anything. Maybe I can't help it, though."

Not long after she was fast asleep, while the beetle hummed drowsily in the afternoon sun, and the wind played with the golden curls and turned over the leaves of the book; and it was not until the maples were casting long shadows across the yard that they found her, hidden as she was in the long grass.

Her grandfather assumed a new interest from that time in the eyes of the child, and she sometimes climbed upon his knee and, putting her arms around his neck, would whisper, "What makes you be a infidel, grandpa?"

As Mrs. Elliott and her mother were influential members of the Church, they often entertained ministers; these ministers often fell into discussions with 'Squire Conway; and Will was always interested in the

---

*John Rogers: An English Protestant martyr (ca. 1500–1555) who was sentenced to death for denying that the real body and blood of Jesus Christ were present in the sacrament.

result of their arguments, even before she could understand much of what they said. Old Mrs. Conway died several years before her husband, and her last breath was a prayer for "father's" conversion. The old gentleman became somewhat deaf, but his mental faculties remained strong and clear till the end. During his last days the beauty and simplicity of his character were noted by all who visited the sick-room. Will was a favorite with her grandfather, and was constantly by his bedside; and sometimes she would come out of the room and burst into tears, saying, "O mamma, he is so lovely and patient, I can't bear to have him die."

The church-people tried hard to turn the mind of Adam Conway at the eleventh hour. They felt that a calm, peaceful death in his own belief would have a bad influence, and the Rev. Mr. Chetham was heard to say that he had no doubt that 'Squire Conway would show such terror at the approach of death, and be so distracted with remorse, that it would be a remarkable warning, and he would be able to point to it and say, "See what the death-bed of an unbeliever is!" but that he should not be afraid to die, and should meet the king of terrors with as much calmness and resignation as if he had lived within the pale of the Church, was not at all within his expectations. They had prayer-meetings in his room, and tried to construe his words into a recantation or acknowledgment of a life-long mistake; but they were disappointed, for Adam Conway died as he had lived, in charity with all men; and we trust that the God who knew his longings after the truth dealt kindly with him, and that the mysteries of the future were duly unveiled to eyes prepared to see them.

Will had been a source of great solicitude to her mother from her birth. Extraordinary vigor of body and mind kept her in the fore front of every sport, and on the verge of every danger; yet there was no lack of native caution in her composition, and, in spite of appearances to the contrary, the risk of life and limb, which she seemed daily to encounter, was less than usual instead of greater. Solicitous neighbors had their hearts in their mouths as they watched her dashing down-hill on her sled with the boys, or out-stripping all but the boldest on the skating-pond, or climbing to the farthest hay-loft; but, fortunately for her peace, the mother slowly discerned the true quality of good sense and prudence that underlay the apparent recklessness of animal spirits, and she was content to give Will the liberty she gave her boys, whose constant companion she became. Nevertheless, the mother's duty of training this daughter for what she appreciated as woman's sphere*7 constantly pressed upon her. To hold the restless, vigorous body to tasks of sewing and darning was more grievous to the parent than to the child; yet it was done, for Mrs. Elliott had extraordinary patience, and was exceedingly conscientious in the performance of that which she considered right, and her path of duty was usually no less clear than her walk in it was steadfast. But to remould and curb the nature, that she only half understood, until her power to mould was past, was her anxious and almost futile task, for the vigorous body fed a brain no less vigorous.

Will was what mothers call a reasonable child, and, approached on that side, there was little or no contest between her and her mother; but, unfortunately, Mrs. Elliott had yielded reason to faith so wholly that, in all matters relating to the moral training of her children, she was incapable of exerting that sway which she could easily have held had she met them on natural ground.

Hers was the task of shaping these children's souls by the line and plummet offered her in the Bible, according to John Milton† and Calvin, or rather by that portion of the Bible distilled into the Westminster Catechism,‡8 which formed the basis of her moral code. Dishonoring human nature by the belief in original sin and total depravity, she was compelled to set herself in antagonism to the children she loved until they, too, accepted her definitions of faith and goodness. And to such a parent, in the perversity of natural things, a child is born with an organic tendency to skepticism; a child whose reason revolted at the formulæ accepted by all about her. The patient mother, as the years drew on, in which she looked for a yielding of her daughter's reason and will to the rule of faith and conduct that guided her, and to which she believed all mortals should yield, found only more and more hostility; but every evidence of Will's waywardness of soul was but a fresh confirmation of her own belief in natural depravity.

*woman's sphere: Most of nineteenth-century society believed that the home was the proper and only sphere of action for women.
†John Milton: The English poet (1608–74), best known for his epic poem *Paradise Lost*, which related the story of the origin of Satan, the creation of Adam and Eve, and Adam and Eve's expulsion from the Garden of Eden. His work reflected the severe Christianity of Calvinism.
‡Westminster Catechism: A catechism is a summary of Christian beliefs; the Westminster Catechism was steeped in Calvinist doctrine.

After much weeping and prayer, the mother nerved herself afresh to the task of subduing this nature, or rather of bringing it into subjection to God, for toward herself Will's temper was one of sweet dutifulness. All that subjection of spirit with which the Puritan held himself in obedience to the stern decrees of a loving but just God, led to the expectation of the same subjection from his children; the family knew but one law, in all the complicated interworking of domestic machinery, the law of the parent's will. Could this great gain but have coexisted with the recognition of the child's God-tending nature, toward whom the parent's hand were only needed to guide, how blessed would be the years of childhood! But, to a nature full of tenderest sensibility, as was that of Mrs. Elliott's eldest daughter, the very loveliness was taken from life by this steady effort to dominate reason and faith, which it was a part of her religion to maintain. For the mother well knew that Will was sweetness itself, in her desire for love; and in the hours of temporary illness, or the twilight moment, when she gave herself up to caress her, she yearned, as only mothers can, to break down the wall of partition which, as years advanced, became more real between them.

And so the burden only grew greater as the years developed the romping, impatient, but loving little girl, into a beautiful woman, whom a mother's pride silently felt to be a radiant contrast to her companions; and it was with only a half-joy that she watched the dancing eye, blue in the skylight and gray in the shadow—the moist, enthusiastic eye, that lighted up a face as mobile as the soul behind it. Will did not know whether she was pretty or not. She felt that she was altogether too large, and, in the condition of semi-hostility to all the conventionalities among which she found herself, was ever ready to admit the worst, in regard to her face and figure. She knew that her smile was bright and her teeth brilliant, and that she was perfectly well and ready for anything; but her brothers never flattered, and Will did not fully know, until years had opened to her the knowledge of the beautiful in art, that hers was a magnificent form, and that her oval Greek face was as faultless in proportion as it was vivacious in expression. Perhaps there was one point of beauty of which she was early conscious and suitably vain, and that was her hand—a large, snowy hand, maybe a trifle too opaque and bloodless, but exquisitely proportioned, and as strong and firm as was her friendship.

The vexed question of religious belief was the cause of the only trouble Will had ever known, and just now, as the story opens, she was in an unusually sore state of mind on that subject. The Sunday before, there had been communion at the Presbyterian church, and, after the regular service, when the communicants were asked to take the middle pews and the others the side ones, it happened that Will was the only one who sat on the side, for the rest of the non-professors went home; but Mrs. Elliott never allowed her family to leave before the sacrament was administered. So Will sat all alone, and tried to look very unconscious while her friends in the middle pews cast solemn and pitying glances at her, and the minister talked about the final separation of the sheep from the goats, accompanying the words with appropriate gestures. Through the open window came the warm, mellow sun, and far off she could see the blue hills. How she longed to leap through the casement and get away from everybody, and walk in the fields, or lie under some tree and think! Everything seemed to her glad and free, except people who went to church and believed in the Bible and Saviour. Her thoughts went back eighteen hundred years, and she seemed to see Jesus walking with his disciples in the fields where lilies-of-the-valley grew, and about which he talked. The face of the Master was one of wondrous beauty, and she thought, if she could only have been one of them and heard him talk, she, too, would have believed and loved him. She saw him again on the shore of the sea of Galilee, and he always had the same rapt expression of devotion as he talked and pointed upward. Finally, she saw him on the cross, and now the beautiful face is distorted with pain. A great crowd are watching to see if he will not perform some miracle, and get away; but he dies, and the people go home, and wonder what will happen next, for it is all very strange. And is this the same one about whom they now talk so much, and dispute concerning his divinity and humanity? She was aroused by the solemn tones of the minister saying: "Take, eat, this is my body. And he took the cup, and gave thanks, and gave it unto them, saying, drink ye all of it." Mr. Reynolds was an old-fashioned Presbyterian minister—one who had never been softened by any of the ideas of liberal Christianity—and one who never temporized to please a mixed congregation. He was of the real old school, whose very shirt-collar seemed to say, "God, having, out of his mere good pleasure, from all eternity, elected some to everlasting life, did enter into a covenant of grace to deliver them out of the estate of sin and misery, and to bring them into an estate of salvation, by a Redeemer." And when he cleared his throat on a frosty Sabbath morning, it sounded as if he said, "All mankind, by their fall, lost communion with God, are under his wrath and curse, and so made liable to all miseries in this life, to death itself, and to the pains of hell forever." And, when he came to make a pastoral call, he always seemed to bring the everlasting fire much nearer; and children never felt quite safe to go on with their play until the reverend gentleman was entirely out of sight. After the sermon to-day, he came and spoke to Will, and told her that he hoped it was the last time she would trample upon the offer of salvation, and grieve away the Holy Spirit, who, he felt sure, was striving with her. But, could he have looked into her heart at the time, he would have called it anything else than a *holy* spirit, that was striving with her. To make matters worse, old Mrs. Johnson had overtaken her on the way home, and told her that she ought to be ashamed, having such a good Christian mother, to hold out so against the means of redemption. There had been many repetitions of such scenes, with variations, during the communion seasons of several years. At first she received their exhortations and reproaches with a guilty feeling that they were in the right, and she in the wrong; but she felt that she would some time come out strong on the Lord's side. Yes, she would join the church, of course, if they would just let her alone a little while, and let her put off the evil day as long as she could. Then, as she grew older, these same exhortations and reproaches made her angry and defiant. What business had they to torment her continually about her soul? Was not her soul her own, and was not its salvation of more concern to her than to them? And, besides, was not she as good in her every-day life as they? Yes, some of them would even do things that she would scorn to do; and she wondered if the Lord really thought as hardly of her as those church-people did. Then she found somewhere among her grandfather's books a copy of Renan's "Life of Jesus,"*[9] which she read with eagerness. Here was a great man who did not believe in the Bible or Jesus as she had been taught, and why might he not be right? Besides, she did not see how a man could be bad who could write such a beautiful dedication to his dead sister as she found in the beginning of the book. This helped to give form to her shapeless doubts and questionings, but she said nothing, for she would not give her mother needless pain. But this unlucky opening of the University of Ortonville by which Will saw the realization of her darling ambition, and her mother's refusal to consent to her going on such grounds, brought all the rebellion of her nature to the surface, and resulted in the disclosure

*Renan's "Life of Jesus": J. Ernest Renan's *The Life of Jesus* (1863) depicted Jesus as a historical figure of flesh and blood rather than a supernatural divine.

of her skepticism above described. So, this glorious afternoon in the early autumn, Mrs. Elliott went to the missionary-meeting with a heavy heart, and Will went up to her own room to think over what had happened.

"Strange," said the girl, as she walked slowly up and down the room, "that the old, old story is so spoiled for me that I cannot bear to hear it mentioned. I wish I had never heard it till now; how beautiful it would seem! And it is beautiful now," she continued, as she paused before a picture of Christ stilling the tempest, that her mother had given her on her last birthday, "when I can separate it from those hard, dreadful things in the Catechism. How glad I am that we have to settle our final accounts with the Lord, and not with the compilers of the Westminster Catechism!

There was a gentle knock at her door, followed by a little pale face, and a voice that said:

"May I come in, Willie? I sha'n't disturb you while you study."

"Oh! it is you, Hally, is it? I thought you were asleep, or I should have been looking for you long ago. I have something to tell you."

Then followed a recital of her hopes about going to college, and how her mother had dashed them, for the moment, to the ground.

"Never mind, Willie, we'll see what can be done about it." And a little white hand caressed lovingly the brown curls. "I've set my heart on your going, too, and I'll talk to mother. Won't it be splendid for you to go and study all the things that Jack Adams talks so glibly about, and said you never could do them because you are a girl? You are so grand and strong, you can do anything you try." And the blue eyes grew bright and the pale cheeks flushed, thinking of the triumphs that her darling sister would win in college.

Harriet Elliott, or Hally, as every one called her, had been thrown from a carriage when a mere child, which resulted in an incurable injury to the spine, and her life always hung on a very slender thread. She was thirteen years of age, a little, pale, patient shadow, with premature habits of thought and reflection unnatural and painful in one so young. To use Will's words, "she had been attacked by ministers and church-people while in such a weak, helpless condition, that they finally brought her to confess herself the chief of sinners; and it really was absurd to hear the little thing, that did not know a wrong thought, mourn over her shortcomings, and question her acceptance and effectual calling."

But there was one subject upon which she was not at all orthodox, where her puritanism failed entirely, and that was in her thorough adoration and approval of her elder sister. No matter what Will did or thought, the little invalid always found ground for forgiveness, if not of approval, and once said in a most heterodox way, when Mrs. Downs was talking of Will's refusal to join the church: "Well, well, such broken-backed creatures as I need a prop of that kind; but I see no use in forcing it on to Will until she feels the need of it."

There could scarcely be a greater contrast than the two sisters presented: the one, tall, fearless, and independent, with bounding step, and glowing face; the other, small, slight, with slow, feeble step, and thin, pale face, always patient, though she had no prospect but a life of pain. To the younger, the elder was everything that is strong, brave, and noble; and Will grew to value more the love and approval of her little sister than of any one else.

Mrs. Elliott was finally induced to give a reluctant consent to Will's going to college. It was with a heavy heart and many misgivings, however, as to the eternal welfare of her daughter, that she packed the large, new trunk, and saw that all her clothes were in good order—careful and loving mother that she was. Some hot tears fell among the piles of clothes in the trunk; for she felt, since the conversation that has been described at the beginning of the chapter, that she would never be brought back to the fold, and being exposed to the miscellaneous beliefs and unbeliefs of a university town like Ortonville made any hope of her conversion still more improbable. And yet the mother had a secret pride when she heard others talk of Will going to college, and predict for her a brilliant career. She gave her a new Bible, and hymn-book, a copy of the "Confession of Faith,"* and, the day before she went, sent for the minister to talk and pray with her.

He talked to her of the dangers and temptations she would meet, and warned her to avoid certain skeptical books. The poor, dear man could hardly have hit upon a more certain plan to insure their early perusal. Will clung to her mother at parting, and whispered: "You will believe in me, mamma darling, that I will do right! You must say so, or I can't be happy," she pleaded; and the mother forgot her creed as she said, "I do believe in you, my precious child." Then there were a rumbling of wheels and a waving of handkerchiefs, and she was gone. "What a happy home mine would be," thought Will, as she leaned back on the cushions of the carriage, "if there were no such thing as religion!"

*Confession of Faith: The *Westminster Confession of Faith* (1646) was one of the forms in which the doctrine of Calvinism made its way to America's first settlements.

54

CHAPTER II

How the Majority
Impressed the Minority

"How fresh was every sight and sound
On open main or winding shore!
We knew the merry world was round,
And we might sail for evermore."
—*The Voyage*

Toward the close of the afternoon Will changed cars for the last time, for they were drawing near the university town; and many got in from villages by the way, whom she took to be students; and, from what she had read, she could easily decide upon the freshmen, from their timid, modest looks; and the sophomores, from their blustering, bullying manners.

Two of the latter class sat not far from her, and presently one of them said to his companion, as he pointed backward with his thumb at Will: "By Jove,* Barker, what'll you bet that girl is not going to enter college? You know they have admitted women by a recent act of the regents, and she just looks like it. All I have to say is, it will ruin the institution; the feminine mind can't stand the pressure, and it will come down to a third-rate boarding-school for boys and girls."†¹

As a matter of fact this same young gentleman had been plucked twice when trying to pass examinations for entering the sophomore class. His companion was not disposed to assent entirely, for, after glancing at Will,

---

*By Jove: In Roman mythology, Jove (Jupiter) was the supreme ruler of the gods. Zeus was his counterpart in Greek mythology. "By Jove!" or "By Zeus!" was a way of invoking the Heavenly Father without blaspheming the Christian God.

†ruin the institution: This claim, used by opponents to express several feared results of the admission of women to the university, included "the loss of reputation and caste among universities, the decline of scholarship, and the corruption of morals."

he said: "Pooh, I don't agree with you at all, Irwin. Although no one can be more opposed to co-education than I am, yet it is not because I believe the feminine mind incapable of doing anything we do in college or anywhere else. Why, I have a sister that can leave me so far behind that I never get sight of her; she is two years younger, and yet she was in my classes in school and did all my problems and translations for me; so, if you object to the movement, do it on reasonable grounds, I say."

Will was much interested in this conversation, and it brought a new phase of the question which she had not thought of before. It had never occurred to her that any of the students could be so selfish and unfair as to be unwilling that the university should throw open its doors to sons and daughters alike, and for a moment she shrank from the thought of meeting so many who would look at her and think, "What under the sun is that girl doing here?" for, who knows, she might be the only one who had ventured to grasp the hitherto forbidden fruit!

Her heart gave a great leap when the name of the town was called out. There was much talking and exchanging of greetings as classmates met again after the long vacations, many cries of "Halloa, Fresh!*² does your mother know you're out?" "What makes you look so pale, Fresh?" etc.

"Drive me to the president's house, please," said Will to the hackman, not knowing of any better place to go, to find out what she must do first. As they whirled along the avenues of maples, she leaned out of the window with wistful curiosity to see the town that was to be her home for the next four years. The driver stopped before a sombre stone house and handed her out, saying, "This is the place, miss," then mounted his box and was off. Will tripped up the steps and rang the bell with a beating heart, for she had a wholesome dread of meeting that high dignitary, the president. A broad-faced Irish girl came to the door, and, in answer to the inquiry for the president, said: "La! miss, the president don't live here; there's his house t'other side the campus; this is the hospital, and we have three cases of small-pox."

Will caught up her valise and hurried down the steps, looking in vain for the hackman who had brought her, and nothing remained but to walk the distance. The wind blew raw and chilly, and a slow, drizzling rain had set in, which added to the unpleasantness of the situation.

"Well," thought Will, "if I were a believer in omens and such nonsense, I should say that the fact of being thus set down before a small-pox hospital

*Fresh!: A derogatory shortening of *freshman*.

was a proof that my college course had not met the approval of the gods; but we'll give them another trial."

The president was not in his residence, but at his office in the university-building, and the maid said she would show her the way; so, once more taking her traveling-bag, she followed the nurse-girl for another half-mile, while the latter wheeled a baby-carriage.

The man of affairs sat at his desk, writing, but looked up with a bright smile as Will advanced and offered her letters of introduction.

He shook hands with her and smiled upon her in the most kindly way as he said: "And you came all the way from C——, alone, you tell me, and are not acquainted with any one here, and you want to enter the university? Why, you are a brave girl, I must say!"

"Have any other young ladies applied for admission, and are there very many boys here?"

"I think that you will not be entirely alone, Miss Elliott, for I hear of several young ladies who are intending to be examined for admission; and, as to your last question, I believe there are more than thirteen hundred young gentlemen in all the departments."

"How do you think the girls will be received in college?" asked Will.

"I can tell better some time hence," he replied, evasively; "and now I will take you to Mr. Benson, the steward, who will find you a good boarding-place."

The president left her in the hands of the steward, a gray-headed gentleman, with a pen over his right ear, and his genial face looked out over a stiff linen collar as he said: "Yes, yes, I have a number of good places down in my book, for everybody keeps boarders here, you know. There is Mrs. Hodges, in William street, No. 94—first-rate place; Mrs. Myers, in Thompson Street; and Mrs. Smith, Jefferson Avenue, No. 59."

"Why, they all seem to be widows here?" said Will, struck with the fact that the heads of the households were women.

"Oh, no; but their husbands always allow them this enterprise of keeping boarders, by which they make their own pin-money and pay the church-dues," said Mr. Benson, with a twinkle in his eye.

Will found out afterward that, in the majority of cases, the women who were allowed the "enterprise of keeping boarders"*³ supported their

---

*enterprise of keeping boarders: As the University of Michigan lacked dormitories, students who did not already live in Ann Arbor traditionally found lodging in boardinghouses.

husbands and families, besides making pin-money and paying church-dues. Mr. Benson sent his little son along, to carry her bag and show the way.

The clouds had lifted enough for the autumn sun to smile for a moment upon the tops of the tall pine-trees in the campus, as Will and her escort set out to find a boarding-place. She thought that everybody was delightfully kind, and that going to college was one of the jolliest things in the world. At Mrs. Hodges's, No. 94, a little girl came to the door, and, on being asked if her mamma had rooms to let to students, she went to speak to that lady, returning with the reply that "mamma don't want girls."

"Well," said Will, with just a little sinking of the heart, "your mamma's prejudices should be respected."

The next was the Myers mansion, in Thompson Street, where the lady of the house came to answer the bell herself. "I could not think of taking a lady-student, it's so odd, you know; we can't tell what they might be like," and the door was closed without further ceremony.

Will's spirits fell perceptibly at this, but she determined to try once more, so she rang at 59 Jefferson Avenue. A little colored servant-boy came to the door, and, after the usual question was put and carried to headquarters, he came back with a grin, saying, "She hathe not a good opinion of ladieths who wanths to come to a boyths' college."[4]

Will returned to the steward's office, and the indignant tears stood in her eyes as she said: "They all look at me as if I were some wild animal, and say they want to take boys; are boys so much better than girls?"

"Oh, oh!" said the kind-hearted steward; "I might have known people are prejudiced, yet, against ladies who come here to college: I did not think what I was doing when I sent you alone. Never mind, I know where I'll take you—strange I didn't think of her before! Mrs. Williamson, a cousin of mine, said the other day she would try lady-boarders if she had a chance."

Mrs. Williamson did take her; and Will was soon eating bread-and-butter and raspberry-tarts, and fast forgetting her tears, as she sat by the open fire and answered the questions of the mother and two daughters about her journey, home, and friends, and how she had the courage to come alone; and she became quite a heroine in their eyes when she told of the repulses she had received in Thompson and Jefferson Streets.

I wish that I could do justice in describing these two girls, Angelica and Samantha Williamson. They were what the college-boys (for there is no subject too sacred for their irreverent tongues to handle) termed "college widows."*5

In every university town there is always a series of these who have depended upon the students for their "chances," and who, after angling patiently in the matrimonial sea for years, are often obliged to give up in despair. They have plenty of bites, but they pull up too soon, or do not conceal the bait effectually, or something interferes with their success. Of this unfortunate class were Mrs. Williamson's two daughters.

Year after year they had watched the tide rise and fall, as each successive class entered and left the sheltering arms of its *alma mater,* but the tide had never risen high enough to float them off the rocks of single blessedness, and they had never even experienced that innocent feeling of rapture and contentment with all sublunary things that comes of being "engaged." They were now in that appalling border-land where, in the rear, they see the path strewed with what once seemed to be golden opportunities, but which proved to be only those fair, false mirages to which every single woman can point as she thinks, "It might have been!" In front lay the vast, desolate plain of old maidenhood, into which they had not yet traveled far enough to feel thoroughly at home, and from which they still had hopes of being rescued.

Year after year they made up bolts of muslin into under-clothes, which they ruffled and embroidered with the greatest industry, and laid away in bureau-drawers to grow yellow and moth-eaten; they had untold supplies of table and bed linen stored away,6 for the good mother would say, as she looked fondly at her girls, "It is best to be ready, for there is no telling what may happen," but it never did happen; and now, as I write, these dear blossoms are still clinging to the family tree, and very probably will never be plucked from that time-honored trunk by a gentler hand than that of the reaper who takes blossoms and grain, alike.

Mrs. Williamson had taken another lady-student several days before, whom she now brought down to introduce to Will, who looked toward the opening door with eager face, for the peculiar light in which "lady-students" were regarded made her curious to look at one from an objective standpoint.

A neat, trim little figure came tripping in, bearing the name of Clara

*college widows: Socially dependent on the male student population, the young women of Ann Arbor may have viewed the new women students as not only beneath their social status but also as unwelcome competition.

Hopkins. She was almost a head shorter than Will, and her plain, gray dress fitted to perfection, while her hair was combed smoothly away from her forehead and gathered in a coil behind. She came forward and seized Will's hand with the most lively enthusiasm, as she said, "I am glad that I am here to welcome you to our ranks."

"What a nice little thing she is!" thought Will; and then they fell to comparing notes, and found that they had gone over pretty nearly the same ground in preparation, although Clara was two years older than Will, and had taught some time in a primary school since her preparation for college. They were soon fast friends, and had agreed to room together; and Will wrote to Hally that night that she had found a "perfect treasure of a room-mate," and that they would get along famously. After they went to their room, and were preparing for bed, Clara said, "Your trunk is not here yet, dear, so you can use my Bible till it comes."

"Thank you," said Will, "I don't care for it;" and she felt as if the wrappings were being taken from an old wound.

The other looked surprised and grieved, and, when she saw that Will did not kneel to pray, she said, "Aren't you a Christian, and don't you love Jesus?" The hot blood rushed to Will's face, as she thought, "As I live, the same old story!" but she replied aloud, "Yes and no." Clara looked puzzled, but said no more.

Will was up early next morning, ready for examinations,* and at eight o'clock she entered the university-buildings prepared, as she said, to run the gauntlet or die in the attempt. The long, bare halls were not accustomed to resound with the tread of girlish feet, and the steps had hitherto been worn only by male devotees in their pilgrimages to the temple of learning. "I can tell," she thought, "just by the way each professor looks at me, whether he believes in girls going to college." She came first to the mathematical-room, where she found an elderly gentleman with a bald head and kindly face, who, as she afterward found, was Prof. Noyes. Beside him sat an assistant or "tutor" with a very large nose, and a half-amused, half-contemptuous look on his face, when he saw a girl place herself among the candidates. The room was nearly full, some working at blackboards, and others being examined orally, while others

---

*examinations: Students who applied for admission were examined for competency in each subject of the course they planned to follow. Students then received "pass" or "fail" slips; if they failed, a tutor would attempt to bring them up to university standards.

still waited for their turn. After waiting patiently for what seemed to her a very long time, the large nose turned to her, and said suddenly, "Miss, can you prove that the whole is greater than a part?"

"No, sir," said Will, promptly and somewhat haughtily, for she was not disposed to look favorably upon any jokes from the tutor.

"Well, then, you may prove that the square described upon the hypotenuse of a right-angled triangle is equal to the sum of the squares described upon the other two sides, and also that the angles at the base of an isosceles triangle are equal." Then followed more propositions, in most of which she acquitted herself creditably. Prof. Noyes,*[7] who had been looking at her work, seemed highly pleased, and began in easy, pleasant tones to ask her some questions about algebra, and Will soon forgot that she was undergoing the dreadful ordeal of examination, for he had a delightful way of asking questions that put her at ease, at once, and she did not feel that she must be all the time on the defensive. He sent her to the board with a problem in quadratics. It was very long, and she worked away until she had covered a whole blackboard, but it would not come out right. She bit the chalk-crayon, in her perplexity, and drops of perspiration started on her forehead, but that did not help the matter. The professor, who had been watching her, now came to her relief by saying: "Your work is very good, indeed, but you have written $^{x}2$ instead of $^{x}4$ in this equation, which, you see, will bring it right; you may consider yourself 'passed' in mathematics, Miss Elliott," and she left the room with a reverence for Prof. Noyes that increased as the months and years of college-life went by. Then, came history, geography, and other things that she considered very easy, and late in the afternoon Latin and Greek.[8] She could not quite decide whether the Professor of Latin believed in girls or not, for he asked her to scan passages in Virgil in a matter-of-fact way without regard to sex, which she liked much better than to have them drag in some allusion to her being a girl, which so many did.

Will had heard that Prof. Borck,†[9] who examined in Greek, was very stern, and bitterly opposed to ladies entering the university, so it was with some trepidation that she entered the awful presence. There were only two candidates left, and, while waiting for her turn, she looked around the room.

*Prof. Noyes: Edward Olney (1827–87) was appointed Professor of Mathematics in 1863.

†Prof. Borck: Probably James Robinson Boise (1815–95), Professor of Latin and Greek Languages, appointed in 1852.

Prof. James Robinson Boise. "Will had heard that Prof. Borck, who examined in Greek, was very stern, and bitterly opposed to ladies entering the university." In reality, James Robinson Boise, the model for Professor Borck, had been one of the few faculty members in favor of coeducation. (Box 1, University of Michigan Faculty Portraits, Bentley Historical Library, University of Michigan.)

The only object of interest, which indeed was enough, was a large oil-painting of ancient Athens, that covered one whole side of the room. Will forgot her anxiety about Prof. Borck, as she watched the beautiful Greek women in their graceful dresses carrying jars of water on their heads, while over all was the soft sky, and she could almost see the wind gently stirring the foliage, when she was aroused by—"Well, miss, what do you know about Greek?" and a pair of large eagle-eyes and a hooked nose swooped down upon her from the rostrum where he sat. She told him what she had gone over—two books of Xenophon's "Anabasis,"*10 Hadley's "Grammar,"† and Arnold's "Composition."‡

"We require three books of Xenophon; but, young woman, it is not so much the amount that I want to know as the way you have done your work"; and he proceeded to find out how she had gone over the ground. He gave her passage after passage to translate, nouns and adjectives to decline, asked for all the comparatives and superlatives of ἀγαθός, and the parts of ὁράω, ἔχω, and other irregular verbs, and might have gone on indefinitely, had it not grown so dark in the room that it was difficult to see the page.

"I've no fault to find with you, Miss Elliott, except that one book of Xenophon, which deficiencies we always require to be made up under a private tutor,[11] and I recommend you to Jerry Dalton, a member of the senior class, who does that kind of work to help himself through college; you will be the first young lady that he has had in that capacity," and, as Will turned to go, he added, "See that you confine yourselves strictly to the Greek." It was too dark for her to notice the flash of humor that was in the eagle-eyes as he said this, and, supposing it was a sort of implication of her necessary frivolity as a girl, she bowed with great dignity as she replied, "I have no other intention, sir."

Prof. Borck turned to his assistant and said: "I do not think it will work at all. Now, I don't know of anything better than to send her to Dalton to make up that Greek, for it is the way we do with the boys; but, if Jerry Dalton can be closeted for an hour a day with that face and eyes and never think of anything but the 'Retreat of the Ten Thousand,'§ he is a very remarkable young man. I'll warrant that before a month he will be partial to the conjugation of φιλέω and ἀγαπάω, and his dreams will not be troubled by the integral calculus so much as by visions of gray eyes and brown hair."

---

*Xenophon's "Anabasis": Xenophon (ca. 444–357 BC) was a Greek historian and essayist. *Anabasis*, or the "The March Up," detailed Xenophon's role in the military expedition of Cyrus to overthrow his brother Artaxerxes II in 401 BC.

†Hadley's "Grammar": James Hadley (1821–72), American scholar of ancient languages and author of *Greek Grammar*, published in 1860 and revised in 1884.

‡Arnold's "Composition": Will is referring to Thomas Kerchever Arnold (1800–1853) and *A Practical Introduction to Greek Prose Composition* (1840), by 1870 a staple in college classrooms.

§"Retreat of the Ten Thousand": A reference to the heroic retreat of the "Ten Thousand" mercenaries who fought for the Greek prince Cyrus the Younger, killed in the battle of Cunaxa between Greeks and Persians in 401 BC. Xenophon describes the retreat in his celebrated prose history, *Anabasis*.

Will had been the unwilling hearer of these remarks, for the door did not latch behind her, and she was delayed in the corridor by looking for her gloves that had fallen from the book; but she only thought, "What an old bird of ill-omen he is!"

This closed her examinations, and she bounded across the campus, eager to tell Mrs. Williamson and the girls her good-fortune. She sprang up the steps two at a time, and, instead of waiting to open the hall-door, she stepped through the window that opened down to the floor of the veranda, and, rushing into the kitchen, seized Miss Samantha by the waist and spun her around, so frightening the cat that she ran out and did not appear again for three days. They all liked this lively girl, and Miss Samantha smoothed her disordered braids with much better grace than if any one else had taken such violent liberty with her revered person.

Perhaps Will's letter to her sister will give the best idea of her first week's experience as one of the girls who first entered the University of Ortonville after the admission of women:

"Dear Little Sis: I'm here, as large as life. I came, I saw, I conquered, and am established as a member of the freshman class of the university, in good and regular standing. Was weighted in the balance, and am somewhat ahead of Belshazzar,* for I was not found wanting, except a little in Greek, which I have to make up under a private tutor, and I must tell you about him. Imagine a pair of legs of tremendous length and the pants making vain endeavors to equal their linear dimensions, arms to match, and the coat-sleeves having the same benevolent intentions as the pants, but failing in the same way; these surmounted by a head-piece adorned with yellow hair and a mushroomy-looking mustache, and you have, in outline, my private tutor. He is a fine fellow, although he holds girls in great contempt. He is President of the Young Men's Christian Association,†¹² and is going to be a Methodist preacher. He knows a great deal about books and such things; but to put him in a parlor would remind one of the famous quadruped in the china-shop. You ought to have seen him when I was first introduced to him and told him that I wanted a little coaching in Greek: he thrust his great arms into his pants-pockets and looked down at me from his immense height with a most pitying expression, partly because

---

*Belshazzar: Also spelled Belshezzar (sixth century BC). This Babylonian general appears in Xenophon's *Anabasis*.

†Young Men's Christian Association: A nonsectarian Christian organization founded in London in 1844.

I was a freshman, but mostly because I was a girl, for he is very orthodox on the girl-question, and doesn't believe in them doing or being anything except 'chaste keepers at home.' But he is as bashful as possible when you bring him to close quarters; and, when he first heard me recite, he sat in one corner of the room and I in another, and from that distance he hurled questions at me; but now he is thawing out a little since he finds that I can acquit myself honorably on Greek roots, in spite of my petticoats; but I cannot tell you any more about him, although he is a fertile subject, for I have so much else to say.

"I have not begun this in chronological order, I see, as I have not told you about the opening morning in chapel. It was terrific, and I did not know as there would be a vestige of me left to send to you. You see, we have prayers every morning in the law lecture-room, as our hall is not done yet; it is an immense room, and the freshmen sit on one side and the sophs on the other, so that the two combustibles are separated by the grave upper-classmen. We girls (there are nine of us) went fifteen minutes before time, and, when we entered the door, we heard the most uproarious din,[13] and, on coming up the stairs, found the fresh and sophs joined in mortal combat, while, above all, rose the chorus, 'Saw freshman's leg off—*short!'* We were terribly frightened, thinking that some one would surely be killed; but at last we were all in the room and no lives lost.

"There are one hundred and fifty boys in our class, and more than a hundred sophs; then the other classes, together with the law and medical students, make an imposing assembly.

"We, poor little wretches, did not know where to sit, of course, and not one boy was polite enough or dared to face the crowd and show us a seat; so we kind of edged around into not much of anywhere, but found to our cost that it was in direct line of the missiles between the hostile classes, which missiles consisted of hymn-books, sticks, anything movable; a great apple-core struck me right in the eye, which caused me to see a whole solar system of stars; but I bore it bravely, feeling something of that rapture that the old martyrs must have felt—for, was I not suffering in the cause of co-education?

"I thought that I was used to boys; but I must say that I never met boy in his most malignant form until I came to college.[14] In looking at my own class, every variety can be seen—long boys, short boys, fat boys, lean boys, boys pious and boys impious, gathered from one hundred and fifty families all over the land, from Maine to Mexico, a most heterogeneous collection, fused into one solid mass by the common bond 'our class.' Every one of them is, doubtless, some 'mother's darling'; but I never before realized how much poor as well as good material is worked up into these same mothers' darlings. Oh, yes, we have a Sandwich-Islander, too, born under the very shadow of old Mauna Loa;* and a Japanese with funny, long almond-eyes and yellow skin, who is being educated for a missionary.†[15] The girls are not expected to have much class-spirit yet, but are supposed to sit meekly by and say 'Thank you' for the crumbs that fall from the boys' table; but, in spite of that, I feel my bosom swell with pride when I look at these one hundred and fifty heads, and think that I, too, as much as the best of them, am a member of the freshman class of the University of Ortonville. But I've wandered from the chapel-scene. As soon as Prexy‡[16] (that is what the boys call the president, for short) came, there was a general lull; he is a magnificent-looking man, called here from the presidency of——, and this is his first year here. One by one the faculty came and formed a most reverend collection of wise heads, with here and there a tutor sprinkled in. They gave out the hymn—

'How firm a foundation, ye saints of the Lord,' etc.;

then the choir of fifty boys stood around the organ, while twelve hundred voices poured forth a volume of sound grand and tremendous; our poor feminine voices were completely drowned. Then the president made a delightful prayer, in which he asked the Lord to watch over and protect those we had left behind, in our homes, and who were making sacrifices that we might come here and drink at the fountain of knowledge; and other pretty things of like kind he said. There was no particular outburst of the belligerents during the prayer, except now and then a wily soph would hiss 'Fresh!' and the fresh would hiss in reply. I suspect that the faculty have to wink at a great many such things, for this time-honored animosity

*Sandwich Islands and Mauna Loa: The Hawaiian Islands were formerly known as the Sandwich Islands, so named in 1778 by explorer James Cook after the Fourth Earl of Sandwich. Mauna Loa is the main volcano on the largest of these islands, Hawaii.
†a Japanese with funny, long almond-eyes and yellow skin: Given contemporary American prejudices against Asians, Will's description of the Japanese student was common, even "polite" for the times.
‡Prexy: Short for the University of Ortonville's President Hannaford and for James Burrill Angell (1829–1916), president of the University of Michigan on whom Hannaford was based.

President James Burrill Angell. Angell, an ardent defender of coeducation, was the model for "Prexy," President Hannaford: "He has to be all things to all men, and to women, too, now, under the new dispensation." (Bentley Historical Library, University of Michigan, BL003652.)

between those two classes, silly as it is, cannot be stopped at once, and, in such an institution, the reins have to be held very judiciously, or they would blow the whole faculty up with gunpowder and think nothing of it. After this, the freshmen were called up, one by one, to receive their papers, upon which was written either 'Passed' or 'Not passed,' and you might have seen one here and there turn pale as he sank into his seat, his paper containing the fatal 'Not passed,' which meant that his examinations had not been satisfactory, and he could not be admitted. Then we all dispersed to the different recitation-rooms to have lessons assigned.

"Yesterday the freshmen and sophs had a 'rush,' which I will explain. They meet wherever the spurt seizes them, and, with the best intentions, plunge at each other like mad in a hand-to-hand fight, and often an arm is broken or an eye knocked out, which is simply 'hard luck.' We were just coming out of Latin while the sophs were going up to trigonometry, and they met on the stairs and went at it.[17] One sweet-faced boy said, 'For Heaven's sake, Phelps, wait until the girls get out of the way!' but that worthy replied, 'Damn 'em, they have no business here anyway, and let 'em take their chances!' I was on the last step hurrying to get out of the crowd, when I was pushed violently against the bannisters, making my nose bleed in a most ghastly manner, and, of course, I had no handkerchief, which, you know, is my fortune always in an emergency (you remember the time I did not dare to cry at Percy Ames's funeral, because I did not have that indispensable with me?); but the girls came to my relief and helped me home, and all the while the martyr-fire burned brightly in my breast, and I only laughed at my bruises. Now, there is not one of those boys but, if you find him out of college, would have run to a lady's assistance and begged a thousand pardons for having had any hand in such an accident; but, would you believe it, not one of those two hundred and fifty boys offered any help or sympathy, simply because they feel that we are trespassing upon their domains!

"You would be amused, too, to see how the people in town regard us; for I never go on the street without hearing some such remark as—'See, there is one of them; look at her!' This will all change in time; but it makes it hard for the pioneers who have to bear the brunt of the battle.

"But I do enjoy our work so much; we are reading Cicero's discourse concerning 'Friendship,' in Latin;*[18] and, in Greek, Isocrates's 'Panegyricus,'†[19] which is very beautiful but quite hard. I still think a great deal of my room-mate, although she is churchy; her father is a Methodist minister, and, of course, poor; and she has taught, to get money to come to college,[20] which is very noble; and she is a fine, ambitious scholar. If she will not bother me too much on religion, we will work well together; but, you know, that's my sensitive point.

"I hope it will not tire you to read this fearfully long letter. Will you miss

---

*Cicero's discourse concerning "Friendship," in Latin: Marcus Tullius Cicero (106–43 BC), orator and statesman of ancient Rome and generally considered to be the greatest Latin prose stylist.
    †Isocrates's "Panegyricus": Isocrates (436–338 BC) was a Greek orator and philosopher.

me much if I do not go home Christmas? You know that I am so far away and have so much to do, that I thought I would not go home again till the end of the year.

"Get well fast, and be able to run over the hills with me in the summer.

"Ever your loving old sister,

"Wilhelmine Elliott."

CHAPTER III

Freshman Experiences

"The tongue which like a stream could run
Smooth music from the roughest stone,
And every morning with 'good-day'
Make each day good, is hushed away—
And yet my days go on."

—MRS. BROWNING

To those at home the winter passed more slowly. The events in Hally's life were her sister's letters, which she kept under her pillow, and over which she laughed and cried by turns; and Mrs. Elliott, too, felt less anxiety than she had expected to feel, in view of the bold step her daughter had taken; and, although she thought that she had cast her burden upon the Lord, yet her confidence was more truly the result of a growing insight into her daughter's character, and in part the reflection of Hally's enthusiasm.

The little invalid grew weaker and paler as the weeks went by, but she always wrote in the most cheering manner to her sister; how she hoped to be able to join her in rides and walks when vacation came, but, even as she wrote, the hope died within her, for her heart told her that she was to have no more of such pleasures with her darling sister. She never allowed her mother to write anything that might alarm Will, for she said, "What's the use? it will only worry her and not help me." All the while the young student, busy with the trials and triumphs of college-life, never thought that Hally could ever be anything else than the dear, patient little angel, and in her dreams of the future the little one always formed one of the chief characters.

A freshman year in college is full of trials for a boy; but, for a girl, who enters an institution where boys have held undisputed sway for generations, every day brings persecutions which he never feels.

He enters a field which has been his without dispute from time immemorial, for his father and grandfather were there before him; while for *her* every step costs a battle, and every innocent action is the subject of unkind criticism. She is presupposed to be loud, masculine, and aggressive, until she proves herself different.

So the nine girls of the University of Ortonville did not find their path strewed with roses, but they were mostly brave, high-minded girls, and hoped to disarm criticism by their daily life and work, rather than by angry retorts, and by degrees they succeeded.[1]

The first concession in their favor was changing the name of the "Young Men's Christian Association" to the "Students' Christian Association," and several of the girls joined. After some weeks they were called upon to lead in prayer, and, after two or three years, were occasionally asked to conduct the meeting.[2]

An incident occurred about this time that weakened the bond between Will and her room-mate, which result was due to Clara's excessive zeal in trying to proselyte.

Will had concluded that she would not go to church any more, so for several Sundays she staied at home and read her dear Carlyle,* much to the grief of Clara, who thought that no person could be good who did not go to church. But the force of habit was so strong upon her that she did not feel quite at ease when she saw others going. So the next Sabbath she ventured into the Presbyterian church, where she heard a sermon from the text, "The wicked shall go away into everlasting punishment, but the righteous into life eternal"; and it was closely defined who the wicked and who the righteous were. She plainly saw that, according to the minister's definition of each, she would be classed with the wicked. The next week, when she was preparing to settle down for a quiet day at home, Clara said, "Go with me to my church to-day, won't you?"

"Oh, I'm sick of churches; it will take me a month to recover from last Sunday's sermon, it was so hideous."

"But I want you particularly to go to-day, for we have class-meeting."

"I don't know much about you Methodists,†[3] but I suppose they are off

---

*Carlyle: Thomas Carlyle (1795–1881), British essayist, historian, and philosopher best known for his two-volume *The French Revolution* (1837) and *The History of Friedrich II of Prussia, Called Frederick the Great* (1865).

†Methodists: A Protestant religion founded by John and Charles Wesley in England in 1743 as a revivalist movement within the Anglican Church of England.

the same piece with the rest; it is always 'Believe what I say or you'll be forever lost,' and doubtless your minister, in addition to that fundamental principle, will denounce Calvinism and every other ism not his own. No, I'm going to stay at home and read Emerson's 'Oversoul.'"*[4]

"And you will not go even to oblige me?" said Clara, in an injured tone.

"Yes, if you put it in that way, I'll do it to accommodate you," she replied, putting on her hat.

Clara had an indefinite idea, as many of her belief have, that, if you can only bring a sinner under direct fire of the gospel, by some happy chance he may be pricked to the heart, and brought to see the truth; so, with a prayer in her heart that her poor, misguided chum might be brought under conviction, they went to meeting.

There were perhaps forty persons in the class to which Clara belonged, ranging from children of twelve to gray-headed men and women, the leader being brother Ramsey, a deacon of the church.

They began by prayer, after which each one was called upon to give his or her experience.

Will noticed that the women spoke and prayed.†[5] This was something quite new, for she had been accustomed to hear no one speak in church but the "holy men," and she did not quite know whether she liked it or not, for it was so strange.

Each one who spoke had some particular friend or acquaintance for whom he asked the prayers of the rest. Clara arose and said that she had a very dear friend who was living without the Saviour, whom she begged that they would remember at the throne of grace in an especial manner.

This irritated Will, when she perceived that Clara was aiming at her, for her interest up to this time in the meeting had been entirely impersonal.

She saw that Mr. Ramsey called on all, and took them in the order in which they sat. She began to feel a little uncomfortable, when she heard him call upon those nearest her, but she thought, "He will not call upon

---

*Emerson's "Oversoul": Ralph Waldo Emerson (1803–82), American poet and essayist. Over-Soul was Emerson's name for the supreme spirit of the universe, "the eternal One."

†the women spoke and prayed: From its beginnings, Methodism allowed women all rights and privileges of membership, ministry, and leadership that were accorded to men within the church.

me, for I'm a stranger;" but he did, saying, "My daughter, what have you to say on the side of the Lord?"

"Nothing, sir," replied Will, growing very red, as she felt the eyes of the whole room upon her.

The good man looked disappointed, and immediately he began to pray for her, begging the Lord to pluck this brand from the burning, and she was portrayed as a poor wretch living without hope and God in the world. At one time she would have been frightened at hearing herself held up in such a light; but now she was only indignant, first, because Mr. Ramsey had called upon her, and then because Clara had insisted upon her going. That was the first and last time that she ever went to a Methodist class-meeting, and she resisted all Clara's coaxing to remain during the rest of the service.

On her way home she was overtaken by one of the girls, whom I have not yet mentioned by name, but who, more than any other, exercised a lasting influence upon Will's character. At first glance you would say that she had not a single element of beauty. Her hair was red, and her nose had a decided inclination to turn up; she had freckles and light eyebrows, and yet no person ever became acquainted with Nellie Holmes[6] who did not think her beautiful; and, before her college-life was over, more than a dozen boys had fallen hopelessly in love with her, and raved about her beauty, while she was a paragon of loveliness to all the girls in the class. She often spoke of her own homeliness in a playful way, and sometimes she would say—and the playfulness was mingled with a tone of regret—"I think Dame Nature might have been a little more generous with me."

To-day she was in fine spirits as she came up to Will, and said: "We have had such a beautiful sermon to-day! Dr. Bingham always preaches so beautifully; the text was, 'The truth shall make you free.' Won't you go with me to hear him some time?"

"What church is it?" asked Will, feeling shy on the subject of churches.

"The Unitarian—that is the one I like the best."

"The Unitarian!" said Will, musingly; "let me see; they do not believe that Christ was God: what do they think of him?"*[7]

"That he was a great, grand brother man, who seemed to get nearer to the soul of things than the rest of us. Come home and spend the day with me, and we'll talk about it—come."

*The Unitarian: Unitarians believe in the unipersonality of God, as opposed to the orthodox Trinity, and thus in a subordinate Christ.

Alice Freeman [Palmer], Class of 1876. Freeman may have been the model for Nellie Holmes. As Anderson described her: "Nell had been brought up from childhood to believe in the equality of woman, and accepted it all as a matter of course." (F99–537: Class of 1876, Classes by Year, Individual, University of Michigan Photographs Vertical File, Bentley Historical Library, University of Michigan.)

"Do you know," said Nell, as they walked along, "you remind me of 'Jo' in 'Little Women'?*[8] only you are prettier than Jo," and she looked admiringly at Will's brown hair and fine profile.

"I'm not as good as Jo; but I wonder what she would have done if she had been made to learn the catechism, and go to prayer-meeting when she did not want to?"

*'Jo' in 'Little Women': A reference to Jo March, the tomboyish character in Louisa May Alcott's popular novel Little Women (1869).

"Is that the way you were brought up? how sorry I am for you!" said Nell, pityingly.

By this time they were at her boarding-place, and she brought Will in and set her down in a rocking-chair before the grate, where a cheerful fire was burning, and said: "Now, I'm going to read you some of *my* religion;" and she took up a volume of Whittier's poems, and read "The Eternal Goodness."

"How beautiful that is!" cried Will, as she repeated:

"I know not where his islands lift
Their fronded palms in air;
I only know I cannot drift
Beyond his love and care."

Then she read "Our Master,"* and Lowell's "Vision of Sir Launfal,"† and ended with Gerald Massey's "Final Harmony."‡

"Yes, those are all very lovely, but they are only poetry," said the skeptical Will; "for how do we know anything about God or a hereafter, or whether there is any?"

"What a little atheist you are!" said Nell; but you will come out all right; I've never had such a struggle as you, for I was never taught to believe in any but a God of love and mercy, and I have never questioned him for a moment."

"No, I'm not an atheist," said Will, a little frightened at the word, "for there must be something at the bottom of things; but as to there being one who looks out for each one of us personally and hears prayers, I don't know, I'm sure."

"I can't remember the time when I did not believe in a God who loved me and listened when I spoke to him. But don't worry about these things too much; you are not to blame for what you think, but I believe you would

*"Our Master": A work by John Greenleaf Whittier (1807–92), American Quaker, poet, reformer, and fiery orator on the causes of abolition and woman suffrage. *Our Master* (1856) reflects his interest in spirituality.

†Lowell's "Vision of Sir Launfal": James Russell Lowell (1819–91), American author and diplomat. His romantic epic poem, *Vision of Sir Launfel* (1848), was based on the legend of King Arthur's quest for the Holy Grail.

‡"Final Harmony": A poem by Gerald Massey (1828–1907), author of *A Tale of Eternity and Other Poems* (Boston: Fields, Osgood, 1870) and a writer on theology, spiritualism, and other religious matters.

be happier if you felt as sure of things as I do. Here is a book that I wish you would read—'The Religion of Humanity.'"*

"That sounds nice, and I'll read it for your sake, if nothing else."

Clara looked doubtfully at the book when Will showed it to her, and she said, "I'm afraid it will only help you farther on the wrong way."

"I'll risk anything being injurious that Nellie Holmes recommends," said Will, with a little touch of resentment, for she had not forgotten the class-meeting of the morning.

It is only due to Prof. Borck's far-sightedness to state the result of Will's lessons with her private tutor. Young Dalton, by degrees, recovered from his bashfulness, and, instead of sitting at the farthest corner of the room, he even, sometimes, forgot his book, and had to look over with her. He also recovered from his contempt for girls so far as to say, "Really, Miss Elliott, if all girls were like you, I should not have the slightest objection to their going to college."

As the days went on, his admiration warmed into quite a personal regard for his promising pupil; and then, before he was aware of it, he was in love, and exhibited some of the most common of the manifold and multiform symptoms which indicate that condition of mind. Sometimes he blushed when she spoke to him, and sometimes affected indifference. Sometimes, when she happened to be a few moments late, he would walk in the direction she was sure to come, and of course was very much surprised to meet her.

One morning he came resolved: stern determination sat upon his brow until he came in sight of the object of his disturbance. The lesson went on as usual, until he found that his text of Xenophon differed very materially from hers, when he laid it down and looked on with her. She was bending with all earnestness over the book, when he suddenly drew her head upon his shoulder and kissed her lips, saying, "It's no use—Miss Elliott, I am going to tell you anyway." If he could only have knelt gracefully upon one knee, and poured forth his soul in words of burning eloquence, his feelings might at least have been spared; but to be unceremoniously kissed like a country lass at an apple-paring was not at all in accordance with Will's ideas of the fitness of things. Poor Dalton! Hamilton, in his

*'The Religion of Humanity': A work by Auguste Comte (1798–1857), a French philosopher, who developed a secular religion (positivism), which emphasized reason and logic. Fully developed, Comte's religion mirrored Catholicism, with priests and a calendar of saints.

"Metaphysics,"* had never told him how to declare himself acceptably, and in all the labyrinths of his calculus he had met nothing that threw light upon the subject; so he trusted to the inspiration of the moment, and threw himself from his high pedestal of a tutor to the level of a very awkward lover. Will thrust his arm aside and stood before him, her face flushing angrily as she said:

"I employed you to teach me Greek, and not make love to me.† Everybody says that we come here just to flirt with the boys; and, when we are going along quietly trying to mind our own affairs, you make fools of yourselves, for which we get the blame. Why, such a scene as this just now is enough to throw disgrace upon the whole cause of co-education in its present uncertain state," and she smiled, in spite of herself, at the extreme character of her statement.

"I—I—did not mean to do any thing wrong; and, if I have, I hope the Lord will forgive me!"

"Doubtless he will, Mr. Dalton; but I think you had better ask my pardon first. I guess we have had enough Greek for the present; so, whenever you are ready, present your bill."

I would not convey the impression that Will was remarkably prudent, or more sensible than girls of her age, maybe; for, had she been in love with the tutor, I'm afraid the cause of co-education would have been secondary; but she was not, and that made the difference.

She read the rest of her Greek alone, and went up to be examined in it; and, as no questions were asked about Dalton, no person knows to this day of the scene that was enacted, for which Xenophon would have been to blame had it injured the cause of the higher education of women.

Finally, the semi-annual examinations came at the end of the first *semester's* work, and, when the professors were asked how the young ladies stood in their classes, they were compelled to say that they had done their work as well as the best in the class, but they always added, "Their health will break down either during the course or after." When the girls heard of it they were highly amused.

"They have changed base somewhat," said Nell, merrily; "at first the cry

*Hamilton, in his "Metaphysics": Sir William Hamilton (1788–1856), Scottish philosopher, whose four-volume *Lectures on Metaphysics and Logic* (1859–60) encompassed his life's work in philosophy and mathematics.

†make love to me: In the nineteenth century, this phrase meant to pay amorous attention to one's beloved or sweetheart, especially during formal courtship. The phrase did not, as it does today, mean to have sex.

was that we were mentally incapable, now we are only 'physically incapacitated.' Strange, isn't it, that we will either die during our college-course or after, and we will not have a head or finger ache for the next decade that can't be directly traced to the higher education? We must not die a bit sooner than fourscore years, either, or it will be because we read Isocrates in a boys' college, but they may make an exception in favor of those of us who are struck by lightning or killed in a railroad-accident."

The rest of the year passed quietly, with only one or two incidents in Will's life worthy of mention. It happened one night in February that Wendell Phillips came to lecture on "The Lost Arts," and Will had no company that night with whom to go, for Clara had a beau, and no others from the house were going.* It is only fair to say, in regard to Clara's beau, that he followed her from her native town, so that it was not an attachment for which the institution was to blame.†9 Will could not miss the lecture, but it was not the right thing to go alone, at least it was not customary; and, although Clara intimated that "Herbert" would not object to her going with them, still, as Herbert said nothing to her, she could not consent to inflict herself upon them.

It was drawing on toward eight o'clock. She stood at the hall-door with cloak and hat on, and looked out into the night. There was a blustering wind that blew scuds of clouds over the sky, giving no certain indication as to whether it would rain, snow, thunder and lighten, or what, but pretty certain that it would do something unpleasant. She thought of the brilliantly-lighted room, where hundreds of "laws and medics" would look curiously at her from the galleries because she came alone.

Now, strong-minded reader, do not smile with contempt because she did not without a qualm seize her umbrella and start for the scene of conflict. She was very young yet, and, to use a term of the spiritualists, had not yet been "developed" into a strong-minded woman, though the material for one was all there.‡10 She had come from a town where one

---

*Wendell Phillips: American orator and reformer (1811–84) who became a leading abolitionist with William Lloyd Garrison's Anti-Slavery Society. After the Civil War, Phillips continued agitating for prohibition, woman suffrage, and penitentiary reform.

†an attachment for which the institution was to blame: Even advocates of coeducation harbored fears of scandalous classroom "romances" resulting from the admission of women to the University of Michigan.

‡had not yet been "developed": Spiritualists believed that a woman "developed" into a medium, an individual who communicates with the dead. A medium could in turn identify and develop the innate talent in others.

who had espoused "woman's rights" would have been shunned as if she had been the victim of small-pox;* so she could not bloom out at once into freedom and absolution from conventionality, even were such a thing desirable. She half turned to go up-stairs, but stopped to reason with herself: "Shall I give up hearing Wendell Phillips's lecture simply because I have no one to tow me along? No, it would not sound well," and she hurried out before the impulse would leave her. The usher took her away up in front, and, as it was late, everybody was there to see her come alone. Some said, "She has grit," and others, "She is too bold," while none guessed her struggle on the stairs. She soon forgot herself in the eloquence of the speaker, and always says with particular satisfaction that she did hear Wendell Phillips lecture on "The Lost Arts."

One other incident, while it lessened somewhat her belief in the necessarily "refining influence of education," at the same time taught her a lesson in prudence, which, perhaps, she lacked. One Saturday night, the mail was late on account of heavy snows, and, as Will was expecting her home-letter, she felt that she could not wait until Monday before hearing from the office. There was no one to send, and, as Clara was sick with sore-throat, she must either go alone or wait. She had not learned to wait, so she went alone. The office was fully a mile and a half from their rooms, and the way was lonely, for the houses were set far back on the lawns, and besides it was after ten o'clock. "Pshaw! what is there to be afraid of in this land of bibles and Christian privileges?" she said, as she drew on her cloak; but the bibles and privileges did not deter her from taking her little pearl-handled revolver from its morocco case; and, putting two cartridges into it, she slipped it into her cloak-pocket, taking care that Clara did not see her, for her room-mate would have been more afraid of a loaded revolver than of anything she might meet on the way.†¹¹

It had been given her once as a prize at a shooting-match, and she had always considered the exquisite little instrument more for ornament than use, and had never loaded it before. She reached the office in safety, and was rewarded by the wished-for letter. Thinking to make the way shorter, she took a street even more lonely than the others, and was hurrying

*"woman's rights": This meant not only suffrage, or the right to vote, but a whole range of rights (e.g., inheriting property, custody of children, equal rights to divorce, and access to the professions) without which women remained second-class citizens.

†pearl-handled revolver: Next to the derringer, the pocket revolver was the concealed weapon of choice for women.

along, when she heard a quick step behind her, and the next instant a hand was laid rudely on her shoulder, and a voice, close to her ear, said: "I have long waited for just such an opportunity of becoming acquainted with you, Miss Elliott."

She turned, and, by the light of a street-lamp, saw the ill-favored visage of a medical student, whose name she did not know, but whose impudent leer she had often encountered going to and from recitations.

"Thank you, sir. I know the way perfectly well, and would prefer to go alone, and she quickened her pace.

"Not so fast, my dear," he said, growing more familiar, and putting his arm round her waist. She grasped the revolver with her right hand, and cocked it, while, with her left, she pushed him from her, saying, as she faced him, "If you touch me again, sir, I'll fire!"

"Oh—ah—I—I—meant no harm, miss; but it—isn't it too late for a lady to go alone?"

"I'll give you until I count three to get from here to the corner!" at which the nonplussed disciple of Æsculapius* took to his heels, muttering, "Who would have supposed she had a revolver?" and his fellow-students thought, next day, that Baggs was unusually quiet, and had not his customary amount of "buncombe,"† as he worked over his "cadaver."

One evening, in early June, Will sat poring over her books. In a few days the final examinations for the year would take place, and then—hurrah for home! There was scarcely a moment that she did not think of home, and the probable changes in the town, and Hally's joy at her coming, and the days were passing rapidly with the pleasant anticipations. There was a knock at the door, and a letter was handed her, on which she recognized her mother's writing. She was not expecting her home-letter so soon, and it startled her somewhat, for they came so regularly. It simply said, "Hally is not at all well, and we think you had better come home as soon as possible."

---

*Æsculapius: The Greek god of medicine, whose skill in healing the sick and raising the dead aroused the wrath of Zeus. Fearing that Æsculapius might make men immortal, Zeus slew him with a thunderbolt. His attribute, a staff with a serpent (a symbol of renovation) coiled around it, remains the symbol of the healing arts.

†buncombe: Sometimes spelled bunkum, the word is American slang for insincere or foolish talk, bragging, nonsense, or anything said for mere show. It originated in 1821 with a congressman from Buncombe County, North Carolina, who, despite the impatience of Congress to vote on the Missouri Compromise continued his speech, declaring "that the people of his district expected it, and that he was bound to 'make a speech for Buncombe.'"

"There, I know it is worse than they pretend, and they have kept it from me all this time," she said, with troubled face, as she hurried down to find out when the next train would leave, and to tell Mrs. Williamson that she must go. There would be no train until eight next morning. As they sat at tea, the door-bell rang, and a boy, with a yellow envelope in his hand, asked for Miss Elliott. The ominous envelope had "Western Union Telegraph Co." on the outside; and the brief dispatch said: "She is dying; come!" A few moments after, Clara found her leaning against the bannisters, and the message had dropped to the floor. She pointed to it, and Clara, after glancing at it, put her arms around Will's neck, as she said: "It is hard, dear, but the Lord gave, and the Lord hath taken away, and we must learn to say, 'Blessed be the name of the Lord!'"

Will writhed as if each word had been a dagger-thrust, but only said, "Please don't, Clara, if you love me!" but Clara, thinking that now was the time to press home "the truth," continued: "That is often the way the Almighty Father deals with us, his erring children; for, when we set our affections upon earthly things, he takes them from us, that we may be drawn toward him. If your sister is taken from you, I shall feel certain that it is intended for your eternal welfare—to draw you nearer to the Saviour."[12]

Will stood up very straight, and, with a hard look on her pale face, said: "Clara Hopkins, if you don't want me to hate you, never talk to me that way again. Affections on earthly things! What does he give us affections for, and objects to set them on? What harm is it doing the Lord, that I have some one who always believes the best things of me? If that is the way your God treats those he loves, I don't want to know him. Pretty way to fill up heaven, by making earth so lonely and cold and wretched that we don't want to stay! Oh, it is too hideous to think of!"[13]

She left Clara sitting on the stairs, while she walked out into the moonlight. The shadows of the maple-leaves lay thick along the walk, but she did not see them; she passed groups of students, who looked curiously at her, but she did not hear their jests.

She wanted to get away from everybody, and think about it. One of the most secluded walks was through the cemetery, down to the river, and this she took. After all, Hally might get well, she thought; many people had been considered dying, and yet recovered and lived many years; but sober reason told her that there was scarcely a hope of its being so in this case.

She wondered if it would do any good to pray.

To whom should she pray? The stars, and blue sky, and moon, did not look as if they knew or cared anything about it, and what else was there away up yonder? At any other time the white tombstones and stillness of the cemetery would have brought up all sorts of ghost-stories to her mind; but now there was no feeling of terror as she walked along the winding paths with rows of graves on each side. Why should she be afraid? Was not Hally soon to be one of those who lie so still, and would she not soon read her name on a stone like that; and how could she ever be afraid where Hally was? When she came to the little river, she threw herself down upon the bank, and looked up through the willow-branches at the sky. The water had a gurgling, contented sound, that annoyed her for a time. What right had anything to be contented and happy in a world where there is so much trouble?

But when Will felt her heart beating against the warm earth while all around myriads of living things were starting up into joyous life, where only a few months before everything was cold and frozen, a feeling of trustfulness came over her, for a moment, and she felt certain that there was a loving hand somewhere that would guide everything aright. But it was only for a moment, for the old pain came back when she arose and faced the hard reality: Hally dying away at home, and twelve mortal hours to be passed before she can even start.

Nell was there waiting for her when she came back. She only said, as she pressed Will's hand: "We are all so sorry, Will dear; I've been to see the professors about your examinations, and they say it will be all right, and for you not to be troubled about them. Prof. Borck said lots of nice things about you, and expressed more feeling than I thought the dear old fossil was capable of. Now Clara and I will pack your trunk after I put you to bed, for we have bought your ticket and ordered the carriage, so you have nothing to do but rest until you go;" and, bringing her night-dress, she did not leave her until she was snugly tucked in bed.

. . . .

It is again night, and the eastward-bound train is sweeping into C——. At one window is a pair of eyes strained to catch familiar objects. Yes, there are the mill and the water-works and the gas-factory, and yonder on the hill is Mr. Hitchcock's new house, just where it was nine months before. There was no one to meet her as she stepped upon the platform, and Will was glad of it, for she dreaded to know the truth. "Driver, please hurry—won't you?" and he looked at her wonderingly as she added, "I may be in time." But the last hope was crushed as she went up the well-known steps, for she saw crape tied with white ribbon swaying in the evening breeze.*

Yes, 'twas all over; and what was the use of going in? So she sat on the steps until they came out and found her, an hour after. Mrs. Elliott met Will with unusual tenderness, for grief had softened her greatly, and she drew her gently into the parlor, where the little rosewood casket was standing by the open window. There, among the soft satin linings, lay the same patient, pale face, much thinner than when she saw it last; but the blue eyes did not open, nor the lips unclose with a glad smile of recognition as she bent over it with endearing words. "If you could only have been here this morning," sobbed the mother, "it would not have been too late; she wanted to see you so much, and, when she was too weak to speak your name, her face would light up when the door opened and then fade with disappointment when she did not see you; she gave me this little note yesterday to give to you if you did not get here in time." Will put it in her bosom, while she stood transfixed, gazing at the waxen face until it seemed to smile and almost speak.

People came in and looked at the dead and passed out, but she saw nothing except the little still figure that was once her sister. Finally, they came and took her away, and she went up to her own room.[14]

Everything was just as she had left it, except the vases on the mantel which were full of fresh flowers, and she found that this had been done daily by Hally's orders since the flowers came. There was the picture of Christ stilling the tempest, and on the other side the deer pursued by the hunters. Over the bureau was the little skeleton rifle that Hally had given her one Christmas, after she learned to shoot.

Then she took the little note from her bosom; it had been written with the greatest difficulty by the weak, trembling hand, and the letters were very uneven; it said:

"Willie darling: I'm so tired that I'm afraid I can't wait even to see *you*. Don't blame any one for not letting you know sooner, because I would not let them tell you, for I was so sure that I could last until your vacation; but, this morning, I know that my story will be told in a few hours.

"It will be so hard not to see you once more; I wished to hear your bounding step in the hall again, and wanted you to carry me out under the

---

*crape tied with white ribbon: Black crape signaled to visitors and all who passed by of a death in the family.

trees in your dear, strong arms, but it is too late. Don't feel too hard and bitter because I have to go, Willie, for you know I never was of any account, and would only be a burden to you and mother.

"All the grand things that I have hoped to do and be, I leave for you, my precious sister, and remember that I always believe in you whatever comes. Somehow, I think I will not be far from you, and when—"

The last lines were almost illegible, and the pencil fell from the thin fingers before the last sentence was finished; and the next day, at the same time, the same little hand was still, and folded over the heart that had throbbed so tenderly, as she painfully traced the last words of love to her absent sister. The next morning, Will arose early, and walked a long way to a certain spot where wild-violets grew, for Hally had always loved them, and, gathering a small bunch, she returned, and clasped them in the dead fingers.

The funeral took place in the afternoon. There were offerings of flowers by the girls in Hally's Sunday-school class; then the ride to the cemetery in the warm June sunshine, where they left her beside her father, under the old beech-tree that stood in the corner of the Elliott lot. Then they came back to the quiet rooms in the old house, and life went on pretty much as before. Many of the good church-people looked for Will's conversion after such a dispensation of Providence, which, they were sure, was sent for that purpose, and they saw with disappointment the vacation passing away, and still she made no "profession." Although she was not converted in the Calvinistic sense of the word, yet Will was different, after Hally's death, in many respects. To be sure, the change was not seen in her unqualified acceptance of the Apostles' Creed,* nor in a warming toward the Shorter Catechism.† She lost none of her buoyancy of spirits, nor her love of adventure, but with her gayety and freedom there were mingled a tenderness and forbearance for all weak, helpless things, more thoughtfulness for those in trouble, and a keener appreciation of beauty, both in the outer and inner world. Everything beautiful was unconsciously associated in her mind with Hally, and for a long time the little grave

*Apostles' Creed: The basic creed of Protestant churches, the Apostles' Creed dates from the days of the early church, a half century or so after the last writings of the New Testament.

†Shorter Catechism: In most Protestant catechisms, there is a larger version for adults and a shorter one for children. The Westminster Shorter Catechism consists of 107 beliefs in the form of questions and answers.

under the beech-tree exerted an influence more powerful than the voices of the living.

Will said that she would remain at home a year after Hally's death, but Mrs. Elliott saw that it would be a great sacrifice for her to drop out of her own class, and, as the eldest son was coming home again to live, she encouraged her to go, and thus Will became a sophomore.

CHAPTER IV

Sophomoric and Other Opinions on
Some Important Social Topics

". . . . Thereupon she took
A bird's-eye view of all the ungracious past;
. . . Till, warming with her theme,
She fulmined out her scorn of laws Salique,
And little-footed China."
—TENNYSON

"The glorious hour has come at last—
Sophomores, we're sophomores!"
—College Song-Book

"By Zeus! we're euchred, Sandy, and it all comes of introducing that topic of the girls. I can't play cards and discuss them too, so let's throw up the cards and make the discussion general. I propose the question: 'Our girls, are they a fizzle or not?'—affirmative, Randolf and Sanderson; negative, Burton and Crooks; how's that Ran?"*

"Don't bother me with any questions about college-girls, for I'm sick of hearing them discussed. Every one I met all summer button-holed me about the girls in college; did I like them, and did they keep up in the class, and were they pretty and womanly, or homely and masculine, and had I fallen in love with any of them—till I swear I never wanted to see a petticoat again!"

"I was bored that way, too," said Crooks, "but I puffed 'em up, I tell you; for, on the whole, I think it was a good move for the institution to let 'em come."

*are they a fizzle or not?: Meaning are the women students a failure? *Fizzle* was also American college slang for flunking a course.

This conversation came from an upper room in Fifth Street, where four gay young sophomores were assembled to have a good time, and talk over prospects for the year that had just opened. Randolf, the largest of the four, would have been handsome but for a supercilious and cynical look that he always wore; he was an excellent student, and plunged into everything with a sort of desperate enthusiasm, so that the girls, among themselves, had dubbed him "The Devouring Element."* Charles Burton was two years his junior, a tall fellow, with a fine sensitive face and scholarly bearing, who, when the conversation took the present turn, sat with an amused smile, but said nothing, until Crooks, a jolly fellow, about whose face there was nothing striking, turned to him with—"Burton, we have not heard from you yet."

"Oh," said Randolf, with a curl of his mustached lip, "Charlie is in the situation of a fellow when he has married one of the girls in a family, and so is bound to stick up for all the rest, good, bad, and indifferent; of course, he will vote their whole ticket."

"As to that," said Burton, blushing; "I have not changed my first position in regard to co-education by acquaintance with the girls here, and if I had forty sisters I would have them all here."

"Come, come," said Frank Sanderson, a merry-faced boy with red cheeks and black eyes that sparkled with fun, "your talk is too general, and we must come down to particulars—that is, to the girls of '70. We'll take them in alphabetical order. I'll do Misses Allston and Bowers," and, lifting his eyes with a mock-heroic air, he said, "O my Muse, wilt thou vouchsafe to mortal man to sing the praises of his Mary Ann!" and then he continued: "I hear Miss Allston is a splendid dancer, and I'm dying to get an introduction to her; and isn't she pretty though, her lips look like fresh strawberries, and wouldn't I like to kiss her; and, in short, she is a decided success, for she gets her lessons first-rate—not one of your digging sort,†[1] but light, airy, fairy-like, you know. Then Miss Bowers enjoys the distinction of being the homeliest girl I ever saw, but she doubtless has the feminine virtues in excess to make up for it—scholarship faultless, etc. There, Crooks, you take Misses Collins and Davidson."

"Well, boys, I'm going to get out my Greek for to-morrow," said Randolf, going to the table and taking the lexicon and a copy of Homer,

*"The Devouring Element": A popular dramatic description of fire, one of nature's four basic elements.
†your digging sort: American student slang for a diligent or plodding student.

"for Old Toughy will invoke the Muses in a different way,* if we don't know all the Homeric forms"; and he pretended to hear no more of the conversation.

"I'm not poetical like you, Sandy, so I'll do mine in plain prose," said Crooks. "Miss Collins strikes me as being a very sensible sort of girl, and don't you remember her elegant translations in Thucydides?† I used to wish that I could run words off my tongue as she did; as to Miss Davidson, I don't know much, for she did not recite in my section, but she has magnificent hair and complexion, which will carry her through. But my favorite among the college-girls, is Nelly Holmes."

"Stop! you are ahead of time," said Sanderson, "for we next come to the chef-d'oeuvre of the class of '70, the Queen of the Amazons,‡² the 'coming woman,'§³ Miss Will Elliott, and no one of us can do the subject justice but Randolf," and he nudged Crooks's elbow. Randolf looked up and frowned.

"Don't get me started on her, for I can't bear her style."

"She admires you anyway, and that shows good taste, for she was anxious to have an introduction to you last year," said Burton, winking at the others.

"She does?" said Randolf, feeling flattered; "well, I'll not throw myself under her chariot-wheels; why, I'm afraid of her: she is brilliant and all that, but so cold and sarcastic and independent, and then she has such a way of aping boys; her very name is boyish—'Will'; if she wants to shorten Wilhelmine, why don't she have it Mina or Minnie, or something feminine? Then her hats are always the same boyish style. You know we fellows don't like to see anything in any woman that we would not want to see in the woman we would marry; and I'd as soon think of marrying an iceberg or the north-pole as Miss Elliott. She is the first girl that I can't

*invoke the Muses: In Greek mythology, the nine Muses were goddesses of inspiration, learning, the arts, and culture. Usually summoned for inspiration, they could also be invoked to punish, which is the "different way" to which Randolf is referring. "Old Toughy" is Professor Borck.

†Thucydides: Thucydides (fifth century BC), Athenian historian, best known for his History of the Peloponnesian War.

‡Queen of the Amazons: By calling Will the Queen of the Amazons, the college boys are insulting her as an "unsexed" woman, a term often applied to suffragists and activist women in the nineteenth century.

§the coming woman: A derogatory term that appeared in a sarcastic 1870 editorial regarding the admission of women to the University of Michigan: "The 'Coming Woman' is to give the home and home-life, the kitchen, dining room and nursery, a wide-berth, and deal with naught but the affairs of State."

understand; she sets herself on a pedestal, and she may stay there, for all o' me."

"I think you entirely misjudge her," said Burton, warmly; "for I had an excellent opportunity of becoming acquainted with her last year, and I do not think there is another girl in the class that has more real womanly feeling than Miss Elliott; and as to her independent ways, I admire them, for they are out of the common run, and her hats are peculiarly becoming to her style, the broad brim and high crown *à la Kossuth.**4 It seems to me it is time for us to lay aside the prejudice that requires women to be cast in the same mould. I think Miss Elliott a splendid specimen of a sound, healthy girl, morally and physically."

"So say we all of us," said Sandy. "By-the-way, I hear she has lost a favorite sister; you remember she was called home before last term was out; perhaps that will soften her to the consistency Randolf likes."

"I shall be careful not to get into her clutches," said the latter worthy.

"How nonsensically you talk," said Burton, "Will Elliott, of all others, is the last to want to clutch you or any one else. I think her independence of masculine help is perfectly sublime. Ran wants a girl to twine around him, for he is still befuddled with the oak-and-vine picture."

"Don't let us show so much disposition, boys," said Sanderson; "I hear Misses Fitzgerald and Baker are not to return—one has gone to Europe, and the other's father has failed, so that leaves only seven of the fair sex."

"I say, Burton," said Crooks, "are you and Nelly Holmes going to hold up the Unitarian choir this year? You are a lucky fellow to have the chance of singing off the same book with her twice every Sunday."

"It's plain to be seen where Crooks's trouble lies," said Sanderson, "but let's have something to drink"; and he poured out a glass of cider from a pitcher on the table, and raised it to his lips, saying, "Here's to the pioneer girls of the University of Ortonville—long may they wave!"

"What do you think?" said Crooks; "Brown, the medic, told me to-day that several women have matriculated in that department, which certainly looks like business."

"Gracious Heaven! Female medics?"†5 said Randolf; "the male medic is bad enough, but from the female medic may Zeus preserve us!"

*à la Kossuth: In the style of Louis Kossuth, a Hungarian freedom fighter and political leader who toured the United States in 1851–52 and drew huge crowds wherever he went.

†Gracious Heaven! Female medics? The first female medical students at the University of Michigan were called "hen medics" on campus and in town.

"You think," said Burton, a sarcastic smile playing round his lips, "with the scientific preacher in one of Charles Reade's novels,*[6] that woman is high enough in the scale of creation to be the mother of God, but not high enough to be a saw-bones?"†

In another part of the town, at 45 Clinton Street, four sophomore girls were settling themselves for the year in two suites of upper rooms in the family of Mr. and Mrs. Lewis, a middle-aged couple, who proved to be a father and mother to the girls, and made a home for them which they always left with regret, and returned to with pleasure.

People were not so afraid of taking college-girls this year; in fact, the Meyerses and Hodges, in Thompson and Jefferson Streets, actually advertised for girls. They had heard that girls were not so noisy as boys; that they took better care of their rooms; that they did not smoke and injure the wall-paper, nor spit tobacco-juice on the furniture; that they did not reel up-stairs half-seas over, and go to bed in their hats and boots. In short, college-girls were no longer ostracised, except in families where there were marriageable daughters, where, of course, nice young men were preferred.

The four girls in Clinton Street are Will and Clara, Nelly Holmes, and her room-mate, Laura Davidson. There are two sitting-rooms, and two bedrooms, cozy and nice; and they have just finished unpacking their trunks, and are putting up their book-shelves and little brackets that they have brought from home, to add to the pictures and other things with which the rooms are decorated. Before one of these pictures Will stands with folded arms. "I like this one," she said, pointing to a fine steel engraving called "Pharaoh's Horses." "What magnificent heads, with flowing manes, fiery eyes, and nostrils dilating as they are driven into the sea by the royal charioteer! But what a queer one *this* is; see, it is one of Cole's 'Voyage of Life,'‡ in which youth is starting out. There he stands at the prow, with beautiful long hair, and innocent, hopeful face; is it a boy or girl? either, I guess; behind him, in the stern, sits old Father Time, with

*Charles Reade's novels: Charles Reade (1814–84), English novelist and dramatist. Popular in Anderson's time, Reade's novels were written with a moral purpose.
†saw-bones: Surgeon.
‡Cole's 'Voyage of Life': Four canvases by Thomas Cole (1801–48), American landscape painter. The series depicts the four stages of life—baby, young adult, middle age, old age—symbolically represented by a lone figure in a boat floating down a river against a changing landscape. Wildly popular, the series hung in many homes as engraved reproductions.

his scythe and hour-glass ready to cut him down at the wrong time; and see, stretching away in the dim distance is the river of life, running in among the trees, and banks lined with beautiful things; but he does not see them, for his eye is fixed on that vague shadowy object which looks like a temple of some kind, for there are towers on it; but it is all so dim, like a dream: is that what we are all chasing, I wonder?—*Mater sanctissima!* there goes eight o'clock,* and I have not looked at my Trig nor Greek yet—have you Nell? I don't want to begin the year by flunking."

"By what?" said Clara, pausing, with a duster in her hand.

"Why, haven't you heard the boys talk about flunking? I think it is one of the most expressive words in the English language; it means a failure, a fizzle, a want of ability to answer when you are asked. Now, how very incomplete it sounds to say: 'The prof called on me, and I was unable to respond from want of knowledge of the subject; or, not being conversant with the topic, I was obliged to remain sitting!' but just to say I 'flunked,' covers the whole ground, including the dreadful feeling of shame and the desire to get through a very small place that must come from a failure in recitation."

"I wish," said Clara, "that you would not fall into the boys' manner of expressing things, for they are so full of slang."

"I don't at all agree with you, for I think that a judicious use of slang is very effective, and I intend from time to time to transplant some of the choicest of the boys' phrases into my own; it is greatly superior to girls' slang; why, one of my girl-friends went to Vassar, and came home full of such as 'I'm dying to know it; I'm furious to see him,' and the most trifling things were horrible, or splendid, or gorgeous, and every other sentence began with, 'I vow!' and, if you don't see that boys' slang is superior to that use of English, I don't admire your taste. For instance, 'cheese it,' 'that squelches me,' 'I'm smashed on her,' 'up on your ear,' or 'that's cheeky'— jewels every one of them, 'five words long, that sparkle upon the stretched forefinger of all time forever'; then, when you add to these the many invocations of the Olympian Zeus, and other classic oaths, you have at once a diction elegant and imposing," continued the provoking Will.

The next time that Clara was alone with Nell, she said: "Don't you think the freedom of our life here is having a bad effect upon Will? She seems to take so naturally to boys' ways."

Mater sanctissima! Literally, "Most Holy Mother!"

"I'm not alarmed about her," said Nell, "and I like every one of her odd ways; she is a character rarely met out of books, and is decidedly refreshing. She is the most delightful mixture of boy and girl that I ever met: she has all the daring, independence, and strength of a boy, and yet the grace and tenderness of a woman. Isn't it too funny to see her try to sew? She has no more idea how to use a needle than if it were Neptune's trident."*

"Yes, and for that very reason she needs taming and curbing a little, for she is inclined to be too boyish."

"Well, I don't want to see her tamed, and she sha'n't mend any stockings or gloves as long as I can get into her trunk—the dear old bother!"

The sophomore year began much more pleasantly for the girls than their freshman, because they had outlived much of the prejudice against them, and began to feel more at home.

Several more girls entered with the freshman class, and, instead of hazing them, and trying to make them feel their nothingness, the sophomore girls received them with open arms, and tried to make the way for the younger members smoother than their own had been. They had, for the first *semester*, Sophocles's "Antigone,"† Horace's "Odes,"‡[7] and trigonometry, besides lectures on English literature and composition. It was a year full of interest in many respects.

In the first place, the question of woman suffrage was to be submitted to the State of S——, for it was about to revise its constitution, and it seemed the fitting opportunity for a decision to be made whether, as John Knott[8] once said, in a very "knotty" speech, "the fair sex should be allowed to vote, to hold office, drink cocktails, and ride astride." The leaders of the woman-suffrage movement§[9] made the university town a basis of operations, and Will was one of the earliest converts.

She had never heard the subject fairly presented, and had not thought

*Neptune's trident: A three-pronged fish spear that is the attribute and scepter of the Roman sea god Neptune.

†Sophocles's "Antigone": *Antigone*, a play by Sophocles (ca. 496–406 BC), is his best-known tragedy, notable for its focus on a strong and defiant woman.

‡Horace's "Odes": Quintus Horatius Flaccus, or Horace (65–8 BC), Latin lyric poet and satirist of the Roman Empire during the reign of Augustus. The most frequent themes of the *Odes* are love, friendship, and the simple pleasures of life.

§the woman-suffrage movement: The movement to secure the vote for women emerged with renewed vigor after the Civil War. In 1874, the Michigan State Legislature put a woman suffrage amendment on the ballot; it was defeated handily.

much about it, but with the spirit of Paul, as soon as she knew the right, she followed it with the greatest enthusiasm.

Mrs. Livermore, Mrs. Howe, and Mrs. Stanton,[*10] beside a host of lesser lights, lectured during the campaign. Part of the university-girls were bitterly opposed to the movement. Nell had been brought up from childhood to believe in the equality of woman, and accepted it all as a matter of course. Clara was not decided, but Will talked, thought, and dreamed of woman suffrage with all the ardor of a young convert.

Debates were required of the sophomores on questions chosen by themselves, and Will got permission to have the question, "Shall the ballot be given to woman?" if she could find three others to take part in it. Plenty of boys were willing to take the negative, but she had trouble in finding some one to assist her on the affirmative. Nell would have taken it, but she protested that, like Moses, she was slow of speech, and would only bring disgrace upon the cause, while the other girls talked reprovingly to her, and said that it was highly improper, and wanted her to give it up.[†] Finally, one young gentleman took it, for the sake of argument, for the boys thought it would be fine fun. The next week was chosen for the discussion, and so many from the other classes had permission to come in and hear it that the room was crowded. Only fifteen minutes were allowed to each speaker, and if one was inclined to run over time he was called to order by the professor. The first affirmative was good, but lacked spirit, plainly showing that the young man did not feel deeply the cause for which he was speaking. The first speaker on the negative had evidently read and thought on the question, and his arguments were well presented, consisting of all those objections now so hackneyed, but then comparatively new, at least to college-students who had never given serious thought to the subject. He sat down amid a round of applause, and there was a general murmur among the boys of "Let's see her beat that, if she can"; "She can't come up to that," etc.

Will arose quietly and took her place upon the platform. She was dressed in simple black, with soft lace in the neck, that made her look more girlish than usual, while her rippling hair was gathered into a coil behind, without ornament.

*Mrs. Livermore, Mrs. Howe, and Mrs. Stanton: Mary Ashton Livermore, Julia Ward Howe, and Elizabeth Cady Stanton were leaders of the suffrage movement and well known to the women of the University of Michigan.

†said that it was highly improper: Most Americans still disapproved of women speaking or debating in public.

She was a trifle pale, and a little frightened, for she knew that the majority was against her. Her voice trembled at first, but grew steady as she forgot herself in her subject, and a bright flush rose to her cheek, so that even the surly and skeptical Randolf whispered to his neighbor, "I never knew before that she was so handsome." She took up the arguments of her opponent, and answered them one by one, occasionally pointing the argument with a flash of wit which made the hard, unsympathizing faces relax; and, as her tones grew earnest and eloquent, every eye became fixed upon her with real, kindly interest, instead of the cold sneers that she encountered when she first began.

The fifteen minutes lengthened into half an hour, and she took her seat amid the most enthusiastic applause, which continued until she came forward and bowed, while the last speaker on the negative refused to speak at all. After they were dismissed, many of the boys with whom she had never spoken before came forward and declared themselves converted to her standard in spite of their former prejudices. She rather hoped Randolf would speak to her too, but he did not.

When they reached home, Nell threw her arms around Will's neck, exclaiming:

"You dear old girl, I'm so proud of you, for your speech was perfectly magnificent, worthy of Susan B. herself.* We are going to crown you."

And, seating Will upon an ottoman, she ran to the conservatory and cut a sprig of ivy, which she twisted into a wreath, saying:

"We do hereby bestow upon you the title of 'Defender of the Faith.'"

The comments of the boys, as they went home in little groups, were various.

"Boss speech that," said Clarke.

"What a way she had of making a fellow feel like Judas himself, for ever having said a word against woman's rights!" said Hawley.

"She beat Gardner all hollow," said Kimble.

"But what a magnificent voice and style she has on the platform—so modest and yet so impressive!" said Ralston, a gentleman of artistic tastes.

"Well, I never liked her half so well before," said Crooks.

Randolf said nothing, but the image of a black dress and white lace at

---

*worthy of Susan B. herself: Susan B. Anthony was a founder of the woman's suffrage movement. Along with Elizabeth Cady Stanton, she formed the National Woman Suffrage Association. In 1872, Anthony and her supporters were arrested for trying to vote.

the throat crossed his mental vision oftener than he would have been willing to confess.

Charlie Burton came down that evening to call on the girls, and he greeted Will with the most genuine boyish enthusiasm concerning the "speech."

"I knew, just by the way you looked when you got up, that you were going to say the right thing."

From this time there sprang up between Will and him a most lively friendship, free from the nonsense that usually marks friendships between young gentlemen and ladies; and Will used to say that she had at last found a good, square boy who would never make love to her, and who never thought she was dreadful because she could not sew, and who seemed always to understand her without explanations; while Charlie wrote home that he had found the oddest, jolliest girl, so charmingly boyish, and, at the same time, such a true-hearted girl.

Now, reader, do not look wise and say: "Yes, the old, old story; of course they fall in love before they know it;" for, to spare all false conjectures, I'll just say that such a thing was never thought of by either party, although they discussed everything, from "the tender emotion" to "the immortality of the soul," but their hearty friendship lasted throughout the course; and even now, although Charlie is married and involved in business cares, he still writes letters of the sincerest friendship to Will, and speaks with the old warmth of his girl-friend in college.

A few weeks after the year began, Nell came home in a high state of excitement, holding up a book as she said:

"See what I've found!—Dr. Clarke's book on 'Sex in Education,'* bearing pat on the question at issue. Mr. Fiske says he has sold more than two hundred copies, though they only came yesterday, and that the book bids fair to nip co-education in the bud."

"Ba, ba, black sheep!" replied Will, looking up; "but sit down, Nell, and read it aloud, for I'd like to know what the dear old humbug has to say against girls."

"Why," said Laura, with a shocked expression, "Dr. Clarke is one of the most eminent physicians in Boston."

"Don't care if it were Æsculapius himself returned from Hades with his shroud on, I would not believe him if he tried to make girls out weak and

---

*Dr. Clarke's book on 'Sex in Education': a reference to *Sex in Education; or, A Fair Chance for Girls* (1873), written by Dr. Edward H. Clarke.

good for nothing. But read it, Mark Antony, read the will, Cæsar's will;" and the impetuous girl made a snatch at the book, but was forestalled by Clara, who took it and began to read aloud, while Will paced the floor with rising excitement.

"Come, my young war-horse," said Nell, "don't shake your mane so defiantly," and she drew her down on the sofa. "Just look at it calmly, and, if it is true, accept it; and, if it is not, there is no need of growing angry about it."

"Well," said Will, only half appeased, "what does the precious doctor propose to do with us after he has cajoled us into believing that we are born and predestined to be invalids from the foundation of the world? Send us home to embroider chair-covers and toilet-sets,* I suppose."

"I hardly think any one will be so rash as to accuse *you* of being an invalid, or making a chair-cover," said Nell, laughing; but Will went on without paying attention to the remark:

"Women have washed and baked, scrubbed, cried and prayed themselves into their graves for thousands of years, and no person has written a book advising them not to work too hard; but just as soon as women are beginning to have a show in education, up starts your erudite doctor with his learned nonsense, embellished with scarecrow stories, trying to prove that woman's complicated physical mechanism can't stand any mental strain. I'll venture that Miss A—— and Miss C——,† etc., whose early decline he bewails, had not sense enough to enjoy good health, or their mothers had not before them."

"Now, that is going too far, when you say that every one who has not such health as you have is lacking in common-sense; even I can't stand that," said Nell.

"Well, well, I'll take it back: they all have the best of sense, from Eliza Ann to Dorothea Maria, and their mothers before them. There, isn't it handsome of me to come down so in favor of the fair sex? But, girls, I like what he says against corsets,‡[11] and the abominable way women dress; for I've been of the same opinion since I have been reading about dress reform

---

*toilet-sets: Articles used in dressing, such as brushes, perfumes, cosmetics, and other such personal care items.

†Miss A—— and Miss C——: Dr. Edward H. Clarke's anonymous examples of women whose health was damaged by coeducation.

‡corsets: Close-fitting inner bodices stiffened with whalebone or the like and fastened by lacing; worn chiefly by women to give shape and support to the figure.

in the *Woman's Journal;*[12] I am going to burn those new corsets you made me get last week, Clara, and make my dresses shorter; and I'm going to prove to you that the corset, with its concomitant train of evils, has killed more women than ever Noah's flood destroyed. Ninety-nine hundredths of all diseases on record belong to women, and they all arise from her mode of dress. What would you think of tying up a race-horse that way and starting him on the course? It's just as absurd to expect a woman to run this race of life creditably in her present style of dress!"

"A speech, a speech!" said Clara; but Will continued:

"Corsets have a moral significance, too, or rather an immoral one, for they have been the means of making women do the most improper things. Take, for instance, the terrible example of Dr. Mary Walker!"†

"What did corsets have to do with her style of dress?" asked Laura.

"Why, haven't you heard how she came to dress so abominably?" said Will, with a mischievous sparkle in her eye.

"No, no," cried they all; "how was it?"

"She was once a most lovely, gentle girl, with laces, and ruffles, and drapery, that floated around her girlish form, soft as gossamer. She read Tennyson,‡ and talked sentimental things under the moonlight; she vowed to love, and be faithful and obedient; but, alas! behold the domestic vampire—the ruthless destroyer of her peace—for on the day when she, a 'sweet girl graduate,' was sweeping up the stage to take her diploma, she tripped upon her train, and, as she fell, her corset-stay ran into her, inflicting a dangerous wound. She arose from the floor a changed woman; she waited not for congratulations or condolences of friends, but hurried home, and took refuge in a complete suit of her brother's clothes, and has never been induced to leave them, except for repairs. What is to blame that she now strides over the country, from platform to platform, in male attire, except the corsets? In view of all these facts, I now proceed to burn

---

*dress reform: As part of the woman's rights movement, a campaign for less restrictive women's clothing reappeared with renewed vigor after the Civil War.

†Dr. Mary Walker: An American physician and feminist (1832–1919), Walker was also an abolitionist, prohibitionist, and dress reformer. After serving in the Civil War as a field surgeon and possibly as a spy for Union forces, she became the only woman to receive the Medal of Honor. After abandoning dress-reform outfits, she wore men's clothing for the rest of her life.

‡Tennyson: Alfred Lord Tennyson (1809–92), the English romantic poet, based much of his verse on classical or mythological themes. He held the title poet laureate of England from 1850 until his death.

Dr. Mary Edwards Walker. "'Why, haven't you heard how she came to dress so abominably?' said Will, with a mischievous sparkle in her eye." Walker, shown here wearing the short dress and trousers promoted by the dress-reform movement, later abandoned even this radical style for a man's suit. (Carte de visite photograph by M. J. Powers, Plumb Gallery, Washington, D.C., 1860–70. Courtesy of the Library of Congress, Prints and Photographs Division, LC–USZ62–112180.)

the prisoner at the bar, on the charge of woman-slaughter and as a corrupter of public morals," and she threw the corset into the grate.

"Why, I never heard that story about Dr. Mary Walker," said Clara.

"I never did, either," said Will; "but I think it is a reasonable way of accounting for the doctor's little idiosyncrasy in the way of dress, and so I put it in; for you know, in law, it is no difference whether things are true or not, so that you make out a strong case."

"Well, for my part, I don't see any point in all this talk about dress reform," said Laura; "my corsets are always loose enough to put both your fists under,[13] and, as to long skirts, I like them, and would not have them any shorter for the world."

"Oh, you're like Ephraim,* joined to your idols, so you'll have to be let alone," said Will.—"But, girls, there is another subject of more importance to me just now. I don't get exercise enough, and I feel Dyspepsia with his bony fingers making a dive for my devoted digestive apparatus,† and my liver is fast making me believe in the total depravity of the human family."

"Yes, you do look as if you were in a rapid decline," said Clara, smiling.

"Well, look at the exercise the boys have—foot-ball, base-ball, gymnastics, and lots of such things; while all the recreation we get is to poke to and from recitations.[14] May be you don't feel the need of it, but I do, and I'm going to ask Mr. Lewis if I may split wood on Saturdays."

"How ridiculous, Will! You would be talked about all over college."

"It's a question of life and death with me;" and, true to her word, she spent the next Saturday forenoon in the wood-shed sawing and splitting wood, to the great amusement of the other girls, who looked in now and then to see how she was progressing, and occasionally to bring her a hot doughnut from the kitchen where Mrs. Lewis was frying them.

The next college paper contained this notice: "People are requested to keep their children indoors, for the great *Megatherium Amazoniense* is

---

*Ephraim: In the Old Testament, Ephraim was the second son of Joseph: "When Ephraim spoke, men trembled; he was exalted in Israel. But he became guilty of Baal worship and died" (Hosea 13:1). Baal was an idol of the Phoenicians, the god of the sun.

†Dyspepsia with his bony fingers: Will is personifying a chronic or more severe form of indigestion that involved weakness, loss of appetite, and depression of spirits. It could be quite debilitating. Americans in the 1870s were just beginning to recognize the health benefits of regular exercise. Women, confined to corsets and the limiting culture of "woman's sphere," suffered most from the ill effects of physical inactivity.

loose,* in the person of a sophomore girl who saws and splits her own wood;[15] the Board of Health think best that every one be on his guard until this interesting specimen is caught and domesticated, measures for which are in rapid progress."

Dr. Clarke's book was discussed in the next few weeks by more than the girls in Clinton Street. The boys read it, and delivered their opinions at length among themselves. The president and the faculty read it, and shook their heads doubtfully about the "experiment of co-education."[16]

The ministers of the place took up the question, and particularly the pastor of the Presbyterian Church, Rev. Edmund Allison, felt himself called upon to give his views at length; so, taking Dr. Clarke's book as a basis, he inveighed against the whole woman movement, both in lectures to his Bible-class and in sermons from the pulpit. It was against the canon of the Holy Scriptures that women should follow the pursuits of men, and that she should wield the saw and scalpel was to the last degree unfitting, for, however much she might try to conceal the hateful fact, she was inherently weak, and her persistent efforts to do that for which God never intended her, would only result in misery to herself and evil to the race. Thus spoke the Rev. Edmund; but still the ladies of the University of Ortonville went daily to the dissecting-room, to the law-lectures and recitations, and still the world moved on.

---

* *Megatherium Amazoniense:* A megatherium was a giant ground sloth that lived in South America eleven thousand years ago. Within the context here, a megatherium is anything of huge or ungainly proportions. When paired with *Amazoniense,* this fictional scientific name implies that Will is a freakishly unsexed specimen of a female suffragist.

CHAPTER V

———≫●《———

Choice of a Career

"One likes a beyond somewhere."
— GEORGE ELIOT

"Love is it? Would this same mock-love and this
Mock Hymen were laid up like winter bats,
Till men grew to rate us at our worth!"
— TENNYSON'S *Princess*

"Girls, here is an invitation to go skating tonight; Charlie and two or three of the other boys are going, and they want us four to go."

"Hip, hip, hurrah!" cried Will, as she turned a hand-spring over the table, and sent Godwin's "Moods and Tenses" spinning to the other end of the room;* "I feel as if I could skate fifty miles to-night! I have not had a chance yet to try my new club-skates,"† and she ran to the closet to get them, while she hummed a part of the skater's song—‡

"Bound to the steel we love, ever and on we go!"

---

*Godwin's "Moods and Tenses": Probably a reference to William Watson Goodwin's (1831–1912) *Syntax of the Moods and Tenses of the Greek Verbs* (Boston: Ginn, 1870).
†club-skates: In the 1870s, ice skates were blades fastened to a pair of boots. Older skates had a wooden base that strapped onto the boot and screwed into the sole. Club-skates, an improvement, could be adjusted to fit the sole by means of clamps. Their broad blades and slightly curved edges made them more suitable for figure skating than speed.
‡the skater's song: Expressing the romance of the sport, composers wrote many songs about ice skating in the post–Civil War era. With Americans' increasing devotion to athletics and outdoor recreation in the late 1800s, ice skating grew into a professional sport, with figure skating and speed skating becoming competitive events.

"It will not be so much fun for those of us who do not understand the art very well," said Nell; "but it will be nice to watch the others."

The river was in fine condition. Recent winds had swept the snow from the ice, leaving it very smooth, and the broad, shining track sparkled in the moonlight as the merry party with shout and laughter buckled on their skates. Will had decidedly the advantage of the other girls, for she was quite at home on skates, while they were only learning, and she said, laughingly, when one of the boys offered to help her put on her skates:

"Oh, don't mind me, but devote yourself entirely to helping the weaker ones, for I can take care of myself," and, hurriedly fastening her skates, she shouted, "I'm going to see if I can't go to the bend and back before the rest of you are ready to start!"

"You must not go alone," said Clara; "it is not prudent."

But there was no one ready, and Will was off; bowing a good-by as she glided swiftly backward, then turning, she was soon out of sight, and the voices of those she left behind grew fainter, until, finally, there was no sound but the sharp cutting of her own steel upon the ice. In some places it was very thin, and swayed as she flew over it, but the sense of danger only made the blood leap faster through her veins. She reached the bend—which was a mile from where she left the party—and stopped to take breath before starting back.

Hearing voices approaching, she glided into the shade of a clump of willows as three juniors rushed by, evidently skating a race. There was a fourth, but his skate had become loose, and, in stopping to fix it, he fell heavily, the thin ice broke with a crash, and the next moment he was struggling in the water, which was much beyond his depth. Will heard his frightened cry, and darted from under the willows in time to see the face of Phelps disappear under the ice, the same who had sworn at the girls on the stairs when she was a freshman, and had pushed her against the bannisters, and who had never hesitated to say unkind and mean things about the college-girls. There was no room in Will's mind for resentment now, for every thought was bent on saving him. She hastened to the spot, and, lying full length upon the ice, leaned over trying to catch him, but the treacherous ice broke from under her, and it was by an almost superhuman effort that she regained her footing.

She hesitated but a moment, while the despairing cry came from the drowning man, "Miss Elliott, can't you save me?" then springing up the bank and across a ravine to a fence, she seized the topmost rail, which was frozen fast, and which it took all her strength to loosen, dragged it to the spot and flung it across the hole in the ice, all the time chiding herself for not doing it more rapidly. She crept out upon the rail and caught his arm, but poor Phelps was too far gone to help himself, and she had not strength enough to draw him out. She begged him to catch hold and try to pull up, but he was so nearly insensible that he scarcely heard her while she was doing her best to keep his head above water.

She listened in vain for voices, that she might cry for help; but all was still, for the companions of the young man had either not missed him, or thought that he could take care of himself.

Her heart leaped with hope as she heard the sound of sleigh-bells passing on the road above, and she shouted with all her might. Her voice was wonderfully clear and strong, and it rang out now on the still, frosty air, startling two gentlemen, who were riding leisurely along, so that one exclaimed: "Hark! wasn't that a woman's scream? Hold the lines, Roberts, till I run over and see. It came from the river." The other, hastily tying the horse to the fence, followed, and in a few moments Will was released from her post, and Phelps was saved.

He could not speak, but was rolled up in robes and put into the sleigh, while Will told of the accident in a few words. She declined riding, and said she would skate back to keep warm, after which she disappeared like an apparition in the moonlight.

When she came back to where she had left the party a little while before, the girls cried, "Where have you been, Will Elliott?" "We would have sent some of the boys after you," said Nell, "but we are all such novices that we can't get along alone on skates. But what has happened?— for your skirts are frozen stiff as boards!"

"Yes, I had a little accident, and got in," said Will, but she could not be coaxed to give further information.

The next day it was talked all over college how Miss Elliott had saved Tom Phelps's life.

The girls came home from recitations in a great state of excitement about it, saying, "Why didn't you tell us last night, you naughty girl, how you came to be so wet, instead of letting us hear from outside?"

"But wasn't it perfectly grand?" said Nell; "for that fellow has said so many ugly things about you; it is an instance of the moral sublime;" and they talked away very fast, while Clara came and threw her arms around Will's neck, exclaiming, "I'm proud that you are my chum."

Will stood blushing, not knowing what to say, until finally, with an impatient gesture, she said: "I shall have to request you to 'cheese that' now, much as such language goes against my feelings, for you talk too much about a little thing that any one of you could and would have done under the same circumstances."

A few days later she received a letter from the father of the young man, which ran as follows:

"My dear Miss Elliott: We have just learned of your heroic conduct by which you have restored an only son to the arms of his glad and grateful parents. To be candid, Miss Elliott, I must confess that, while I was in the Legislature, I worked against the admission of women to the university, because I felt it my duty; but, if I am forgiven for that, my influence will hereafter be on the other side, and 'tis you who have converted me.[1] How could I consistently stand out against a movement, the results of which have made me to-day the happiest father in the State? And if you are a representative of college-girls, I'm glad that my son has the honor and privilege of being in the same institution with them.

"I know that reward is not to be spoken of in the case, for such a deed is beyond price; but, if ever you are in need of help in carrying out your plans for life, remember that you will find in me one who will feel honored by being able to assist you in any way that lies in his power. Tom's mother unites with me in the deepest gratitude, and warmest wishes for your welfare. Sincerely yours,

"Edmund Phelps."

"The old gentleman is quite gushing," said Will, as she threw the letter into Clara's lap.

From that time young Phelps was the warm friend and defender of Miss Elliott, and, whenever her peculiarities were spoken of in an unpleasant way, he always said:

"It will do very well to talk like that when it's smooth sailing, but wait until you get under the ice and are saved by such a woman, and you will change your tune."

One evening, as Will and Clara sat by their own little fire cozily talking, Will said, assuming a confidential tone:

"Do you know, I believe Charlie and Nell are engaged! I've been confirmed in the belief ever since the night we went skating; his manner toward her was so different from the way in which he treated the rest of us."

"I should think," said Clara, "that he would tell you all about it, for you are such great friends."

"Well, I think he has been on the point of telling me several times, but could not get up courage. And don't you think Nell has changed wonderfully?"

"I don't quite see in what respect you mean."

"Well, now, she used to talk so enthusiastically about our college course, and had so much class spirit; we all used to say, you know, that we never could survive if anything should happen that we could not go on with the class, and we used to talk about what grand things we were going to do and be when we got through, have careers, etc.: now she talks so calmly and contentedly about everything, and she never says anything more about a career. I don't think she even takes the interest in her studies that she used to—not that she does not always have good lessons, but she does not go at them with the same spirit, and always acts as if she had something better in prospect, and was simply waiting to get there, taking this by the way. I'm half provoked with her for giving up so easily, but, if he is her affinity, as they say, why it must be all right. I tell you nothing takes the starch out of a girl like being engaged. She loses ambition right away, and don't amount to anything forever after."

"What would you have girls do? Don't you believe in their being engaged and married?"

"Oh, yes, I s'pose so," said Will, yawning, "but that always seems to be the end of them, they settle right down and lose their individuality, and are as good as dead and buried. Now, I can't think of anything more prosy than being married, for then the future is fixed, and any one can foretell your life from that to the end of the chapter. The pleasant uncertainty is all gone, and the grand possibilities of the future are all narrowed down to the stupid reality of being some man's wife; read Jean Ingelow's 'Songs of Seven,'* and you have it all. I think it is so dreadful to get to the end of things, and have nothing more to look forward to than what your mother and grandmother did before you."

"What are *you* going to do?" asked Clara.

"Oh, I don't know," said Will, impatiently, "but I want to do

*Jean Ingelow's 'Songs of Seven': English poet and novelist Ingelow (1820–1897) wrote these seven poems (1863) depicting the seven epochs in a woman's life. Very popular, they went through several printings; the poems were set to music, sold as sheet music, and sung in parlors across America.

something, have an object, be somebody" (and she struck at the air with clinched hands as if fighting an enemy); "I want to choose some trade or profession for life, as the boys do, and work."

"Then you do not intend to be married?"

"I don't know, but I s'pose I'll have to be sometime; for to think of being an old maid and growing old and gray with no one in particular to love, is horrid. They say that a woman can't have a profession and take care of a family well, and I'd like to show that she can if it is possible. I wish that I had some particular talent for something, so that I could know what I was made for; deciding upon a work for life is no easy matter. Have you decided what you are going to be?"

"No, but I want to work somewhere for the Lord, if he wants me."

"Yes, you'll marry some missionary and go to China or India, and wear your life out teaching the heathen the way of salvation according to John Wesley,* and that is more than most of us will do, I doubt not," and Will, seeing from Clara's last remark that she was veering around to the religious question, hastily took up her books, and the subject of future careers, for the time being, was dropped.

Not many days after, Will burst into the room with radiant face, exclaiming:

"I've at last found my ideal woman—perfectedly grand she is, and I'd do anything for her, live for her, die for her!—and she has helped me decide what I'm going to be."

The girls were all together in Will's and Clara's room, and, as they were accustomed to Will's outbursts of enthusiasm, they all looked up with expectant but not astonished faces.

"Her name is Evelyn Lane; she is in the medical department, and the professors all say she is the smartest in the class. I'm going to be a doctor, for I think there is no calling in life so grand. To save people's lives and make them well and happy, what could be more magnificent! To think of having people confide in you, and believe that you can save their dear ones; to have a mother take your hand with tears of gratitude in her eyes, and tell you that you have saved her darling, to have pale faces grow brighter at your entrance, what lot in life could be sweeter?"

*John Wesley: The eighteenth-century founder of Methodism. To reach as many people as possible with the gospel, Wesley began to travel and preach, commission lay preachers, open chapels, minister to the sick, establish charities, and do other such work that spread Methodism. The later work of Methodist missionaries in foreign countries extended Wesley's personal evangelical zeal.

"You precious girl, what an old romancer you are!" said Nell.

"Romancer!" echoed Will, indignantly; "maybe you think I'm in fun about it?"

"Oh, not at all; only you have a way of idealizing people and things wonderfully; but your choice is grand, and we all give you a God-speed, and three cheers for Dr. Elliott and the new career!" and they gave three cheers in pantomime, so as not to disturb Mr. and Mrs. Lewis below.

"I'll finish in the literary department, and then go right into the medical, for I think I have just about enough money to put me through and keep me until I have passed the starvation period, which always comes before a doctor or lawyer is established. I'll depend upon you girls to get me into practice, for you will each take me for your family physician, and I'll carry the young Bartons and Joneses and Smiths through the whooping-cough and measles in the grandest style. But, oh! my doctor-lady, she is divine; and, what do you think? she kissed me—actually kissed me, all undeserving as I am—and such a mouth and lips!*² It will make me happy for a month! I never realized how much there is in the art of kissing before. Here, Clara, I'll begin on you, and try different kinds for practice. This is the kiss of your city cousin, who cares nothing particular about you, but is obliged to like you because you are her father's sister's child; she leaves behind a delicate odor of Hoyt's German cologne or Lubin's extract,† and on the whole is rather nice. Here is your Sunday-school teacher, who is greatly interested in your eternal welfare; it is sincere and pleasant accordingly. Here is the kiss of your big brother, who gives it from a sense of duty in a matter-of-fact, business way, while around his mustache is the lingering fragrance of a fine Havana—not at all bad.‡ Here is the kiss of somebody else's big brother, which makes your heart beat faster, and is very unlike all the others—so I've heard, for I do not speak from experience. But what makes you blush so, Clara? Does it bring up reminiscences of the past? I beg your pardon."

"Upon my word," said Nell, "I've never heard such an elaborate analysis of the art in my life. I think you will have to write a book on the subject."

"Oh, I'll bring it in as an appendix to my book on 'Women in Clothes.'"

*she kissed me: Expressions of physical love—kissing, hugging, "crushes," or sleeping in the same bed—were fairly common among nineteenth-century women.

†Hoyt's German cologne or Lubin's extract: Popular toiletries of the late nineteenth century.

‡a fine Havana: A high-quality cigar made in Havana, Cuba.

Clara took an early opportunity of saying to Will that, as she now had chosen her life-work, she hoped that she would take Jesus for her helper, otherwise she feared for her success. Clara's solicitude for Will's well-being was sincere and genuine. She was of a very affectionate disposition, and she yearned over Will with the feeling of an elder sister. She admired, too, the gay, dashing girl, and even tried to imitate some of her feats, and thought her splendid; but when it came to questions of religion she felt the weight of her great responsibility. She was, as has been said, the daughter of a Methodist minister of small income, and had been brought up to habits of the most rigid economy. She kept all her accounts in a most methodical way, and added them up carefully at the end of each week, which Will declared made her nervous.

She was a close student, and entered into the minutest particulars of everything; viewed every text from every conceivable side, and would sometimes take up half the recitation-hour, to the annoyance of the rest of the class, discussing some preposition or particle with the professor, its probable meanings, or the shade of difference between that and some other. She was a general favorite among the professors, for she was not only a fine scholar, but she seemed always to strike the points that pleased them most. No man can be a college professor for any length of time without having one or more hobbies, and a right appreciation of the merits of these hobbies on the part of a student is a sure passport to favor. Sometimes it is a particular manner of demonstrating a proposition, or of rendering a passage, or the pronunciation of a word. Clara was always fortunate in remembering these, and bringing them in at the right time, to the great delight of the professor in the chair. It is a wonder that Will and Clara lived together four years as they did; for Clara had a disposition which was sometimes exacting and even imperious, and her room-mate was made of very combustible material. They did have a good many ups and downs, and sometimes high words full of bitter feeling passed between them, but they always made it up, and were heartily ashamed of it afterward; but two such dispositions should never live together, for they mutually dwarf and cramp each other. Will, with her large, restless nature, was made impatient and more restless by Clara's exact way of doing everything. Clara was a "limit-lover," while Will was a "limit-hater," and, instead of each yielding something in order that they might meet upon a common platform, each pulled more decidedly her own way. They would have lived more comfortably, however, had it not been for the ever-

recurring question of religious belief; and Clara had something of the spirit
of persecution mingled with her love for Will, which made her feel that
she must hold the subject before her continually. She sometimes wrote
home requesting their prayers, and was in the habit of saying that she
would not feel that she had done her duty if she left a word unspoken that
might fall upon her room-mate's heart with the weight of conviction. In
such cases Nell was always Will's refuge, and she never failed to find
comfort from the quiet but decided words of her friend.

Do not imagine that Will and her room-mate were always in a state of
domestic ebullition, for there were times, and many, too, when they really
enjoyed each other; they had gay walks and strolls, they read books
together, and even laid girlish plans for the future, in which they were to
be associated in some way, but, as has been said, they were never intended
to live together; and when, after four years of daily contact, they separated,
Will felt no aching void in her heart made by Clara's absence. She thought
often of her, and with the kindliest feelings and warmest wishes for her
welfare, but she never had that feeling of want and desolation that comes
when we have parted for an indefinite time, and perhaps forever, from one
with whom we have been long associated and have come to regard almost
as a part of our own life. When Will was in trouble it was not Clara of
whom she thought first, but it was to Nell's arms that she longed to fly, and
into her ear that she longed to tell her troubles; but there was real
loneliness in Clara's heart as she bade Will good-by for the last time, and
felt that the great stormy and sunshiny nature was gone from the reach of
her voice forever, and it was a real sorrow to her that she seemed to go so
easily and with no apparent regret.

CHAPTER VI

Ortonville versus Vassar

"Ortonville, *February* 24, 187—
"Dear Mame: You have asked me, ever since I came here, to write you a descriptive letter telling all about the university, the professors, the boys and girls, and so on. I've never found time to do it until now, so here goes. I must begin with our faculty, of course, as they are the crowning glory of the whole, and may Jove hurl one of his ever-ready thunderbolts at me if I do not deal justly with them! There are more than forty men in our faculty, including our president, senior professors, assistant professors, emeritus professors, and "toots,"* as the boys call them. Our Prex's name is Hannaford, and we all dote on him. It is a hard position to fill, that of president of an institution of this size. He has to be all things to all men, and to women, too, now, under the new dispensation. He is a perfect Chrysostom in eloquence,† and the baccalaureate addresses delivered by him will be long remembered by the classes who heard them. To be sure, our class owes him a little grudge for expelling one of our boys for hazing, but then we know it was just, for he almost killed a freshman by holding him under the pump one freezing night, so that he had convulsions and meningitis afterward. Then comes lovely Prof. Atkins,‡¹ who occupies the chair of Latin Language and Literature. There is an air of refinement and culture about his every movement, and in every line of his sensitive face. He has spent many years in Europe, and is as familiar with the city on the Tiber as with his own native town. There is some talk of his resigning, on account of poor health, while young Prof. Lathrop will take his place;§² he

---

*toots: Tutors.
†a perfect Chrysostom: St. John Chrysostom (ca. 347–407). The saint's eloquence as a preacher posthumously earned him the surname Chrysostomos, which means "golden mouthed."
‡Prof. Atkins: This is a reference to Henry Simmons Frieze (1817–89), Professor of Latin Languages and Literature.
§Prof. Lathrop: William Charles Flamstead Walters (d. 1927).

is engaged to Prof. Atkins's daughter, and bids fair to become a giant in the world of learning. Dear, old, sour Prof. Borck comes next,* who is our exponent of Greek language and customs. His sourness is mostly on the outside, for under his frowning exterior there beats a heart as tender as a woman's. They say he has domestic trouble. Poor man! Do you notice that many of our great men are unfortunate in their selection of companions for life? Prof. Borck has traveled over the classic soil of Greece, but it was in his early manhood. He has strolled in the groves of Helicon,† and drunk at the fountain of Hippocrene.‡ He has visited the supposed site of ancient Troy, but it was before Dr. Schliemann's discoveries,§3 so he did not see the body of Agamemnon,**4 nor the fan with which Helen is supposed to have carried on her flirtations with the handsome Paris.††

"Our assistant professor in Greek is a bachelor, and has not had matrimonial infelicities to account for his bad temper, so we conclude it is physiological. I always used to believe that love and reverence for a teacher were the best incentives to study, until I knew him; but I don't believe that any amount of love or reverence would have started us out of bed at four o'clock on cold winter mornings to look up Homeric forms, half so soon as the inevitable certainty that a deficiency in these would be met with cutting sarcasm and scathing words of reproof from the professor in the chair. We used to call him '῍Πόδας ὂκυς Achilles, Homer's ferocious old boy.'‡‡5

"I must tell you a little incident that happened in class, just to show how he used to take fire. The word ἕν (pronounced *hen*) occurred in a

*Prof. Borck: Prof. James Robinson Boise (see chap. II).

†Helicon: A mountain range of Boeotia in ancient Greece celebrated in classical literature as the favorite haunt of the Muses. A temple adorned with beautiful statues and a sacred grove stood on the fertile eastern slopes of Helicon.

‡fountain of Hippocrene: "The fountain of the horse," the fabled spring on Mount Helicon. The winged horse Pegasus, who loved to browse there, created the spring by stamping his hooves.

§Dr. Schliemann's discoveries: Heinrich Schliemann (1822–90), a German archaeologist.

**Agamemnon: In Homer's classical epic the *Iliad*, Agamemnon was the leader of the Greeks at Troy.

††Helen . . . Paris: In the *Iliad*, the Trojan prince Paris carried Helen, mortal daughter of Zeus and the most beautiful woman in the world, to Troy, thereby precipitating the Trojan War.

‡‡Achilles, Homer's ferocious old boy: In the *Iliad*, Achilles was a half-immortal hero of the Trojan War. The assistant professor of Greek is probably Martin Luther D'Ooge (1839–1915).

passage, one day, and he went on to explain its use with great zeal. He began, 'Gentlemen, I want you to notice that the construction of this *hen* is very singular.' To be sure it was very trifling in the boys to smile and think of poultry when the innocent ἕν was under discussion, and when a passage from a great poet was being analyzed, but boys will do trifling things.

"The professor noticed their merriment, and grew nervous—was something the matter with his collar or necktie that caused it?—and he put up his hand to see, but he was dressed with his usual precision, so that could not account for it. He began again: 'This *hen* has been the subject of a great deal of discussion,' and again the naughty boys smiled louder than before. He grew very angry, turned first red, then purple, till one of the girls whispered to me, 'I'm afraid he's going to burst.'

" 'Dismissed!' he roared, shutting the book, and it was not till several days after that one of the boys told him the cause of the laughter.

"Next I come to Prof. Noyes;* but how can I ever do justice to the embodiment of the higher mathematics? I could not hope to, if this same embodiment were not, at the same time, a great-souled, warm-hearted man, made of flesh and blood. He is the terror of the idle wretch, while ever the true friend of every honest inquirer after mathematical truth. He has a calm, gray eye, that solves problems and completes curves at a glance, that we cannot more than see through when he explains them to us.

"The boys call him 'Old Ironclad,' from his traditional severity in examinations, but yet every faithful student feels that he will be justly dealt with when Prof. Noyes has him in hand. A fine demonstration makes his face kindle with pleasure, while a poor or badly-worded one jars on his fine mathematical nerves like the striking of a wrong note on a musical instrument.

"Now I must tell you about our lovely Dr. Golding,†[6] who has the chair of Moral and Mental Philosophy. The old doctor has had a checkered life. He was born in England, educated at Oxford, and destined by his father for the ministry. But this did not suit the young man, who decided that mercantile life would be more to his liking than the sacred calling, and he accepted an offer from a business-house in Australia.

*Prof. Noyes: Prof. Edward Olney (see chap. II).
†Dr. Golding: Dr. Benjamin Franklin Cocker (1821–83), Professor of Mental and Moral Philosophy.

Dr. Benjamin Franklin Cocker. Cocker, chairman of the Department of Mental and Moral Philosophy, was the model for the kindly Dr. Golding: "We love every hair of his white head, and we love his old-fashioned vest and coat." (Box 1, University of Michigan Faculty Portraits, Bentley Historical Library, University of Michigan.)

"After several years he failed in business, and took to the sea. Once he was thrown among cannibals, and they drew lots between Golding and his companion for their dinner, and the lot fell on the other man. Before another meal he was rescued, and this incident set him to thinking that he had been spared in order that he might bear witness for the Lord, and he entered the ministry.

"For several years he had charge of a congregation in Sydney, Australia, where he married the daughter of an English merchant.

"After a while, upon starting for America, their ship was wrecked in sight of land, and the Rev. Caleb Golding, with his wife and children, was saved by the life-boat. They came to Ortonville with nothing in the world but the clothes on their backs and love in their hearts.

"As they walked up the street, whom should they meet but an old college friend of the doctor's? And in less than a week he was established as the pastor of the Methodist Episcopal Church of Ortonville, where he continued for several years.

"Then the chair of Metaphysics in the university was made vacant by death, and he was called to fill it, and that is the way our dear Dr. Golding became a college professor.

"He has been, now, fifteen years here, and no one would guess from his saintly face that he had ever been a wild, somewhat reckless youth. But we love every hair of his white head, and we love his old-fashioned vest and coat. His very 'Good-morning' carries a blessing with it. I think he is just what Christ would have been had he lived in this age of the world—the embodiment of truth and goodness. It is strange about him, too, for when he gets into the pulpit in the Methodist church he can shout as loud as any one, and talk about the wrath of God against sinners.

"He is only himself in the class-room; there he becomes as wide as the universe itself, and belongs to no sect, but includes them all. I don't think it would be a surprise to any of us to see a real halo of light around his head, or to see a white dove hover about him, or any such token of his kinship with the world of light.

"Have you ever seen Nast lecture?*⁷ You remember one of his first pictures is man as a laughing animal. I never saw any one that looks so much like that caricature as Prof. Markham.†⁸ His great, round face is ornamented with a fringe of short, black hair; this meets his beard on both sides, thus completing the magic circle. His anterior development is such as yearly to threaten him with Falstaff's fate in regard to his knees. But here the comparison between Prof. Markham and man as simply a laughing animal ceases, for he is master of the most sublime of sciences— astronomy. Although his body is doomed to earth by the attraction of two hundred and seventy pounds av., yet his mind lives among the stars. He is always busy in the observatory sweeping the heavens with his telescope, and no poor, innocent asteroid can lay claim to legitimacy without first reporting itself to the ever-watchful professor. Planets and comets are his

*Nast: Thomas Nast (1840–1902), an American editorial cartoonist.
†Prof. Markham: James C. Watson (1838–80), Professor of Astronomy.

playthings, and he speaks of the changes that will take place in the heavenly bodies millions of years from now, according to computation, in as matter-of-fact a way as if he were speaking of to-morrow or next week. Oh, such a memory as he has! He can fill a whole blackboard with logarithms so fast that it makes one dizzy to watch him, and carries the figures of long computations in his head in a way that seems nothing short of miraculous. We wish sometimes that he would not be so wrapped up in his celestial thoughts, for he hasn't much time to spend on classes, although he is destined by the curriculum to waste an hour a day for three months over the sophomore class, trying to initiate them into the simplest mysteries of his science, and we feel considerably aggrieved when he is too busy to let us have nothing but a hurried peep through the big telescope. What is the pleasure or profit of a set of striplings when compared with an entanglement of Jupiter's moons, or a transit of Venus? So we settle back upon the conclusion as previous classes have done, that the observatory[9] was built for the benefit of the university in general, and Prof. Markham in particular.

"Prof. Schlötterbach is our teacher of German.* I shall have that next year. His immense schmeerbauch and large round face are a living example of the health-giving properties of lager-bier, pretzels, and Limburger cheese, however much that last-named article has been defamed by sensitive nostrils.† He is generally good-natured, but, when angry, he is terrible. His first exclamation on seeing our class was, 'Mein Gott! poys, dees class must pee deevide.'

"The boys sometimes take unfair advantage of his imperfect knowledge of our manners and customs, and of his English, which he speaks *sehr mangelhaft.*‡ If I should attempt to give you in full the virtues and excellences, and I must say the faults, of our faculty, Gabriel's trumpet would still find me bending over my unfinished task, but I must tell you of Prof. Leclere,§ the French master, with his delicate little cigarette always between his lips when out of the class-room, and his irresistible accent of English—his reci*p*rocal, pro*b*ably, impos*s*ible, etc.—which we would not

---

*Prof. Schlötterbach: As there were several language instructors during Anderson's years at Michigan, we have been unable to identify the model for this character.

†schmeerbauch: A colloquial German term literally meaning "jelly belly."

‡*sehr mangelhaft:* German for "very unsatisfactorily."

§Prof. Leclere: The model for this professor has not been identified.

have him correct for anything. And Prof. Gray,* emeritus, who, after serving the university for thirty years, has retired to private life. He comes among us sometimes, leaning upon his cane, and sheds upon us the mellow beams of his declining sun. Then, there is a long line of tutors, each with his budding wings of genius—and you have in brief our faculty.

"Now, you wanted to know about the boys—whether they pay us much attention. You old girl, don't I know what a flirt you are? What clover you would be in here, where there are thirty boys for every girl! Well, I'll just tell you that you could not carry on many flirtations, and keep up your standing in class too. Some of the girls tried it, but found they must give up one or the other; and, with remarkable good sense, they chose their books instead of the boys. Yet, from the way the wind blows, I should not wonder if one or two matches were made in our class. Well, what could be more natural and fitting? Where can men and women learn to know each other better than by reciting in the same classes? Why did not your father let you come here with me, instead of sending you off to an old boarding-school, where you don't see a fellow once a month, and are always watched by some old corridor-spy?

"I never could stand such a system of espionage as that,†[10] and would, no doubt, be expelled before one term was out; while here, where we have the most unbounded liberty, I am a pattern of decorum.

"I see that you shy at the word 'club,' and say some pretty things about home-life, and I want to set you right on one or two points. I have not tried club-life yet, though I expect to next year; but I know what it is from those who have tried it. It is simply this: a company of students, boys and girls, club together and get a woman to cook for them, and have a steward to attend to marketing. In this way they can make their expenses as much or little as they choose.[11] It is just going out to meals. Next year we will have our rooms at Mr. Lewis's, just the same, but they cannot board us, so we are going to club it. We have the best motherly woman to cook for us, and our company is very select—made up of boys from our class (the best ones, of course), ourselves, and some freshman girls. That is a great beauty of

*Prof. Gray: Probably Dr. Abram Sager (1810–77), Professor of Obstetrics and Diseases of Women and Children and Chair of the Medical Department for thirty-two years. He retired in 1874 and was then appointed Professor Emeritus and Honorary Dean of the Medical Faculty.

†such a system of espionage: A reference to the heavy regulation of women students' lives, both in and out of the classroom, at women's colleges and boarding schools.

clubbing; you admit those only whom you want, and make your club just like a family. The only difference between your table and ours is, that instead of a lot of girls, with a pair of spectacles at each end of the table looking to see that you eat what is digestible, and that you behave decorously in the mean time, we have a jolly set of girls and boys, and flatter ourselves that we behave a great deal better than if some one were watching us. You want to know, then, what I would have in place of boarding-schools for girls. I would have the girls distributed around into as many good families where it is taken for granted that they will conduct themselves properly without surveillance, and have the college provide for nothing but their intellectual wants. For those who cannot stand such liberty, if they must be sent from home to learn something, I'd send them to the house of correction. But I am growing too didactic, and I hope you will not consider my comparisons odious, since you asked for everything in full. You ask if all the boys are reconciled to our being here yet? Most of them, I think, are willing, now that we are really established, to 'give the thing a trial.' It is very amusing to hear a boy of nineteen or twenty years define woman's sphere, and mark the line which she shall walk or ought to walk.

"Boys know a great deal from fifteen to twenty-one. Of course, the boys here do a great many silly things for our benefit—for example: when we have experiments in physics, the room is often darkened, so that there is not a ray of light for some minutes; then some boy makes the sound of a loud kiss, which will pass round the room. It is suggestive, but harmless; so we pay no attention to it. They do lots of outlandish things, and go to a great deal of trouble to tear up sidewalks and move gates, and, don't you think, one day they managed to get a live donkey up-stairs and set him on the platform in the chapel, and, when we came to prayers, he stood looking over the Bible as solemn as if he were reading a funeral-service instead of eating the hay they provided for him. It is the Fresh and Sophs who do such things. Juniors and Seniors are too elegant and dignified to engage in that kind of sport, and they generally have flirtations enough on hand, with the girls in the city, to occupy their extra time. You want to know if there are still 'disagreeable' things that we have to encounter. We have outlived the most of them, I guess. There is one disagreeable thing, though, that I must speak of. I hope that, before I have a daughter old enough to go to college, they will have expunged from the classical course some of the selections from authors to which they now cling, and it will be

The Chaucer Hash Club, 1876. "I have not tried club-life yet. . . . It is simply this: a company of students, boys and girls, club together and get a woman to cook for them. . . . In this way they can make their expenses as much or little as they choose." More than a way to save money, these clubs permitted men and women students to socialize on terms of equality. (F55–454: Eating Clubs, University of Michigan Photographs Vertical File, Bentley Historical Library, University of Michigan.)

well for them to use a little carbolic acid as a disinfectant in the process. I know they say people ought to be pure-minded enough to read those things and still not have any definite idea of wrong suggested by them; but I want to know where the good is in trailing classes along, year after year, through the indelicate thoughts of certain authors because they are considered good examples of the idiomatic use of the language when there are plenty of other selections that might be taken, and that would illustrate just as well.

"Now, my dear, if you will pardon this ridiculously long letter, you will give an illustration of your usual amiability. If you do not have time to read it all at one sitting, you can keep it by you for light reading. Tell me all about your life there at Vassar,*[12] and forgive me if I have been too hard on boarding-schools, but I can't believe in any of your one-sided institutions, Matthew Vassar to the contrary notwithstanding. Write to me very soon, and believe me, ever yours,

"Wilhelmine Elliott.

"P.S.—What do you think of Dr. Clarke's book? The way he makes you Vassar girls faint and lop around on all occasions is perfectly funny. In my opinion he makes a great ado about nothing, and fails to hit the point. 'It's flat burglary, and I go to prove it.'

W. E."

"Vassar College, *March* 15, 187—

"My dear Will: I received your splendid long letter more than two weeks ago. If it were any person but you, I vow I would resent some of the things you said, but you always have a way of saying what you please, and everybody lets you. Some of your assertions are based on ignorance; therefore you are, to an extent, excusable; for, when you speak of this institution as nothing more than a 'boarding-school,' it simply shows that you know nothing about it.

"Your theory about having the girls put out in families to board might be a good one, but it is exceedingly unpractical. You are so carried away, dear, with the idea of co-education that you only see one side. Well, you know that I never was radical in anything, and least of all on this subject. I do not believe in mixed schools, for, as you yourself admit, both the boys and girls might be tempted to neglect their work by being together. For all you protest that you are a 'pattern of decorum,' I can't imagine it; and I doubt not a little judicious watching would be good for you.

"But we are as free here as it is possible to be in an institution of the kind. I'd like to see you put four hundred girls together, and leave no particular rules and no one in particular to see that they behave! I would not trust even 'patterns of decorum' in such a case. Oh, no; with all your fine talk you cannot make me believe in your precious hobby. You can't make me believe that it is a good thing for a few stray girls to be mixed up with such a tremendous crowd of boys as you have there, and the unequal

*Vassar: A college for women, founded in 1861 in Poughkeepsie, New York.

proportion will exist for a long time, and maybe always. Their 'refining influence upon the ruder sex'[13] is purchased at too great a cost to themselves. How preposterous to think of seven girls in a class of one hundred and fifty boys! As to the competition between the male and female mind being the best incentive to study, that, again, is all talk, for you can't find more competition and enthusiasm in study than we have here among the girls. Again, you say that, since we have to live all our lives with them, it is absurd to be separated in education.

"Bless me! that's just an argument in favor of one-sided institutions, as you are pleased to term them; when we are destined inevitably by the Fates to eat three meals a day with some John, George, or Thomas, the four years of college when we see nothing of them ought to be counted clear gain, and I prefer to put off the comparison of the relative merits of the male and female intellect until my education is finished. I'm glad to be informed about 'clubs,' though I can't help shivering a little at the word yet, but hope to get over it.

"I feel tolerably safe about you now; but at one time I expected to hear that you girls at Ortonville were playing foot and base ball, hazing freshmen, and engaging in other manly sports. I'm glad there is one thing we can agree on—Dr. Clarke's book. A lady-physician, who lectured for us the other night, said that he had drawn very sweeping conclusions from very narrow premises, and that most of the evil he lays at the door of the school could better be traced to the improper training and habits of young children; in other words, that it is in the nursery where the foundations are laid for failing health in womanhood. I don't dare to say a word to the folks at home, though, against Dr. Clarke; for, you know, he was our family physician when we lived in Boston, and mother and Aunt Jane swear by him in everything.

"Don't stop telling me things because I scold you, for that is one of my privileges.

"Ever your loving friend,

"Mary Palmer"

CHAPTER VII

A Call from the Minister

"I do not believe it; God's kingdom is something wider,
Else let me stand outside it, with the beings I love."
— GEORGE ELIOT

"I know not; one, indeed, I knew
Perplexed in faith, but pure in deed:
At last he beat his music out,
He faced the spectres of the mind,
And laid them."
— *In Memoriam*

One day Will came in and threw herself down upon the sofa in Nell's room with a very disconsolate air, exclaiming, "I just wish I were dead, so I do!"

Nell looked up from her work with a smile, for she was accustomed to Will's moods, and did not think it worth while to stop then, but intended, at her leisure, to find out the cause of her recent disgust with life. By-and-by a great sob came from the sofa, which decided her, at once, to look into the merits of the case; so she came and knelt down beside her, and said, coaxingly, "What is it, dear? Tell your old auntie all about it."

No reply, but another sob. Nell was an adept at managing such things; she pressed the question no further, but stroked the hair from her forehead gently, and said nothing. Ere long a voice came from the depths of the pillow:

"I want to be like other girls; I'm tired of being odd and queer."

"Why, we would not have you different for the world; we all like your oddities, and, as to wishing yourself like other girls, it's quite stupid."

"Maybe you girls do like me, but the boys don't."

"Oh, as to that, the boys who know you do like you, and the others are afraid of you; but they all admire you sincerely."

"Admire! I'm tired of being admired. I want people to love me—I can't live without love;" and the voice was choked by an application of the pillow, and again there was silence. The intermittent grief soon found vent again in speech: "As I was going down-town to-day, I saw Randolf coming up the walk, and I thought, 'Now I'm going to speak to him;' but, don't you think, he sailed by and never looked at me!"

"Have you ever had an introduction to him?"

"No; but it seems to me, if three or four daily recitations together for a year and a half do not give one license to speak to a classmate, fifty introductions would not either. I have spoken to several of the boys without having been formally introduced to them, some of the good, brotherly sort who did not seem to stand on ceremony. Why, we meet them constantly everywhere, and it seems so silly, for instance, to stand and warm your fingers for half an hour over the same register with a classmate, and never say a word, because you have never been ceremoniously presented to each other. Oh, it is clear in Randolf's case that he does not want to speak because he does not like me;" and again there was a resort to the pillow.

"Do you want me to state your case as it seems to me?" said Nell.

"Yes, go on; I can bear anything, I s'pose."

"Well, in the first place, you say you are tired of being called odd; now, there is no denying that you are odd and different from the majority of girls, but let us see if that is to be regretted: you have better health than most girls, and an amount of life and vivacity that leads you sometimes to indulge in extraordinary gymnastics, but they are done in your own room and before those who understand you. I can't see any earthly harm in turning a hand-spring or coming up-stairs four steps at a time if it isn't before a miscellaneous crowd. Your manners in company are unexceptionable, as far as I see. The next point is your *physique*. There is truth in the charge that your features are strongly marked, and might be even called a little masculine, but you can't help that, and would not want to, for you know that your face is striking and your features handsome, and that you would not exchange for one of the heavy-eyed, pale faces we see every day. I must confess that your little eccentricities in dress, although they would never be noticed in another girl, do give you an appearance of oddity. For instance, you wear a hat that will stay on your head without an elastic, and you pull it off on many occasions when other ladies would not do the same; but where is the merit or demerit in that? I like it because it is you who do it; in another girl, very probably, it would not be becoming. Then you wear your dresses short enough to keep out of mud and dust; and who is there that would not commend you, although they might not have the courage themselves? Now we come to that intangible, indescribable, irrepressible something—your very own self. You ungrateful girl, to talk about no one liking you! when there is no girl of my acquaintance who has the warm love of women and girls as you have. You get as many love-letters from your different girls as a belle of the period from her suitors, and I know of no better recommendation for a woman than to be a favorite with her own sex. As to boys, they all like you when they know you, but, until then, they stand in awe of you, unless they happen to be geniuses like Charlie Burton, who can read character and interpret it correctly. I don't think there is any great misfortune in so inspiring the average male biped with awe that he admires at a distance; it is pleasanter, in nine cases out of ten, to have him there than to risk a closer encounter, because it saves you a great deal of trouble that we of the less striking sort are liable to—"

"But I would prefer to be of the less striking sort, and would risk the trouble," interrupted Will.

"But," continued Nell, in a tone of playful raillery, "your weariness of life all seems to hinge on the fact that Guilford Randolf takes no notice of you: why, you are as bad as Haman, who was so upset because Mordecai would not do him homage,* when he had all the rest of the kingdom at his feet. Here we all are bending the knee to you, but you count it as nothing because Randolf is not marching in your triumphal procession. You must make allowance for the young man, for he has been brought up with a mother and sisters who are leaders of fashion, and always stand upon ceremony; you appear in his horizon as something entirely new, with your independence of dress and manners, and you must not blame him if he cannot take you all in at once. But, bless me, what a lecture I've given her, to be sure!" and she kissed Will's cheek, where the tears had gradually dried, as she became interested in Nell's delineation of her character, and she now threw her arms around her neck as she said:

"You dear old gospel, you always make me think better of myself when

---

*as bad as Haman . . . because Mordecai would not do him homage: In the Old Testament (Esther 3:1–6), Mordecai, a Jew and one of King Ahasuerus's servants, refused to bow before Haman, a prince promoted to a favored position by the king. Angered by this slight, Haman ordered all Jews in the kingdom killed.

you take hold of me in earnest. By-the-way," continued Will, after they had sat silent a few moments, "they are going to have a revival in the Students' Christian Association, and I've promised Clara that I would go with her to-night."

"Yes, she has been asking me to go, but she knows that I am as firm in my belief as she is in hers, so she does not press the question with me," replied Nell. "They need not try to convert me by it, for I long ago made up my mind that if I am ever converted it shall be in calm weather, and not during any religious excitement; I don't believe in those religious whirlwinds one bit,*[1] for they never last; one thing that I have to be ashamed of is that, when I was very young, I was really worked up so that I went out to what they called the anxious-seat. I was visiting my aunt at the time in a little country town, where they were all Methodists, and they were right in the midst of a revival in which everybody was converted: all the young people with whom I was acquainted, without one exception, "got religion," as they called it, and they all went to work at *me;* I went to meetings with them, and one evening, with their shouting, groaning, and praying, I was so upset that, when they asked those who were seeking to come forward and kneel at the altar, I yielded to the coaxing of friends and went out. I was not fairly fixed on my knees at the altar, when I was ashamed, and wondered what I was there for. When I saw the bishop making for me, I got up quickly and said that I had made a mistake, and went back with a very red face, to the great disappointment of my friends. They took more than a hundred people into the church, but in six months they were all following the ways of the world worse than ever, and, in my opinion, you scarcely could have guessed that there had been a revival."

"What did your Presbyterian friends think of that?"

"My mother did not like it much when she heard that I had been out, for Presbyterians are cold-blooded, you know, and don't believe in excitement. I like that in them, too, for there is not so much danger of being mistaken about the coming of the Holy Spirit when the temperature is not allowed to rise above a moderate height."

"I think it is so strange," said Nell, "that you have been led by your reason in a path so widely apart from the one in which you were brought up—when you are so young, too. Now, I go right along as I've been trained, and if I'd been brought up in orthodoxy it would have been just

*those religious whirlwinds: Nell is referring disparagingly to revivals or camp meetings.

the same—I should have stuck to it; but you seem to have cut loose from everything, and made your own way. I don't quite understand it."

"Well, I sometimes wonder at myself," said Will, "and think that perhaps, after all, it is a pity. I don't want to feel so cut off and apart from people; I don't want to be looked upon by all the sweet, pious folks as a dreadful, dangerous heretic, as I suppose I am; but what am I to do about it? I can't make their theology seem reasonable, and they won't let me be pious unless I take their creeds and speak their shibboleth.* If they had just let me alone, I presume I should have fallen into the traces."

"But you are not out of harmony with God and the great and good minds, my dear, and some day you'll find your path leading up to theirs, where you can join them."

"Do you think so? I don't know, I'm sure; the world has always been made so black to me outside the pale of the Westminster theology, that I am not more than half emancipated yet. I do want to believe something positively, and that is what I can't say that I do. I presume I'll swing round, and finally, like Heinrich Heine,† be seized with a heavenly home-sickness, and die clinging to the old faith in which I was born."

This conversation will serve to show the uncertain state of mind in which Will was at this time. She had been unable from constitutional inability to accept the old faith, but had nothing in place of it, and her nature was not such as to be contented long with a mere negative belief; for, perhaps more than most others, she needed something to cling to and believe with her whole heart. Neither Nell nor Clara could quite appreciate her state of feeling, for, although they believed so differently from each other, still each was faithful to her home training, and Will found that, after all, she must have her struggle alone.[2] It was in this frame of mind that she was met again by the wave of a religious revival.

All the various denominations of Ortonville were bending every energy to the awakening of religious interest, hoping it would culminate in a glorious work of grace, such as had never been seen there before. They had meetings every evening, and Will was at last persuaded to go, to please some of the girls, for this freethinking, independent girl was at the same

*speak their shibboleth: The mode of speech (i.e., jargon, terminology) distinctive of a profession, class, or in this case a religious sect, intended to be comprehensible to members only.

†Heinrich Heine: A German-Jewish poet and journalist (1797–1856) and also a famous cynic, who wrestled with his Jewish faith throughout his life. On his deathbed, he said, "God will pardon me. It is His trade."

time one of the most coaxable and yielding; while by her mental constitution she found herself stepping outside of all sorts of boundaries, social and religious, to be left out by the will or even the indifference of those about her was a grievous thing. Like most strong heads, hers was fed by a warm, tender heart, and her desire to please the girls was at once her weakness and her strength.

The meetings were impressive, and great numbers of students, among whom Will recognized "hard cases," arose and requested the prayers of the meeting. She was silent and respectful, but not impressed, for she had constantly in mind the time when she went up to the altar and had been ashamed of it afterward; and, however deeply she craved some rest for her faith, she felt now, more than ever, that there was nothing offered her by by storm of sentiment. Some took her silence for a token that she was thinking deeply, and the girls, without her knowledge, asked one of the ministers to call upon her next day and talk with her. So she was greatly surprised when the door-bell rang and she was told that the Rev. Mr. Allison was waiting to see her in the parlor.

"To see me?" said Will; "I guess there is some mistake, for I never met him. I had a letter of introduction to him, but I never presented it."

"There is no mistake," said Clara, "for he asked me yesterday where you lived, and said he was coming."

Will hurriedly smoothed her hair, and with a little fluttering of the heart went down to the parlor.

As she entered, a tall figure in black arose and gave her his hand. Edmund Allison was a man of not more than thirty-five years, but he looked fully fifty, for from continued ill-health his face was sallow, and his long beard streaked with gray. His dark hair was parted away from a broad pale forehead, and the hand he gave to Will was slender, cold, and feeble; yet his eye burned with fervor, for he had come to speak in the cause of his church. Mr. Allison had entered the ministry at twenty-four, with shattered health partly inherited, partly contracted during the years in which he had toiled through his academic and theological course, with insufficient good, and without any of those social pleasures that youth needs for building up a healthy manhood. He stood at this time of his life, with all the sternness of his will and the strength of his intellect, one of the few stanch defenders of the ark of the covenant in the midst of all sorts of assaulting Philistines.

"Miss Elliott, I was requested by some of your friends to call upon you for the purpose of talking with you on religious subjects, and I gladly embraced the opportunity, for I have known you by sight and reputation for a long time, and have hoped to see you a faithful worker in the cause of Christ; I believe that you have unusual ability, which, if turned in the right direction, would make you a great power for good."

"Thank you," said Will, blushing deeply, partly from embarrassment and partly from indignation, that the girls had thus without her knowledge planned a religious conference for her, into which she had been innocently led; "if I had known of their design, I should not have allowed them to trouble you."

"I was led to think from what they said that you were thinking deeply upon the subject; indeed, Miss Elliott, I had strong hopes of finding you under conviction."

"I have given them no reason to think that I am in any such state," said Will, trying to be respectful, while the same old bitter feeling of rebellion came back that she had not known since she left home for the first time.

"I learn that you have been brought up in a Christian family."

"Yes, sir, I was brought up a Presbyterian."

"Have you found anything better—anything that satisfies your spiritual needs more fully, may I ask?"

"I am only trying to find something to believe," said Will.

"Believe in the Lord Jesus Christ, and thou shalt be saved."

"But, sir, must I not also believe in all the articles of the catechism?"

"It would be impossible to accept Christ openly without subscribing to the articles of faith as held by some branch of the Church, and I believe you can nowhere find God's justice and mercy, in his great scheme of redemption, more correctly stated than in the catechism adopted by the Westminster Assembly, and accepted by the Presbyterian denomination in all parts of the world."

Will hesitated to reply. She felt in one moment all the stinging sense of injustice to a world of striving, aspiring, though erring mortals, which was the one conviction she had ever brought away from her study of the Shorter Catechism, every line of which was engraven in her memory. She felt as if she could blaze into a defense of God against it, but respect for his age, and the clerical habit, which Mr. Allison wore in all its old-fashioned precision, restrained her.

"But I have not found any satisfaction in thinking of God's scheme of redemption, by my study of the catechism—it always repels me," she said, gently.

"Oh, my young friend, let me assure you that you are standing on the most dangerous ground, and I pray God that I may be the humble instrument of bringing you back to the fold from which you have strayed."

"But, so far as I know, I am only yielding to the perfectly honest conclusions of my own reason and sense of justice. Is it so dangerous to think? I am compelled to think about everything else; it seems to me that this is a subject upon which I should not decide rashly."

"Miss Elliott, you are wrong in saying that it is not a subject to be decided at once, for every moment you hesitate makes your chances of salvation less: now, now is the accepted time, and now is the day of salvation. It is not a subject for the exercise of reason, but of faith—faith in the God of Abraham, and his Son, who was sent into the world to save those who are lost. There is no objection to your looking at the question from all sides, if first you are firmly rooted and grounded in the truth, for then there would be no danger of being led away from it, but, in your condition of mind, it would be fatal for you to read works on infidelity, for the heart, naturally prone to evil, will turn to unbelief as the sparks fly upward."

Will's keen sense of the logical was so much amused at this argument that she smiled a little as she said, looking hard at a small copy of the "Last Supper" that hung behind the minister's chair, "But how can I search and try the truth, if I must first accept some statement of it that binds me sacredly to fixed conclusion?"

Mr. Allison began to feel the pique of an unexpected firmness and clearness of opposed convictions in his questioner, notwithstanding the quiet repression of her manner and words; but, with no intention of intellectual contest, he waived a direct answer to her remark, saying only: "It is safest for erring human nature to throw aside reasoning, and accept by faith the Saviour crucified. You know the alternative he offers, 'He that believeth shall be saved, but he that believeth not shall be damned.'"

Will began to grow restless under this gospel fire. A door of unpleasant memory was suddenly opened. Having avoided the Presbyterian church since she had been at college, she had not heard the stern statements for nearly two years, and they recalled sickening scenes of mental conflict and the only unpleasantness that she remembered of her home-life.

She began to feel that she had grown so much in the interval that she could clearly and completely refute the clergyman, but she was very unwilling to take up the contest. Nevertheless, it was not in her nature to hide, or to seem to accept, what she disbelieved or doubted, and, if the minister continued to press her, she felt that she must offend him by her replies.

"You know these texts, Miss Elliott; you are familiar with the Bible?"

"Yes, sir, I am very familiar with those texts," she said, and out of the struggles of the past how could she command a tone that had not in it a shade of irony? The keen sense of her questioner caught it at once.

"What!" he exclaimed, "do you mean to imply that you have gone so far as to disbelieve the Bible, Miss Elliott?" and he gave her a searching look.

"I have gone so far as to wonder if it is the only word of God to man, and the only rule of faith; yes, I'm afraid I should not agree with your definition of its inspiration."

"How is it possible for a student, who is daily weighing evidence in all departments of science, to withhold assent to a truth so self-evident as the inspiration of the Holy Scriptures," exclaimed Mr. Allison, "of which they bear the most overwhelming proof in the faithful portraits of life and manners, in their unswerving truth to the foibles of the men they paint, their evident freedom from all glosses, to say nothing of fulfilled prophecies?[3] Human nature stands before us in the Bible with its weaknesses and crimes unconcealed, as profane writers would never have dared to portray it."

"But, Mr. Allison," replied Will, in a long pause which the minister made, as if to take in a full sense of her heresy, "it appears to me that the Bible ought to be valuable in proportion as it helps to nobler views of life and offers us examples for imitation, and inspires us with a love for what is high and pure; it does not seem to me that the Bible helps me very much in these respects. I have gained more, I think, of such inspiration from history than from the Hebrew Scriptures."

"History and modern philosophy, my dear young lady, are *ignes fatui* that have led thousands to destruction;* but one of the greatest facts of history is the fact of the power of the Scriptures, which have brought life

---

*ignes fatui: Figuratively, this Latin phrase means "will-o'-the-wisps," "delusions," or "something misleading." Literally, it means a phosphorescent light that hovers or flits over swampy ground at night, possibly caused by spontaneous combustion of gases emitted by rotting organic matter.

and immortality to light, and have shone upon a people sitting in darkness and the shadow of death, until a modern civilization has sprung up under its beneficent beams. But, since you have made up your mind about the Old Testament," said Mr. Allison, with a slightly perceptible sneer, "you have hardly been so bold, at your age, as to fling aside the inspiration of the New also?"

"Oh, certainly, I think the apostles were inspired with a love of their Master; I think they were very heroic and true; but then," she added, after a moment's doubt whether to say it or not, for she perceived the growing heat of her antagonist, "so was Xenophon who wrote of his master, who was also a great teacher, and suffered for the truth he taught."

"But Socrates* did not leave a record attested by the combined testimony of a band of disciples. It is in the remarkable agreement of our four evangelists that we find our source of proof of our New Testament story. The harmony of the four gospels is a rock of strength, such as no heathen teacher has ever boasted."

"Is it?" replied Will, musingly. She was listening not to Rev. Mr. Allison, but to the voice of her mother's pastor, whose reasoning on the harmonies, whose defense of every outpost of his faith, had been the chief food for her youthful skepticism.

"Here we find the highest proof of the complete inspiration of the sacred Scriptures, in the story of his miracles, the record of his sufferings and death; but what think you of Christ?"

"I think he was a teacher come from God, and I try to follow his example, but I come far short of it. I like to read his life—"

"But if you do not think him God himself, then you make him a mere impostor, for in his own words he claims oneness with God."[4]

"You have made the Bible your life-study, Mr. Allison, and of course you are perfectly familiar with it; but I somehow feel as if I could get at other meanings of Christ's words, which I take from them just as they read, and it does not seem as if he claimed divinity for himself; but then there are so many chances for different constructions to be put upon the leading passages that one becomes confused. I have heard the best and most sacred texts denounced as interpolations by learned men, until it has finally

*Socrates: A Greek (Athenian) philosopher (470–399 BC) known for his method of inquiry, called the Socratic method. The Rev. Mr. Allison is correct: Socrates left no writings. His two disciples, Xenophon and Plato, and references in the writings of another Greek philosopher, Aristotle, provide all that we know about him.

seemed to me that I must judge of the meaning of the Bible for myself. I think it is a privilege every one ought to be allowed."

The clergyman was surprised and disappointed, but the sweet reasonableness of the girl was as little provoking as any species of resistance could possibly be; and, interested in her frank, lively mind, he set himself to the task of conviction, little doubting that he could easily break down the slight fortifications of unbelief her short experience had set up, so he recommenced in a dry, pulpit tone: "My dear young lady, I have come to set forth the claims of God in Christ upon you, and to urge you to make your own the merits of that atonement by which alone you can be justified. You believe that all have sinned and come short of the glory of God, and that he hath sent forth his Son to be a propitiation through faith in his blood. Without the shedding of blood there is no remission of sin, and by the offering of the Lord Jesus is prepared the open and manifest way by which God may be reconciled to men. Should God forgive sinners without an atonement, justice would be sacrificed, the law would cease to have any terrors, and its penalty would be annulled; but God has appointed his Son to be a substitute in the place of sinners: what he endured on the cross was such as to accomplish the same ends as if those who shall be saved by him had been doomed to eternal death. 'What he endured no tongue can tell!'"

"Mr. Allison," interrupted Will, in a tone of excitement that she could no longer repress, "I can't *bear* this doctrine of atonement—I long ago rebelled against it,[5] and nothing can make me think that I shall be better by believing that an innocent being bore a load of penalty and shame for me; it degrades me, however it may exalt him. I can find comfort and inspiration in his teaching, however, and I mean to try to obey his precepts."

"What right have you to find comfort in his teachings, when you reject his divine atonement?"

"What right have I? Would you take him away from me simply because I do not believe on him as you do? Do you not want me to have help in my daily life from his example? It is a great deal more to me to think of him as a brother man than as God incarnate. That answer to justification in the catechism always disturbed me even when I was a child,* and I've never

*justification: Justification is the process through which God's grace makes sinners righteous. Theologians do not agree, however, over the nature of justification and how it is achieved.

since been able to see any fairness in it. You know it says, 'Justification is an act of God's free grace, wherein he pardoneth all our sins and accepteth us as righteous in his sight, only for the righteousness of Christ, imputed to us and received by faith alone.' The catechism gives me nothing but unlovely ideas of God and heaven. Do you think that people can be happy in heaven without their friends?" she said, softening a little, and appealing to the heart of the man by her almost childish earnestness.

"I have no expectation of deriving my happiness in the eternal world from any earthly fountains; I am not sure but we will be so constituted that our joys will be heightened by the contrast of the miseries of the lost, even as we are sensible, on earth, of a keener enjoyment of comforts, when we reflect that many are deprived of them."

"O Mr. Allison," said Will, shuddering, "that is really the most dreadful thing I ever heard."

"We do not know—we do not know what God has prepared or what is included in his future; we only know that he that believeth shall be saved, and he that believeth not shall be damned."

"I beg to be spared further persuasion, Mr. Allison," exclaimed Will, with a face full of indignation. "I shall never be brought to become a Christian on the terms you present; they only repel my affections and degrade my reason."

Mr. Allison rose to go. He had expected to find a young lady in a very troubled and anxious state of mind—one to whom he could tell the old, old story with his own comments, and finally pray, and leave her in penitent tears over her depraved nature; but to find instead a youthful antagonist who had decided ways of expressing herself, and who asked questions and said things that were hard to refute, was not at all to his liking, and, when he saw that his talk had had no effect but to arouse her opposition, it was too much for his Christian grace.

"Miss Elliott," he said, as he slowly walked to the door, "never in the whole range of my ministry have I met with such a confirmed case of unbelief as I find in you, and, considering your youth and early training, it is marvelous how you came to stand where you do. You profess to be a seeker for truth, and yet you are firmly determined that you won't see it. I would rather bury my daughter than have her as you are to-day! You have adopted the egotism of the party you represent."

"I did not know, sir, that I represented any party. I do not claim to, at least."

"You belong to those who are serving Mammon,* who are trying to pull down daily what we are trying to build up; and, Miss Elliott, if it were not for the protection which we of the Church throw around you, you would to-day be classed among the immoral and lawless of the land, for thither your conclusions lead. It is simple truth," continued the man, growing more and more angry, "and I say again, count up your friends and see how many of them, who believe as you do, are examples of true grandeur and nobility of soul, and how many of them would stand by you in times of need. The smallest number, I can tell you, for your true friends all belong to our side; but there will come a time when even they ought to leave you to the destruction you have chosen, and withdraw their protection from you."

His persuasion had not succeeded, so he thought to try intimidation by drawing a frightful picture of her future.

"You do not mean to say that such men as Mr. Bingham and Mr. Hart are not noble examples?" she said, referring to two men of high standing in the Unitarian Church.

"They, doubtless, are good men, but I say that *we* protect them from the consequences of their own beliefs. Ah, Miss Elliott, look at the death-beds of unbelievers if you want an awful proof of the truth of Christianity— their ravings of despair, and the worm of remorse gnawing at their hearts, because of their denial of the truth."

"I have seen the death-bed of an unbeliever," said Will, quietly, and in a few words she told of the beautiful life that she had watched pass calmly out into the great unknown, and for the moment she forgot the reverend gentleman as the face of her grandfather passed before her mind.

"How do you know that he did not repent on his death-bed?"

"Repent of what?" asked Will.

"That he had rejected the Saviour all his life. Such a case as that of your grandfather is hard for us to judge, Miss Elliott, but, if the Bible is true, we must believe that he is lost forever."

"Then I don't *want* to be saved, sir; but somehow I feel that the Lord will judge him better than any one else can," and there was a tender expression in the gray eyes that the minister could not see, for the gathering twilight.

*Mammon: Riches or materialism in general. The Rev. Mr. Allison is referring to the single-minded pursuit of monetary gain and conspicuous consumption that characterized the Gilded Age.

"It is needless to say, Miss Elliott, that I feel deeply and earnestly interested in you, not only for yourself, but for the great good you might do for the cause of Christianity if you were only one of the chosen; and then I think of the great harm you will do if you continue in the present state of rebellion and opposition to the light. I will bear you to the throne of grace in prayer."

"Thank you," said Will, mechanically, and they shook hands and parted.

CHAPTER VIII

Heavy and Light Shading

"Give me a look, give me a face
That makes simplicity a grace,
Robes loosely flowing, hair as free;
Such sweet neglect more taketh me
Than all the adulteries of art;
They strike mine eyes, but not my heart."

—BEN JONSON

"For her physician tells me she hath pursued conclusions
infinite of easy ways to die."

—SHAKESPEARE

One day in early March of Will's sophomore year the university was electrified by the report that Hattie Worden, a girl in the freshman class, had committed suicide by shooting herself.[1]

"How could she?" "Why should she?" "What was the matter?" "She was a splendid scholar!" were the bursts of astonishment as the girls hastened to inquire concerning the truth of the report, and offer any assistance that might be needed. They found a frightened group around the bed upon which lay the unfortunate girl, while the doctor was trying to ascertain whether life was entirely extinct. Two round, dark spots, one on the neck and the other on the temple, showed the path of the cartridges, while on the stand was a small revolver, the innocent cause of the tragedy. Her room-mate sat crying, with her face buried in her hands, as she moaned, "If I had only come a moment sooner, I might have prevented it!" A little note was found on the table, which explained after a fashion the unnatural deed. It said:

"My dear Friends: You have never suspected that, while I have been going in and out among you, I have been a monomaniac on the subject of suicide, and no one has ever known it, not even my precious mother, whose heart I will break by the deed that I have at last been compelled to commit. I had an uncle once who shot himself, and I know that I inherited the tendency to suicide, so that my life has been one constant, silent struggle with that temptation; but I can bear it no longer. Do not go to searching for a cause for this act; there is none except this hereditary taint, for I have the kindest of parents and friends, and God knows that I would not give them this sorrow if I could help it. Often and often when I have been apparently studying and seemingly absorbed in my books, I have been wrestling with the wish to put an end to my existence. I thought that by coming to college, and throwing myself wholly into a busy student's life, I might forget it; but, like a stern Nemesis, it has followed me. The college-girls will feel disgraced, I know, and I would gladly save them from it, but I cannot. Telegraph, please, to my uncle, John Worden, in Madison County, and let him break the news to my mother. Once more begging you to deal kindly with my memory, I am, truly yours, Hattie Worden."

"Very extraordinary, indeed!" said the doctor, after the letter was read; and, stepping across the room, he began a conversation in a low tone with Miss Easton, the room-mate of Miss Worden, in which he asked if she knew anything of Miss Worden's previous life; whether she had not been disappointed in love; for, he said, "you will find that at the bottom of trouble like this nine cases out of ten."

Miss Easton professed her ignorance of any such condition of affairs. The afflicted parents arrived the next day to accompany the remains to their home, which was in the western part of the State. The mother said that Hattie had always been peculiar from a child, but that they had never suspected any predisposition to suicide. The self-upbraidings of the mother for not having better understood her daughter's nature were painful to hear.

The newspapers took it up, and there were various reasons assigned for the deed. Some said that she had studied too hard to keep up with her class, and thus the evil effects of co-education were early becoming manifest. Others said that she had fallen in love with a classmate, and, because it was not reciprocated, she had found life too great a burden to be borne; and another moral was drawn concerning co-education. A few accepted the truth, which was that Hattie Worden was the victim of an hereditary mental disease which shows itself in a continual wish to take one's own life.

Following close upon this sad event came another not so tragical, but none the less sad. It was the death of one of the girls in Will's class from typhoid fever.[2] She was quite a favorite, and had particularly endeared herself to the girls by her lovely, winning ways. She was ill for two weeks before the disease proved fatal, and every morning the girls, with anxious hearts, heard the president pray for the sick one, for they were not allowed to see her lest they might be infected with the contagion. One morning it was whispered from seat to seat that Alice Winthrop was dead, for the president prayed for the bereaved family this time. It was the first break made in the class by death, and was deeply felt by all.

The class was excused from recitations for one day, and accompanied the remains to the depot with the relatives, and all wore crape on their hats for two weeks. Again it was said that the evil effects of the higher education of women were proved by this event, but this assertion seemed to be offset by the fact that a brother of the young lady had died, a few years previous, of the same disease, being also a member of the sophomore class, and then of the same age. This satisfied some that sex had nothing whatever to do with it, while the majority maintained their first opinion.

To be entirely candid, it must be confessed that toward the end of the sophomore year one or two of the girls did give evidence of having worked too hard, and the pale cheek and hollow eye pointed to an early decline. But it would hardly be fair to attribute it to the fact that they were studying in a "boy's way," for had they been in a female seminary the same thing would have happened. The same pale cheek and sunken eye were to be seen here and there among the boys at this period in the course, which only proves that neither the delicate boy nor girl should attempt a college-course, but should leave it for those who have brain and muscle in more equal proportions. But four more healthy girls than the sophomores in Clinton Avenue were not to be found. Will came into the waiting-room one day (the waiting-room was a refinement that had sprung up since the admission of the girls, by which they were saved the tedious delay in the cold halls) with the announcement that she was going to have her hair cut. A burst of disapproval came from all sides of the room.

"Will Elliott, you are not in earnest! You would look like a fright; don't do it, please!" and they formed a supplicating circle around her.

"It's just this way," she said: "I've been coming to it for a long time, and this morning, when a hair-pin got crosswise and spoiled the whole lecture for me, I thought things had come to a crisis," and she drew off her switch and flung it across the room, while she shook down her own heavy but not very long hair. "I suppose the fashion will change before long, so that my own hair done up in a little pug behind would not taboo me from fashionable society; but when I tried leaving off my switch the other day you all made so much ado that I had to put it on again.*3 Now, girls," she continued, smiling, "you know that I'd do anything to please you that is not a sacrifice of principle, but this hair takes too much of my time—it shackles me, abridges my freedom, and I must be free; so come off it must!" This declaration was met by a groan from the girls. "I don't believe I'll look so bad, either; for it will wave round my head like Harriet Hosmer's,† and, besides, if you don't like it I will wear a wig till it grows out; but you know you'll have to like it. I'll hurry home and leave my books and rush to the barber's while the voice of the δαίων is still fresh, or you will lure me on to the rocks of destruction by your siren songs," and she bounded merrily away.

Acting from impulse, as she so often did, she hastened to a barber and gave him directions,4 just how short she wanted it, how it was to be on top and behind; to all of which he grinned a "Yes, miss; all right." What possessed the dusky son of Ham has never to this day been made clear—whether it was temporary mental aberration or malice aforethought that prompted him to use his scissors as he did.‡5 After giving directions, Will sat in the chair with perfect faith that he would do as she had told him; she gave herself no further thought; and, in fact, the whole time she was repeating a Latin ode that they were to commit for the next day. When, finally, he said, "It's all right, miss," she hastily threw her scarf over her head for fear of taking cold, and hurried home, not daring to look in the glass until she should reach her own room. Arriving there, she found all three girls anxiously awaiting her. As she threw aside her scarf they all shrieked, "Will Elliott! what have you done?—you're ruined!" She gave a hurried glance into the mirror, and all her courage forsook her at the sight.

*switch: A long bunch or coil of hair, often made of false materials, worn by women to make their hair look fuller.

†Harriet Hosmer: American sculptor (1830–1908). Raised as a boy, Hosmer was encouraged by her widowed father to ride horses, shoot, and otherwise compete in the male sphere. Hosmer was famous for her short hair, preference for men's clothing, and casual adherence to conventions of gender respectability.

‡dusky son of Ham: In the Old Testament (Genesis), Ham was the second son of Noah. Ham was believed to be the Egyptian word Khem (black), the native name of Egypt.

He had actually cut it so short that one could not catch it with thumb and finger—the style the boys call "dead-rabbited."* She threw her arms round her head and sank into a chair, with the despairing cry: O girls! he has ruined my head for life—ruined!" she repeated, in a perfect frenzy of disappointment. "I told him how to cut it, and see what he has done!" The girls, seeing that she was as much astonished as they, came to the rescue, and, as it could not be helped by any earthly means, tried to make the best of it.

"Oh, it will soon grow out again," said Nell; "but how will you go to recitations?" and they all looked at each other as if to say, "Sure enough, how will she?"

"Can't we contrive some sort of a head-dress?" suggested Laura; "they will think that something is the matter with your head, and that the doctor ordered it cut."

But how lame and impractical seemed all the suggestions to Will, who sat with her poor, cropped head bowed, the very embodiment of wretchedness! Her great resort in time of trouble was to go to bed, and she soon buried her dishonored head in the pillows, but not to sleep. What should she do tomorrow? How could she face the whole class with that head, and yet how could she miss a lesson for such a cause? Meanwhile, the girls were discussing the case among themselves with no less interest, and they could see no better way than that she should plead a slight indisposition for two or three weeks and remain at home. That thought had not once occurred to Will as she lay tossing on her bed until her face burned with feverish excitement and dread of to-morrow's ordeal. They brought up her supper, while Mr. and Mrs. Lewis came to condole, and there was as much mourning over her as if she were dangerously ill. Not a word of blame or reproach came from any one, for they saw how much she suffered.

"You are all so kind to me that I can't stand it," she said, with quivering lip; "if you'd only scold me thoroughly, I would feel better."

"We have been thinking," said Nell, quietly, "that you had better not think of going to recitations for two or three weeks, until your hair has come out a little; we will make a satisfactory excuse for you."

Will sat bolt upright at this.

"Stay at home? Miss recitations for a month, and have them all think me sick or something? Indeed, I'll do no such thing! I'll go if it kills me,

*dead-rabbited: Cut close to the scalp.

and take the full consequences of my own foolishness!" and, she added, with a burst of petulance of which she was instantly ashamed, "If you girls are afraid to be seen with me, you can go alone, and so will I!"

"Come, my dear," said Nell, while a flush of anger tinged her cheeks for a moment, that Will should attribute to them such motives for the suggestion, "you are doing the unfair thing by us when you suspect that we will be ashamed of you. Every one of us is glad to stand by you whatever you may do, and you know it."

"Forgive me, darling!" said Will; and she laid her hot cheek against Nell's, whose neatly-brushed hair formed a striking contrast to the shorn head where the white scalp shone through with almost ghastly clearness. Mr. Lewis declared that he would go and horsewhip the barber;*[6] but, as that could not restore the brown, wavy locks nor bring peace to the troubled mind, it was given up.

Charlie came down in the evening, but Will would not see him.

All night she dreamed about beautiful heads with long, curling hair, but when she put out her hand to touch them they vanished, and she awoke with her hand on her own bristling head. As often as she fell asleep there was a repetition of this dream, until finally, when it first began to grow light, she arose, determined to bury herself in her lessons, and forget if possible. She succeeded so well, as she sat poring over her Sophocles, that finally she said: "There, I can scan that choral ode perfectly; and now I'm going to comb my hair!" and she actually went to the bureau to get her switches, when a glance in the mirror brought it all back. The cunningest feminine art could not fasten a switch on now. The knowledge that she had no hair to comb as she had yesterday morning—the fact that one of the simplest acts of every-day life was now beyond her power to perform— brought a feeling of desperation entirely aside from the other disagreeable features of it. She had aimed at freedom; but she now felt that it had its disadvantages.

The girls made no allusion to it in any way, but quietly waited to see what she would do. As nine o'clock approached, Will put on her cloak, and finally tried her hat; it fell down over her eyes, and looked very strange. She flung it aside, and wrapped her head in her scarf. When they entered the waiting-room, the freshman girls were already there, and the rest of the girls in her own class.

*horsewhip: The horsewhip was the common tool of punishment for slaves; it symbolically placed them on a par with horses, which were also "property."

"Now, girls," she said, standing before them, "when I unwrap my head I don't want you to say a word in my hearing. There has been a mistake, and talking won't help it."

This was said in a stoical tone, but, when she saw the looks of sympathy and real friendship as they crowded around her, her stoicism failed; and tears sprang to her eyes as a little freshman threw her arms around Will's neck and said:

"I love you anyway; and your head is handsome without any hair!"

They all smiled at this, as did Will herself. But the hardest trial was yet to come, for she had all the boys to face. When the bell struck they went in, and as Will passed down the aisle there was an instant of terrible silence; then a murmur and buzzing, as one and another looked at his neighbor and asked:

"What under heavens has she done that for?"

"By Jupiter! wouldn't epaulets become that crop?"

"Let's call her Captain Elliott!"*

"Gee-rusalem! she heads us off at the barber's as well as in class."

"Well, I'd like to wring that barber's neck!" said one or two, who had heard of it from Charlie.

The professor gave just one glance, and went on without further notice.

As she sat down, a tiny note came to her, passed from seat to seat, saying:

"Never mind, Will; it's a step in the right direction—only a trifle too short! Charlie."

In a few weeks Will's hair had grown out, and fell in graceful waves over her head, so that the girls said:

"She does look a great deal better with her hair short, for all we made such a hue and cry when she talked of having it done."

Will kept up her gymnastics faithfully (for she had improvised a sort of gymnasium),[7] and frequently declared that she would have been in her grave had it not been for the parallel bars and rings. But that was not her only exercise. One day in the early spring, still in the sophomore year, Mr. Lewis came home leading a large, beautiful bay horse, and the girls rushed down to look at him.

"What is his name?" they asked.

*Captain Elliott: Will's short hairstyle has unsexed her in the eyes of many of her male classmates and made her the object of ridicule. Long hair was one of the main signs of femininity.

"I'll let you name him. I've just bought him, for his style pleases me."

"Yes, he is magnificent," said Will. "Let's call him Lord Chesterfield;* for he is so proud, and carries himself so grandly. We can call him Chester for short."

They all thought it was a good name.

"And you will let me ride him?" said Will, in her most coaxing tone.

"You ride him!" echoed Mr. Lewis, looking at her in astonishment. "Why, he'd never let you get on him. The man of whom I bought him told me particularly that he did not like women around him."

Will turned red with vexation at the reply, but stepped up to pat Chester's neck without making any answer. He gave an impatient toss of his head, and his eyes looked fiery, seeming to prove the truth of Mr. Lewis's statement of his disposition toward women. She withdrew her hand, saying, "You foolish fellow! I won't hurt you." But there was a determined look on her face which said plainly, "I'll tame you yet, see if I don't!" and her eyes sparkled with the anticipation, while she pretended to be reconciled to the fact that she could not ride Chester.

Next morning she was up at the usual time; but, instead of going into her gymnasium, she went to the stable to try and make acquaintance with the new horse.

As she approached the manger he started back with a snort, as if he would break the halter. She spoke soothingly to him, and offered him a wisp of hay, of which he took no notice; but, after a time, he stopped tugging at the halter, and even let her stroke his nose, while she talked to him all the time, calling him pet names. She went cautiously around him and stood by his neck. He did not mind it much, and she left the stable well pleased with her success. She felt just a little guilty when Mr. Lewis, at the breakfast-table, said, with fatherly solicitude:

"Girls, if you ever go into the stable when Chester is there, be sure and don't go round his stall, for he is not to be trusted."

Mr. Lewis sometimes turned him out in the field, and there Will tried her hand at catching him. It was a different thing from petting him in the stable, for now it depended entirely upon his royal pleasure whether he would allow her to come near or not. She walked slowly up to him, and he watched her curiously until she came within a few feet, when he threw up

*Lord Chesterfield: Philip Dormer Stanhope, Fourth Earl of Chesterfield (1694–1773), English statesman and author whose letters to his son were the source of popular advice books and many famous quotations.

his heels and bounded off in the most tantalizing equine style. But he did not seem quite satisfied with himself, for pretty soon he came trotting up again, and walked round and round her as if attracted by some unseen power, and yet not daring to come closer.

When she tried to approach, he would toss his head coquettishly and go away a few steps, yet never far. Soon the circles he made around her grew smaller and smaller, until he was within reach of her hand.

"Come," she said, "we've had enough of this; why can't we be friends?"

He seemed to understand the spirit of her remarks, for he allowed her to put her arms around his neck and lay her head against his glossy mane. A pretty picture they made as they stood in the early morning sunshine—the grand horse, with his tremendous muscles, submitting to the caresses of the slight girl! She finally tried fastening the saddle upon him, and waved a skirt round his heels to see how he would take it. She fixed the next Saturday for her ride, and so adroitly had she managed her visits to the meadow and stable that no one knew of her friendship with the horse. Saturday came at last. Her habit was of dark-blue cloth, with close-fitting basque,* that set off her figure to good advantage. Her cap was of black velvet, which fitted close to her short curls, giving her quite a dashing air. After Mr. Lewis had gone down for the noon mail she hurried on her habit and ran to the stable. Her fingers trembled with eagerness as she fastened the girth and adjusted the bridle. For a moment, and for the first time, a feeling of dread came over her. Was she doing right? What if she were thrown and killed? But when Chester laid his head lovingly against her arm her courage returned, and she said:

"Forgive me, old boy, I'll never wrong you by doubting you again."

She opened the door and led him to the fence, from which, with a bound, she was in the saddle. The grand animal trembled with eagerness for the race, but waited for her word. She gave it, and he sprang forward. As they dashed by the open window she shouted, "Good-by, girls!" and touched her velvet cap.

"If there isn't Will on Chester!" cried Laura.

"Oh, it can't be!" said Clara, starting up with a frightened look; but there was no mistaking the merry laugh that floated back on the breeze. "She will certainly be thrown and killed!"

---

*basque: The continuation of a lady's bodice slightly below the waist, forming a kind of short skirt.

"I have an idea that Will knows what she is about," said Nell, "or she would not have tried it."

The pair created quite a sensation as they dashed through the streets, Chester performing all sorts of pretty, graceful curvetings,* and looked as if he intended to throw his rider over his head; but she knew that he had no such intention.

Mr. Lewis heard, while on the street, that a young lady was riding his new horse, but he thought it must be a mistake. However, he came home sooner than usual, and immediately went to the stable, where of course he found an empty stall, with saddle and bridle gone.

He came into the house in great excitement, exclaiming, "Where is Chester?" The girls told him all they knew. At first he was very angry. "Just like the harum-scarum girl,† to go and get her neck broken!" and he paced the floor a moment or two, then went down-stairs, and out on the street, where he gazed up and down in hopes of seeing her; but, at the moment, she was trying Chester's speed more than three miles from the city limits.

A little before tea-time she came cantering up, her face aglow with pleasure and triumph. They all came down to meet her, when they heard hoofs on the gravel-walk, Mr. Lewis being too much relieved at her safe appearance to be very angry, but he wore a very stern look, until Will came and threw her arms round his neck, saying:

"Papa Lewis" (the girls called him papa), "I knew that you had given Chester too bad a name when you said that he did not like girls."

He kissed her flushed face, and only said, when he saw the horse follow her to the stable like a kitten:

"I never saw the like!"

It was about this time that the university received a visit from the State Legislature *en masse*. They came unannounced, for the purpose of making investigations which it was perfectly proper for them to do. In the first place, they wish to see if there were any sectarianism taught in the institution; then they wished to learn for themselves how the girls were doing; and, besides, they had some business pertaining to the financial department. The first object, however, was the most important. Since the revival it had been rumored that several of the professors had been trying to inculcate their own religious views with their teaching, and that the State would not permit. Not that the State in which Ortonville was

*curvetings: Any leaping or frisking motion of a horse.
†harum-scarum girl: A flighty person.

situated was a godless one, nor were the legislators godless, but they all felt that the surest way to prevent any one denomination from getting the upper hand was to establish and maintain the university on purely non-sectarian principles.*[8] They all filed into chapel that morning just as the singing began, and a very imposing assembly they made. Like State Legislatures in general, they included men of every stamp. There was the smooth, slippery, many-sided politician, side by side with the hard-handed rustic who had been taken from the plough and sent to represent his district because of his well-known integrity.

The hymn was "Stand up for Jesus!" and, as no mention was made of any particular church in which it was best to stand up for him, they could scarcely find an objection. The prayer was wide and universal enough to suit the most liberal. It was asked around, from seat to seat, "Would they visit the recitations?" Why, certainly they would; and perhaps there was a little sinking of the heart here and there as the vision of an unsolved problem or an untranslated passage came to a student's mind. After the chapel exercises, the Legislature resolved itself into squads of half a dozen each, to visit the different rooms. Dr. Golding's room was suspected of being the place,[9] above all others, in which some particular ism might be taught, so they went there, expecting to confront it on the threshold. But they found the class quietly discussing the composition of mind, the coördination and integration of correspondences,†[10] the nature and growth of intelligence, instinct, and memory.

Another half-dozen went to the Greek-room, where Will's class was reciting. Randolf sat in front of Will, and, as the recitation went on, he saw that the last passage in the advance was coming to him, and this, by some accident, he had neglected to look up. He leaned over to ask Russel, but Russel had been sick and absent, and so was not prepared. Randolf's uncle was one of the visitors, which made him dislike more than ever to fail. "Bother it," he muttered, "it is the very first time that I ever neglected a passage, and to think it must come to me! I don't want to flunk before my uncle, but I s'pose I must."

Will saw his perplexity, and, although they had never spoken to each other, she ventured to tear the margin from her book, upon which she

*purely non-sectarian principles: Not favoring one sect of Christianity over another.
    †the coördination and integration of correspondences: From the Doctrine of Correspondences, a tenet of Emanuel Swedenborg (1688–1772), a Swedish scientist, philosopher, and mystic.

wrote the translation of the passage, and timidly touching his arm she gave it to him. He took it, and was complimented for the fluency of his translation by the professor.

The girls did themselves credit, and the six legislators retired well pleased. After they were dismissed, Randolf came to Will and thanked her very warmly, saying that she had saved him a great mortification; he explained that he had been interrupted the evening before, and had not had time to finish his lessons. On the way home he thought, "She is a kind-hearted girl, and has quite the girl's way of blushing, after all, when a fellow speaks to her."

That evening Charlie said to Nell: "Do you know, I think that if Randolf were only acquainted with Will he would like her exceedingly; and can't we manage in some way to have them meet each other?"

Charlie's engagement with Nell was a settled thing, so that they had time for a little innocent attempt at match-making among their friends.

"Oh, yes, we can manage it easily, I guess; he plays croquet,* does he not? The weather is getting warm now, and Mr. Lewis says we can put up the arches any time. There is nothing like a croquet-ground for getting acquainted. Let's ask him down to-morrow evening."

So Charlie conveyed the invitation to Randolf with all due ceremony. Oh, yes, Randolf said that he played croquet, and was glad of an opportunity of meeting the young ladies. Charlie rather wondered that he did not say something uncomplimentary about Will, for he did not know of the little incident in class that morning.

Perhaps Will took unusual pains to look well, and possibly it never entered her head; but she did manage to look very pretty that evening on the play-ground. She wore a white cambric trimmed with light blue,† and her slippers each had a little bow of the same shade. One would never have supposed, to look at her then, that she believed in woman-suffrage, or had decided to study medicine. Yet the *tout ensemble* was odd. There was an inexplicable something that made her different from the others. Perhaps it was the superior grace and symmetry of her figure, which was never embarrassed by any tight-fitting garment; it might have been in the pose of her head, from which she now and then raised her hat to run her fingers

---

*croquet: A popular lawn game involving the use of wooden mallets to drive wooden balls through iron arches, or "hoops," fixed in the ground in a particular order.

†cambric: A kind of fine white linen originally made at Cambray in Flanders.

through her curls, a trick that she had acquired in defiance of the remonstrances of the girls, and one which displayed her unusually fine form with a remarkable effect of which she was entirely unconscious.

All the sweetness and brightness of a June day was around and above them as they came gayly to the croquet-ground. The old locust in the corner of the lawn was gay with its blossoms, and roses of many hues were blooming luxuriantly, while robin-red-breasts hopped saucily upon the grass with a familiar air, as if they felt perfectly at home.

"Will is our champion here, Mr. Randolf," said Nell, as they took up their mallets; "I hope you will bring down her pride by beating her, for all last season she never lost a game, and her contempt for the rest of us grew quite noticeable: long continuance in power is sure to make one impudent, you know," she continued, laughing. At heart she was proud of Will as she remembered her masterly strokes.

"Don't believe it, Mr. Randolf, for I'm not at all formidable; occasionally I make a good shot, but it is more accident than skill."

"I used to play a good deal with my sisters, and they called me a fair player; but what you say of Miss Elliott makes me very timid about entering the lists," said Randolf.

It was decided that Will and Charlie should play against Nell and Randolf.

"Well, Charlie, you and Mr. Randolf pink to see who goes first."

"Pink—how's that?"

"Oh, you both take balls and place them about the same distance from the stake on opposite sides, then the one that strikes nearest the stake has the choice of going first or last; otherwise we can't decide readily."

"Oh, Mr. Randolf's stopped nearer than Charlie's."

"Well, I suppose there is some advantage in going last, which of course we must take—so, Burton, lead off," said Randolf.

Charlie was a fair player, but did not get farther than the centre wicket, where he stopped in position. Next came Nell; she was a nervous player, sometimes making brilliant strokes and sometimes very poor ones. She took Charlie's ball out of position and came to within one arch of the turning-stake, but struck the side of the wicket without going through. Will came next. She shot through the first two arches, then made for Nell's ball.

"Croquet, like war, makes monsters of us, for it obliges us often to abuse those we love best," she said, as she sent Nell's ball flying away out of bounds; then she took Charlie's and played upon it until she went clear round, and became a rover, after which she sent him into position and stopped near him. "I think that is the very first time in my life that I ever went clear round at one stroke," she said, apologetically.

"Croquet is like marriage," said Charlie—"you take your partners for better or worse; and yours, Will, is for the worse, for you see, if you hadn't me on your hands, you'd have gone out on that stroke: so much for working double with a poorer half."

"Oh, how very modest we are!" said Will, mockingly.

Randolf's play was almost equally brilliant, for he scattered the enemy's balls, put his partner in position, and was confident of making the last two arches at one stroke, but only went through one, then away out of position for the other, so he had to come back. Randolf had sent Will so far that he thought it impossible for her to hit any of the balls at one stroke, but she took a rapid aim at him as she said, "I feel it in my bones that I am going to hit, and that never fails."

"By Zeus!" said Randolf, involuntarily, as the ball sped across the ground and struck his with a sharp, decided ring.

"You see, my only hope is to keep you from being a rover,* Mr. Randolf."

As she stood with the toe of her slipper on her ball ready to croquet Randolf away out of bounds, Charlie stepped up close to her and said, with a mischievous smile:

"What monsters croquet *does* make of us, to be sure, causing us to abuse those we love best!"

"You impudent boy! you almost made me miss that, and I did not send it half as far as I intended"; and she snatched a rose from the trellis and threw it with such good aim that it struck Charlie on the tip of the nose, which was a remarkably large one.

"Oh, I surrender, if you take to missiles!" he cried, "and most humbly beg your majesty's pardon."

"You may prove your sorrow by holding an umbrella over me until the sun goes behind the house, for I'm getting burned."

Randolf liked to see that she cared about her complexion, and, when it was Charlie's turn to strike, he gallantly offered to hold the umbrella,

---

*rover: A croquet term meaning a ball that has gone through all its hoops and is ready to win; it also refers to the player whose ball is a rover. Coming from Will, who is being coy with Randolf, *rover* also means an inconstant lover or a male flirt.

which offer she gracefully accepted. The game lasted more than an hour, and Will and Charlie came out ahead. It was too late to play another, so they stopped, with the understanding that they were to have another very soon. When Charlie and Nell were alone, he said:

"Who ever would have supposed that there was so much artfulness in Will Elliott? Why, she acted the perfect coquette there this evening, with her smiles and blushes, and I know Randolf is smashed.* Did you notice how he took every opportunity to chat with her under that umbrella? *Ille habet*, as Terence says,† and I'd have it myself if I did not know some-body better," and he kissed Nell's hand.

"Oh, it can't be called artfulness; it is a feminine virtue, and Will has all the feminine virtues, besides many of her own manufacture. You see, her pride has been wounded for a long time because Randolf seemed to ignore her, while he was pleasant to the rest of us girls, and it is human nature to want to conquer an enemy and bring him to your feet."

The Legislature, after visiting a few days, went away highly pleased; and, when that body convened in the State Capitol, many eloquent things were said about the university being the pride of the State; toasts were drunk at many dinners to its long life and success, and liberal grants of money were made for additional buildings. During their visit they had had a private interview with the president concerning the girls, the result of which was not definitely known, but it must have been, on the whole, favorable. Very probably the president said that, as scholarship went, they were a decided success; but as to the mooted question of health, as far as he could yet tell, too much had been made of it. Not long after, the president overtook Will on the street, and, after greeting her in his usual pleasant manner, he said:

"Miss Elliott, I've been using you as a sort of trump-card, for, when the legislators asked concerning the health of the young ladies, I pointed to you, and asked them if they wanted a better answer than that; and now you must not fail me, for I'm relying on you."[11]

"I wish I felt as sure of everything as I do of my health," said Will, as she came to her own gate.

"And I wish all the young ladies took as much pride in their health as you seem to," he replied, as he tipped his hat and passed on.

*smashed: Infatuated.

†*Ille habet*, as Terence says: Charlie Burton is telling Nell that Randolf "is smitten" with Will. The phrase comes from the *Andria*, a work by the celebrated Latin playwright Publius Terentius Afer (ca. 185–160 BC), known popularly as Terence.

CHAPTER IX

A Possible Result of Co-Education

"The sense of the world is short,
Loud and various the report—
    To love and be beloved:
Men and gods have not outlearned it,
And how oft soe'er they've turned it,
    'Tis not to be improved."

—EMERSON

A year has passed since the events of the last chapter. It is again June, and the roses bloom on the trellis in Mr. Lewis's yard, and the croquet set is again on the front lawn, whence it had been taken during the long winter. In the house things looked about the same as we left them a year ago.

The pictures of "Pharaoh's Horses" and "Youth starting on the Voyage of Life" still hang on opposite sides of Will's and Clara's room, and the four girls are there busy with their studies, as when we saw them last. It has been a year of hard work. They have wrestled with the conic sections; they have begun to enjoy the masters of classic literature, besides having had a little French and German. Two ladies have graduated from the law department, of whom one was admitted to the bar in a Western State, while the other went into an office with her father, both having passed their final examinations with honor. Several ladies have also taken diplomas from the medical department. Among the number was Miss Lane, the object of Will's rapturous admiration, who went as a missionary to India, but, her health failing, she returned, and died not long after.

Others went immediately into practice, and to-day are respected physicians, having fought their way through all sorts of bigoted opposition from men,[1] but more particularly from women themselves, who, above all others, one might suppose, would hail the advent of women physicians with unbounded delight. The first ladies who entered the medical school of the University of Ortonville had harder battles to fight than those of either of the other departments.[2] The character of their work, which had hitherto been considered as preëminently man's work, made their position peculiarly trying. People were slow to believe that a woman could be truly womanly and work in the dissecting-room, attend clinics, and hear lectures on all sorts of dreadful subjects. It was once darkly rumored, too, that a woman of actually bad character had smuggled herself into the department, but had been promptly expelled by the officials. That, of course, was charged as a direct consequence of the admission of women; for, if they had not been admitted, *she* never would have come.

Think of it! One solitary, misguided woman had actually strayed into the medical department of the University of Ortonville, where yearly, without censure, are harbored dozens of male profligates, who are turned out at the end of the course to poison public morals. How much those will have to answer for who made such a condition of things possible by the admission of women!

The girls in the literary department had steadily maintained their reputation for scholarship. They had joined the literary societies,[3] but the secret fraternities were something to which they could never hope to attain.[4] The mysteries of the Psi U's, the ΔKE's, the Alpha Deltas and Sigma Phis, must remain to them forever sealed. But, notwithstanding this inherent disability, they manage to have pleasant times, and are even quite happy over their work and prospects for the future. Just now Will is sitting by the open window, with a German reader in her hand and lexicon in her lap. Soon she breaks out impatiently:

"This 'Diver' of Schiller's is a bothersome thing to translate smoothly;* it is easy enough to see what he means, but when you want English to express it, the words are hard to find."

Let us take her face in a moment of repose, and see if it has changed. There is the same fine profile, the dark eyebrows and lashes, and the same bright smile, as she turns to answer some pleasantry of the girls. Perhaps the expression is a trifle more thoughtful than that of a year ago, and maybe even sad for a moment, as she gazes out of the window. She is not thinking of the landscape without, but of the future, and how in one more year her class will be making preparation for their entrance into the world from the

*'Diver' of Schiller's: Friedrich Schiller (1759–1805), a German poet and dramatist, wrote a ballad in 1798 called "Der Taucher" (The Diver), which was later set to music by Franz Schubert.

Old Library Interior, the University of Michigan, 1870s. "People were slow to believe that a woman could be truly womanly and work in the dissecting-room, attend clinics, and hear lectures on all sorts of dreadful subjects." Here a lone female student makes herself at home in the all-male atmosphere of the library. (Bentley Historical Library, University of Michigan, BL003686.)

sheltering arms of their alma mater, as the seniors now are doing. She used often in those last days to say: "I don't see how I lived, girls, before I knew you; and how I'm going to give you up and sally out into the world alone, is more than I can tell." She turns from the window now, and, laying her books on the table, says: "I've finished the 'Diver,' but that 'Chamountfal' of Goethe's is too much for me to-night.* I have not done anything improper for a long time, girls; I'm afraid I'll forget how; I am actually spoiling for a scrape. Come, my old blessing, can't you help me?" and, throwing herself full-length upon the sofa, she put her head in Nell's lap.

*'Chamountfal' of Goethe's: Johann Wolfgang von Goethe (1749–1832), politician, humanist, scientist, writer, and philosopher. We have been unable to identify this poem.

"I guess you will not have to call in help to get up some mischief," said Nell, as she played with Will's hair. "I should think that you were in a sad decline if you needed help for that."

"I have it," said Will, as she came quickly to a sitting posture. "The man who works in the museum told me,[5] the other day, that if I would bring him some birds he would stuff and mount them for me; and I'll write a note to Randolf requesting the pleasure of his company on a shooting-excursion next Saturday. It's leap-year,*[6] and what's the good of having it, if we don't use it?"

"Aren't you afraid of shocking his delicate nerves?" asked Clara.

"Precisely what I want to do, for it must come sooner or later—as I am destined to give each of my friends a shock some time or other, it seems, and the sooner it is over the better. I think I'll write in French; that is the language of diplomacy, isn't it? It will be good practice; besides, such an invitation will not sound so bold in French as in English. Come, help me with it. Let me see—how shall it begin?

"Monsieur Randolf: Est-ce que j'aurai le très-grand plaisir de vous accompagner Samedi prochain d'aller faire tour à la campagne pour tuer des oiseaux?

La vôtre,

"Wilhelmine Elliott."†

Randolf was not shocked—which showed the ground they had gained in acquaintanceship. He was amused and pleased; in fact, he was pleased with almost everything, lately, that Will did. They had seen a great deal of each other in the last year; they had studied, walked, and rowed together, and rumor had been busy coupling their names for some weeks. Randolf liked her; yes, he more than liked her, yet he could not say that he was in love. He was in that uncertain state in which some sudden crisis was necessary to show him where he stood. The young man has changed more than Will in the years that have passed. His face has lost the sarcastic expression, and he is handsomer and more manly-looking. But he is still impetuous and boyish, which is not an unpardonable sin in a youth of twenty-one. He criticises Will a good deal mentally, but in a very different spirit from that of a year ago. If he had put his thoughts into words, he

*leap-year: Will is referring to an old custom that allowed women to take the lead in courtship (and even to propose marriage) during a leap year.
†"Mr. Randolf: May I have the very great pleasure of accompanying you next Saturday on a country outing for some bird hunting? Yours, Wilhelmine Elliot."

would have said that he liked Will best when she was the most womanly; and he meant, by that, in her quieter moods, when she was gentle and confiding, when she clung to his arm as they passed some rough-looking character on the street at night, and he would silently wish, in a general way, that she felt the need of protection oftener. In her gay, brilliant moods she dazzled him, but he did not like her then so well. Yet, with all her faults, he preferred her to the others. He was as much a skeptic on matters of religion as she, yet he often half wished that Will were a Christian, for he had an idea that a woman needed that to soften her. He answered Will's note in French that compared very well with hers, saying that he would be most happy to accompany her. They were to start promptly at eight o'clock, for they had a long ramble before them. Randolf was there on time with his gun and game-bag, looking quite sportsmanlike. Will, dressed in a suit of dark-green plaid, fashioned something like the page's costume of Robin Hood's Maid Marion, seemed half boyish; yet, from her arching foot to her hunter's cap with its floating feather, there was only bewitching girlishness and grace.

"We would ask the rest of you to go, but we know you could not stand the walk and would faint by the way," said Will, as they stood on the veranda ready to start. "We will not find any scarlet tanagers this side of Barker's Woods, and that is four or five miles at least."

"Oh, you're welcome to your tramp!" said Nell. She was glad that Will could walk and shoot, although she had no ambition for herself in that direction.

"Let me carry your gun until we get out of town," said Randolf.

"Well, I had intended to carry it myself," said Will, teasingly, for she knew he would not like it; "but, after all, I guess you had better take it. I don't want to wound Mrs. Grundy needlessly, for the old lady has been quite considerate toward me of late."

With a basket of lunch that Mrs. Lewis had put up for them, they strolled out into the bright June sunshine, forming a part of the joyous young life that throbbed on every side. There was one peculiarity in Randolf's treatment of Will, and that was, he never objected to anything she did in the way of overstepping the bounds of conventionality when they were alone. He would say:

"I don't care what you say or do when you are with me, for I understand you."

"You are not the only one that understands me. Charlie Burton was my first friend among the boys, and I think he knows me better than any one of them." She was a little vexed at Randolf's masculine self-assertion and conceit, in thinking that he understood her better than any one else. "Do you remember how you used to treat me and talk of me in our freshman year?"

"I don't think it is quite kind of you to bring that up."

"Well, I did not mean any harm, only I wanted to show you how long it took you to do me justice. But don't let's quarrel. Will you hold my gun, please, while I vault that fence?" and she darted on ahead of him, and was over with one bound, leaving him to follow.

"Where did you learn that vault?" he asked, in surprise at the feat.

"Oh, my brothers taught it to me long ago, and I see I have not forgotten it."

They had by this time walked far from the sight and sound of the town, and had struck across the green fields into the woods.

"I've heard so much about your skill in shooting, now let's see if you can hit that squirrel yonder on the white oak," said Randolf.

"Oh, we've started out for birds, and I don't want to kill anything that we have no use for; it's hard enough to kill them for scientific purposes."

"Yes, but I want to see if you can hit the squirrel," he persisted.

It was a little red squirrel, that had run up an oak and now sat peering over one of the topmost branches, with nothing but his head visible.

"I can hit him, if the gun is good for anything—and his blood be upon your head," she said, as she took aim and fired.

The squirrel fell from branch to branch until he reached the ground.

"Splendid shot!" exclaimed Randolf, in genuine admiration.

"I never feel a bit of satisfaction in anything killed without a purpose," said Will, "although I confess that slight excuses have sometimes satisfied my conscience."

"There is the bird we are looking for!" cried Will, as a little scarlet tanager flitted across the arching branches above their heads. "How pretty it looks, darting among the green leaves!—and there is his mate; let them die together. You take one, and I'll take the other."

The reports were simultaneous, and two little lifeless bodies fluttered to the ground at their feet.

"Oh, your shot are too large!" said Will. "You have completely riddled yours, and broken its legs and wings. I had fine shot, and look, you can't see where it was hit. I don't believe yours can be mounted, but we'll take it for the sake of its mate." And the birds were rolled carefully in paper, and put in the game-bag.[7]

By this time the sun was overhead, and, as it was very warm, they decided to rest and have their lunch. They found a spot where a cool stream meandered through the heart of the forest, and fallen trunks covered with moss offered inviting seats.

"I wonder what Mrs. Lewis has given us," said Will, as she began to unpack the well-filled basket. "Well, if she hasn't put in coffee, and sugar, and a little bottle of cream! She seems to understand picnicking. Do you like coffee, Mr. Randolf?"

"Yes, immensely; but can you make it?" he asked, doubtfully.

"Why, of course I can. Do you suppose my precious mother would let me grow up without knowing how to make coffee, and bread, and such things? But you don't deserve any for doubting my ability to make it. However, it was a sin of ignorance, and I'll forgive you if you'll bring me a pail of water."

"I'm your most obedient servant," he said, making a low bow, as he took the little tin pail and started for the brook.

A fire was soon crackling on a flat stone, and when there were coals enough she put the coffee to boil in the pail while she went to spread the table. Randolf threw himself upon the grass, and pretended to be much absorbed in his memorandum-book, while in reality he was watching Will as she flitted to and fro from the fire to the mossy log where the table was to be. Now and then she lifted the cover to see how the coffee was doing, then gathered wild-grape leaves from a vine that hung low from the branches of a tree, and upon these she placed the sandwiches and other articles with which the basket was filled.

Randolf, like most men, was easily brought to a tranquil state of mind by the immediate expectation of something good to eat; and as the fragrance of the coffee was wafted to his nostrils, he fell into a dreamy reverie, in which he pictured himself in a home of his own, and some one moving to and fro preparing things expressly for him because he liked them; some woman with light hair, long—yes, it must be long hair, he guessed, and yet short, curly hair was pretty—maybe it would be short, after all; then a soft, white hand would bathe his head when he was tired; and he glanced up at Will, half expecting that she would read his thoughts. But she was busy ornamenting the table with green boughs, and displaying a great deal of artistic taste in the arrangements, as far as the appliances within reach would allow.

With a burst of boyish enthusiasm Randolf said:

"Let's pretend that we are Adam and Eve, and I'm resting after my work in the vineyard."

"Yes, I dare say it was one of Adam's principal employments, resting around to see what Eve was getting for dinner. The Lord used to come down and call on them in the evenings, too; but I don't feel ready to receive such distinguished company." It was just such speeches that Randolf could not bear to hear her make. "There is one thing," continued Will, "in which Eve had an advantage over us, and that was, she had no abominable skirts to bother her," and she gave hers an impatient twitch, which, short as it was, had caught upon a fallen limb. "I'll never be happy in skirts," she went on, her face flushing with anger as she saw that the braid was torn from the bottom and dragged along in an unsightly string behind.

Randolf's luxurious dream was broken, and he sat upright with cloudy brow.

"I do wish you would not scold so much about woman's dress. I never am with you an hour that you do not say something against long dresses and hating woman's way of doing things. What under heaven would you do—wear pants? What will you be happy in? Other girls are not always complaining as you are, and I do wish you would give it up!" He wanted to add, "for my sake!" but did not quite dare to; for why should she stop it for his sake?

"Oh, yes; you like to see a woman like Mrs. Guild, with trains a yard long wiping up the dust. Well, I hope your wife will be all your fancy paints in the way of long skirts, Mr. Randolf. But come," she said, suddenly realizing that she had allowed her temper to get the better of her, "our coffee will get cold. Don't let's say any more about it, for it doesn't make me feel a bit different on the dress-question, and only spoils my temper, which is none of the best."

The coffee was pronounced delicious, and Randolf's spirits returned as he took cups of the steaming beverage from her hand, and heard her talk with a wise air about making bread and biscuits. He forgot the unpleasant affair of the dress, and thought how charming she was. The sunlight played through the branches over her hair, which seemed prettier than any chignon or waterfall that he had ever seen.

"We have not brought anything to read while we are resting after dinner," observed Will.

"Can't you recite something?" asked Randolf.

"Let me see: I've just been learning Tennyson's 'Voyage,'* in odd moments, and I like it very much."

Randolf was not familiar with it, and, of course, would like to hear it; so she repeated that charming little poem with great spirit, and evidently to the satisfaction of her auditor, who applauded her at the end. There was a silence of a few minutes, when Randolf said:

"That's the whole of life in a nutshell, isn't it?"

"Yes," said Will; "what vision are you chasing—what are you going to do for a life-work?"

"Oh, I'm going to be a lawyer; I decided that long ago. What are you going to do? In this era of woman's rights you can enter one of the professions with perfect propriety, I suppose," he said, with a slight air of raillery.

"I don't know what I shall do, I'm sure," said Will, looking fixedly on the ground.

Why did she not speak of her intention to study medicine? Was it because she knew that he would not approve it—because it would shock his sense of propriety, so that he would like her less? She was hardly willing to make this admission. At all events, she did not speak of it. They were so busy with their talk, they did not notice that the sun no longer shone through the tree-tops and made shadows with the leaves, nor did they see the great black clouds rolling up in the west, until a rumble of thunder made them sensible of an approaching storm.

"I think I know a shorter way home than the one we came," said Randolf, as he hastily caught up the basket and guns, while Will followed close after him, and they hurried through the wood. They walked in silence some distance, when Randolf stopped suddenly and looked around with a bewildered air, as he said: "I don't remember this hazel copse at all. I'm afraid we are not on the right track; but if you will wait here a little while, I'll see if there isn't a house somewhere. I don't like to take you around on an uncertainty." The thunder had, all this time, grown louder and nearer, and lightnings began to play through the sombre shadows of

*Tennyson's 'Voyage': "The Voyage" (1864), a descriptive poem of an ocean journey, was a romantic allegory for "Life as the pursuit of the Ideal," or in this context a "vision" of the ideal.

the forest that they had just left, giving the trees a strange, unearthly aspect.

Will did not like to stay alone, for, although she was naturally brave, she had the instinctive dread of solitude that braver natures than hers have felt at an approaching storm. She wanted to follow Randolf, but was afraid he would laugh at her for being so timid. She congratulated herself that they had gotten out from under the large trees of the forest, but she did not notice the tall poplar that stood near the spot where Randolf left her. The storm now burst in all its fury. There was a blinding flash, and the poplar was shivered from top to bottom, but Will did not see nor hear it, for she lay very pale and still upon the ground. Randolf had gone to the edge of the thicket, where he saw a log-house set in a little clearing—the same one at which he had stopped a year or two before when he was hunting with some of the boys; but, approaching it from another side, he had not recognized the locality till now. He started back for Will as fast as the thick bushes would allow. He shouted, but there was no answer save the dismal creaking and groaning of the tree-tops swayed by the wind. A vague terror seized him as he reflected that the lightning had struck somewhere very near. He parted the bushes with desperate haste, and his breath was almost suspended with apprehension lest something dreadful had happened to her.

"Ah, there she is! But, my God, she's dead!" he gasped, springing forward.

Had the circumstances been different, he might have paused to admire the artistic beauty of her position; but it came back to him, long after, with great vividness. It was the easy attitude of one having thrown herself down to rest. The right arm, from which the sleeve had become unfastened at the wrist and had fallen open to the shoulder, was thrown over the head, the tips of the white fingers just touching the damp curls. The left still grasped a little bunch of forget-me-nots that he had given her on the walk. One foot was drawn under her, while the buttoned boot of the other was just visible through the leaves of wild-columbine among which she had fallen. Her wet garments clung to her in folds like marble drapery, as they shrank to the still form. The face was very white, and the long, dark lashes looked darker still as they lay upon the bloodless cheek.

Randolf had never been able to say, up to that moment, that he loved Will Elliott; now he did not say it, but felt it. He snatched her from the ground as if her weight were nothing—for he was a powerful fellow, and now his feelings helped to make one hundred and twenty pounds imperceptibly light. He strode over the brush like a giant with his burden, for he had a gleam of hope that she might yet be restored with proper care.

The woman in the log-house was somewhat startled when she saw them enter the clearing, and called to her daughter, a girl of twelve, "Mirandy, I b'lieve somebody's been struck when the poplar went, for here comes a young man a-carryin' something;" and she hastened to undo the fastening of the door, which had been closed when the storm began.

Randolf laid Will upon the clean but homely bed, and begged the woman to do what she could. For this she needed no urging, for she had already brought some brandy, with which she began to rub her limbs.

"Young man, make me a fire in the kitchen-stove, and get me some hot water," she said to Randolf, who sprang eagerly to do her bidding; for action of any kind was better than waiting in suspense.

The mother and daughter worked over Will with intense energy.

"She's a-comin' to," said the woman.

A faint color began to steal over Will's face. Randolf, hearing the words, came and bent over her. She opened her eyes with a dreamy expression, and the color deepened into a blush when she recognized him.

He turned away, murmuring, "Thank God!" and, following the woman into the kitchen, he poured forth his thanks with boyish eloquence.

"Tut, tut, young man! She's your sister, likely?"

"No," he answered, simply.

Randolf then said that he would go home and bring a carriage for Will in the evening. So, taking one more glance at her, as if to reassure himself that she really was alive, he started.

Mrs. Curtiss—for such was the woman's name—after performing several little needless offices of kindness, such as smoothing the pillow and tucking down the spread, sat down with her knitting near the bed.

She was very curious to know about the strangers, for their coming was quite an event in the monotonous life of the log-house. The bright young girl with her odd hunting-suit, the tender devotion of the young man who was not her brother, was material enough for the imagination of as practical a woman as Mrs. Curtiss.

Will lay very quietly looking about the room. A wide fireplace was on one side, the outlet of which was a clay chimney built on the outside of the house. On a rude mantel was an old-fashioned clock, with a picture of a woman's head on the door with her hair done up in the style of Martha

Washington. Just over the bed were some woodcuts of Grant,* Colfax,†
and other worthies, cut from the illustrated papers.‡

Slowly it all came back to her: how they hurried to get shelter from the
storm, and how she wished Randolf would not leave her alone, but was
ashamed to say so; then the rest was all blank, until she awoke in this queer
room. Her eyes finally settled upon Mrs. Curtiss and her knitting.

"I've put you to a great deal of trouble," she said. "What was the matter?
Did I fall?" And she passed her hand over her forehead, as if trying to
remember.

"No trouble at all," said the woman, glad to begin the conversation; for
her curiosity was worked up to such a pitch that she would soon have
begun it herself if Will had not opened the way. "You see, you was too near
the poplar when it was struck, and you got sort o' stunned-like. Do you live
far from here?"

"In Ortonville. How far is it?"

"Five miles, my man calls it."

There was a pause, in which Mrs. Curtiss was revolving the best way of
broaching her relations with Randolf.

"The young man looks a heap like you—enough to be your own
brother."

"Does he? He is only my classmate in college."

Ah! here was new light.

"What! be you one o' them girls as has come to the college in
Ortonville, that they made such talk about a year or two back?"[8]

Will replied that she was, smiling at the woman's new interest.

"La, now! I've been a-wantin' this long time to get a sight o' them; for,
from all I heerd tell, I thought they must be queer-lookin' things. But I don't
see that you look so powerful strange," she continued, looking Will over
from head to foot. "The huntin' is a little odd, but I don't see no harm in it."

"I'm the only one of the girls that uses a gun," said Will, anxious to put
the college-girls in the best possible light. "I learned to shoot at home,
with my brothers."

---

*Grant: President Ulysses S. Grant (1869–77).

†Colfax: Schuyler Colfax, vice president during the first term of President
Ulysses S. Grant (1869–73).

‡cut from the illustrated papers: People of lesser means often decorated their
homes with framed lithographs of scenes and famous people cut from popular
illustrated newspapers of the day such as *Harper's Weekly* or *Frank Leslie's
Illustrated Newspaper*.

"Where was you brought up?" asked Mrs. Curtiss, anxious now to know Will's antecedents.

"In C——."

"Have you parents?"

"I have a mother, but my father was killed in the army."

"Do tell! Is it so? What a pity! My brother Enoch was killed, too! Heap o' sufferin' that war made!"

There was another pause, after which Mrs. Curtiss said, assuming a facetious air:

"You'll be a-fallin' in love with some of them young men in college, of course."

"That is not what I came for," said Will, laughing.

"Well, there's somebody thinks a heap o' you, I can tell you. The way that young man hung over you to-day, pretty nigh crazy when he thought you was dead; then, when he found you wasn't, almost wrung my hand off, he was so glad!"

"Oh, of course it would have been awkward for him to have taken me home a corpse," she said, indifferently, while in her heart she wanted the woman to go on and tell her more about Randolf. Had he really hung over her with more interest than he would have shown for any girl thus thrown under his protection? And had he really carried her all the way to the house?

"It's my opinion you'll know it 'fore long how much he thinks o' you. And you'd better take him, too, for he's mighty handsome."

Will would not have borne it under ordinary circumstances to have her affairs thus probed, but now she was only amused at the curiosity of the woman; and, besides, these assurances of Randolf's love for her were far from unpleasant, though coming from the hostess of the log-house.

"Then you believe in women being married?" said Will, not caring to drop the subject.

"La, yes! What else would you have 'em do? Now, my man ain't no great shakes, but he's a heap better'n none. I hain't no kind o' patience with women as wants to vote, and do everything men does. I believe in the Scriptur', that women ought to stay at home, and not go preachin' around in public."

"You at least believe in women being doctors?" said Will.

"Indeed I don't! It's man's work, and a woman that'll do it is not modest."

Will did not care to enter into a discussion of the point, so she only said: "Do you think so?"

She was able to sit up after a while, but her head felt dizzy and strange. She grew impatient for Randolf's return, for it seemed so long since she had left home in the morning; but when she reflected that he had to walk there, she knew that he could not get back with the carriage until evening, so she passed the hours as best she could.

Mrs. Curtiss was quite won to her by the interest she took in duck-raising, the price of eggs and potatoes, and the probabilities of the wheat-crop. Meanwhile, Randolf was making his way to the town. The sun had come out after the storm, and again the shadows played across his path, while sparkling drops hung from every leaf and branch. As he passed the place where Will had fallen, he saw a little black-velvet bow that she had worn at her throat lying on the grass. He picked it up, and, pressing it to his lips, thrust it in his bosom. If any one had told Guilford Randolf, the year before, that he would ever go into raptures over one of Will Elliott's ribbons for the owner's sake, he would have considered nothing more impossible. How very different were his feelings now compared with those of a few hours ago, when he had come along that very path! Then the bright, impulsive girl at his side, while she charmed, yet perplexed and annoyed him with her outbursts against conventionalities and woman's way of dressing. Now he thought of all those things, not exactly with approval, yet with a tender feeling in which there was no reproach. He was happy in thinking of her just as she was, with all her oddities of speech, dress, and manner.

In this frame of mind he reached the town, and told the girls at Mrs. Lewis's, who were thrown into a great state of excitement at the narration, and could scarcely wait until Will was with them again.

Randolf procured a carriage, and, well provided with robes and wraps, returned for Will. The sun was sinking behind the log-house when they bade their kind-hearted hostess good-by, and Will was handed into the carriage. She was yet very weak, and it was a novel situation for her, leaning on some one for support, and she said, smiling:

"What sort of an invalid would I make? Is it becoming?" They rode in silence for some time, when Will said: "I wonder how it would have been, now, if I had been killed to-day?"

"I should have nothing to live for, then," said Randolf, frankly.

She was a little startled by the reply, and she knew from the tone that he was in earnest; but, not noticing it, she went on:

"Mr. Lewis would have telegraphed to my mother before this time; our class would have a holiday, and the president would say beautiful things about me in chapel; then half a dozen of you boys would be appointed to take me to my mother; then—"

"Oh! don't talk that way," he said, with a deprecating gesture; "it makes me desperate. I could not live without you, Will." It was the first time he had ever called her that. "I love you better than anything else in the world;" and his handsome face glowed with earnestness as he leaned toward her.

She was looking at the landscape as it lay spread out in the moonlight, with here and there a farmhouse, in which moving lights glimmered through the trees. She answered, calmly:

"I wonder—if what you say can be true—I wonder if it is possible to love one whom you have once disliked, as you certainly have me?"

"Oh, why will you speak of that?" he asked, very much pained by the allusion; but she went on, unheeding:

"I was here two years before you ever spoke to me, and all that time I heard of unkind things that you said about me. Now, is it possible for one to change so utterly in so short a time?"

"It is possible," he said. "I was blind those years; I did not know you. You are as different from my first impression of you as day is from night. But it is very cruel to doubt me, when I have repented in sackcloth and ashes."

"Have I been cruel?" she asked, kindly. "I am sorry, and will never be so again."

Randolf hardly knew whether his repentance had been accepted or rejected, but the feeling that prompted him to say thus much was now beyond control, for he felt that everything depended upon winning her, and, yielding to the moment's impulse, he drew her closer to him and kissed her lips.

The next evening, at twilight, Will lay on the sofa in the parlor listening while Nell played Beethoven's "Moonlight Sonata." She was yet weak from her experience of the day before, and she lay rather pale and languid, very unlike herself. When Nell was through, Will said:

"Won't you stay with me to-night, instead of going to church? I want you."

"Why, of course I will! for how could I refuse anything to my precious girl who was so nearly taken from us yesterday?" and, bending over, she tenderly kissed her.

"I want to tell you something, Nell," said Will, as she drew a bassock close to the sofa and sat down:* "Guilford Randolf is in love with me."

"Yes? I admire his taste; in fact, I've seen it for some time. Are you going to tell me all about it?"

"Yes. He did not seem to care so much for me until after the accident yesterday."

"Oh," said Nell, laughing, "Venus's son had to bestride a thunderbolt before he could reach the young man effectually.† Well, are you in love with him?"

"Yes, I'm afraid I am, and that is what troubles me. You know that I had made up my mind to study medicine, and now here I am drawn off the track like any other girl. Somehow I feel as if it were very weak, but I can't help it. Like old Bishop Somebody, I hereafter count nothing human foreign to myself, so I shall do the very natural and proper thing of forsaking a professional career for the one I love, and give up dreams of fame as master of the healing art."

"I suspected as much, and, on the whole, I'm glad of it, for a professional life would be so lonely for you, grand as it would be. But why can't you take a course in that, while he is in the law department? What did he say when you told him of your intention to study medicine?"

"I—I—have not said anything to him about it, for I know he can't bear anything of the kind."

"Well, I should broach the subject the next time you have a chance, and find out what he thinks. He has no right to be too exacting. I think it would be splendid for you to study a profession; then, if you are ever left a widow, you can support yourself."

The girls talked far into the evening about their hopes for the future. Nell told how she and Charlie were to be married at the end of the course; then they were going to live in one of the Western States, where Charlie had had a position offered him in a college as soon as he was through.

Will determined to tell Randolf about the medicine at their next interview, and an opportunity came in a short time. They were out rowing, one evening, on the river; they had started with a party, but soon found themselves alone in one of the little skiffs. They pulled up the river for a while, keeping near enough to the other boats to join in college-songs,

---

*bassock: Another way of saying *hassock*, a thick, firm cushion used as a footrest.
†Venus's son: Cupid (Eros), the Roman god of love.

whose meaningless words and rollicking measures, mellowed by the water, floated softly across to either shore. Will sat in the stern, with the tips of her fingers in the water. She had entirely recovered from the accident in the wood, and now her laugh rang out merrily as the boats hailed each other in passing. After a while, becoming separated from the others, Randolf rested his oars, and they floated down.

"I think I never told you, Guilford," said Will, as she caught a water-lily in passing, "that I had fully determined to study medicine before I knew you."

"You had!" he exclaimed, and looked at her. "Well, I'm glad to be your savior from such a fate."

"I was wondering," she went on, "if you would not think it nice for me to go through the medical department while you are in the law; we could be together then, you know."

A strong expression of disgust came over his handsome face, as he said:

"Do you suppose that I would ever have a wife who had been familiar with all the disgusting details of a dissecting-room? Bah! she would never get rid of it."

Will felt a hot flush of indignation at this reply; his arbitrary tone and utter want of sympathy with her cherished plan hurt her deeply. Randolf evidently had no perception of the sacrifice it might be to her thus to submit to him a darling scheme, and the bluntness of his reply shocked her extremely.

"You have no right to talk to me in that way," she replied, "and I can't understand your continued prejudice against professional women, when you see such noble examples as Miss Lane and Mrs. Hartly. After all the avowals of devotion you have made to me, I don't see how you can treat with disrespect a thing that once lay so near my heart, and which I should have carried out had I not loved you well enough to give it up."

The closing part of the speech pacified him. "Forgive me!" he said; "I'm an old bear, to speak to you so." Yet, while he thus rebuked himself for having wounded her, the thought uppermost in his mind had been that he would save her from a life of hardship, and he wondered that she did not see this. Her eloquent talk about the grandeur of a life spent in healing the sick and smoothing the paths of the dying made no impression upon him. It might do for some women, but the one he cared for must never hold a scalpel or know anything about diseases.

Yet he was not more selfish, perhaps, than most men, in being unable to see that the woman he chose could wish to indulge any plans or wishes that might conflict with him. Will did not feel quite happy, for she was disappointed. Randolf had not met her confession with the frankness and generosity she had expected, and, notwithstanding his apology, she still felt uncomfortable. But he talked very gayly as they strolled up the bank, arm-in-arm, and during the remaining days of the term he was so devoted, that she almost succeeded in forgetting this disturbance of her feelings.

CHAPTER X

———◦《◦》◦———

Another Phase of the Story

"She is cunning past man's thought;
Would I had never seen her."
— SHAKESPEARE

"My eyes are open to her falsehood; my whole life
Has been a golden dream of love and friendship,
But now I wake."
—*Ibid.*

Three years after Will had left home for the first time she is again in the westward-bound train, on her way to Ortonville. Familiar faces are now seen at every station, for it is the day before college opens, and the students are gathering in from all directions. Instead of a freshman, trembling with dread of examinations, she is now a senior, returning to college after her junior vacation spent at home. It is not as a stranger that she is now whirled along the streets, for all things, even the buildings, look like old acquaintances, and the hackman knows where to drive her without any directions. She knows, too, that warm hearts are waiting for her on Clinton Avenue, for Clara and Nell were to have come yesterday.

Randolf and Will have kept up a lively correspondence during the vacation. He had spent the summer with his mother and sisters at Newport, and his letters were full of amusing descriptions of the people he had met; but Will was most pleased with his last letter, in which he said: "All the women I've met this summer are so tiresome compared with you, and I long to be with you once more." Will had spent a pleasant time at home. Mrs. Elliott had slowly learned to respect her daughter's independence of thought, and they had long, earnest talks in the summer twilight, so that Will became happy as a child in her mother's confidence. She told her mother about Randolf, and read his letters to her, so that the mother grew young and lived over again the happy days of her own love, as she watched this devotion to an absent classmate, only known to her through Will's descriptions. They found that they had many points of common faith in their struggles after the better life, and Will spoke of her doubts in a frank, fearless way, that once could not have failed to call forth the most bitter reproofs from the maternal lips. What had so changed Mrs. Elliott? She held the articles of her creed just as faithfully, and prayed as earnestly for Will's conversion, but the hardness that had so repelled her child in previous years was gone. Hally's death had begun the change, for almost the last words she said to her mother were, "Promise me, mother darling, that you will be gentle with Willie, when I'm gone, about believing things in religion, for she means to do right"; and she had promised, as she held one of the little dying hands.

The softening effect that advancing years have, upon a nature in which there is real sweetness, had made the keeping of the promise easy, and Will felt that this last vacation spent at home was the happiest time in her life.

The future looked very bright to her this beginning of her senior year. She had won a place of high standing in her class; she had been restored to her mother's trust and confidence; she was so well and strong, that simple existence was joy and every breath a pleasure. Then, over all these causes of happiness, Randolf's love for her shed a rosy halo, that consciously or unconsciously heightened every other pleasure.

Their studies were to be elective this year, and she and Randolf had decided to take nearly the same things, that they might study them together. The first *semester* she took Theoretical and Practical Astronomy, because he wanted her to; and he took Greek and German, because she wished to keep up those studies.

The class of '70 was once more visited by death,[1] and this time the victim was Arthur Dennison, a young man greatly beloved by the faculty and his classmates. It was a month after the opening of the year that he was taken with some kind of malignant fever, and in one short week from the time his manly voice was last heard in the class-room the news came that he was dead. His home was in the country, ten miles from Ortonville, and his class-mates went out in carriages to pay the last offices of love and respect to their departed brother. It was in October, when the trees were gay with their autumn dress—when summer, even yet loath to take its leave, looked back regretfully, and still poured its wealth of golden sunshine upon the shorn meadows and shocks of yellow corn.

Charlie and Nell drove out in a large double carriage with Will and Randolf. Arthur's home was an old-fashioned country-seat, with a wide veranda running across the front; over this flowering vines had climbed, but now they were yellow and withered, and the leaves fell to the ground with every breeze. There was the swing in the big apple-tree, that Arthur had put up for the younger children in his last vacation. How they all looked forward to Arthur's vacations! They were the events of the year at the farmhouse. But that is all over now, for he will never come home again at the holidays, although he will be no farther away than the little churchyard just down the road.

The procession had already left the house and gone to the church when the carriages from Ortonville arrived. They were to have a sermon, and a large crowd had assembled, for the young man had been a universal favorite in the neighborhood, and many of the good people had looked forward to the time when they would see him stand in that pulpit and proclaim the way of life, for he was intending to be a minister. Dr. Golding conducted the services. He spoke of the lovely Christian character of the boy; of the mysterious dealings of Providence in thus taking away a life that already in the bud gave promise of such eminent usefulness in riper manhood. Then they sang,

"How blest the righteous when he dies!"

And when they sang the last verse–

"So fades a summer cloud away;
So sinks the gale when storms are o'er;
So gently shuts the eye of day;
So dies a wave along the shore"—

Will thought that Death was not the grim, terrible spectre her childhood had fancied, for Dr. Golding made it so certain that Arthur was not dead, but only gone before, and they could almost see him standing on the other side, smiling, and beckoning them to follow. Then the soft air came in at the open windows, and gently rustled among the immortelles which the girls of the class had brought and laid on the rose-wood casket; while the tinkle of a distant sheep-bell and the cooing of doves in the forest-trees near the church completed the peacefulness of the scene. The class, walking two-and-two, led the procession to the grave, and, there parting, the bier was borne between the rows of young, uncovered heads, the usual burial-service was said, then the gray-haired sexton began to throw in the clods of earth, and their dull, hollow sound fell on bleeding hearts, just as it has ever fallen in years past, and will in years to come.

Dr. Golding rode home in the carriage with Will and Randolf. Will always felt as if she were in the presence of a saint when she was near him, and to-day she could almost see a halo around his venerable head as they left the graveyard and drove homeward. Not a word was spoken for some miles, for each was busy with his thoughts; finally Will said, suddenly,

"Dr. Golding?"

"Yes, my child," and the silvery head turned toward her with fatherly interest.

"How do we know that there is anything more of Arthur Dennison than that we put in the ground to-day?"

"In other words, you wish to ask what proofs there are of the immortality of the soul?"

"Yes, sir—whether there is any beyond, and how it can be proved outside of the Bible."

"That which comes first to my mind as an answer is, the indestructibility of force. We have all heard the ringing voice and seen the sparkling eye of him whom we followed to the grave to-day, and we have all loved and honored the mind and soul that were behind them; that force still lives somewhere, since it is indestructible."

"Yes, but does that prove that we have an individual existence, where we remember the things of the past?"

"No, not exactly; but let us see if we cannot find something that will touch that point. Take again the young life that has just gone from us, with its unfulfilled hopes and longings: does it seem reasonable to you that these should never have a chance to be satisfied or realized? Then take the millions whose lives are a perpetual struggle for bread, whose every aspiration has been crushed under the iron heel of poverty: can you believe that there is nothing brighter for them beyond—no place where their better selves, which now lie dormant, will bloom and expand under the genial warmth of a heavenly clime? Oh! there must be a real heaven for the poor, if for no others. You have had friends die, Miss Elliott, have you not?"

"Yes, sir."

"Do you think that your hopes and desires of seeing and loving them again have been given to you by some superior Being, that he may mock you with their fruitlessness in the end? It cannot be."

Nothing more was said, and they all again relapsed into silence, which was unbroken until the horses' hoofs resounded on the Ortonville pavements. Randolf was very tender and loving as he drew the robes around her, for fear the night-air would be chilly, and Will was happy in spite of her doubts concerning immortality. It seemed as if she could face any possibility with Randolf by her side. The idea of death was not pleasant, but then it was so far away, and would come only at the end of long years spent with the one she loved. The thought of any possibility more unpleasant than death did not enter her buoyant mind.

Not long after this, Randolf said to Will, one day: "I have an acquaintance here, a young lady, who is taking special studies; she is a particular friend of my younger sister, and as such, of course, I am bound to pay her some attention, and I want her to know you very soon. When will you go with me to call upon her?"

"Oh, 'most any evening."

So they went to see Helen Durant. Will found her a very gay young lady, of about her own age, with brilliant black eyes, and dark hair done up *à la mode*,* abounding in the most approved of society small-talk. Will felt that she was being weighed in the balance, as she several times found the black eyes trying to read her with a gaze full of curiosity, which was politely withdrawn when she saw that it was noticed. She felt kindly toward Miss Durant, because she was a friend of Randolf and his sister, but there was an inexplicable something that she did not like; the glances from the black eyes did not make her feel at ease, and there was something in the tone of voice that impressed her as not quite sincere.

The next time Randolf saw the young lady he asked, affecting indifference, how she liked Miss Elliott. She laughed as she said: "Isn't she funny?—so odd, I like to look at her and study her, as a naturalist would a rare specimen. She is magnificent, and all that, but, in my opinion, she is living a century or two in advance of her age, she is so ultra in everything. Of course, she believes in woman's rights?"

"Well, I don't really know, for I think she has modified her views since coming to college, and I take a little credit to myself for having brought it about," said Randolf.

*à la mode: In the current style.

"Ho, ho! she has been under your tutelage, has she? Now, really, that grows interesting; but I advise you to influence her to let her hair grow and wear her dresses longer."

Randolf's face flushed with vexation as he replied, quickly: "I would not have her style of dress changed at all; she is the most sensible girl I know."

"Oh, yes, indeed—sensible to the last degree, you know! and that is against her ever becoming a woman of society. She is splendid to talk to, but she is not such a one as a man would want for a wife—for no man wants to marry an oddity, you know; and, since the making a fine match is the chief thing in a woman's life, I call her style unfortunate."

Randolf's greatest weakness was a dread of ridicule, and it often had the effect of overmastering entirely, for the time being, his better judgment. In reply to Miss Durant's last assertion, however, he said, with warmth: "If you call it unfortunate to have a true heart, a fearless love of right, and unflinching courage in carrying out principles, then Miss Elliott is indeed unfortunate."

Poor Randolf! that was the bravest speech that he was destined to make for some time before his sister's friend, in defense of the woman he had asked to be his wife. After this first talk with her there was no difference in his treatment of Will, only, perhaps, he was more devoted than ever, as if to assure himself that criticism had made no difference in his feelings.

Miss Durant returned Will's call, and seemed very pleasant, but she always left an impression of insincerity, so that Will did not have any inclination to pursue the acquaintance further than exchanging formal calls.

Randolf said to her, once or twice, "Why don't you cultivate Miss Durant? You can learn a great deal from her that is useful, for she is a perfect lady of society;" and Will answered:

"I don't know why it is, Guilford, but I can't believe in her very much, and, somehow, I feel that she does not like me; in short, there is no congeniality between us whatever."

Once he ventured to say to her, when they were going out somewhere in the evening, "Why don't you wear your dresses long, as the rest do? And can't you contrive to put your hair up in some way, like the others?"

"Why, Guilford, you've told me so often that you liked my hair!" she said, looking at him in surprise.

"Yes, yes, I do; but it's odd, you know, and we owe it to society to conform to its ways."

"Well, I'll let it grow, if you like it better; but wouldn't it be well to wait, now, until the end of the year, for there will be an uncomfortable period when it is neither long nor short, and it will be quite unmanageable."

"Maybe it is best," he said, reluctantly, "but I should think you might contrive some way with a switch, as they call those things they pin on."

"Oh, but they are so heavy, Guilford, and make my head ache so!"

"Well, well, don't do anything that will make you wretched; but you can at least wear trains,*² like the others."

"I have such a horror of trains; I feel so crippled in them!"

"But we must conform to the rules of good society, and I hope, the next time we go out, you will wear a longer dress."

Will felt intuitively that Randolf had been listening to recent criticisms of her, and she said, with considerable feeling:

"You are an apt pupil of Miss Durant; she is always talking about conforming to the usages of society."

At the end of the first *semester's* work the president gave a reception to the senior class, as was his custom.³ The president's receptions were always regarded as the great affairs of the season, and, when the evening came, the brilliantly-lighted rooms were gay with the assembled beauty and fashion of Ortonville. Miss Durant was radiant in corn-colored silk, which glistened and shone beneath the folds of a black lace over-dress, looped and draped in an indescribable manner by elegant artificial flowers; her diamonds flashed in the gaslight, and her magnificent hair, gotten up after the latest Parisian mode, set off to advantage her really aristocratic face.

"You are most intensely yourself again to-night!" said Randolf, in a not unpleased tone, as he gave Will his arm at the door of the dressing-room.

She wore a white cashmere, cut square in the neck, and the lace around the throat softened her strongly-marked features. Her glorious head, free from "all the adulteries of art," was a marked contrast to the elaborate head-gear of the ladies in the parlors below. A gentle, pleased light shone in her eyes as Randolf's gaze rested on her, for she could see that he admired her, although he had so often remonstrated because she was not more like others.

---

*trains: An elongated part of a skirt that trails behind on the ground. Trains were especially fashionable in the 1870s and were worn by women in formal day and evening dress.

"Ah, there goes the *Valse à deux temps* and *Galop!** We are too late for it, and I am engaged for the next dance to Miss Durant," said Randolf.

"And I am engaged to Tomlinson," said Will.

"Seems to me you dance with him a great deal lately," replied Randolf, with a slight twinge of jealousy, as he remembered how Tomlinson had monopolized Will at Mrs. Foster's party, the week before.

"Yes, he says that he likes to waltz with me better than with any one else."

"He does? The villain! I'll fix him!" was the laughing reply, as they entered the parlor and were presented to the president and his lady.

After the waltz, while Tomlinson stood fanning her, Will glanced across the room to where Randolf and his partner were standing in earnest conversation before a small photographic copy of Nydia.†* Will noticed an expression on Miss Durant's face that she had never seen there before—a look of unconcealed devotion, of which, up to this time, she had not had the faintest hint. The truth flashed upon her: Helen Durant was in love with Randolf, and that was the reason of her dislike and continual criticism of herself. It is all so plain now; why had she not seen it before? She tried to see Randolf's face, but his back was toward her. She was so occupied with the thoughts that came with this new revelation, that she forgot her partner, who had been talking away to her very busily, while she said "yes" to everything mechanically, until Tomlinson showed himself injured by her evident abstraction and lack of interest in his conversation. Watching for a moment when she could go unnoticed, she stole out into the yard, for she wanted to get away from the lights and music, where she could be alone and think.

There was no snow, and she walked around the winding paths until the house was hidden by the evergreens. It was not moonlight, but the sky was very clear, and myriads of stars looked down upon her as she wandered on, unmindful of her slippered feet and uncovered head. She felt sorry for her rival, because she thought it must be hard to love any one and not have it returned; and she felt so certain to-night of Randolf's faithfulness to

---

Valse à deux temps and *Galop!*: Popular dances of the time. Valse à deux temps is a round dance in triple time, a waltz. The Galop, a lively dance in 2/4 time, was originally an independent dance but became part of a set of quadrilles.

†Nydia: From a scene inspired by a British novel, Nydia, the blind girl of Pompeii, was made famous as a marble sculpture by Randolph Rogers in 1860.

herself, that there was scarcely room for any feeling of jealousy. She could not pardon the way in which Miss Durant had tried to injure her in his eyes, yet she had great pity for her, which she could well afford to give, feeling sure that she herself stood first in his affections. Hearing voices, she stepped into a summer-house, which was still covered with dead vines and leaves, and where she could not be seen by those passing on the walk. As they came nearer, she recognized Miss Durant's laugh, and her heart leaped to her throat as she heard her own name spoken by that young lady.

Yes, it was she and Randolf, and they were talking about her. Would it be honorable to listen? She could not now get out unperceived, for they were very near, and she would not have Randolf see her wandering out there all alone, for he would be vexed at the impropriety.

They were talking very low and earnestly, and, when near the summer-house, paused before turning around.

"Yes, yes," said the girl, "she is very artistic, but so odd. Why don't you induce her to do and think as people of society do, since you have so much interest in her? It would be a missionary-work, really, Mr. Randolf."

Randolf answered, in a hurried and rather impatient tone:

"I don't see, really, Miss Durant, why you find so much fault with Will Elliott. She seems to have the benefit of all your excellent criticism. Are there no others whose style you can disapprove, and give her a rest for a while?"

The reply was in a still lower tone:

"It is my interest in you, Mr. Randolf, as the brother of my dearest friend, that makes me wish Miss Elliott were a different style of woman, for I know of your warm interest in her." Then assuming an air of raillery, she continued: "Imagine yourself, now, the husband of a woman like Miss Elliott!5 Bless me, wouldn't I like to see it! She would come home from her woman-suffrage conventions, where she had been presiding, and ask you how Johnny's whooping-cough was, and what you were going to have for dinner. You would have to turn your attention to domestic economy, for there must be one such in a well-regulated household, you know. By-the-way, if you want any recipes for cakes, custards, and such things, I shall be happy to supply you, after you have become well established as a housekeeper."

She had touched the weak point, which she always did when she resorted to ridicule. Will waited breathlessly for the reply, for she knew that the arrow had struck home.

"Miss Durant, your remarks seem to imply that my interest in Miss Elliott is more than that of a mere friend, and I now, once for all, beg to set you right on that point. I have a great respect for Miss Elliott as a girl of rare talent, but as to ever marrying her, the idea is absurd!"

He said this all in a hurried tone; then there was a low reply, as they started back again toward the house.

Will rubbed her hand slowly across her forehead, as if to assure herself that she was not dreaming; then she stepped out again into the starlight. How strange everything looked now! The very stars twinkled mockingly, and the waving pine-tops seemed to whisper to each other Randolf's last words, "The idea is absurd!"

It had only been a few minutes since she left the parlor, and yet it seemed so long. She felt ten years older as she slowly ascended the stone steps; her face is very white and her lips are tightly closed. They were going to dance the Lancers,* and she had promised to be Randolf's partner, but she could not do it now. She never wanted to see him or take his hand or touch his arm again. Seeing Nell in the conservatory, chatting with Phelps, she went to her and whispered:

"Won't you please ask Charlie to take me home quick?—my head aches so!"

Nell looked in surprise at the pleading face, and, seeing that she really was suffering, replied:

"Certainly; and I must go, too, and get something for your head."

"No, I want you to take my place in the Lancers, and excuse me to my partner and escort. Do not feel alarmed; I'll be better in the morning," she said, trying to look cheerful.

So Charlie took her home, and left her with many regrets on account of the headache, though he felt sure that something had happened between her and Randolf, for he had a wonderful way of knowing things without being told.

Randolf's feelings, after he had denied his love for Will to Miss Durant, were those of a traitor; and yet he did not hasten to correct the impression made upon her, but listened silently to her playful congratulations as they walked toward the house. He thought, "I'll go down to-morrow and tell her the whole truth, and she can sneer as much as she pleases," and thus he satisfied his conscience for the moment; and it was with his usual

---

*the Lancers: A type of quadrille; also the music proper to this dance.

composure of manner that he came in, and went to find Will for the Lancers. He was a little startled when Nell met him and delivered Will's message, but the real cause, of course, did not cross his mind; and, with some expression of anxiety in regard to her health, he gave his arm to Nell and led her to their place in the quadrille.*

The next morning he went to call on Will, and was met by the servant with a note addressed in her well-known hand. What could it mean? Was she too sick to see him? It had never happened so before. He turned to go, and opened the note as he stood on the steps. It said:

"Mr. Randolf:" ["By Hercules, that's cool!"] "I cannot see you any more, so please do not take the trouble to call for me. Your book of logarithms I'll send by Charlie. Wilhelmine Elliott."

He tore a blank leaf from the "Oedipus Tyrannus" that he had brought to translate with her for Monday's lesson,† and wrote:

"For God's sake, Will, what do you mean? Can't I see you a moment? I must—you owe it to me! I'll wait in the parlor."

Maggie, the Irish servant-girl, looked very much interested as she took the note from the hand of the young man, who bade her take it instantly to Miss Elliott, and wait for an answer. It came:

"No further words will be needed, when I tell you that, by an accident, I was in the summer-house last night when you and Miss Durant walked by. Do not take the trouble to explain, for my mother-tongue needs no translation. W. E."

Here was a new situation for Guilford Randolf, and a painful one; for, when out of reach of Miss Durant's fire of sarcasm, he loved Will as devotedly as when he had carried her in his arms to the log-house during the thunderstorm. Now, in the clear light of this Saturday morning, he had felt so strong—had vowed that no woman should ever say another word against Will in his presence. Will's figure had flitted before him, too, when he first awoke, in white cashmere with the soft lace. The classic head, and, above all, the unassuming manners, in striking contrast to the affection of

---

*quadrille: A square dance, of French origin, usually performed by four couples. It contains five sections, or figures, each of which is a complete dance in itself. It is also called a set of quadrilles.

†"Oedipus Tyrannus": Greek tragedy by Sophocles about a powerful and wealthy king whose pride brings ruin and dishonor upon him. In Randolf's hands, it is intended to mirror his own fall from grace.

other girls, never appeared to him so lovely as now, in this mental picture the morning after the party; and he was impatient for nine o'clock to come, that he might take his books and spend the forenoon bending over them with her by his side. Now, it was all dashed to the ground, and worse than that: he stood in the light of a deceiver and liar in the eyes of one who, he knew, scorned any compromise of truth in word or deed. He read the note slowly several times, as if to find some other meaning less hard and unbearable; but the decided, bold hand could only be read in one way, and each word stood out almost in relief against the white paper, like the very sentence of doom. He took his books and left the house.

CHAPTER XI

End of the Preparation.—
Beginning of the Career

"Large interests keep the soul free; like the great ocean-
currents which interchange the climates of the globe, they
balance the nature and modify all excess."
—*Anon*.

When the second *semester* began, Will elected her studies without
consulting any one except Nell. She secretly hoped that Randolf would
not be in the same classes, for then she would rarely see him, and that, she
thought, would be a great relief. She decided to take history and analytical
chemistry, and she kept on with Greek and Latin. When she went into
Professor Roemer's room to get the list of historical questions, the first one
she saw was Randolf, who had come for the same purpose. "Why, of
course," she thought, "I might have known he would take history! And
maybe, after all, it is a little cowardly for me to be unwilling to meet him
in recitations."

Nell took chemistry also, and they made themselves large aprons, and
engaged tables at the laboratory side by side. The first morning, when they
were arranging the bottles on the shelves and washing test-tubes, Will
glanced across to the next row, and on a card above one of the tables she
saw Randolf's name, which meant that he had engaged it for work. It was
rather a coincidence that Randolf should have chosen practical chemistry
too, and she was more amused than annoyed at the fact that their tables
were so situated that she would see the back of his head whenever she
looked up. Randolf had chosen a course in toxicology as a probable help in
his future work, so that Will's motives and his were the same in electing
work in the laboratory; for she had returned to her original intention of
studying medicine, and for this a course in chemistry was the first requisite.

Will had not spoken to him since the reception, and had returned his notes unopened.

One day, in the history-class, the topic for discussion was the policy of the Tudors.* The class was resolved into a kind of debating-club, of which the professor was president, and the questions were all historical. Each day some one was appointed to present the question in the form of an essay, giving at the same time his or her own views, after which each member was expected to speak, and either approve or condemn the essayist. This time it was Randolf's turn to open the discussion, and he read an essay in which he defended the mendacious policy of Elizabeth—that policy by which, as a recent historian says, she hoodwinked the statesmen of Europe for fifty years.† He contended that the security of England and the prosperity of her reign were brought about by her artfulness, and he praised the duplicity which in another would have seemed a mere vice.

When he was through, the professor turned to Will with a smile, and said: "I see that your view is somewhat different from Mr. Randolf's, Miss Elliott; will you favor us with it?"

She arose, and, looking steadily at Randolf, said: "Mr. President, I cannot listen calmly to a defense of lying. I believe that lies, either political or social, are wholly evil; and it pains me to hear a classmate, usually distinguished by his championship of everything that is noble, thus defend a wrong. Perhaps *he* has never suffered from the effects of a lying tongue, that he so eloquently pleads its usefulness. In spite of the brilliancy, eloquence, and dash of this celebrated queen, her falsehoods, as well as those of less distinguished women, were her weakness, and not her strength. I believe that Elizabeth's strength lay in a different direction. It was her real love for her people and her deep sense of their dependence upon her, and an overruling purpose to bring about their good, which was the basis of her policy; and it was this loyalty to her people that was the main-spring of the prosperity of her reign."

She went on at some length with growing enthusiasm, to the great

*the Tudors: The royal family of England from 1485 to 1603, beginning with Henry VII and ending with the reign of Queen Elizabeth I (1558–1603). The ascension of the Tudors to the throne marked the beginning of major religious and political reform in England.

†the mendacious policy of Elizabeth: Will uses the debate over Queen Elizabeth's foreign policy as a metaphor for Randolf's betrayal of her to Miss Durant. In other words, while Randolf lauds deceit as an inventive means to an end, Will argues that loyalty and love are the only true strength.

delight of the class, who always felt sure of something good when Will grew interested in a discussion.

Randolf was rather pleased than otherwise that she had thus taken him up, although he winced under her allusions; for anything almost was easier to bear than the cool, total indifference with which she lately regarded him. He wondered if she would not speak to him about the discussion after class, but she sat down; and when they were dismissed her face wore again a look of haughtiness, so that he did not dare to be the first to break the silence.

Do not think that, because Will entered into her college-work with apparent enthusiasm, the experience through which she had just passed was anything but a most trying one, and one that required all her strength of character to endure. To give up her bright dreams of the future, that she was to have spent with Randolf, cost her many a struggle, for she had loved him with all the warmth of her impulsive nature.

Almost an equal source of pain was the disappointment that arose, on finding that one whom she had believed to be true was false at heart; for, although she knew Randolf's weakness, she could not think that his dread of ridicule could ever have led him to deny his love for her in that way, if he had loved her truly. She determined, by throwing her soul into her work, to forget her disappointment; and she hailed with joy the return of the old enthusiasm as she was introduced to the mysteries of the laboratory, and delved among the musty volumes of the library to look up references on historical questions.

Several weeks after the discussion in the history-class, Will was working diligently in the laboratory, one afternoon, over her little boxes of "unknowns." She was looking for iodine, that she felt sure was in one of them, but the test would not bring it out clearly enough until she had tried several times. Finally she held up the test-tube in great glee, exclaiming, "See, Nell, there it is—there are the purple globules!" and she tapped the tube with her finger, to see them rise and fall. Hearing no reply, she glanced at Nell's table, which was all cleared up, as they were accustomed to leave them for the day, and her hat and cloak were gone. Why, to be sure—Nell had told her that she must go at four, and now it was after five. Only a few scattered ones were left, who, like herself, were working over puzzling boxes, and could not bear to leave them unsolved.

Just then there came a crash of shattered glass, but as that was a very common sound in the laboratory, she did not even take the trouble to look around to see whence it came, but hurriedly emptied the tube, and began to clear away her table.

Soon she heard a suppressed groan, and, on looking across to the opposite row, she saw Randolf leaning against his table, looking deathly pale, while he tried with his handkerchief to stanch the blood flowing from his arm.

A glass retort with which he had been working had burst with great violence, and a piece of the glass had been driven into his wrist, severing the radial artery. Will was by his side in an instant. She knew that the first thing was to stop the flow of blood; so, pressing her fingers tightly over the wound, she held it while she called to some ladies at the farther side of the room, who were in the pharmaceutical department, and who had also remained later than usual. They came hurriedly; but one, seeing the pool of crimson that had already begun to coagulate on the table, became faint, and was obliged to go away, while the other helped Will to tear her apron into strips, which she tied around the arm, drawing the knots with all her strength. Then they supported him to an old sofa that stood near the entrance, having already dispatched Thomas, the janitor, for Dr. Jewitt, whose office was in the next block. He came puffing in, and, on examining the bandaging, asked:

"Who did this?"

"I did my best at it, sir," said Will.

"Well done! well done!" and, as he proceeded to make a ligature preparatory to tying the artery, he added, "You have saved his life by your prompt action, Miss Elliott."

"This is my first surgical operation, doctor. Do you think that I will be a disgrace to the profession if I study hard?" asked Will, laughingly.

"Do you really intend to study medicine?" he asked, pausing a moment in his work, while he looked at her in surprise.

"Yes, sir."

"I am heartily glad of it, and I welcome you to our ranks," he said, cordially.

When it was all done, and the wounded arm carefully adjusted in a sling, the doctor said he would take Randolf home in his carriage, as he was yet very weak from loss of blood. When she could help no more, Will turned to go, and had almost reached the door, when Randolf raised himself on his elbow, and called:

"Wi—Miss Elliott!" but his voice was weak, and she did not hear.

"Miss Elliott!" shouted the doctor, "this young man has something to say to you;" and, suddenly remembering that he had some business at the other end of the room, the good doctor strode away, muttering, "It's plain enough that young man is in love with her; his pulse was quicker whenever she came near. I guess her practice of medicine will be limited to one household."

It was with great reluctance and embarrassment that Will came back. She had sprung to his rescue without a thought of anything but saving life, but now, when that excitement was over, the old personal feeling of wrong returned, and made it very hard for her to turn and go toward the sofa to hear what Randolf wished to say, and she was sorry that Dr. Jewitt had left them alone. Randolf's pale face flushed as Will came near, and he said, in a low voice:

"I thank you, Will—I beg your pardon!—Miss Elliott. I—I did not deserve this from you, and I—"

"Oh, I should have done it for any one; there was nothing personal in it," she said, with a shade of sarcasm in her voice.

Randolf would have given worlds if he could, then and there, have had a reconciliation with her and have obtained her forgiveness; but there was something in her manner that made it impossible to utter the words of affection and remorse that sprang to his lips.

Will, on the other hand, while she looked at the handsome, boyish face, knew that she loved him as truly as ever; but, not being willing to betray any weakness, she choked the feeling, and her pride helped her to assume an air of indifference, while she said:

"If I can be of any assistance in a professional way, Mr. Randolf, I hope you will let me know," and, without another word, she left the room.

Randolf fell back upon the pillow with a hopeless groan, as he murmured:

"I have lost her! She seems so far away, that, while I look at her, the words freeze on my lips. And yet," he gasped, as with sudden energy he arose and staggered across the room to the window, hoping to get another glimpse of her, "she shall know that I am true, if it takes my whole life to prove it."

The doctor came up at the moment, and said:

"How's this? You'll start that to bleeding again if you are not quiet."

He saw that it was some mental trouble that caused Randolf's agitation, and he only said, as he helped him into the carriage, "Don't worry yourself into a fever, for the arm will be all right in a few days."

Randolf was put to bed, according to the doctor's orders, and soon fell into a troubled, restless sleep, in which the gay figures of an evening party flitted before him. Among them were two whom he recognized: one with black eyes and flashing jewels, who stood talking to him; the other with frank, happy eyes, that looked confidingly into his as she passed and repassed in the figures of the dance, her loveliness of form and complexion set off by the soft folds of her white dress. He was blinded for a moment by a flash from the black eyes, and when he again looked for the trustful face it was no longer there; but instead was the stern, proud form of an injured woman, whose glance seemed to chill his very soul. Then he awoke, unrefreshed and feverish, to find his arm out of the sling, and his chum asking, "What under the canopy are you dreaming about, that you thrash around so?"

It was drawing on, now, toward the end of the term, and each senior was beginning to wonder how life would seem outside of college. Some would immediately go into professional study, some into mercantile life, while a large proportion expected to teach, as a stepping-stone to some other life-work. Clara was going as a missionary to South Africa,*[1] under the auspices of the Methodist Church; one of the girls intended to study law with her father; Nell was to be married; and Will was looking eagerly forward to the study of medicine, and her return, the next year, to the university for that purpose.

One day she came into Nell's room, and threw an open letter upon the table saying, "Read it, Nell; my plans are upset, as usual," and she paced the floor in an excited manner. The letter was from her uncle, who had been appointed her guardian at her father's death, and who still continued to manage her finances. It said:

"My dear Niece: The enterprise in which, with your consent, I had invested your money, has failed on account of financial pressure. It sweeps away your little fortune, and I am left worse still, being many thousands in debt. It is with the greatest sorrow that I write you this, for I know of your plans for the future, and would gladly have saved you this disappointment had I been able.

"Your affectionate uncle,

"John Elliott."

*missionary: No longer limited to married women, missionary work in foreign countries for the Methodist Church was part of an ever-expanding woman's sphere.

"Poor Uncle John! My trouble is small compared with his, because he has a large family depending upon him!" said Will.

"You will not let it discourage you so that you will give up medicine, will you?" asked Nell. "Just think of your glorious health, and now splendid education! With far less material many have worked their way to success and distinction."

"I ought to be ashamed, that is true, to be so easily discouraged; I was intending to go right on without stopping, you know, but I can teach, or do something, and it will only postpone the medicine;[2] for I am determined to put it through, in spite of the frowns of Dame Fortune."

The only honor conferred by the University of Ortonville for scholarship and general standing was an appointment to speak on commencement-day. The faculty were accustomed to select ten from each graduating-class for this purpose; but from a class like that of '70 it was a difficult task to choose ten who stood preëminently superior to all the others, and were therefore entitled to the honor of being asked to speak. The class had, as freshmen, contained one hundred and fifty members; but, as the years had passed, they had dropped out from one cause or another, until now, a month before graduation, the number was one hundred and fifteen men and five women. Probably there was not a man in the class who did not feel sure of getting an appointment, for each one thought that the faculty could not be so blind as to overlook his merits.

There was much laying of wagers among the boys as to who the lucky ones would be, and the excitement grew more intense as the last of May approached, for that was the day for the announcements. The boys all felt sure that Will Elliott would be one of the speakers, and they did not see how they could fairly take more than one girl, when the number of girls was so small in proportion. The work of deciding the rival claims of one hundred and twenty ambitious students might have appalled any ordinary body of men; but the faculty of the University of Ortonville *was* no ordinary body, so it undertook it with the full assurance that justice would be meted out to the expectant scores. Each student, on the other hand, was ready to uphold the decision of the faculty if he were one of the chosen, and ready, on the contrary, to be sorely injured if he were not among the elect.

On the evening of the 31st of May the August body convened, and the next morning Jacob, the postman, was almost mobbed by the boys as he took the letters to the office; but he withstood their assaults by a judicious use of his cane. The letters reached their destination, and were ready to be taken from the hand of the postmaster in the orthodox way.

At noon Nell burst into the room with:

"Oh, Will, there is your faculty-letter! You're the only girl that got one, and I'm so glad they have taken you! You will represent the girls splendidly! We'll all be so proud of you, for you are such a magnificent speaker!"

Will listened to this torrent of compliments with remonstrance, as she opened the letter and read:

"Miss Wilhelmine Elliott has been chosen by the faculty as one of the speakers for Commencement,[3] and she is requested to report at once at the president's room, No. 9.

"Signed, by order of the faculty,

"James Morrison, *Secretary*."

"I don't deserve it any more than the rest of the girls; and, besides, how can I do it? Won't they excuse me, Nell?" and Will leaned her head wearily upon her hand.

"Excuse you! I should think not. Why, it will be *the* thing of the day— the only lady! And all the girls are so glad that they've taken you, for the rest of us could not do it at all. No, indeed; you must hold up the cause of the girls by making one of your masterly strokes. But why don't you ask who your distinguished company is to be—the other fortunate nine? You have no curiosity at all."

"Well, who are they?"

"Oh, Randolf, of course—and Charlie, Pendleton, Hooker, and I don't remember the others. Now, what are you going to write about?"

"I'm sure I don't know. What do they expect in a Commencement-speech?"

"Oh, don't take the Union of the Saxon Heptarchy, nor the Rise of the Dutch Republics, nor the Fall of the Roman Empire. Take some topic of the day, into which you can throw your whole heart."

"Well, since you girls wish it, I'll try and do my best," said Will, as she folded the letter mechanically and laid it on the table.

. . . .

It is now the Sunday evening before Commencement, and Will is lying on the sofa in the parlor, while Nell is playing snatches from Haydn to her in the twilight. The soft June air and the breath of roses came in at the window, just as they did a year ago.

"Nell, do you remember you stayed at home from church one night last June, to talk to me?"

"Yes, I remember;" and she came again and sat beside the sofa. "Do you want me to stay with you to-night?"

"Yes, please; I want to have one more talk with you before we go, and the last few days there will be such a rush that I will not be able to have you alone."

"Have you decided what you will do when college closes?" asked Nell.

"Yes, I have been offered a position in Wisconsin as instructor in Greek and Latin, and I am to go there immediately on the close of college. Do you know, that fine position at Colton, that was offered me, they refused to let me have when they found that I did not belong to any church, and I hear they have given it to Roberts; he is a member of the Episcopal Church, you know."[4]

"To Roberts!" echoed Nell. "Why, he has ponied right through every recitation since he came to college,*[5] and he has no standing among the boys at all."

"Oh, well, I'm well enough satisfied as it is, and I'm glad I'm not to go there," said Will.

"Is your mother willing for you to go off so far alone?"

"Yes, mother is very considerate; and she has confidence in me, I guess, that I will do about right."

"I'm glad that your mother understands you better now," said Nell. "I used to be sorry for you when you told me how you were opposed in your religious beliefs."

"Yes, that is all over now; but, Nell," and her voice grew sad and bitter, "I don't believe much in anything now; I don't believe there is a loving God who feels sorry when we suffer. If I believe in any almighty Power, it is in one who delights in our wretchedness—who loves to make us trust in people, and then show us how foolish we are to do so. You are the only hold I have on truth and goodness, and soon you will be gone—then I'll have nothing," and she clung to her as if it were, indeed, the last good-bye.

"Will, dear, you must not talk so! it is dreadful—it makes me shudder!"

Will had never mentioned Randolf's name since the reception, and,

---

*ponied: To use secretly a literal translation of a foreign text in preparing or reciting lessons. In this context, ponying was considered to be a form of cheating, getting by on someone else's work or using a cheat sheet.

although Nell understood it all in a general way, she knew nothing of the particulars.

"Don't you want to tell your old Nell all about it?" she asked, coaxingly, thinking that it would be a relief to her feelings to talk it over, instead of keeping it so closely to herself, and affecting indifference.

"Yes, I can tell *you*"; and, nestling her head on Nell's shoulder, she told all the incidents of the reception, from the time she left Randolf at the parlor-door until his conversation with Miss Durant. Her voice was calm and steady through the whole narration until she came to Randolf's last words, "The idea is absurd!" when her lips quivered, as she said, "I don't want to hide anything from you, Nell, and I know it is very weak, but I love him as much as ever, and I'm afraid I always will"; and, burying her face in Nell's lap, she gave way to a passionate flood of tears. Nell did not try to check this outburst of grief, but waited quietly until the sobs became less frequent, when she raised the bowed head, and, holding it close against her cheek, said:

"I think that you are just a little unfair in not giving Guilford a chance to explain."

"Do you think that I could ever believe him again?" cried Will, flashing up, while all the time Nell's words only echoed a hope in her own heart that somehow, after all, he might be made to appear less blameworthy.

"You must remember what a jealous woman can do when she determines to; and I have no doubt but that woman's tongue has been like a fly-blister to Randolf, and in a moment of irritation he said that for which he would feel the most bitter remorse. You know how impulsive he is."

Will listened to this with a secret feeling of satisfaction, while at the same time her pride would not allow her to admit, even to herself, the possibility of an explanation. Nell told her of talk that she had heard among the girls, that Miss Durant was in love with Randolf, and how it was believed that she came to college with the intention of breaking his engagement with Will. Then their conversation turned upon Commencement-day, and Nell asked:

"Have you finished your speech?—and what is it about?"

"I took 'Women in the Professions.'"[6]

"Good! I knew you would choose something that would take well with an audience."

"That is a subject upon which I have thought a good deal since I took up the idea of medicine; but I dread to speak, and I don't have the enthusiasm about it that I ought to have."

"That will come with the occasion, and we are all expecting you to cover us with glory, as a representative college-girl, you know."

Never did June sunshine play over a greener campus, and never were June skies more soft than on the Commencement-day of the class of '70.[7] Long before ten o'clock seniors might have been seen hurrying to and fro, big with importance; while the gay uniforms of the band, who were to supply music for the occasion, gave a holiday-air to the scene.

The large hall was rapidly filled, for every one in Ortonville was anxious to attend the exercises, and especially to see the first girls graduate.

There was to be no distinctive salutatory or valedictory, and the speakers were to be taken in alphabetical order; but, as Will was the only lady, she was allowed to select her own place on the programme, and she chose to come about the middle of the list. When the programmes were distributed, the exclamations and remarks were something as follows:

"Ah! we have one girl-speaker, Wilhelmine Elliott. Who is she?"

"Oh, she is a sort of brilliant oddity—very talented—a splendid scholar! I used to hear of her often when she was a freshman. She thought nothing of taking her gun and bringing in a brace of quail for breakfast. There is a sort of romance about her lately, but I do not know how true it is. They say one of her classmates fell in love with her, and, because he did not like it, she gave up her gun and made concessions to society for his sake; but something came between them, and now she has gone off on a tangent about studying medicine, and they don't even speak to each other. There she is now!" said he, as the procession entered, the girls coming first, "the tall, handsome one on the right. What a superb head she has! Let me see, what is her subject?—

'Women in the Professions.' Whew! that will be 'woman's rights,' of course."

The ten speakers passed into the waiting-room at the back of the stage, upon which the faculty had already arranged themselves. The band played a spirited air, and the day began.

The anticipation of the audience seemed to centre around Will's name, and curiosity was on tiptoe as, after the music which came between the speeches, she advanced to the front of the stage. She was dressed in black, with only roses for ornament; and as she came forward there was a modest,

Class of '75, in front of Haven Hall, 1875. "There she is now!" said he, as the procession entered, the girls coming first, "the tall, handsome one on the right. What a superb head she has!" Although Olive Anderson stood out at her graduation as the only woman commencement speaker, she is less conspicuous in her class portrait. (Bentley Historical Library, University of Michigan, BL003640.)

half-timid air about her, very becoming to her girlish face and form, which won the hearts of the audience before she opened her lips.

Those who expected from the subject a torrent of invective against the "gray preminence of man" were disappointed, for it was only a calm, earnest argument for an "open career for talent." She made it appear so suitable, and even desirable, by her clearness of statement and straightforward eloquence, that women should occupy places in the professions hitherto monopolized by men, that even the sternest opponents of such a movement yielded to the spell, and acknowledged, for the moment, the truth of her conclusions. She won her hearers not more by her words than by the richness and pathos of her voice. There was in it a sympathetic quality which could only have come from a deep personal feeling. The experience of the last six months had, unconsciously to herself, developed the tender part of her nature, which only those realized who knew her best.

Randolf made a brilliant and effective speech on the "Hellenism of Modern Thought." His was the last.[8]

Then came the conferring of degrees, a short address from the president, and one hundred and twenty B.A.'s and B.S.'s were given to the world, for better or worse.

An admiring crowd of friends gathered around Will for congratulations, but she prized, more than all, the words of affection that came from the girls in the class, and she felt repaid when they expressed their unbounded satisfaction with her speech.

"Where are all your bouquets?" asked Nell.

"They are in the waiting-room, and I am going to send some one to carry them home; but there is one basket that I must carry myself," and she went to get it.

The basket in question was one that had been arranged with the most exquisite flowers by her classmates, and she did not want to trust it in any hands but her own. As she stood a moment inhaling the fragrance that came from the mass of flowers, there was a hurried step on the stairs, the door opened, and Randolf stood before her.

"They say you are going away to-night, Will. You cannot deny me a last word. I must have a chance to redeem myself; I must know there is hope for me."

"Guilford Randolf," she said, looking steadily in his face, "you have been the cause of the happiest and the most wretched moments of my life; and now, to-day, when I was beginning to realize that there may be pleasure aside from living with and for you, when I was learning to forget you, it was cruel for you to come and bring up again the past that is so painful!"

There was something in her voice that gave him encouragement in spite of the bitterness of her words.

"God knows your words are just, Will, but not merciful. I can scarcely dare hope to be taken back to the place I once held, but I want you to believe that I am true at heart—that in a hasty moment I said something that I would gladly have wiped out with my life's blood. Do you believe me?"

The longing to be reconciled to him almost over-mastered her; but pride, and a yet lingering suspicion of his truth—the one sentiment she could never reconcile with love—struggled still.

Her trembling lip and pale face showed to the young man how intense this struggle was; but this only aroused his fears that, after all, he should lose her.

"Do you believe me?" he repeated, passionately, as he caught her hand, that rested upon the basket of flowers she was holding.

"I want to believe you, Guilford," she said, looking steadily into his eyes.

"You must, you shall, believe me! You must not go out of the reach of my hope. Will you?"

"I am going away to teach—going into a distant State, where you would not care to come. Good-by!" she said, gently withdrawing her hand from his grasp.

"No, I will not say 'good-by.' I will follow you until you can again give me the place I lost by my dastardly conduct. Don't be unmerciful, Will! You will write to me?"

"Yes," she said, frankly, now offering him her hand, but this time she did not dare to meet his eyes. Then she hurried after Nell and Clara, who were still waiting for her below.

That evening a little group stood on the platform of the railway-station, bending to catch the last glimpse of a disappearing train. Among them are Mr. and Mrs. Lewis, Nell, and Clara.

"May the Lord bless her!" said Mr. Lewis, dashing something like a tear from his eye.

"Well," said Clara, "that's the last we will see of Will Elliott, until she comes out a splendid physician."

"She is a dear girl," said Nell, "and will be splendid, whatever she does."

"Bless my soul, does that girl think she is going to study medicine?" said Mr. Lewis, with an amused laugh. "If she don't marry that pair of handsome eyes that used to be forever coming to study off the same book with her, I'll miss my guess!"

"Oh!" said Mrs. Lewis, "you men are so conceited! You think a woman never has an aim in life that she won't leave to go at your beck and call. I have more faith in our Will than that, and we'll see if I'm not right."

The next year other girls were in the upper rooms of Mr. Lewis's house in Clinton Avenue, but for a long time the old people thought that there could be no girls like those of '70.

The end.

Note from the Editors

In editing this novel, we have corrected all identifiable typographical errors from the original printed version. We have tried to identify every writer and piece of literature or source of a quotation; we also noted the few we were unable to identify. We have explained contemporary idiomatic expressions. We have sought in the annotations to illuminate the educational context at the University of Michigan in the 1870s and to relate events and people in the university's history to Anderson's experience.

We owe a debt of gratitude to several individuals who helped us with this project. Classicist Claude Nicholas Pavur, S.J., helped us track down the quotation from Terence in chapter III. Jamie Schmid of the Saint Louis University library, Nancy Baird of the Western Kentucky University library, and W. Eric Nelson assisted with other obscure searches. Carolyn Reitz and Karen Manners Smith gave intelligent and helpful readings of the introduction. An early consultation with James Reische of the University of Michigan Press led us to LeAnn Fields, who believed in this project from the start. Allison Liefer of the press provided us with a digitized version of the novel, which made our editing much easier than it might have been. We appreciate the constructive advice given by the press's anonymous reviewers of the original proposal. The Bordin/Gillette Researcher Travel Fellowship facilitated a trip to the Bentley Historical Library at the University of Michigan, where we found many previously unexploited primary sources. Karen L. Jania and William K. Wallach of the Bentley were especially helpful. Profound thanks to you all!

—Elisabeth Israels Perry and Jennifer Ann Price

Notes

CHAPTER I

1. In January 1870, the Board of Regents voted five to three in favor of the following resolution: "Resolved. That in the opinion of the Board no rule exists in any of the University statutes which excludes women from admission to the University." *Proceedings of the Board of Regents (1864–1870), University of Michigan*, 326, Bentley Historical Library, University of Michigan (hereafter *Proceedings, 1864–1870*).

2. In her twenty-page manuscript memorial, Sarah Dix Hamlin gives 1854 as Anderson's birth year. This cannot be right, as *The Chronicle*, the University of Michigan's student newspaper, lists Anderson's age as twenty-two years nine months at the time of her graduation in 1875, putting her birthday around September 30, 1852. Anderson was almost nineteen years old when she entered the University of Michigan in the fall of 1871. Sarah Dix Hamlin, "Olive San Louie Anderson, Class of '75, Obituary" (June 5, 1886), Sarah Dix Hamlin Paper, Bentley Historical Library, University of Michigan (hereafter Hamlin Paper, 1886, BHL); "Statistics of the Class of Seventy-Five, University of Michigan," *The Chronicle* 6, no. 18 (July 3, 1875): 211.

3. Calvinism provides the foundational theology of the Congregational, Reformed, and Presbyterian churches in America. Calvinists relied strictly on scripture as the foundation for Christian faith and practice. The Synod of Dort (1618–19) defined the five points of Calvinism as follows: "(1) humanity is by nature totally depraved and unable to merit salvation; (2) some people are unconditionally elected by God's saving grace; (3) God's atonement in Christ is limited in its efficacy to the salvation of the elect; (4) God's transforming grace, ministered by the Holy Spirit, is irresistible on the part of humanity; (5) the saints must persevere in faith to the end, but none of the elect can finally be lost." Daniel G. Reid, ed., *Dictionary of Christianity in America* (Downers Grove, Ill.: InterVarsity Press, 1990), 211.

4. Anderson had an older sister, whose illness "so absorbed the mother's attention that [Anderson] was allowed to grow up very much as she pleased." Hamlin Paper, 1886, BHL.

5. Writing to a university regent in 1870 regarding the search for a new university president, Dr. Benjamin F. Cocker, Professor of Moral and Mental Philosophy at the University of Michigan, voiced a similar fear of "irreligion." "You are no doubt aware," he wrote, "we have a few men here who will not rest until the University is dissevered, both in name and in fact, from all religion that has any claim to evangelical character. . . . This would be a great calamity. . . . Perhaps I am too much alarmed, and there is no immediate danger. But with the popular agitation just now to exclude the Bible from

schools and colleges, I fear that a movement to give us a President disconnected with the Church, might prevail." B. F. Cocker to Regent Edward Carey Walker, September 18, 1870, Folder: 1870, Edward Carey Walker Correspondence, BHL.

6. Boarding schools taught such subjects as etiquette, painting, French, and music. They were not meant to be institutions of higher learning equal to those of young men. In 1809, The Philadelphia Academy for Young Ladies considered "The modesty and amiableness of . . . the well-bred woman" should never be sacrificed to "the affectation and conceit of scholastic attainments." Indeed, "it should be her constant study to avoid an ostentatious display of the decorations of her mind." By 1878, the reputation of such boarding schools had not changed. Dorothy Gies McGuigan, *A Dangerous Experiment: 100 Years of Women at the University of Michigan* (Ann Arbor: University of Michigan Press, 1970), 11.

7. The Industrial Revolution brought with it a spatial division of labor between most middle-class men and women. Women tended to stay home to mind domestic concerns and men went to work outside the home. This division of labor became so embedded in the culture as to seem natural. Limited mostly to the home, woman's sphere also included some limited public roles in churches, charities, and schools, where women's presumed moral superiority and nurturing qualities could serve society well.

8. Catechisms are usually set out in the form of questions and answers designed to make doctrine more easily taught and committed to memory by those seeking Confirmation or Baptism. The Westminster Catechism was just one of the several brought to America by English and other European settlers. It began with a brief introductory summary of what it meant to be a Christian, then moved on to explanations of the Apostles' Creed, the Ten Commandments, the Lord's Prayer, and the meaning of the sacraments. Reid, *Dictionary of Christianity in America,* 231.

9. Stripped of his divinity, Renan's Jesus was the hero of a powerful sentimental narrative about a man who triumphed over adversity through suffering, resignation, and pure love. Considered heretical at the time, Renan's Jesus reflected the skeptical mood of the day regarding traditional religious faith, as well as Anderson's own religious feelings, with which she imbued her character Will Elliott.

CHAPTER II

1. *Proceedings of the Board of Regents (1870–1876) University of Michigan,* BHL (hereafter *Proceedings, 1870–1876*), 76.

2. The traditional rivalry between freshmen and sophomores renewed itself each academic year. Although the competition rarely moved beyond good-natured baiting and contests, the two classes occasionally brawled. Later in the century these spontaneous skirmishes became more ritualized. Lawrence R. Veysey, *The Emergence of the American University* (Chicago: University of Chicago Press, 1965), 282–83.

3. Many Ann Arbor women kept student boarders as a means of earning income without having to leave home. Nevertheless, they were reluctant to take in the university's first female students. Ruth Bordin, *Women at Michigan: The "Dangerous Experiment," 1870s to the Present* (Ann Arbor: University of Michigan Press, 1999), 12–13.

4. The lisping, grinning servant boy may derive from blackface minstrelsy. The

grin on the boy's face suggests the social mask that most African Americans learned to wear in the presence of whites (especially white women) as part of a survival technique. Here, though, Anderson has thrown in a stock minstrel character to administer the final humiliation in Will's initial search for a place to live. See Eric Lott, *Love and Theft: Blackface Minstrelsy and the American Working Class* (New York: Oxford University Press, 1993).

5. As Madelon Stockwell, the University of Michigan's first female student, relates in a letter to Lucinda Stone: "The young men of my class were, without exception, very kind to me throughout the course. But this I can hardly say of the young women of Ann Arbor during the first few months after I entered. I once attended a senior party of about two hundred, and not a woman except the hostess and her daughter spoke to me during the whole evening. The members of the senior class, however, seemed very kindly disposed, and by their agreeableness atoned as they could for the slights offered me by the other side." Mary Louise Hall Walker noted, "there were a few noble women in Ann Arbor at that time, who at the risk of losing caste, always befriended University girls." Belle McArthur Perry, *Lucinda Hinsdale Stone: Her Life Story and Reminiscences* (Detroit: Blinn Publishing Co., 1902), 116–17; Mary Louise Hall Walker, "Early Days of Co-Education," *The Inlander*, April 1895, 278.

6. A young woman traditionally stored away family heirlooms, special handmade linens and clothes, and other precious and personal domestic articles in preparation for marriage. Sometimes these articles (her "trousseau") would be kept in a special trunk, or "hope chest," set aside just for that purpose.

7. As *The Chronicle* reviewer of Anderson's book wrote: "Prof. Noyes, the 'elderly gentleman with a bald head and kindly face,' who came to the relief of the perplexed lady candidate with 'Your work is very good, indeed, but you have written x^2 instead of x^4 in this equation, which, you see, will bring it right,' has endeared himself to more than one among us by some kind suggestion, when we have stood at the dusty blackboard vainly striving to recall thoughts which seemed to have fled through the windows and out away over the fields." *Proceedings of the Board of Regents (1837–1864), University of Michigan*, BHL (hereafter *Proceedings, 1837–1864*), 1064; "An American Girl and Her Four Years in a Boys' College," *The Chronicle* 9, no. 8 (February 2, 1878): 117 (hereafter *Chronicle* review).

8. The subjects that Will Elliot studied at the fictional Ortonville were the same ones Olive San Louie Anderson studied at the University of Michigan. In 1870, the university followed the classical course pattern of European universities and was especially strong in the teaching methods (i.e., the German seminar) of the Prussian universities that were in vogue in the 1860s. As for the particular subjects studied, McGuigan writes: "Greek and Latin were still the basis of a liberal education. Class discussion was minimal. There was no question as to whether the courses one studied were relevant to one's life or not" (McGuigan, *A Dangerous Experiment*, 42). Englishman Charles Wentworth Dilke, who visited the university on a trip around the world, found it to be "probably the most democratic school in the whole world—cheap, large, and practical. There are at Michigan no honor lists, no classes in our sense, no orders of merit, no competition" (ibid., 43). It was true, writes McGuigan, that "students were given no grades; they either passed or failed a course, or were 'conditioned'—which meant they might try the exam again within a specified period of time" (ibid., 42).

9. Although some unknown person penciled a note in a copy of *An American Girl*

naming Boise as the model for the character of Prof. Borck, Boise had resigned in 1868, three years before Olive San Louie Anderson enrolled at the University of Michigan. Martin L. D'Ooge replaced Boise and would have been the Greek professor who examined Anderson when she entered the university in 1871. But Boise seems to have endured in the memory of the institution and may have been the real Prof. Borck after all. Formerly with Brown University in Rhode Island, Boise was the only member to go on record favoring the admission of women in 1858. His daughter, Alice Boise, informally attended classes at the University of Michigan before women were admitted, taking her father's Greek class from 1866 to 1867. Alice Boise later wrote of her experience in the University's student magazine, *The Inlander:* "Just when the thought formed itself in my father's mind of taking me into his class room, I do not know. I remember, however, vividly, an event which occurred at the close of our last public Greek examination in the high school, in June, 1866. Our teacher, Professor Lawton, stood near his desk; at his right stood President Haven of the university; at his left my father; before him President Haven's son and my father's daughter. Suddenly my father laid one hand upon the shoulder of young Haven, and one upon me; then, gazing earnestly at President Haven, he said in impassioned tones, 'And your son can go on, but my daughter can not!' None of my father's colleagues in the faculty, except his assistant, Professor Spence, approved of the admission of women." *Proceedings, 1837–1864,* 522; Bordin, *Women at Michigan,* 6; Alice Boise Wood, "How Michigan University Was Opened to Women," *The Inlander,* April 1896, 273; Perry, *Lucinda Hinsdale Stone,* 115.

10. Beginning Greek language students often read Xenophon's writings, especially the *Anabasis.* Will may even be referring to the popular James Robinson Boise (Prof. Borck) edition, *Xenophon's Anabasis, with Explanatory Notes, for the Use of Schools and Colleges* (New York: D. Appleton, 1856). It was revised and reprinted in 1873.

11. The fictional Jerry Dalton was based on a real private tutor in Greek. As *The Chronicle* reviewer of *An American Girl* wrote: "Nor . . . is the 'tutor with a very large nose and a half-amused, half-contemptuous look on his face,' unknown to fame in Michigan University." Four years at the University of Michigan could be expensive for the mostly middle-class students it attracted. Although in the 1870s the university's fees were very low (about 10 dollars per year), books and living expenses could increase that cost to as much as 350 dollars. A bachelor's degree could cost almost 1,400 dollars, "a considerable sum for a middle-class family of the time," according to Ruth Bordin. Thus, to earn extra money some students became tutors. *Chronicle* review, 117; Bordin, *Women at Michigan,* 16; *Proceedings, 1870–1876,* 66.

12. The Young Men's Christian Association (YMCA) provided young men a safe haven in the city, meeting rooms for reading and Bible study, help with lodging, and Christian companionship. In 1851, the YMCA came to Boston, where it became more aggressively evangelical. Along with preaching the gospel, members cared for the sick, ran Sunday schools, advocated temperance, and distributed Bibles. The YMCA was at the forefront of the social gospel and physical culture movements of the 1880s. Reid, *Dictionary of Christianity in America,* 1299.

13. In a letter to his father-in-law, James B. Angell described a similar state of disorder in the chapel. He considered his handling of the problem a "crucial test" of his authority during his first week as president of the University of Michigan: "It has been the traditional custom for years for the students to be very noisy before and after devotional exercises, and disorderly during them. The first few days of the year the

sophomores and freshmen have usually thrown missiles at each other, shouted, sang, etc., etc., so that the chapel was a bedlam. The first day this year, before the faculty went in, the usual disgraceful performances went on. Dr. Cocker officiated. After the services I made a brief address. I was very cordially received, but while going out, the boys were very noisy. The next day I went in early. Soon two sophomores began to pitch nuts at the Freshmen. I kindly, but firmly requested them to desist. They obeyed instantly. There was some shouting, which I did not then interfere with. I thought I would limit myself to the throwing. The janitor afterwards picked up a large collection of missiles, which they left quietly under their seats. The next day, there was no throwing and no noise. The services were beautifully impressive. The college choir sang beautifully. I took occasion at the close of the service to make a few remarks on the whole subject of disorder in the chapel, which were received in the best spirit. And there has since been no slightest manifestation of disorder." James B. Angell to Dr. A. Caswell, September 27, 1871, Folder 11, Box 1, James B. Angell Papers, BHL.

14. Sophomore Mary Marston made a similar observation in a letter to her father: "They say—'boys will be boys,' which seems to mean 'boys will be horrid.' At any rate, they never say it when boys are agreeable. Still, our boys are pretty good on the whole. I like them much better collectively than I do individually though." Mary Olive Marston to "Pappa," December 20, 1874, Mary O. Marston Papers, BHL (hereafter Marston Papers).

15. Mary Marston mentioned a Japanese student, Mr. Toyama, in Prof. Olney's math class. Americans in the 1870s had just begun to show interest in the trappings of Japanese culture—fans, porcelain, fine art, and kimonos. Love of Japanese culture culminated in 1885 with the wildly popular light opera, *The Mikado*, by the British team of William S. Gilbert (lyricist) and Sir Arthur Sullivan (composer). Like many racial minorities in nineteenth-century America, however, the Japanese people themselves faced a prejudice ranging from rude curiosity to acts of violence. Mary Olive Marston to "Mamma," May 23, 1875, Marston Papers, BHL.

16. James Burrill Angell came to Michigan from the University of Vermont, beginning his long and highly respected tenure in 1871, the same year in which Anderson joined the Class of '75. As McGuigan notes, he was a dedicated administrator and educator, handling his own correspondence, acting as dean of the Literary Department, teaching classes on history and international law, and traveling often to give speeches. Above all, he was beloved by faculty members and students alike. Angell was also an outspoken advocate of coeducation, and, as Bordin writes, "he gave his full support to the university's new commitment to coeducation." Under Angell's leadership, "women students found a secure place in all departments, including medicine and law." McGuigan, *A Dangerous Experiment*, 40–41; Bordin, *Women at Michigan*, 9.

17. Although Will Elliott gets caught up in the "rush" on the stairs at fictional Ortonville, the women students at the University of Michigan, according to Ruth Bordin, did not participate in the traditional rivalry and occasionally violent skirmishes between freshmen and sophomores. In its "Class of '75" memorial issue, *The Chronicle* describes the event as follows: "On the Saturday following occurred the first collision between '74 and '75 which will always be remembered as the 'rush on the stairs.' In the midst of the enjoyment, when we were just discovering the fact that '74 men made very good playthings, a part of the faculty appeared, and one reckless professor venturing to mingle with the crowd soon found himself making a bodily

demonstration of horizontality, while from his lips in broken accents came the mandate to 'desist.' But it was evident to all that he could vociferate as loudly on his back as on his feet, and finding they could have no peace with him the rushers did desist for the time being, and went in to prayers. In chapel the pea-nuts, hymn-books, shot, and eggs were hurled with unusual precision." Lucy Salmon, a contemporary of Olive San Louie Anderson, remembered it slightly differently, writing that "banisters were broken down, [and] the floor was completely covered with hats, buttons, neckties, etc." Instead of being caught up in the chaos, the women, at the urging of the faculty, confronted the men involved, hoping their presence would end the violence. It did. Bordin, *Women at Michigan*, 15; "Class History, '75," *The Chronicle* 6, no. 18 (July 3, 1875): 212–13; Louise Fargo Brown, *Apostle of Democracy: The Life of Lucy Maynard Salmon* (New York and London: Harper Bros., 1943), 49.

18. Cicero's discourse on friendship, entitled *Laelius de Amicitia* (Laelius on Friendship), dates from around 44 BC. He defines *friendship* as "a complete identity of feeling about all things" and "the greatest of all the gifts from the gods."

19. An opponent of Plato, Isocrates believed philosophers should attend to immediate problems in reality rather than speculate on metaphysics and epistemology. In *Panegyricus*, Isocrates urges Hellenic unity (panhellenism) against Persia.

20. Many women taught school before going on to college. As Bordin writes: "Many students took some responsibility for their own support. Both men and women frequently left the campus for a semester to teach, and many already taught briefly and saved some money before entering Michigan." Alice Freeman left in her junior year to serve as a high school principal in Illinois. Bordin, *Women at Michigan*, 16; see also "Introduction," n. 29, this volume.

CHAPTER III

1. Eleven women enrolled in Olive San Louie Anderson's class in 1871. Nine graduated from the Literary Department with Anderson in 1875. These were Anderson, Emma Cornelia Andrews, Martha Angle, Angie Clara Chapin, Emily Persis Cook, Caroline Irene Hubbard, Lelia Alice Taber, Ella Thomas, and Harriet Lavinia Winslow.

2. The "relatively staid" and coeducational Student Christian Association met weekly in the largest lecture hall as well as separately by graduating class. Among the eight officers of 1875, two were women. Bordin, *Women at Michigan*, 15.

3. Methodists believed in a rigid adherence to liturgy. In the United States, they eschewed "vices" such as drinking, gambling, and dancing and took highly moral positions on social and political issues. Methodist conversions took place in revivals or tent meetings, which became important forms of evangelization in nineteenth-century America. Reid, *Dictionary of Christianity in America*, 732–33.

4. A leading intellect of transcendentalism in New England, Emerson believed that by communing with nature one could find spiritual renewal, or transcendence. He described the "Over-Soul" as "That great nature in which we rest as the earth lies in the soft arms of the atmosphere; that Unity, that Over-Soul within which every man's particular being is contained and made one with all other." Ralph Waldo Emerson, "The Over-Soul," *The Essential Writings of Ralph Waldo Emerson* (New York: Modern Library, 2000), 237.

5. The founder of Methodism, John Wesley, personally made the decision to equalize women's roles in the church. His decision had far-reaching consequences, as Methodist women developed leadership skills that led them to play important roles in the abolitionist and women's rights movements.

6. Alice Freeman Palmer (1855–1902) may have been the model for Nellie Holmes. See Ruth Bordin, *Alice Freeman Palmer: The Evolution of a New Woman* (Ann Arbor: University of Michigan Press, 1993).

7. The Unitarian Church resulted from a split within Massachusetts Congregationalism between orthodox Calvinists and liberals in the early nineteenth century. In 1825, the liberals formed the American Unitarian Association in Boston. The split centered on two key issues: "the nature of biblical interpretation and authority, and the extent of human capacity for spiritual development." Unitarians also advocated a rational reading of the Bible and the cultivation of the spiritual self. Reid, *Dictionary of Christianity in America*, 1196–97.

8. In one scene, Jo declares, "It's bad enough to be a girl, anyway, when I like boys' games and work and manners! I can't get over my disappointment in not being a boy. And it's worse than ever now, for I'm dying to go and fight with Papa. And I can only stay home and knit, like a poky old woman!" Olive San Louie Anderson's friends nicknamed her "Joe," after Alcott's popular character. Louisa May Alcott, *Little Women* (Boston: Roberts Brothers, 1868); Hamlin Paper, 1886, BHL.

9. As President Angell observed just a few months into his tenure: "Our girls do fine and I have seen no slightest trouble arising from their presence, though we have no laws on the matter. I have not seen a young man once walking across the ground with a young woman. Their demeanor in this respect is admirable." James B. Angell to an unknown correspondent [probably his father-in-law, Dr. Caswell], December 10, 1871, Folder 12, Box 1, James B. Angell Papers, BHL.

10. American spiritualism began in 1848 at Hydesville, New York, where two young sisters, Margaret (Maggie) and Katherine (Kate) Fox, allegedly conversed with the dead by interpreting the spirits' rappings or knocks. As the two toured the country holding "séances," more women became "mediums," finding in spiritualism an authoritative voice they rarely enjoyed elsewhere. Because some spiritualists advocated radical ideas about marriage and sexuality, by the 1870s spiritualism had become synonymous with "radical" feminism. See Ann Braude, *Radical Spirits: Spiritualism and Women's Rights in Nineteenth-Century America* (Boston: Beacon Press, 1989).

11. A century earlier, women in dangerous professions, such as tending bar or prostitution, carried a "lady's muff pistol." As women's sphere expanded in the mid–nineteenth century, more women began to carry handguns, although, as Will suggests, guns still carried an "unladylike" stigma. Most women preferred the derringer, a single-shot, nonreloading pistol small enough to fit in the palm of a hand. Women such as Will, who traveled alone, often carried such handguns for self-defense. She has a pocket revolver, small enough to conceal in a cloak pocket but capable of firing more than once if necessary.

12. Clara is reciting to Will the first stages of Christian mourning and the effect that grief is supposed to have on the mourner's soul. As Karen Halttunen writes, the act of grieving "resembled the crude morphology of conversion that characterized nineteenth-century evangelical revivalism"; mourning manuals reminded readers of its healing powers. The mourner was supposed to feel first "a strong sense of his own spiritual insufficiency." Out of the grief "came a deep sense of the vanity of earthly

happiness," including the pleasure the mourner had taken in the company of the departed loved one during their life. As Clara believed, "God visited death upon the spiritually careless to remind them that their day too would come." Karen Halttunen, *Confidence Men and Painted Women: A Study of Middle-Class Culture in America, 1830–1870* (New Haven: Yale University Press, 1982), 129–30.

13. This kind of religious belief, that everything, including death, has a purpose, contradicts Will's (and Anderson's) belief in a loving and merciful God. As Sarah Dix Hamlin wrote of Anderson: "God was to her a loving, gracious presence, filling her soul with light and joy, and to be worshipped with the mind as with the spirit. All interpretations of Him, as found in the religions of the world, were to her but translations of the paeans of praise and worship emanating from the life of humanity. So broad was she in her spiritual outlook that she could only accept a religion which is eternally the same." Such views found sympathy at the University of Michigan. "[I]t is refreshing," *The Chronicle* reviewer of Anderson's book wrote, "to read a novel which introduces religious discussions in the story without converting all the characters to orthodoxy in the last chapter. Not a few of Sola's readers will be reminded of a similar experience of their own in reading that noble and out-spoken chapter introduced by George Eliot's heroic lines: 'I do not believe it: God's kingdom is something wider, / Else let me stand outside it, with the beings I love.'" Hamlin Paper, 1886, BHL; *Chronicle* review, 118.

14. Because of the new emphasis placed on mourning the dead in the nineteenth century, the wake (the time allowed for mourners to view the body of the deceased and pay their respects) increased in importance. This required the work of an undertaker to embalm the corpse, close the eyes and mouth, tint the face with flesh-colored liquid, dress the body, and apply other techniques to make the deceased appear to be "asleep." Then families could put the corpse on display to mourners for several days in the family home, where the ritual viewing usually took place. A final photographic portrait (memento mori) might be taken of the deceased at that time. Halttunen, *Confidence Men and Painted Women*, 170.

CHAPTER IV

1. As the *New York Weekly Witness* observed in 1894, "The student who earnestly pursues his scholastic studies is held to be a scrub, or grind, or dig." Mary Marston writes, "I have not worked so here, that is, I have not done so much of what we call here *digging*, but I believe the eyes of my mind have been opened a little, and I have found out a good many things that I didn't know before in addition to what I have learned in the classroom." Mary Olive Marston to "Pappa," June 20, 1875, Marston Papers, BHL.

2. The Amazons were an ancient legendary (either historical or mythical) nation of female warriors led by a queen and believed to have lived near the Euxine (Black) Sea. According to legend, Amazons cut or burned off their right breasts so as to use their bows more freely. One antisuffragist used it as an insult, saying: "Now woman has rights, . . . but she has no right to be *man*. Yet, no wonder 'tis, if amid the stirring enterprises and new discoveries of the age, some half-amazon, should defy the customs of social life, and assume the right of levelling all distinctions between the sexes,

walking forth *à la Turk* [in trousers], and becoming the gazing-stock of the street." Prof. J. H. Agnew, "Woman's Offices and Influence," *Harper's New Monthly Magazine* 3, no. 17 (1851): 656.

3. *Michigan Argus* (Ann Arbor), January 14, 1870, clipping in the Albert Yates Scrapbook, BHL.

4. John Nicholas Genin, a New York hatter, cashed in on Kossuth's popularity by beginning a hat craze in his honor that soon swept the nation. The hat itself was a black or brown, low-crowned, soft hat, with the left side of the brim fastened to the crown and ornamented with a long black feather. The hat was very similar to the military dress hat worn by officers on both sides of the Civil War. Thus, for her male classmates, Will's Kossuth hat reflects not just her independence but also her willingness to disregard gender norms.

5. In 1870, the medical course consisted of two six-month terms. Just after the Board of Regents passed the resolution formally admitting women to the university, a committee of the faculty of the Department of Medicine and Surgery submitted a "Memorial on Female Medical Education" that explained their position on the subject of medical coeducation. The committee was not against women attending medical school, nor were they against female physicians. "In [our] judgement," it wrote, "the medical *co-education* of the sexes is at best an experiment of doubtful utility, and one not calculated to increase the dignity of man, nor the modesty of woman. [We] believe that it must be obvious, even to the casual observer, that a large portion of medical instruction cannot be given in the presence of mixed classes without offending the sense of delicacy, and refinement, which should be scrupulously maintained between the sexes." Thus, as Ruth Bordin writes, "When eighteen women enrolled in the Medical Department in the fall of 1871, they were placed in segregated classes." Because this arrangement was costly, however, it lasted only a year. In 1872, women joined their male classmates in the lecture hall, although they were still seated separately. Anatomy labs continued to be segregated by sex until 1908. McGuigan, *A Dangerous Experiment*, 41; "Memorial on Female Medical Education," March 25, 1870, Coeducation—Michigan Collection, BHL; Bordin, *Women at Michigan*, 15, 23; see also, "Introduction" in this volume.

6. Reade's first novel, *It's Never Too Late to Mend* (1856), shed light on prison abuse and encouraged reform. An advertisement by the publisher of Anderson's *An American Girl* in the *Cornell Era* (Cornell University's student newspaper) used Reade's main character in *A Woman-Hater* (1877) as a point of comparison: "Charles Reade's recent creation, 'Rhoda Gale,' was drawn from imagination alone; but 'An American Girl' is a life-original of one of those unique productions of girlhood, due to our special institutions, customs, and civilization, written by 'one of themselves;' and her 'Four Years in a Boys' College' is full of interest at the present day." *Cornell Era*, March 1, 1878, v.

7. "Horace is beautiful," Mary Marston wrote to her mother. "We have read twenty-seven odes so far. I like the scanning particularly. Just wait till you hear me quote 'em, and see if they don't sound nice. Next summer I must begin to make an impression on people. I don't think I did this summer. Horace will be just the thing for that." Mary Olive Marston to "Mamma," November 1, 1874, Marston Papers, BHL.

8. We have been unable to make a certain identification of John Knott or discover the source of his "knotty" (a pun for "naughty"?) quip. At first, we thought he

might have been a local legislator, but no such person by that name existed in Michigan at that time. Anderson may have heard his speech or read about it in a local newspaper.

9. The opinion around the University of Michigan can be gleaned from Mary Marston's letter to her mother after the midterm elections of 1874: "The only interest I took in the election, was in the matter of suffrage. We had considerable fun about it at the table. Professor Adams said he would do as his wife said, but she declined to advise him. He voted against it, as did all the members of the Faculty, I believe, except Professors Merriman and Cocker, and Mr. Berman and Mr. Blackburn. The majority in this ward was only six against it, but it's a pretty bad defeat throughout the state." Mary Olive Marston to "Mamma," November 8, 1874, Marston Papers, BHL.

10. Elizabeth Cady Stanton spoke in Ann Arbor in November 1869, just prior to the Board of Regents' formal admission of women. As University of Michigan student Josiah L. Littlefield noted in his diary: "Mrs. Stanton lectured this evening. It was to women principally, 'Our Young Girls' being the title. She spoke about the manner in which women dress at the present day, and showed conclusively that health and happiness are destroyed by tight lacing. She also showed the importance of having girls properly educated for different kinds of work. Her lecture was sound in every point and delivered in a clear and distinct voice." Mary Ashton Livermore presided over the American Woman Suffrage Association in Chicago in 1869 and founded that same year *The Agitator*, a periodical devoted to woman suffrage and temperance. It merged a year later with the *Woman's Journal* (Boston). Will mentions reading about "dress reform" in the *Woman's Journal* later in this chapter. In October 1874, Julia Ward Howe (author of "The Battle Hymn of the Republic") also spoke in Ann Arbor at the Unitarian Church. Sophomore Mary Marston reported that "we four girls had curiosity enough to go down and hear her. But we were all very much disappointed. She has an exceedingly unpleasant voice, and her lecture was pretty poor." Diary of Josiah L. Littlefield, Ann Arbor, October 1869–May 1870, BHL; Mary Olive Marston to "Mamma," November 1, 1874, Marston Papers, BHL.

11. Corsets were the main target of the dress reform movement, especially after the Civil War, when fashion dictated tighter lacing. Dr. Clarke called them "artificial deformities strapped to the spine . . . that embrace the waist with a grip that tightens respiration into pain." Edward H. Clarke, *Sex in Education; or, A Fair Chance for Girls* (Boston, 1873), rpt. (New York: Arno Press, 1972), 23.

12. Activists first denounced women's "hobbling and irrational fashion" in 1850 as "a dress which imprisons and cripples them." Elizabeth Smith Miller had invented a bloomer costume (Amelia Bloomer publicized them) consisting of a short skirt over long Turkish trousers. Bloomers not only failed to catch on, they were widely ridiculed. After the war, with more women in positions of cultural authority, such as physicians, professors, and college administrators, dress reform began to be taken more seriously. Like Dr. Clarke, women physicians directly attacked fashion's ill effects on women's health. While still unconventional, the reform dress they offered was less radical; it was simply a looser and shorter version of the fashionable dress of the day. As Sarah Dix Hamlin observed of the women at the University of Michigan: "As a rule, they dress healthfully, are not ashamed to show that they can take a long breath without causing stitches to rip, or hooks to fly; they do not disdain dresses that are too short for street-sweeping; they have learned that the shoulders are better for sustaining the heavy skirts

than the hips, and they are finding that, especially in this climate, healthful though it is, one must be prepared with suitable clothing for all the exigencies of the weather." Abba Louisa Goold Woolson, ed., *Dress-Reform* (Boston, 1873), rpt. (New York: Arno Press, 1974); McGuigan, *A Dangerous Experiment*, 57; Sarah Dix Hamlin, "University of Michigan," in *The Education of American Girls, Considered in a Series of Essays*, edited by Anna C. Brackett, 314–15 (New York: G. P. Putnam's Sons, 1874).

13. Most women replied thus when confronted with the unhealthy facts about wearing corsets. As dress reform advocate Dr. Caroline E. Hastings wrote in 1873: "'But I do not wear my corsets too tight,' every lady is ready to answer. I never yet have been able to find a woman who did, if we accept her own statement; and yet physicians are constantly called upon to treat diseases which are aggravated, if not caused, by wearing corsets." Woolson, *Dress-Reform*, 57.

14. Sarah Dix Hamlin confirms Will's complaint, writing that "there is no regularly prescribed exercise. Most of the young women have rooms some distance from University Hall, to which they are generally obliged to go two or three times a day, so that they, of necessity, have considerable walking—in which some of those here have shown remarkable powers of strength and endurance." Hamlin, "University of Michigan," 315.

15. *The Chronicle* mentions a female student who chopped her own wood, although the date and the rank of the student would seem to exclude Anderson. Nevertheless, the female wood chopper was deemed noteworthy enough for the gossip page of the student newspaper. "A lady sophomore saws her own wood, quite to the chagrin of her brother sophomores. It is even reported that when certain ones of the aforesaid did assail her wood-pile and reduce it to a length suitable for burning, she disdained to touch a stick of it, and continued to use none but what had been sawed by her own hands." "Things Chronicled," *The Chronicle* 3, no. 7 (December 16, 1871): 82.

16. Clarke's book caused widespread controversy in New England, generating several prominent polemics against the doctor's views. By contrast, the book produced very little written comment at the University of Michigan. See Introduction, 15–17.

CHAPTER V

1. In 1867, the Michigan State Legislature approved a joint resolution favoring the admission of women to the University of Michigan, stating that "the high objects for which the University of Michigan was organized will never be fully attained until women are admitted to all its rights and privileges." Three years later, the University's Board of Regents passed its 1870 resolution formally admitting women. Bordin, *Women at Michigan*, xxvii.

2. Victorian society accepted physical expressions of love between women more readily than it did similar behavior between unmarried heterosexuals. Will's disquisition on the art of kissing embarrasses the pious Clara and thus serves to sharpen the differences between them. On emotional bonding among Victorian women, see the classic article by Carroll Smith-Rosenberg, "The Female World of Love and Ritual: Relations Between Women in Nineteenth-Century America," *Signs: A Journal of Women in Culture and Society* 1 (Autumn 1975): 1–29.

CHAPTER VI

1. As acting president of the university in 1870, Frieze presided over Michigan's transition to a coeducational institution. Of Anderson's description of Prof. Atkins, *The Chronicle* reviewer writes: "There is no mistaking the man and the face; clear-cut as a cameo, making even the most lawless junior as he gazes upon it repent of his acts and feel that to be a gentleman is man's noblest aim, which called forth such enthusiastic praise from 'Will's' pen. The Greek room and the painting of Athens are familiar objects." Not a strong proponent of coeducation, Frieze believed, according to one newspaper, that "The admission of ladies might injure the reputation of the University among college men, who are generally prejudiced against such a policy, thinking that it lowers the standard of education. Women often want to pursue special courses of study, and many of them would leave the University without taking any degree.—The institution might thus degenerate into a mere high school for the education of young ladies. He did not think, however, that the small number who would come to take a full course would injure the reputation of the University, provided the standard is kept up to the present grade. He thought it would not be possible to get along with young ladies in the medical department, and recommended the amendment of the resolution to make this exception." *Chronicle* review, 117; Newspaper clipping, Willard Family Scrapbook, BHL.

2. Walters replaced Frieze in Latin Languages and Literature upon Frieze's retirement. He authored and coauthored numerous classroom texts on Greek and Latin, including *First Steps in Continuous Latin Prose* (1897), *Hints and Helps in Continuous Greek Prose* (1897), and *Ad Limen: Being Reading Lessons and Exercises for a Second and Third Year Course in Latin* (1917).

3. Conducting most of his archaeological work in Greece, in 1873 Schliemann believed that he had discovered the ancient city of Troy in a trove of ancient fortifications, ruins, and gold jewelry. He published his findings in *Troy and Its Remains* (1875). Although he was later proved wrong, Schliemann was quite celebrated at the time of Anderson's years at the University of Michigan.

4. After the war, his wife (Clytemnestra) and her lover (Aegisthus) murdered him. The two also murdered Cassandra, the daughter of King Priam, whom Agamemnon had acquired as his concubine at the end of the Trojan War. Orestes, Agamemnon's son, would later avenge his father's death. The homecoming of Agamemnon and its aftermath were favorite subjects for Greek tragedy.

5. When Achilles's mother dipped him as a baby in the River Styx to make him invincible, she held him by the heel, leaving that one spot unprotected. Paris killed him when the god Apollo guided his arrow to Achilles's weak spot (the Achilles' tendon or heel). Professor D'Ooge, the author of *Oration of Demosthenes on the Crown* (Chicago, 1875) among other works, replaced Professor Boise in 1868 and was Anderson's Greek professor. In contrast to Will's characterization, Mary Marston enjoyed D'Ooge's Greek class: "We have also finished the seventh book of the *Iliad*. There are lots of funny things in Homer, that is, opportunities for comical translations; and it is a temptation to make them. But I just can't tell you how much I enjoy the hour of Greek recitation. It is really something to look forward to, all the rest of the time." Mary Olive Marston to "Mamma," November 1, 1874, Marston Papers, BHL.

6. Today we would call the subjects Cocker taught psychology and philosophy. Cocker was appointed by the Board of Regents in 1869 and quickly became a favorite

among the students, even officiating at the marriage of Madelon Stockwell, the first woman student, to one of her classmates, Charles K. Turner, after her graduation. Cocker was a prolific lecturer, scholar, and supporter of woman suffrage. His published works include: *Lectures on the Truth of the Christian Religion* (1873), a compilation of lectures "delivered before the students of the University of Michigan on Sunday afternoons"; *The Theistic Conception of the World: An Essay in Opposition to Certain Tendencies of Modern Thought* (1875); and *Some of the Characteristics of Modern Scepticism* (1881). *Proceedings, 1864–1870*, 377.

7. Nast earned fame for his anthropomorphic caricatures of Gilded Age political figures and power brokers. Best known for creating the Democratic Party donkey and the Republican Party elephant, Nast also used his art to help bring down the corrupt leadership of William March Tweed, the "boss" of New York's Democratic Party machine and its headquarters, Tammany Hall.

8. An 1857 graduate of the University of Michigan, Watson remained as an instructor and professor of mathematics and astronomy until 1863. That year the university named him director of the Detroit Observatory, a position he held until 1878, when he left to head the Washburn Observatory at Madison, Wisconsin. In 1870, he was awarded the prestigious Lalandegold medal from the French Academy of Sciences for the discovery of the most planets in the decade. In 1874, while Anderson was in her junior year at the university, Watson led a successful expedition to China, where he "observed the transit of Venus." Watson was the author of several books and numerous articles on astronomy, including *A Popular Treatise on Comets* (1860). According to *The Chronicle* review of *An American Girl*, "The picture of Prof. Markham, . . . requires only the addition of 'Order gentleman, is Heaven's first law' to become so perfect that even the dullest junior that ever 'ponied' through Astronomy could not fail to recognize it." *Science* 1, no. 22 (November 27, 1880): 270; *Proceedings, 1870–1876*, 73; *Chronicle* review, 117.

9. The Detroit Observatory, built around 1854, was the pride and joy of the university's first president, Henry Philip Tappan. It was funded mostly by "a few liberal friends of science in Detroit" and so named in honor of them. The telescopes in the observatory were then among the largest in the world. President Tappan recruited Franz Brünnow, a German astronomer, as the observatory's first director. Tappan's desire for an observatory illustrates the slow but gradual shift within institutions of higher learning toward more scientific and research-based curricula in the late nineteenth century. *Proceedings, 1837–64*, 3; Veysey, *The Emergence of the American University*, 135–37; see also Patricia S. Whitesell, *A Creation of His Own: Tappan's Detroit Observatory* (Ann Arbor: University of Michigan, Bentley Historical Library, 1998).

10. An article entitled "Apron Strings" in *The Chronicle* described the consequences of such overly strict rules for students at women's colleges: "The legitimate result of such Paulina Pry guardianship is either a passiveness and tame acquiescence which is ignoble in man or woman, or an evasive, deceitful habit of action, which easily becomes a prominent characteristic. It fosters that airy insipidity, that absence of and contempt for womanly earnestness and honesty, which men generally expect in boarding-school misses, and very young men affect to admire in the same, and it savors of extravagance to have institutions which do not produce much of anything else. . . . Our fair co-workers in Michigan University are quietly elaborating a practical and complete refutation of the principles on which these boarding-schools and their 'self-

reports' rest; they are proving in themselves their ability to walk alone, to act alone, and all this with womanly modesty and an amount of common sense, which to the ordinary economical boarding-school girl would seem lavish extravagance." T. H. Johnston, "Apron Strings," *The Chronicle* 5, no. 5 (November 29, 1873): 52–3.

11. According to Ruth Bordin, "Occasionally a group of students, both male and female, followed a practice long used by men of forming an 'eating club,' hiring a cook, and dividing the expenses." Bordin, *Women at Michigan*, 13–14.

12. The college was founded by Matthew Vassar (1792–1868), who had little formal education but was a voracious reader and had amassed a fortune as a brewer by his mid-forties. His niece, Lydia Booth, had inspired in him the idea of founding a "real" college for women, that is, one that was the academic equal of men's colleges. Thus, Vassar was founded not as a boarding or "finishing" school, but rather as a "separate but equal" institution for women committed to the same intellectual rigor that characterized the all-male colleges and universities of the time. He gave half his fortune and two hundred acres of land for the college, which formally opened in 1865. University of Michigan graduate Lucy Maynard Salmon became a professor of history at Vassar in 1887.

13. This was an early argument for admitting women to universities. As one critic of Anderson's novel put it, however: "[T]he women who first came to the University probably do not care to be called 'heroines of civilization.' Nothing in their fate seems to demand this sort of 'poetic justice.' So far as available sources of information are to be trusted, the first one was a woman who respected herself in every way, and therefore she was treated with entire courtesy. It is altogether likely that the young men here at that time did not at once adopt the manners of the drawing room, whenever she hove in sight along the corridor. Nor did they play at football in dress coats and kid gloves. Suppose women have had occasional annoyances in college, all that can be said is, that such things are not to be met here only; and, unfortunately, matriculation does not change an ill-bred man into a gentleman." "Correspondence," *The Chronicle* 9, no. 11 (March 16, 1878): 167; Bordin, *Women at Michigan*, 15.

CHAPTER VII

1. Held at regular intervals by itinerant clergy of several Christian denominations, including the Presbyterian, Baptist, and Methodist, revivals lasted from a week to as long as a month, depending on the size of the local population. They usually generated great religious enthusiasm and energy in the citizenry. Penitents would confess sins, seek forgiveness from the membership, testify, pray, and experience conversion. Nell's characterization of revivals reflects a certain class snobbery on her part. Reid, *Dictionary of Christianity in America*, 1012–13.

2. Anderson was very much like her character Will. Hamlin wrote of her: "Many a time she did seek if a special theological creed could satisfy the requirements of her nature better than that intense practical religion that she lived in her daily life. It was the 'truth of truth' she sought with all the earnestness of a nature which came from Puritan stock, and there was in her character a loveliness which meant nothing but devotion to duty and consecration to high aims, which made her life a religion in itself." Hamlin Paper, 1886, BHL.

3. Mr. Allison is equating scientific proof with biblical proof, an equation that in

the 1870s was becoming increasingly less valid in universities. In fact, science and religion had begun to diverge seriously in universities in the decade after the publication of Charles Darwin's *On the Origin of the Species* in 1859. Some academics openly resisted the ascendancy of science (especially evolution, or "Darwinism"), believing that it "conveyed a tone . . . which the older phrase, 'natural philosophy' had comfortably muffled. Science paraded nakedly, seemed vulgar; it appeared to denigrate the position of man in the universe." Most academics, however, were ambivalent and thought that "science, as well as religion, should recognize its appropriate sphere, acknowledge the limits and boundaries of its realm, and stop when it reaches them." Like men and women, science and religion should occupy separate spheres. In this context, Mr. Allison represents an older worldview, while Will reflects the scientific future and the growing crisis of faith in religion and universal truths. Veysey, *The Emergence of the American University*, 41–42.

4. Christology, the theological study of the nature of Jesus Christ as both human and deity, has fueled an ongoing debate among the various Christian sects. In this scene, Will is espousing what was then a specifically Unitarian view of Jesus as a great prophet and teacher ordained and sent by God but not the deity himself. This rejection of Jesus as God incarnate also entailed a rejection of the Trinity. Nineteenth-century Unitarians made the humanity of Jesus a central pillar of their beliefs. Reid, *Dictionary of Christianity in America*, 1196–97.

5. The doctrine of atonement originated with Calvinism and its emphasis on original sin, in which God could not easily forgive sins nor could sinners atone for their own sins. The Rev. Mr. Allison still adheres to this older, yet waning doctrine of atonement that Will "can't *bear*."

CHAPTER VIII

1. A sophomore did try to commit suicide during Anderson's junior year, 1874. Sophomore Mary Marston wrote of the incident in a letter to her mother: "A very sad thing happened here last Sunday. A Miss Sykes, who entered college two years ago, and was out last year, came back to complete her course. But she was seized with a fit of monomania to which she has long been subject and shot herself through the head. She is still alive, but there is little hope of her recovery. President Angell this morning in chapel gave a brief statement of the facts, speaking of her as a girl of 'excellent character and excellent mind.' Of course, it makes us all feel sad." She reports in her next letter to her father that "poor Miss Sykes . . . is recovering." Mary Olive Marston to "Mamma," September 29,1874, and Mary Olive Marston to "Pappa," October 4, 1874, Marston Papers, BHL.

2. Hamlin wrote of this woman's death in an essay defending the health of the University of Michigan women. It appeared in a book of essays rebutting Dr. Clarke's popular indictment of coeducation: "The class of '75 had, on entering, eleven women. Of these, one has died, an apparently healthy girl, who passed from us in the second year of her college life, shortly after her return in the autumn. We do not know the cause of her sickness, but we do know that it was not the result of overtaxed mental powers, since it occurred but a little while after the long vacation of the summer, and the disease was one which had carried off a number of members of the same family in former years, viz., typhoid fever, alike unsparing of age, sex, or condition. With this

exception, this class has been remarkably healthy." Hamlin, "University of Michigan," 310–11.

3. Dr. Clarke called switches "artificial deformities . . . piled on the head." Mary J. Safford-Blake, M.D., wrote of the fashionable masses of false hair: "Many invalids, who are unable to lift a broom, habitually carry weights upon their heads . . . that the Humane Society would think cruel if laid upon animals." Clarke, *Sex in Education*, 23; Woolson, *Dress-Reform*, 25–26.

4. African Americans had succeeded in, and in some cities dominated, the barber trade since before the Civil War. Barbers formed part of a small class of black entrepreneurs, some of whom became quite wealthy catering to white customers. In the 1870s, whites still patronized black-owned businesses such as barbershops, butcher shops, catering firms, and other service-oriented establishments. The end of Reconstruction (1876), however, signaled the beginning of a more rigidly observed (and often violently enforced) segregation, which encompassed all aspects of society. August Meier, *Negro Thought in America, 1880–1915* (Ann Arbor: University of Michigan Press, 1966), 139–40.

5. According to the racial ideology of the nineteenth century, Ham represented a separate creation for people of African descent. In the United States, this belief helped justify the legal codification of discrimination and prejudice against blacks. Although Darwin's theory of evolution (1859) threw the idea of a separate creation into serious doubt, it endured nevertheless; till his death, the celebrated Harvard zoologist Louis Agassiz stubbornly believed in a separate creation. At the same time, some African Americans embraced the idea of a biblical father of their own. To them, Ham was a figure of racial pride, especially among those involved in the early-nineteenth-century separatist movement, which encouraged black emigration to the new African country of Liberia, and later in the struggle for citizenship rights. Thus, Anderson's phrase can be seen as a term of educated prejudice. Meier, *Negro Thought in America*, 51–52.

6. This form of punishment had become so racialized that Mr. Lewis's first response to what he sees as a violation of Will and white womanhood is to threaten to horsewhip the African American barber.

7. The students of the University of Michigan had been agitating for a gymnasium since the 1860s, but the state legislature refused to see the need. It was not until the early 1890s that a Detroit philanthropist, Joshua Waterman, donated half the money needed to build a gymnasium, the other half to be raised by the university. Despite Waterman's declaration that the gymnasium should be open to both men and women, the women students eventually had to find the funds to build a separate one for themselves. McGuigan, *A Dangerous Experiment*, 59.

8. The university's rituals remained generally Christian in tone. Acting on accusations of sectarianism at the University of Michigan in 1873 (especially in Dr. B. F. Cocker's classroom), a committee of Michigan state legislators visited the university to investigate. Their report concluded: "We are unanimously of the opinion that the general charge of sectarianism is a mistaken one. The teachings of the University are those of an enlightened and liberal Christianity, in the general, highest, and best use of the term. This is not in our opinion sectarian. If it is, we would not have it changed. A school, a society, a nation, devoid of Christianity, is not a pleasant spectacle to contemplate. We cannot believe the people of Michigan would denude this great University of its fair, liberal, and honorable Christian character as it exists

today." "Christianity and Michigan University," [unknown newspaper,] July 24, 1873, Scrapbook, Vol. III, p. 19, Box 22, Alexander Winchell Papers, BHL.

9. The complaint of sectarianism at the University of Michigan to the state legislature in 1873 singled out Dr. B. F. Cocker's Department of Mental and Moral Philosophy as "a very dangerous one, that a great deal of sectarianism can be taught through it." Ibid.

10. The doctrine stated that every natural object symbolizes or corresponds to some spiritual fact or principle, which is, as it were, its archetype or prototype, and that the scriptures were written in harmony with these correspondences. Swedenborg's doctrine had its greatest influence on nineteenth-century culture.

11. James B. Angell refuted Clarke in an article in the *Woman's Journal* (the main organ of the woman's rights movement) by extolling the excellent health of the women at the University of Michigan: "I have made it an object of particular examination and scrutiny, and I am thoroughly convinced that there is no danger which need be considered worthy of mention, in any young woman, in tolerably good health, pursuing the regular course prescribed, nor has it actually been the case that they have been impaired in health by the course." "Our Young Women," *Woman's Journal*, August 23, 1873, 267.

CHAPTER IX

1. A "Memorial on Female Medical Education" submitted to the University of Michigan Board of Regents in 1870 lists some of the commonly held objections to female physicians and medical coeducation.

2. As one doctor remembered the first women in the Medical Department: "We certainly did not welcome women students! I think we were afraid they'd take away our patients. But our attitude was not personal." On two early Michigan medical students, Amanda Sanford and Eliza Mosher, see the Introduction, 13–14; McGuigan, *A Dangerous Experiment*, 36–38, 41, 63–64; and Bordin, *Women at Michigan*, 33–34.

3. As Bordin writes, women readily joined the existing literary societies. Alice Freeman became an officer in the Literary Adelphi, while Octavia Bates was an officer in the Webster Society for law students. University of Michigan women even created the first all-female society—the Quadratic Club (Q.C. for short), which began in Lucy Salmon's room in 1872. Its object, according to the handwritten "History of Q.C.," was twofold: "literary culture and social intercourse." Salmon also saw the group as a means of alleviating petty class rivalries. As the "History of Q.C." states: "There were three classes of us, Juniors, Sophomores and Freshmen. Each class and indeed each section of the class was interested in its own work, and with most of us, our work took all our time and thought. We learned each other by sight in chapel, but there was no crowded waiting-room, no chance for introductions. Our acquaintance was limited to those few whom we met every day in recitation and even this acquaintance was slight. Surely it was time for us to be something more than so many disconnected human machines." Eventually, the club had women from all four classes, freshmen through seniors. Although it was democratic in theory, a vague criteria for membership existed, as the "History" suggests, in their efforts to secure "for the improvement of the society the cream of each year's Freshman girls." Sophomore Mary Marston wrote often of the

Q.C. meetings in her letters home: "I went to the Q.C. last night, and enjoyed it, as I always do. But the exercises were particularly good. Angie [Chapin] had a fine essay, and there were other nice things. A good many of the Freshman girls have joined already, and some of them promise to be valuable members." According to Bordin, the sixteen members met once a week, "responding to roll call with a quotation from Whittier, Ruskin, or Macaulay and proceeding to discuss 'some high-minded question to sharpen our ideas,' such as dress reform or the advisability of protective tariffs." From the evidence available, Anderson does not appear to have been a member. Bordin, *Women at Michigan*, 16; "History of Q.C.," 1875, BHL; Mary Olive Marston to "Mamma," October 18, 1874, Marston Papers, BHL.

4. The women of the Q.C. specifically shunned the kind of secrecy that fraternities offered. The society's history (written anonymously but possibly by Lucy Salmon) recorded the sentiment: "The lady who now occupies the chair as President (Emma M. Hall) had received a letter from the ladies of Syracuse University saying that they had formed a secret society, and asking us to become a chapter. This aroused some discussion, for some of us were and are, quite strongly opposed to secret organizations, especially as we have them illustrated to us in the gentlemen's college secret societies." The Q.C. women rejected the Syracuse invitation and thus maintained the group's friendly intellectual focus. As the author of the "History of Q.C." commented: "It is astonishing to recall how soon a warmer friendly feeling grew up among us, and that too a genuine one, founded on no secret society sham, but on a true congeniality of tastes and pursuits. I doubt much whether any other society could show a record so clear of petty dissensions or hard feelings among the members." As fraternities grew in popularity in the late 1870s and 1880s, they exerted an enormous influence on campus activities and in many cases took over student events and publications completely. Their growth greatly weakened the mostly coeducational literary societies, which had been so popular with the arrival of the first women at the university, and forced a concomitant growth in all-female societies. As a result, there were five sororities by 1890. "History of Q.C.," 1875, BHL; Bordin, *Women at Michigan*, 22.

5. Will is referring to the university's Museum of Natural History and specifically to Mr. R. W. Corwin, a taxidermist and custodian of the collections. In 1837, the state legislature authorized the university to establish a Cabinet of Natural History. It began with a collection of minerals purchased from a private collector and displayed in a faculty residence. Later it was moved to the newly created Museum of Natural History in the main university building. Its collections ranged from zoological and botanical to geological and archaeological. Museum donors included amateur naturalists, local Ann Arbor residents, and University of Michigan students. Like the Detroit Observatory, the founding of the Museum of Natural History reflected the university's ever-increasing shift toward science and objective learning. *Proceedings, 1837–1864*, 147–48, 205; *Proceedings, 1870–1876*, 355–68.

6. The custom, of unknown origin, dates at least as far back as 1288, when a law was enacted in Scotland stating that during a leap year any woman, rich or poor, was free to propose to any man she liked. If the man declined the proposal, he was fined according to his means. The fine could range from a kiss to payment for a silk dress or a pair of gloves. If he could prove that he was already betrothed to another, he was free to turn down the woman's proposal. France and Italy passed similar laws around the same time.

7. Taxidermy is the art of preserving the integument, together with the scales, feathers or fur, of animals. Birds were the most common animals selected by amateurs for preparation and mounting, as the university museum's list of donated specimens shows. The prepared bird was stuffed, given glass eyes, and fixed to a stand or perch on which it was arranged in the most natural and lifelike attitude the taxidermist could achieve. For display in a natural history museum, the bird was labeled with its scientific name, sex, locality, and date. *Proceedings 1870–1876*, 363–78.

8. The local and national papers were filled with reports of and opinions about the admission of women at the University of Michigan. See Willard Family Scrapbook, BHL.

CHAPTER X

1. Mary Marston related the death of one "Mr. Timothy" in a letter to her mother: "One day last week, the death of Mr. Timothy was announced in chapel. I was very much shocked, though I knew he went away sick some weeks before the vacation, and had heard since that he was very ill. He had consumption and I think his death must have been hastened by lack of proper food and clothing. He always looked pinched. It used to make my heart ache to see him. But he has left a beautiful memory. We thanked God for his life and example in our class prayer meeting [of the Student Christian Association]. Hattie is on a committee with Mr. Bishop and Mr. Barbour to draw up resolutions to be sent to his friends." Mary Olive Marston to "Mamma," January 31, 1875, Marston Papers, BHL.

2. The train was a common target of the dress-reform movement. One reformer called these trailing skirts "the worst form of barbarism in our dress." Not only did they add weight to the already heavy fashion of floor-length dresses, but they were exceedingly impractical. "For women who go thus hampered, there can never be one step free from filth and annoyance of some kind, unless the skirts are clutched and held up by main force." Woolson, *Dress-Reform*, 35.

3. The Senior Reception was an annual tradition held at President and Mrs. Angell's residence just before classes ended for the year. Many seniors went home before returning for graduation week in late June. Mrs. Angell took charge of the occasion, making them especially elegant and memorable affairs. As McGuigan writes, "both President Angell and his wife, Sara Caswell Angell, set an example of personal kindness and interest in the women on campus that did much to banish the prejudice they had first encountered." Mrs. Angell was a particular favorite of the women of the university. She taught Sunday School at the Congregational Church and made a point of greeting students. She was even willing to break the "seniors only" rule of the Senior Reception for her favorite students. As Mary Marston wrote: "Of course, members of lower classes are never invited, but Mrs. Angell said to me, to-day in Sunday School, that she wanted me to come ever so much, but didn't quite know as it would do to send me a formal invitation, but if I would come without that, she would be very glad to see me. Wasn't that kind? I was very much pleased." McGuigan, *A Dangerous Experiment*, 41; Mary Olive Marston to "Mamma," May 30, 1875, Marston Papers, BHL.

4. The fact that Will notices Randolf and Miss Durant standing near a photograph of Nydia is intended to be ironic. In the story, Nydia, a blind flower seller, struggles through the ancient city of Pompeii as it is being buried in volcanic ash from

Mount Vesuvius, straining to hear Glaucus, a nobleman with whom she has fallen desperately in love, and his fiancée Ione. Blind Nydia uses her acute hearing to find the two and leads them to safety at the shore. In despair over the impossibility of her love, she drowns herself. Her tragedy is a reflection of Will's predicament.

5. Miss Durant knows her quarry well. She takes aim at Randolf's vulnerable masculinity by painting a humiliating picture of the sex-role reversal and emasculation that will accompany a marriage to Will. As Karen Lystra writes in her book on nineteenth-century courtship: "Sex-role anxiety after the Civil War was concentrated upon the question of male-female contrast. Gender contrast was a particularly vexing problem for nineteenth-century men, whose sense of masculinity was linked to their ability to counterpose male to female behavior. The necessity to establish a contrast was one of the most pressing claims of nineteenth-century masculinity." She concludes that "the nineteenth-century woman's movement appears to have played a significant role in increasing sex-role insecurity in post-Civil War America" and "contributed, perhaps centrally, to a new level of self-conscious sex-role awareness" and an uneasiness over women's commitment to their traditional sphere. Karen Lystra, *Searching the Heart: Women, Men, and Romantic Love in Nineteenth-Century America* (New York: Oxford University Press, 1989), 147–48.

CHAPTER XI

1. Single women missionaries had been working abroad since the 1830s, some as full-time ministers, and women missionary societies began forming in the late 1860s to support their work. The Woman's Foreign Missionary Society, formed in Boston in 1869, sent two women to India that same year as the society's first missionaries. The society also published the first women's mission magazine in 1869, the *Heathen Woman's Friend*.

2. Graduating with the goal of studying medicine, Anderson never pursued the field. As Hamlin wrote: "At the time she was ambitious to study medicine, and it was believed that she would return and enter the Medical Department of the University. Such was, indeed, her intention, and an exceedingly brilliant future seemed to open before her. The aim of ambition changed in after years, but there was none the less belief that she would have attained to a high position in another chosen field of activity." Hamlin Paper, 1886, BHL.

3. Each year, the faculty chose ten to twenty of the top students to speak on a topic of his or her choice at the commencement ceremony. In 1875, ten speakers made the list, including Olive San Louie Anderson, the only woman among them. Two of the students later declined, making a total of eight speakers on Commencement Day, 1875.

4. Anderson took a teaching job at a Santa Barbara college, where she taught Greek and Latin. As reported in the *Michigan Argus* (October 13, 1875): "Miss San Louie Anderson, of '75, is illustrating the independence and usefulness of Woman, as propounded in her commencement address, by teaching at Santa Barbara, California, for $2,000 a year." While there, according to Hamlin, Anderson wrote *An American Girl*. Albert Yates Scrapbook, BHL; Hamlin Paper, 1886, BHL.

5. As one writer in *The Chronicle* put it, "there are few to whom this system is familiar, to whom it is not a system of concealment, simple deceit excused only upon

the ground of shrewdness." M. F. Hapgood, "Ponying," *The Chronicle* 4, no. 12 (March 21, 1873): 136.

6. Anderson's commencement speech was entitled "The Next Century." *The Chronicle* described her performance: "Miss Olive San Louie Anderson spoke in a somewhat sarcastic vein of the possible solution in the course of 'The Next Century' of many of the vexed questions of the day, including the many-sided 'woman question.'" The *Tribune* summarized her speech more thoroughly: "A piece of music was performed and then Miss San Louie Anderson of Mansfield, O[hio] delivered an oration on 'The Next Century.' She said that our country is still in its childhood and we could not see what was to prevent its becoming all that Fourth of July orators predict concerning it. This age is considered a fast one. Miss Anderson thought that the next century would see some very curious results in the way of the improvement of machinery and the development of faster locomotion. Miss Anderson thought this decidedly an age of reform and of humbug. We have a nervous aristocracy in this country, ever unstable and fierce, because it is uncertain of its tenure. The aristocracy of the old world has the advantage of being certain of its tenure and it is a more decent aristocracy than that of America. Miss Anderson further thought that neither the twentieth century nor the fortieth would see the world redeemed unless women were granted the rights and privileges which belong to them." "The Commencement Exercises," *The Chronicle* 6, no. 18 (July 3, 1875): 225; "The University, Concluding Proceedings of the Board of Regents, the Exercises of Commencement Day," *Tribune* (July 1, 1875), Scrapbook, Vol. III, Box 22, Alexander Winchell Papers, BHL.

7. Commencement Day was just one day in the University of Michigan's traditional Commencement Week, which included much ceremony and celebration, such as Class Day exercises, a concert, the Alumni Dinner, and the President's Reception. The formal commencement exercises for the Class of '75 began at ten o'clock Wednesday morning in University Hall. An estimated 3,500 attended. According to the local newspaper, "The usual procession of the regents, the faculty and the class was formed at half-past nine on the Campus, near the Law School, and marched to the University Hall. Out of a class of over 100 graduates, only seven young gentleman and one young lady were announced to deliver orations. . . . The graduating class was seated in the central seats of the hall, as usual, and the spectators very nearly filled the remainder of the body of the auditorium, and the best seats of the gallery were also filled, largely with ladies. The young gentlemen who were to deliver the orations, were very properly located in the rear of the platform, where were gathered the governor, the regents and the faculty and a large number of invited guests." After a selection by the Bishop Orchestra, President Angell offered a prayer, then the orchestra performed again. Next came the student commencement speakers, who ranged in subject from "The Educating Influence of the Law" to "The Evils of American Journalism" and "The Political Services of Thomas Paine." A poem by J. B. McMahon, "The Fairy of the Glen," provided a fanciful commentary on the results of the admission of women to the university. After the speeches, President Angell conferred the degrees on the graduates. "The University, Concluding Proceedings of the Board of Regents, the Exercises of Commencement Day," Alexander Winchell Papers, BHL.

8. At Anderson's commencement ceremony, the last speaker was James M. Barret of Arlington, Illinois, who "discoursed on 'Government by Discussion.' He said that government by discussion was the deadly foe of absolutism and the foundation of government carried on according to the laws of justice and reason." Ibid.